The Lost Years

The Palumbra Chronicles: Book One

L.D. Fairchild

THE LOST YEARS

Copyright © 2020 by L.D. Fairchild.

For information contact :
https://booksbyfairchild.wixsite.com/ldfairchild

Book and Cover design by MiblArt

ISBN: 978-1-7347172-1-1

To Emma and Carolyn,
who believed their mom
could write a book long before
she believed it herself.

CONTENTS

CHAPTER ONE

A small, white corner protruded from the damp ground, barely waving in the gentle breeze. Smudged and torn and barely visible, it had been there for a long time, but just recently the ground had worn away enough for the corner to break the surface, like a seedling in the spring.

Most people would have walked right by without stopping. It was small, and it was a few feet off the bare dirt path. But on this day, that small, white corner caught Maeve Jackson's eye as she walked home from her occupation training. Curious, she stopped on the path.

At 17, Maeve Jackson had just one year of occupation training left before she would take her place in the city hospital as a nurse − the job chosen for her by the World Government's aptitude test that she, like everyone she knew, took at the age of 16. She was a tall girl with an athletic build. Slim with brown eyes and brown hair, she could run faster and more gracefully than most people. In another age, she would have been a track star, but in this age, the World Government had banished all competitive sports. The only athletic endeavors allowed were the prescribed exercise regimen everyone was forced to partake in once a day. The World Government wanted healthy workers.

Maeve was a girl who noticed everything. She noticed that few people in her world seemed truly happy. She noticed that no one spoke badly of the government. She noticed that if you did happen to speak badly of those in power, you suddenly disappeared. She noticed that though the aptitude test was supposed to put you in a job that fit your skills, it rarely put you in a job that filled your soul. And on this particular day, she noticed a small, white triangle sticking up out of the ground as she walked from occupational training to her home.

A piece of trash was worth noticing because the World Government made sure trash did not make it to the streets of Palumbra. Trash on the streets left the appearance of a government that didn't care for its people. There was a whole crew of people dedicated to making sure trash did not appear, and the fines for littering were so staggering that most of the people in Palumbra would never be able to pay them off, ensuring that they would be slaves (although no one called them that) to the World Government until they died. For all those reasons, Maeve noticed the small, white triangle.

She looked around. There didn't seem to be anyone else nearby that could have dropped the piece of paper. This wasn't a well-traveled path. It was a quick shortcut from the hospital to Maeve's home, but few people used it and no one else had noticed the small, white triangle waving its greeting from several feet off

2

the path. Maeve worried for a moment that someone might think she had thrown trash on the ground, and she had no wish to become a World Government slave at the age of 17.

When she was sure no one was watching her, she lightly stepped off the path and bent down to look at the gently waving piece of paper. The ground was damp from a recent rain, and the dirt around the paper moved easily. As she brushed away dirt and leaves, she realized the small piece of paper was encased in a plastic bag and attached to something much larger. Slowly, the leaves and dirt revealed a square metal box about the size of the box her shoes came in.

Maeve looked at the top of the box buried in the dirt, trying to decide whether to dig it out and see what was inside or simply cover it back up and pretend she had never seen it. She was going to be late getting home, and tardiness was frowned upon. The World Government kept track of where everyone was and how long it took them to get places. While there weren't any cameras in the woods, Maeve knew the WG had other ways of knowing where people were, and wandering around in the woods was not considered a good use of one's time. Someone might begin to wonder where she was. Reluctantly, she started to cover the box back up, trying to come up with a plan to retrieve it that wouldn't land her in hot water with her parents or the World Government.

As she began pushing dirt back over the box, she couldn't resist opening the plastic bag on top of the box. She pulled out a piece of paper and stared at the words printed on it:

> To the people of the future:
> We have left this time capsule for you to open. We hope that what is in this box leads you to the truth.
> The survivors of Preston High School
> November 18, 2125

Maeve wrinkled her forehead. "Survivors?" she whispered to herself. "What does that mean?"

She read through the note again. When she got to the date, her eyes widened. "2125. That's nearly 70 years ago. It's part of the Lost Years. Now, what do I do?"

Maeve jogged along the path. She was going to be in trouble. As she came to the end of the path, she heard a low whistle. Surprised, she glanced around and spotted a figure standing against the lone tree in a muddy patch of ground that served as the backyard for Gray Cantwell's house. The figure raised his hand in greeting, and Maeve quickly made her way over to where Gray stood.

Gray Cantwell's 6-foot, muscled frame leaned lazily against the tree. The wind ruffled his longer-than-regulation-length black hair, and Maeve absently wondered how as a soldier-in-training Gray had gotten away with having hair that long. She would bet the army was going to cut it for him soon. Maeve mentally batted away the stray thoughts of Gray's hair and focused on her predicament.

"I'm late," she said, slightly out of breath from her jog, as she focused on his ice blue eyes and ruggedly handsome face. She shifted nervously from foot to foot.

Gray and Maeve had gone to the same school before they started their occupational training but had never had class together. But all the girls knew Gray because he was one of the most popular and best-looking boys in their class. However, despite living near each other, she had probably never said more than three sentences to him in her life.

"I know, Maeve," Gray replied. "I was waiting for you."

"Waiting for me? Why?" Maeve shook her head. "I didn't know you even knew my name, much less what time I come home from work."

"I've always noticed you, Maeve." Gray sent a quick grin her way as she gave him a puzzled look.

"You have?"

"Yep, but we can talk about that later. You have bigger problems. Men from the WG are at your house."

Maeve's eyes widened, and she twisted her hands together. "WG men? What am I going to do?"

"Calm down, for starters," Gray said gently. He brushed his hand soothingly over her shoulder. Maeve startled a bit at his touch. "Why are you late?"

Maeve looked at the muddy ground. "I can't tell you."

She raised her eyes to watch Gray's reaction. He frowned and gave her a hard look.

"Keeping secrets? That can get you in a whole lot of trouble, Maeve. The WG doesn't like secrets, although they seem pretty good at keeping them. They just don't like for the rest of us to have them."

"Will you help me? Please?"

"Will you share your secret?"

Maeve shook her head. "I barely know you. How could I trust you?"

Gray lifted her chin with his finger so she was looking directly into those blue eyes that seemed to see straight into her soul and made her want to know him better. "You can trust me," he said seriously. He dropped his hand and said brusquely, "You need a good excuse."

Maeve shook off the serious moment, tucking it away to ponder when the danger to her had subsided.

"Can't I just say I lost track of time on the way home?"

Gray raised an eyebrow. "You know that won't work. Since the WG men are already there, you can't just play it off as enjoying the weather or getting lost in thought. You'll need a better excuse, and you'll need to stop looking like you have something to hide."

"What do you mean?"

Gray pointed at Maeve's face. "Your face shows your every thought. Right now, your eyes are telling me you have no idea why I'm helping you and you're scared I'm going to turn you in. But they also tell me you're a little bit interested in me."

6

Maeve gasped. "How did you know that?"

"I told you. It's on your face. We'll work on your trust issues and explore that interest later, though. Right now, you have to get home with a believable excuse."

"What am I going to do?" she asked.

"You need a reason to have made that walk so slowly," Gray said as he scratched behind his ear. His eyes brightened. "I know! You twisted your ankle. It slowed you down."

"How am I going to pull that off? I'll probably forget which foot to limp on."

"Tear your pants," Gray said. "That way it will look like you fell."

"No," Maeve replied, shaking her head emphatically. "I'm not tearing one of two pairs of pants I own just to look realistic. The World Government doesn't hand out the next clothing ration for six months!"

"Well, then rub some dirt on one leg. It will look realistic and will help you remember which ankle is supposed to hurt − unless you really want to sprain your ankle for this exercise?"

"No, dirt will be fine, thanks," Maeve said as she shook her head in annoyance.

"We should get to it then," Gray said as he knelt down to grab a handful of mud and rubbed it haphazardly on her right pant leg.

"What do you mean we?" Maeve asked with some alarm.

"I noticed you when you came limping off the path and chivalrously decided to help you to your house.

Just being neighborly. Plus while you're a terrible liar, I am not. I can help cover for you with the WG men."

Maeve started to protest, but decided having him as a distraction for the WG men could only help.

"All right. Let's get going."

"What were you thinking, Maeve?" Maeve's father asked after the WG men and Gray had left. "You know how important it is to be where you're supposed to be when you're supposed to be there."

"Dad, I twisted my ankle." Maeve pointed to the bandage wrapped around her ankle and brushed at the mud Gray had put on her pant leg.

Maeve's mom glanced at her with doubt in her eyes but remained silent.

Maeve's father just shook his head and went back to reading a report related to his job in construction for the WG. He spent a lot of time working on government buildings, but Maeve never knew what exactly took place inside those buildings once they were built.

Her mom was a teacher at the government-run school, working with the early school kids. She had been Maeve's teacher when she was younger. Maeve didn't know who had been happier when that year had ended.

"I'm just glad you're safe," Maeve's mom said as she patted her shoulder and set a cup of weak tea in front of her. On a normal night, Maeve would be helping with the chores, but tonight she sat in her chair at the table with her leg propped up on the chair next to her. She felt like a fraud, but she couldn't tell her parents the truth.

Her dad set aside his report, stood and shrugged on his coat. "I'm going to go bed down the animals."

Maeve's mom nodded. They both knew her dad would be outside for an hour or more. It was his only time during the day that he got to spend time by himself. In a world where everything was regulated, you carved out what little time for yourself that you could.

As soon as the door closed, Maeve's mom set aside the towel she had been using to dry the dishes and carried her own cup of weak tea to the table. She sat in the chair Maeve's dad had recently vacated.

"Are you going to tell me what really happened?"

"I twisted my ankle." Maeve averted her eyes as she repeated the lie.

"I think you and I both know that's not what happened. You can tell me the truth."

Maeve bit her lip. She loved her mom, but her parents had always taught Maeve that the easiest way to live in Palumbra was to follow the dictates of the World Government, and as far as she knew, her mom had always followed that rule.

The silence stretched as Maeve picked at the mud on her pants. She looked at her mom and shook her head. "I twisted my ankle."

Maeve's mom took a sip of her tea and studied

Maeve with sad eyes. "I love you, Maeve. Your dad and I work hard to protect you, but we can't keep you safe if you don't trust us."

Maeve studied her tea as if it held all the secrets of the future. Her mom sighed. "Whatever it is, be careful, OK?"

Maeve readied herself for bed in the loft area that served as her room and tried to make sense of her day. She felt terrible about lying to her mom, but she knew that her mom would have wanted her to turn over the box to the WG as soon as she heard about it. Her parents loved her and she loved them, but they weren't ones to consider rocking the boat. Their rule for survival under the WG was to do exactly what they were told.

Maeve had lived by that rule, too. Until today. Or maybe it had begun before today.

Recently, Maeve had started to question her parents' rule as she began to notice that anyone who voiced disagreement with the WG just disappeared. One of her friends at school just didn't show up one day last year. The teacher said she had moved, but there was nowhere to go. Palumbra was the only place that had survived The Lost Years.

Maeve had come to realize she didn't really know much about the World Government except that they controlled everything. In school, no one ever addressed why the WG existed. They had learned all about how the

World Government worked (one person was in charge) and had intently studied the system for being placed in a job, but no one ever taught the history of the WG. It was as if no one wanted them to know the truth.

"The truth," Maeve said out loud to the empty room. "That's what the note in that box said. 'We hope that what is in this box leads you to the truth.'"

"Do I want to know the truth?"

Maeve had a feeling whatever was in that box was important, but she didn't know what to do about it. She could talk to her friend Ginger, but Ginger was busy with her new job at WG headquarters as well as taking care of her little sister, Emery.

Maeve's thoughts turned to Gray Cantwell. Despite his uncle working for the WG, she thought he might be someone she could trust. Which made no sense. She knew nothing about him. She should probably just tell her parents and turn the box over to the WG, but Maeve was too curious. She needed to know what was in that box.

Her curiosity didn't explain the urge to tell Gray, though. She thought back to how Gray had helped her fool the WG men, something she knew was wrong. She marveled at his ability to so easily tell a lie. What else did he lie about? She hardly even knew him, and Gray's uncle was one of WG president Arabella Laughlin's closest confidants. She would be crazy to tell Gray about the box.

Maeve crawled onto the straw mattress covered with a well-worn quilt her mother had made for her when she was 8 and blew out the single candle illuminating her room. Her family was not a wealthy family in Palumbra, but almost no one was. The World Government provided clothing and food rations. While they didn't go unclothed or unfed, no one had any extra to spare. If someone in your family defied the World Government, your whole family would suffer with fewer food rations. It was an easy way to keep the general public under control. While everyone grew their own food, the WG could make it difficult by withholding seed or soil additives or they could confiscate your animals.

Maeve lay on her meager bed and pulled the quilt up to her chin to ward off the chill of a fall night. She thought about how Gray had saved her from walking into her house full of WG men without a plausible story. He had stood beside her and lied to make sure she avoided punishment for her tardiness. She remembered the sincerity in his eyes when he had said, "You can trust me." Maeve shivered as she thought about how her skin had tingled when he brushed his hand over her shoulder and wished she could trust him with her secret, so she would have an excuse to get to know him better. But trusting the wrong person with her secret could harm both her and her family.

"I can't," Maeve whispered into the darkness. "I can't trust anyone."

CHAPTER TWO

Maeve tried to forget about the box. She went to her training at the hospital each day. She did her chores at home. She told no one. She almost forgot about her chance meeting with Gray Cantwell. Almost.

There was something about him that made her want to know him better. But in Palumbra, meeting with people you didn't normally see during the day wasn't an option. There just wasn't time because every moment of your day was regulated. There was a reason the WG knew how long it took her to get home every day and showed up at her door when she was late. Not only were there cameras everywhere, you never knew who was spying for the WG. Wariness was a behavior learned young in Palumbra.

Maeve's day consisted of getting up at 5 a.m. and helping to take care of the few animals they were allowed to own. Every family had their own cow, pig and a few chickens. The pig was replaced every year. The chickens were expected to live at least five years, and the cows were supposed to last 15. If your animals died before their expected time, then you had to beg, borrow or do without eggs and/or milk until time for your replacement.

After helping with the animals, Maeve washed up, fixed breakfast for her family and headed off to the hospital. After her shift at the hospital, she was expected to come home, help with the evening animal chores, straighten the house and help fix the evening meal. If there was time after the evening meal, she could sit and talk with her parents or read a book approved by the World Government's Department of Printed Resources.

This had been Maeve's life since she was born. Until this year, she had gone to school in the hours that she currently worked at the hospital because in Palumbra, there was little time for anything else. Everyone worked. If you didn't work, you disappeared − no one seemed to know where.

Despite her best efforts to forget the box she had found, Maeve found herself thinking about it each night before she went to bed in the tiny loft space that served as her room. She tried to convince herself to just leave it alone. Trying to dig it out would only get her in trouble, but there was something compelling about the box. It was as if it was calling to her. And if it wasn't the box calling to her, it was the promise of the mysterious truth the note had mentioned.

The truth. What was the truth? Was life different before the Lost Years? She had heard rumors that it was, and you could see evidence of it in the part of the city that was still in ruins. If it had been different, what happened

14

to create the world she currently lived in?

###

    Maeve took the shortcut home from the hospital. She had tried to forget about the box and her encounter with Gray, but she couldn't.

    Maeve tried to only take the shortcut a couple of times a week like she had before she found the box. She didn't want to draw unnecessary attention to herself. Until she had found the box, Maeve hadn't experienced the WG's intense scrutiny, and her experience that day convinced her she didn't want to be in the focus of their attention again.

    As she passed the spot where the box was buried, she was tempted to stop to see if it was still there. The ground looked undisturbed, but she knew now wasn't the time. Being late again would look suspicious.

    She knew that to dig up the box would require bravery she wasn't sure she had. She would have to figure out how to circumvent the ever-watching eyes of the WG, which meant sneaking out during the night. Even then she could get caught. Maeve had no idea what happened to people who displeased the WG, but she knew they disappeared and never came back. When she was 10, her neighbor Mr. Tomkins had been taken away, leaving a wife and two kids to be turned out of their home. Maeve remembered that day. His wife stood on the doorstep with tears running down her face, and the next day, she and the kids were gone, too.

Maeve knew the consequences for being caught would be steep, and she wasn't sure she was ready to face them.

Thoughts of the box inevitably led to thoughts of Gray. Maeve had caught a glimpse of him just once in the two weeks since she'd found the box. They had rarely crossed paths when they were in school together, and she saw him even less now that they were each in training. Soldiers and nurses didn't interact unless there was a war, and with the WG firmly in control, the likelihood of a war was slim.

As she walked home, Maeve listed off what she knew about Gray.

1. He lived in her neighborhood.

2. He was training to be a soldier.

3. His parents were dead – killed long before she could remember. She had no idea what had happened to them. She only knew this much because her mom had mentioned it the night he helped her home.

4. He lived with his uncle, Night Cantwell, who held some sort of important position in the World Government. She knew he worked closely with WG leader Arabella Laughlin because he was always with her when she made an address to the citizens of Palumbra.

5. She could not forget Gray's kindness to her.

Maeve kicked the ground as she walked. There had to be a way to get to know Gray better. She needed to know why he had helped her when it could have gotten him in trouble. She couldn't do anything about digging up the box right now, but she could find out

16

more about Gray. He lived right down the street, and she had done nothing to thank him for helping her out of a tricky situation. No one would think it unusual if she wrote him a note of thanks and took it to his house.

Maeve picked up her pace and hurried home.

When Maeve got home, there were chores to be done and by the time dinner was over, it was getting dark. Electricity in homes was limited to those who worked for the WG, and candles and kerosene were rationed. Most families went to bed when the sun set and got up when it rose. Maeve vaguely knew that at some time in the distant past, people had all the electricity they could want and were able to stay up well into the night, and she wondered what that kind of freedom felt like.

As the sun set, Maeve went outside to catch the last dying rays and write her note to Gray, but she stared at the blank page. Gray had not sought her out since the day he had helped save her from the WG men. What if he didn't care to hear from her again?

Maeve debated internally for a minute, then decided the worst thing that could happen was she never saw him again, which was exactly how things stood currently.

With that thought, she put pen to paper and wrote:

Hi Gray,
Thanks for helping me home the other night. I don't know how I would have made it without you. I

wish I had something more than words to give you as thanks. My ankle is all healed, and I'm back to walking to and from the hospital every day. Some days I even walk the long way. I appreciate what you did for me.

Thanks again,
Maeve

Maeve read the note with critical eyes, making sure that it gave nothing away about what had really happened that night. If the WG ever got their hands on the note, it would look like a simple thank you. Her goal was to thank Gray and give him an opportunity to catch up with her again if he so chose. Now, it was up to him whether she saw him again.

The next day, Maeve took the shortcut home from the hospital, taking a quick glance at the spot where the box was buried on her way by. She arrived home a few minutes early, so no one else was home. She left a note saying she was running an errand, grabbed the note for Gray and headed to his house.

When she knocked on the door, a distinguished man in his mid-30s answered the door. He was so tall she had to tilt her head back to look him in the face. When she did, she met a pair of striking blue eyes that were identical to Gray's. His eyes were set over angular cheekbones and a slim nose. Jet black hair that touched his shoulders adorned his head. This must be Night Cantwell.

"Hello," the man said. "Who might you be?"

"I'm Maeve Jackson. I live down the street."

"Nice to meet you, Maeve. What can I do for you?"

"I just wanted to drop off this note for Gray. He helped me when I hurt my ankle a couple of weeks ago, and I wanted to say thanks."

"Ah, yes. You must be the young lady that arrived home late. Gray told me about your ankle and your encounter with the WG men. I'm glad you're all healed up. Gray isn't home right now, but I will make sure he receives your note."

"Thank you," Maeve said. "I'll be going now. It was nice to meet you."

"Nice to meet you, too," Night replied. "And Maeve?"

"Yes."

"Try not to be late again."

Maeve's heart sped up, and she tried not to show the nervousness his words created. Night Cantwell worked for the WG. Did he know she hadn't hurt her ankle? Did he know about the box?

"I'll do my best not to twist my ankle again," Maeve said with a slight smile. "Thank you for giving the note to Gray."

"You're welcome."

Maeve turned to walk back to her own house, noticing that Night Cantwell stood in the door, his intense blue eyes following her as she walked down the street, the note for Gray in his hand.

CHAPTER THREE

Maeve wondered if Gray's uncle had given him the note as days passed and she neither saw nor heard from Gray. On the days she passed the place where the box was buried, she wondered what, if anything, to do about it. And every day, she wondered if Gray had gotten her note.

"Well," she thought one day as she walked home, "he's clearly not interested in getting to know me better. That's fine. I don't need him. I can figure things out on my own. Plus, his uncle works for the WG, and I bet he monitors everything Gray does. Who needs that kind of trouble?"

Her decision made, Maeve stepped off the path near her street − and found Gray waiting for her.

Lost in her own thoughts, she nearly walked past where he was standing, fishing pole over his shoulder. It wasn't until he quietly called her name that she realized the object of her thoughts for much of her walk home was standing right in front of her.

"Oh ... hi," Maeve said as she took a step back.

"Hi," Gray replied with a smile.

"What are you doing here?"

"Well, I was about to go fishing." He motioned at the pole. "Thought I'd see if you wanted to join me."

"Why?" Maeve eyed him suspiciously.

"I got your note. I thought maybe we could catch some fish for dinner, but if you're not interested..." He shrugged and started to turn away.

"No, no, I'd love to go," Maeve said quickly as all thoughts of not wanting to get involved with Gray fled from her mind. "I just need to change into older clothes."

"That's OK. I can wait. Meet me back here in 20 minutes." Gray leaned against the side of his house and set the fishing pole next to him.

"OK. Sure," Maeve said as she hurried toward her own house, glancing over her shoulder to see Gray's blue eyes following her movement down the street.

After a quick stop at home to change her clothes, leave a note for her parents and grab her fishing pole, Maeve rejoined Gray at the entrance to the path.

"Ready?" Gray asked.

"Sure," Maeve replied.

Without talking, they walked side by side back the way Maeve had come home from the hospital. It wasn't an awkward silence but a companionable one because despite not knowing him well, Maeve felt comfortable in his presence.

Gray finally spoke. "Thanks again for the note. I was wondering if I'd ever hear from you again."

"Well ... I thought that might be the best way to talk to you again since deviating from my schedule isn't really an option."

"Was fishing on your schedule?"

"Not today, but it is something I normally do."

They were tiptoeing around a forbidden subject in Palumbra – the stranglehold the WG had on its people. Neither wanted to say too much for fear they were still being watched.

"Your uncle seems pretty nice," Maeve said, changing the subject.

"Yeah. He's decent. He's not my mom and dad, but if I can't have them, I'll take Night."

"You don't call him Uncle Night?"

Gray shook his head and shrugged. "No. He's not a fan of that. So he's just Night."

"Night's an unusual name. Come to think of it, Gray isn't that common either."

"Yeah, we're an unusual family," Gray said with a grin.

When they reached the lake, Gray pulled out a box of bait and baited both their hooks.

"I can do that, you know," Maeve said, reaching for the hook.

"I know you're plenty capable." Gray handed the pole with its baited hook back to her. "Now, throw your hook in the water and don't argue."

"Really?" Maeve frowned as she took the pole back. "What would you know about me? Until a couple of weeks ago, we had never spoken."

"Not true. We'd had exactly three conversations before that." Gray stared at his pole as he stated this fact.

"What? I'm pretty sure I'd remember that."

"Nope. We spoke three times before that day on the path."

"When?" Maeve demanded.

"Once in Year 6 when I stepped on your shoe. I said 'Sorry,'" Gray said as he cast his hook into the still, clear water of the lake. "Another time in the lunch line in Year 8. I asked if you wanted some cake. And right before the aptitude test I asked if you were nervous."

Maeve expertly cast her own line into the lake and said, "Those aren't conversations. We barely spoke."

"They were the highlight of my days," Gray said with a grin.

"You're crazy," Maeve announced with a grin of her own.

They fished in silence for the next few minutes until Gray nudged Maeve with his elbow. She looked up from contemplating her line and found his eyes pinned on her. "Why are you so surprised that I remember every time I've talked to you?"

Maeve shrugged. "Why would you? I'm nobody important. There's nothing special about me."

Gray turned to face her, holding his fishing pole with one hand and using the other to tip her chin up to look him in the eyes. "I've watched you, Maeve Jackson. You are most definitely something special. You help your friends, and you're kind to other kids, even the ones you don't like. You follow the rules and you don't rock the boat, even when something bothers you."

Maeve shook her head. "But that's not special. That's just life."

Gray returned his attention to his fishing pole. "Do you ever think maybe there's more to life than just doing what we're told?"

Maeve glanced at him. "You're a soldier. Isn't that what you do, follow orders?"

"Maybe." Gray shrugged. "But maybe there's more than just following orders. Maybe there's another way to live."

Maeve shook her head. "I don't know what you're talking about, but it sounds dangerous. The only way to survive in Palumbra is to do what we're told."

"So why were you late that night?"

Maeve jerked her fishing pole in surprise at the swift change in the conversation. "Why do you want to know?"

"You just told me that the only way to survive is to follow the rules, so I'm curious what would make you break those rules," Gray said quietly.

Maeve studied him thoughtfully then shook her head. "I can't tell you."

"Who can you tell, then?" Gray asked as he gave a hard tug on his fishing pole to free the line that had caught on a hidden snag. "Did you tell your parents?"

Maeve shook her head in frustration. "I can't tell anyone, OK? It's too dangerous!" Maeve slapped one hand over her mouth, horrified that she had revealed too much.

Gray pried her hand away from her face and gently turned her to face him. "All the more reason to share, Maeve. You might need help."

Maeve turned away as she felt a tug on her line.

Slowly shaking her head, she said, "I can't, Gray. I just can't."

No more was said about Maeve's secret as they began to reel in fish. They talked about their jobs and their families and people they both knew from school as Maeve caught four fish and baited her own hook after the first round. Gray finished the hour with two fish. Together, they scaled and cleaned the fish, then washed their hands in the lake, picked up their poles and headed for home.

As they reached the end of the path, Maeve looked up at Gray and said, "Thanks for the fishing trip. My mom will be happy to have something different for dinner."

"No problem, Maeve. Maybe we can do it again sometime." Gray turned his head to look left, then right, then over his shoulder. He took a quick glance up at his house. Dropping his voice and placing his hand on her shoulder, he said, "And maybe next time you'll tell me your secret." He winked at her and started up the walkway to his house, his long legs eating up the distance to the door.

Maeve stood frozen at the end of the path until he reached the door, looked over his shoulder, and lifted his hand in a wave. Maeve slowly lifted her hand to wave back and started toward her own house – her steps much slower than Gray's.

Like most people in Palumbra, Maeve didn't

have a lot of friends. Her only real friend was Ginger, a girl she'd known since they started school. Even when children were young, they were kept busy with school and chores as they were expected to be contributing members of society from the time they could walk and talk. Some of Maeve's earliest memories were of helping her mother gather eggs and wash the dishes.

Life in Palumbra was hard work. The wars of The Lost Years had made it difficult to grow crops on the land, so just feeding a family required an industrious spirit. The soil had to be carefully prepared, and plants had to be tended. Each family only received one allotment of soil additives and a small amount of seed each year, so they had to use them wisely. Maeve remembered learning to read at school out of a dog-eared copy of <u>Growing Crops in Difficult Soil</u>, much like the well-worn copy her family had at home. Schools used it to teach reading because it was the one book every Palumbrian family owned.

Because it took so much time just to survive in the hostile environment of Palumbra, most families kept to themselves. Everyone was friendly enough, but there simply wasn't time to nurture friendships outside of your family.

So it was surprising to Maeve that Gray kept showing up. A week after their fishing trip, Gray caught up with her on her walk home from the hospital. Just as she was passing the spot where the box lay buried, she heard footsteps behind her. Careful not to slow her steps or to even look at the place where the box was, she glanced over her shoulder to see who was walking on the path with her. She immediately caught a glimpse of dark brown army fatigues. Her heart sped up. Had they caught her? Was the WG now sending people to spy on her?

When she looked more closely, she found twinkling blue eyes staring back at her. "Gray! You startled me. I don't usually run into people on this path."

"Well, that sounds kinda lonely. Good thing I'm here." He grinned.

"Where are you going?" Maeve asked.

"Heading home," Gray said and waved his hand in the direction of their houses.

"But this path isn't on your way home. Did they have you doing military exercises outside the compound?"

"Nope. I just thought I might find some company on this path, so I decided to take the long way home."

"You were really looking for me?" Maeve asked with a lift of her eyebrows.

"Really was," he said with a grin as he tapped her on the nose with his index finger.

"Why would you want to spend time with me? You're not spying on me, are you?"

"Why would I spy on you, Maeve?" Gray sounded hurt. He pinned her with his stare. "Maybe I just like spending time with you."

Maeve was silent. She had enjoyed talking with Gray when they went fishing. He was funny and smart, not to mention easy on the eyes. And he seemed to be interested in her, too, since he remembered every time they had met. But when she wouldn't answer his questions about why she was late the day she had found the box, she assumed that would be the end of their budding friendship. Now, she didn't know what to think. Gray's uncle worked for the WG, which made her wonder if the WG was suspicious of her. What if Gray <u>was</u> a spy for his uncle?

Maeve had so much to think about. Until she found the box, she would never have worried about getting on the wrong side of the WG. Her life in Palumbra was predictable but not terrible. She knew about people like Mr. Tomkins disappearing, but she had never thought much about what could cause that to happen. Now, she thought about it every day.

"Earth to Maeve," Gray said.

"What? Oh, sorry. I was just thinking."

"About what?"

"Probably things I shouldn't be," she said with shrug. "Tell me about what you did today."

"We spent the day getting ready for the practice disaster event at the end of the week. What about you?"

"Well, I do work at the hospital, so I helped the sick and injured. Actually, I mostly just carried stuff for people and filed paperwork. Not many new patients today, so the youngest nurses get the grunt work."

They had reached the spot where the path ended in Gray's backyard. Maeve turned toward Gray, noting his brown army fatigues and the empty holster on his hip.

"Do they let you carry a gun during the day?"

"Sometimes. It depends on what we're doing. But we're never allowed to leave the compound with them unless we're out on an exercise."

"Do you really think you could kill someone?"

"I think when you're a soldier, you don't get much choice."

"But who are we fighting? Palumbra hasn't been part of a war since The Lost Years."

Gray glanced around and said quietly, "It might be better for you if that question stays unanswered. Some answers are dangerous."

Maeve gave him a questioning look but was distracted when he took her hand and gave it a squeeze.

"Have a good evening, Maeve," he said quietly. "Maybe I'll take the long way home more often."

He turned aside and walked up the path to his house. Maeve watched him go. At the door, he turned toward her and saluted before going inside, leaving Maeve to turn her steps toward her own home.

CHAPTER FOUR

Gray didn't take the long way home the rest of the week. Maeve tried not to be disappointed.

"It's not like he promised to walk with me," Maeve told herself when Gray didn't show up on the path home the next day. "He's probably busy. Surely, he's not upset because I asked if he was spying on me."

But as the week progressed, Maeve became less and less sure of herself. She nearly forgot about the box as she focused on how she could see Gray again.

Because they weren't already friends, simply going to his house to talk with him would have looked suspicious. She had to figure out another reason to see him. His position as a soldier in training didn't put him in the same places as her training to be a nurse. Any contact with him would have to look spontaneous and natural, but Maeve had yet to figure out how to make that happen.

Going back to get the box was less of a concern because Maeve could always take the shortcut. Every time she passed the box, she glanced over to make sure it was still covered. Keeping an eye on the box wasn't a problem – getting it out of the ground would be because while the shortcut wasn't heavily used, it carried enough traffic that she couldn't just dig a hole and expect no one to notice it. Digging it up on her way home wasn't an option because there just wasn't enough time on her walks to and from the hospital to dig the box out all at once.

As the week ticked by, Maeve became more and more anxious to dig up the box. She worried constantly that someone else would find it and endlessly pondered what the note meant when it talked about "the truth" and whether she really wanted to know the answer.

Friday finally arrived and with it, the joint exercise with the military, where they would practice their response to a natural disaster like a tornado or flood. Maeve wasn't sure why they even did these drills. There hadn't been a tornado in years, and Palumbra didn't get enough rain to cause a flood. All of their food was grown in greenhouses where water and nutrients were carefully administered to the plants. All her life, water had been a precious commodity. Even showers and clothes washing were regulated by the WG.

When the day of the exercise arrived, Maeve walked to the hospital using the shortcut, sparing the box's location a quick glance. When she saw nothing had been disturbed, she quickly covered the remaining distance to her work.

When she arrived, she found what looked like the entire military of Palumbra milling around. Since she was a few minutes early, she stopped on the hill above the hospital and took it all in. There were tanks and trucks and hundreds of people set up outside the hospital. The occasional doctor or hospital administrator could be seen talking with some of the military people. Her eyes scanned the crowd looking for one specific soldier-in-training – Gray Cantwell. From her perch on the top of the hill she could hardly make out individual faces, so with a shrug, she continued down the hill.

As she neared the doors to the hospital, she spotted her boss Nancy Longstreet talking with a soldier. Nancy called her over. As Maeve approached, the soldier turned around, and a pair of startlingly blue eyes met her own, causing her to smile.

"Maeve, I want you to meet Gray Cantwell," Nancy said.

"We've met," Maeve said.

"Oh," said Nancy, her eyes widening. "How do you know each other?"

"Gray helped me out the other day when I twisted my ankle on the way home. We live on the same street."

"Well, that helps since you're going to be working together today," Nancy said.

Maeve raised her eyes to Gray's and offered a quick smile. He quirked his lips in response.

"You'll both be working in the triage area. Maeve, you will be assessing injuries and Gray will be helping to identify the injured and provide you with security," Nancy announced.

"Security?" Maeve asked with a grimace. "Why would I need security?"

"A disaster would be a good time for troublemakers to cause a disruption, so security is part of our disaster plan," Nancy replied.

"OK," Maeve said as if that made perfect sense to her. As far as she knew, the World Government held a tight grip on everything. In her whole life, there had never been an attack on the WG, so why would they need security today? She looked at Gray, but he seemed to be taking Nancy's pronouncement in stride.

"Lead the way, Maeve," Gray said.

Maeve started walking toward where the triage area had been set up in the corner of what was once a parking lot. No need for a parking lot now, though. So few residents of Palumbra had vehicles of any kind that the only ones in the lot were a couple of decades-old cars and the military vehicles ringing the perimeter. To Maeve it seemed like the military was showing a large presence for a simple disaster drill.

The hospital ran disaster drills every six months, but this was the first one that Maeve had been a part of. She had seen them before on her way to and from school, though, and she didn't remember any drill that with this large of a military presence. It wasn't just the vehicles. There were hundreds of soldiers roaming through the hospital personnel — every one of them carrying a gun.

She glanced over at Gray. He, too, had a sidearm strapped to his belt and a rifle slung over his shoulder. She felt a shiver of unease and wondered again what kind of trouble the military was expecting.

"This way," Maeve said to Gray. "Are there

always this many military people at these disaster drill?"

"I don't really know," Gray said. "This is the first one I've been a part of. I do know that we got a lot of instruction on security for this drill."

"Hmm," Maeve said with a lift of her eyebrows.

They reached the triage area and Maeve said hello to Ginger Snell, one of her only friends and a former classmate who was in training to be part of the World Government's technology team. Ginger was probably a genius, and although there were no tests to prove it, she was a whiz with technology. When they were in school, Ginger was the person the instructors asked to fix the school's three ancient computers. Maeve wasn't sure how Ginger had learned about technology since books and computers were scarce, and the only people who had access to computers were those who worked in the WG headquarters.

Despite there being little time to for friendship in Palumbra, Maeve and Ginger had been friends since they started school. Despite their different interests, they were close, and Maeve viewed Ginger as the sister she'd never had.

Since they had left school for their different jobs, though, they hadn't seen much of each other.

Maeve looked at Ginger and asked, "What are you doing here? I didn't think there was much technology to work on out here."

"It's an all-hands-on-deck kind of day," Ginger replied. "All the trainees at headquarters are expected to participate. We're some of the wounded."

34

Ginger held up her arm, which had been made to look as if a piece of shrapnel had been buried in it. It wasn't very realistic looking, but as the triage nurse-in-training, Maeve would be able to determine the severity of the wound and place her in a treatment line.

"I bet you're a terrible patient," Maeve said with a grin as she turned to Gray. "Do you know Ginger?"

Gray took in the petite girl with large gray eyes and waist-length black hair that was pulled into a high pony tail and said, "I recognize you, but I don't think we've ever met. Gray Cantwell."

"Hi, Gray," Ginger replied. "Nice to meet you. I recognize you from school, but I didn't know you two knew each other."

"We don't. Not really," Maeve said, downplaying the times she and Gray had met. "Gray helped me out the other day when I hurt my ankle walking home from the hospital, and we just got assigned to work together today."

An old-fashioned dinner bell began ringing to signal that everyone should get ready for the drill to start.

"That's my cue to go act injured," Ginger said. "Talk to you soon." She bounced away cheerfully into the crowd.

Maeve and Gray moved on to check in with the head nurse in the triage area. She handed them both clipboards and assigned them to check in patients and make an initial assessment of their injuries. Gray's job was to identify those he could and to keep an eye on the security around them.

"Ginger seems nice," Gray said to Maeve once they had found their assigned spot.

"She is. We've been friends since early school. We were two quiet kids in a sea of noisy ones, and we kind of banded together, I guess. I don't see her much any more since she's in training at WG headquarters and she's almost solely responsible for her little sister, Emery."

"How old is her sister?"

"She's 12."

"Where are her parents?"

"Her dad died under some mysterious circumstances, and her mom works double shifts at the factory."

There was no need for Gray to ask which factory as there was only one in Palumbra. The factory made everything that the people of Palumbra needed from clothing to furniture. It was a huge operation, taking up a large swathe of land just outside the city center. The vast majority of Palumbrians actually worked there, and Maeve considered herself lucky to have an aptitude that kept her away from it. From what she knew, which admittedly wasn't much, working at the factory was a difficult job at best.

"I'm glad we got paired up today," Gray said. "I've been trying to figure out how to see you again without raising any suspicion about your tardiness the other day."

"Really?" Maeve asked as she twisted her hands together. "Why would you want to see me again?"

"Maybe because you're smart, pretty and a bit

fun to talk with?" Gray replied.

Maeve looked up from her clipboard, trying to decipher Gray's intention. He smiled at her and waited for a reply.

"Oh. But we hardly know each other."

"We could change that," Gray said with a wink.

Maeve looked at him with serious brown eyes. He seemed sincere.

"I think I'd like that," Maeve said slowly.

Before either of them could say anything else, their first patient arrived. Maeve hurried to look over the young soldier's "injuries" and quickly deduced they were not life-threatening, so he could wait for treatment.

Gray noted the soldier's name and ID number on his clipboard and relieved the soldier of his weapon. They sent him to the appropriate area and moved on to the next patient.

They worked together for the next two hours, cataloging names and injuries and collecting the "wounded" soldiers' guns. They were so busy they barely had time to look around at the rest of the drill or talk to each other about anything other than their jobs. Gray had amassed quite a stockpile of weapons as he took each soldier's gun.

Just as Maeve was about to greet another patient, a huge explosion shook the ground and hurled debris, flames and smoke into the air.

"What was that?" Maeve asked Gray as burning debris rained down around them. "This is supposed to be a natural disaster drill, not a war drill."

Gray pulled her out of the range of the falling debris and brushed ash from her hair. "I don't think that was part of the drill."

As the smoke from the initial explosion cleared, Maeve and Gray could see that half the hospital had been blown away by the explosion. What had been the main entrance of the hospital was now just a sheared-off wreck. Flames and smoke billowed from what was left of the building and bodies littered the ground around it. The heat from the fire kept those left standing from making their way into the hospital to help those still trapped. Maeve and the hospital workers that had been part of the drill stood in stunned silence as they took note of the bodies around them. People who had been thrown to the ground by the explosion began to stir, many moaning in pain.

"What do we do now?" Maeve asked.

Gray was surveying the perimeter of the parking lot near where they were standing. Maeve followed his gaze to the woods at the edge of the lot where she thought she saw movement.

"Maeve, something is wrong," Gray said as he backed up a step.

"Of course, something is wrong. The hospital just blew up." Maeve looked around in confusion, then shook her head and took a step forward to help the wounded. Gray put his hand on his arm to stop her.

"No, I mean I don't think the hospital blew up because of a gas leak or an accident." Gray took another step away from the woods and pulled his rifle around as
38

if ready to shoot.

Maeve looked at him, then at his gun. "What are you talking about? Of course it was an accident."

"Maeve, look at the edge of the parking lot." Gray let go of her arm and motioned in the direction of the trees. "What do you see?"

She tore her gaze away from the shell of the hospital and the score of injured people around it and began to slowly look around the edge of the parking lot.

"Are those people? People with guns?" Maeve shifted uneasily.

"We have to get away from here." Gray turned, grabbed Maeve's hand and began to move away quickly.

Maeve stopped and dug in her heels, refusing to go another step. "You want to leave? What about all the injured people?"

"Those people aren't heading this way just to have a chat," he said as he motioned with his gun toward the advancing group. "They blew up the hospital as a distraction. Nothing good is going to happen if we stay here."

Maeve looked from the group with guns to the still blazing hospital. Her gaze scanned the wounded and dying, and she began to cough as the thick smoke from the hospital blaze wafted toward them. "How do you know this? What if those people are coming to help? What's going on?"

"I don't know, but I do know that if we stay here, we may not live long enough to find out." Gray tugged on her hand and began moving again. Maeve looked again at the devastation around them and slowly began to follow.

As if his words were prophetic, the rat-tat-tat of gunfire broke through the roaring of the flames and the cries of the injured.

"Maeve, we have to go!" Gray's grip on her hand became unbreakable. Maeve stumbled along beside him as he began to jog.

Maeve looked over her shoulder to see a group of people lift their guns and begin shooting at the wounded and those who were trying to help them. Her eyes widened and she quickened her pace.

"They're shooting at the people trying to help! Why aren't the soldiers stopping them?" Maeve cried as she struggled to keep up.

"Do you see any soldiers besides me?"

Maeve scanned the area, looking all around the hospital grounds as she ran. Despite her having sent dozens of soldiers to different areas for medical help, the only uniform within her line of sight was Gray's. She raised scared eyes to Gray's face.

"We have to go," Gray repeated. He grabbed several guns off the pile of the "wounded" soldiers' guns, handed one to Maeve and tugged on her sleeve. He shoved ammunition into his pockets and handed more to Maeve to carry.

"What about Ginger?" Maeve frantically whipped her head back and forth, searching the hospital grounds for her friend.

"Do you see her?" Gray asked as he started

moving again.

Maeve looked around again, praying for just a glimpse of Ginger's distinctive long hair. "There," Maeve said, letting out a sigh of relief and pointing to her left where Ginger sat on the ground, her eyes glazed over, about 100 yards from where Maeve and Gray stood.

"Let's get her and go," Gray said.

CHAPTER FIVE

"**G**inger!" Maeve cried.

Ginger didn't move. She just stared at the hospital, her handheld computer still in her lap.

"Ginger, we have to go!" Maeve tugged on Ginger's hand, trying to get her to move. She glanced over her shoulder. People with guns were closing in on them from all sides.

Ginger finally glanced up at Maeve.

"The hospital," she said. "What happened?"

"I don't know, but we have to move."

"But, people are injured. I have friends in there." Ginger motioned toward the burning hulk of the hospital.

"Ginger, there are people with guns headed this way. We have to go." Maeve tugged again on Ginger's hand, this time with more force.

As they spoke, Ginger slowly got to her feet, holding tightly to her computer. Maeve looked at Gray, who was anxiously scanning the perimeter of the parking lot, looking for an escape route. "Maeve, let's move."

Maeve grasped Ginger's hand and pulled her next

to Gray. Gray glanced at them both and said, "We have to move quickly and quietly. No one is paying attention to us now, but once we start moving, they'll notice us. Stay as low to the ground as you can, and follow me. If anything happens to me, there's a small fishing hut on the far shore of the lake where we fished earlier this week. Go there, and wait for my uncle to find you."

Maeve looked at Gray and cocked her head. She was startled to know Gray and his uncle had a plan for a situation like this.

There was no time give it any more thought, though, as Gray started running in a half-crouch toward the hospital.

"What are you doing? We can't go in there. We'll burn up." Maeve turned to head back the way they had come. Gray placed a hand on her arm to stop her.

"Look," he pointed toward the hospital. "If we stay close to the edge of the hospital building, no one will be able to see us, and we can make our way into the woods. We have to find cover. I don't know what those people with guns are up to, but I do know it can't be anything good."

Maeve kept one hand wrapped around Ginger's hand and her eyes on Gray's back. He had two guns strapped across his back and one in his hands. As he ran, he kept swiveling his head back and forth, trying to see in all directions at once, and she stayed as close as possible without getting in his way.

Gray skirted around the front of the hospital, keeping just out of range of the burning debris but staying in the shadow of the building. Just as they were about to slip into the woods without being seen, Maeve heard a shout and a whistling sound. Something hit the tree next to her with a thunk.

Gray turned and pushed her and Ginger toward the woods in front of him as he returned fire, grabbed Maeve's hand and sprinted the last 100 yards into the woods.

They ran through the woods, with Gray continually looking over his shoulder, listening to the sounds of their pursuers crashing through the underbrush behind them.

He led them in a circuitous route through the woods, but their pursuers seemed to have no trouble following them. Gray stopped and crouched behind some bushes to get his bearings, and Maeve and Ginger did the same.

"How are they following us so easily?" Gray asked. "We're not that noisy, and we had a pretty good head start. We should have lost them long ago."

"But the WG can track anyone," Maeve said.

"Not anyone," Ginger replied. "They mostly rely on cameras and knowing how long it should take for a person to travel from one place to another. And there are no cameras in these woods because they're too difficult to maintain."

"That's right," Gray said. "My uncle told me the WG relies on people and cameras to track the citizens of Palumbra. These woods are one of the places they have trouble with, so we <u>should</u> be safe in here," Gray said as he scanned the area.

"So how are they following us so easily?" Maeve asked.

"I don't know," Gray said. He looked from Maeve to Ginger, and his eyes widened. "Ginger!"

"What?"

"What are you carrying?"

"It's my handheld computer. I thought we might need... Oh." She looked at her computer as realization dawned. Her face tightened as if in pain, then she reluctantly handed the device to Gray.

"We have to get rid of it," Gray said.

"We should use it as a decoy," Maeve said. "If they're using it to track us, we can use it to our advantage."

"Good thinking. I'm going to take it and run one direction. You two run the opposite way. We'll meet up at the lake. Can you girls get there from here?"

Maeve took a few seconds to get her bearings. She had not been in the woods often, but everyone in Palumbra knew how to determine their directions based on the position of the sun. It was the only way to navigate that was available to everyone.

Maeve pointed south. "Head that way, and we should run into it," she said.

"Can either of you shoot?" Gray asked.

Maeve shook her head. There had been no opportunity to learn because access to guns was strictly controlled by the WG.

"I can. I think," Ginger said. "I've only done it in computer simulations. But I know the basics."

"That will have to be good enough," Gray said and

handed her one of the guns. He gave her a 10-second orientation that mostly consisted of "Here's the trigger." Ginger slung the gun over her back and looked at Maeve.

"We're good," Maeve said. "We need to get moving."

"Good. I'll meet you on the far shore. Stay hidden until I get there. Wait 20 minutes for me, then find the fishing hut if I don't show up."

Maeve looked at Gray, suddenly scared for him. "Gray, be careful."

He winked at her and took off at a run into the trees.

Maeve grabbed Ginger's hand and started running, heading south through the trees. The sounds of their pursuers became fainter and fainter. Neither girl said a word. Not accustomed to this much running, both Maeve and Ginger were breathing heavily, and eventually, they had to stop and catch their breath.

"What is going on?" Ginger asked.

"I don't know," Maeve said, pursing her lips. "Who were those people?"

Ginger looked at Maeve and asked quietly, "How do you know Gray? How do we know he's not part of this?"

"He lives down the street from me. We went to school with him, remember? He's training to be a soldier. I twisted my ankle on the walk home from the hospital a couple of weeks ago, and he helped me home. He lives with his uncle, Night Cantwell."

"Night Cantwell?" Ginger gasped. "He's one of

Arabella Laughlin's advisers! We need to be careful."

"Gray won't hurt us. The WG is strict, but they're not out to kill us. We haven't done anything."

Ginger looked skeptical. "Anyway, we don't have any good choices other than to head for the lake. We need to move on."

As they ran, Maeve thought about what Ginger had said. She didn't really know Gray that well, but she couldn't decide on any reason he would have to harm her − unless the WG knew she had found that box. Maeve shook her head. That didn't make sense. The WG would have just dug up the box. Since there was nothing she could do about it now, she pushed the worries aside and focused on running.

They arrived at the lake without encountering any of their pursuers and waited for Gray. She and Ginger knelt behind some bushes to wait, Ginger keeping the gun propped on her lap with her finger on the trigger.

"Do you think you could actually shoot someone?" Maeve asked, staring at the gun.

Ginger's face was grim. "If they were going to shoot me? Definitely. Someone has to be alive to take care of Emery."

Ginger generally took care of Emery because her mom worked long hours at the factory. Maeve loved Emery. She was a tiny thing, with sleek blond hair and a face that reminded you of a doll − large blue eyes, long lashes and pink cheeks. But her china doll appearance masked a strong, determined girl.

"Where is Emery right now?" Maeve asked.

"Hopefully, at school. We need to figure out what's going on, so I can go pick her up."

"Do you think there were attacks anywhere else?"

"I don't know. I'm worried. What if they attacked the school? I need to get Emery. What about my mom and your parents?"

Maeve bit her lip. "I don't know," she said, feeling helpless.

Maeve glanced around, willing Gray to emerge from the trees. What would they do if he didn't show up? Was it even safe to go home? Off in the distance, Maeve could see black smoke rising and knew something was burning. Maybe it was life as she knew it.

"How long have we been here?" Ginger asked.

"About 10 minutes, I think. I guess we give Gray another 10 minutes, then we try to find the fishing hut ourselves."

Without warning, a figure emerged from the trees to their left. Maeve uncrouched herself as if to stand, but Ginger grabbed her hand and pulled her back down. "We don't know who that is," she whispered.

Maeve nodded and returned to a crouch, thinking that she would need to learn to be more cautious. "Do you think it's Gray?"

"How do we know Gray is on our side?" Ginger whispered urgently. "What even is our side? Who are we fighting? Why did they chase us? What is going on?"

"Ginger, I don't know, OK? All I know is Gray got us out of there, so I think we should trust him until he gives us a reason not to."

Ginger arched her eyebrows and gave a brief roll of her eyes. "I think you're being way too quick to trust him. You can't really trust anyone with ties to the WG, but you're right. There aren't any other options right now. But I'm keeping the gun."

"Fine. But why can't we trust anyone with the WG?" Maeve asked.

"Oh, Maeve," Ginger said with a disbelieving shake of her head. "Do you think everyone likes living under the restrictions of the WG? Don't you think there might be people fighting against the government?"

Maeve stared uncomprehendingly at Ginger. She started to speak but Ginger shook her head as a figure emerged from the tree line, wearing brown army fatigues. As he drew closer, Maeve could see blue eyes scanning the area from under the army-issue cap. It was Gray.

Maeve slowly got to her feet, rustling the leaves as she stood. Gray stopped and raised his gun, unsure of who she was. "Gray, it's me," Maeve said quietly.

He lowered his gun and walked quickly to their hiding spot. "Are you guys OK?" he asked as he gave them a quick once over. Ginger and Maeve nodded.

"We're fine," Maeve said. "Just happy to see you."

Gray nodded at Ginger and squeezed Maeve's hand. "Come on. Let's move. We have to get to the fishing hut." He walked briskly to the east.

Gray seemed to have a plan, and since he was the only one of the three of them who did, Maeve and Ginger followed.

CHAPTER SIX

They followed Gray through the woods as he worked his way around the lake. With each crack of a twig under their feet, Maeve worried they would be heard. Gray hadn't said anything about whether he had lost their pursuers. He hadn't said anything since he showed up and told them to move. Maeve didn't know what to think about any of this. While life in Palumbra wasn't good, there had never been any organized resistance to the WG before.

She shook her head in confusion. She didn't know whom to trust. Did Ginger know something she wasn't telling Maeve? Did Gray?

Maeve thought about her mom and dad and wondered where they were. While they weren't a family that expressed a lot of emotion, Maeve loved her mom and dad. Did they know what was going on?

While Maeve thought herself in circles, she continued to follow Gray as Ginger brought up the rear. Both Gray and Ginger held their guns at the ready, looking for the enemy – whoever they were.

Abruptly Gray stopped as the woods opened into a small clearing with a small shack in the center.

No trees or bushes grew in the clearing, which meant anyone could see you as you approached the door. Maeve wondered if that was intentional. The ramshackle building's roof sagged and the paint was chipped, but when Maeve gave it a second look, she could see that the structure itself was standing straight and the glass in the small, square windows was intact.

"Why are we stopping?" Maeve asked.

"Just making sure it's safe to cross the clearing," Gray said.

"Did you lose the people chasing us?" Ginger asked.

"I think so, but I want to be sure. Keep that gun ready. Ginger, you're going to run across the clearing to the side of the fishing hut. Take cover there, then cover Maeve as she crosses. I'll come last."

"OK. Do I run straight there?"

"Kind of zig-zag back and forth as you run. Makes you harder to hit."

Maeve felt Ginger squeeze her hand once, then she said, "I'm ready."

Gray gave a quick nod and made a sweeping "after you" gesture with his hand. Ginger took off at a sprint, weaving back and forth as she ran to the side of the fishing hut. Gray's eyes scanned the clearing for danger, but Ginger made it without incident.

"Your turn," Gray said.

Maeve followed Ginger's path, feeling exposed as she ran with nothing to defend herself. "I need to learn how to shoot," Maeve thought. She immediately shook off the idea. This was just a temporary situation, she told herself. Her life would go back to normal when this was sorted.

Maeve reached Ginger without incident and watched as Gray quickly made his way to them, eyes alert and head swiveling as he ran. Ginger kept a firm grip on her gun and watched intently as Gray ran across the clearing.

"What now?" Maeve asked. "Why didn't we just run straight to the door?"

"We might not be the only ones here," Gray answered. "We don't know how many people might know about this place. Cover me."

Gray crept around the corner of the shack, careful to keep his footsteps quiet. When he reached the door, he motioned to the girls to join him, and they, too, moved carefully around to the door. He positioned them on the side where the hinges held the door in place.

"On the count of three, I'm going to open the door. Maeve, stay back. Ginger, when I open the door, keep your gun ready."

Gray slowly turned the doorknob and eased the door open, letting the nose of his gun lead the way through the door.

Maeve heard Ginger's gasp of surprise as Gray nudged the door open and raised his gun. Ginger did the same. "Keep your hands where I can see them," Gray said.

"D-d-don't shoot," said a male voice.

"Who are you? Why are you here?" Gray asked.

"S-S-Silas. My name is Silas. I come here

sometimes when I want to think. But today I came because the world has gone mad."

Maeve, standing behind Gray's broad shoulders still couldn't see the person attached to the voice, but she was pretty sure she knew who it was. She tapped Gray on the shoulder. "I know him."

Gray looked into her eyes, seeming to judge if she really knew what she was talking about. "I know him," she said again. "He was in my class at school. Let me talk to him."

Gray stepped aside but kept his gun trained on the boy. "Don't get any closer. Talk to him from here."

Maeve stepped through the doorway with her hands turned palms up in front of her so he could see she didn't have a gun. "Hi, Silas," she said.

Silas was huddled into the corner of the fishing hut. His dark face showed evidence of tears, and his slim, lanky body was curled into a ball as if he was trying to become part of the cabin floor. His brown eyes looked at Maeve with hope that she would have some answers.

"M-M-Maeve? Are you with him?"

"Yes. This is Gray and Ginger. What are you doing here?"

"I-I-I was walking home when the bombs started going off. I didn't know what to do. There were people with guns everywhere. Buildings were destroyed. I just knew I needed to get somewhere safe, and this was the only place I could think of. What's going on?"

"I don't know, Silas," Maeve said gently. "The hospital was attacked during the disaster drill, and we just managed to escape. Gray knew about this place. Have you seen anyone else?"

"No. My p-p-parents work at the factory. I don't know if it was hit when the bombs went off."

Maeve looked at Gray. "I think you can put the guns down now. Silas was a year behind us in school, and he's clearly not armed. Why don't you close the door so we can try to figure out what to do next."

Gray motioned to Ginger and they both slowly lowered their guns. Ginger swung her rifle onto her back, but Gray continued to hold his across his chest as they entered and closed the door. Ginger sat next to Silas while Gray prowled from window to window, watching the trees outside.

"Good idea," Gray replied. "Because mine doesn't work."

"What?" Maeve yelped. "You were out there with a gun that doesn't work?"

"Not exactly," Gray reached for the second gun on his back. "This one probably works. Every gun has a computer chip in it. The WG keeps track of all of its weaponry so it doesn't fall into the wrong hands. They can disable the weapon if it gets outside their control. They tell all the soldiers that during training so they don't think about selling their weapons on the black market. Apparently, they disabled mine."

Maeve placed her hands on her hips. "Does that mean the WG can track where we are?"

"Eventually, yes," Gray replied. "But they only register the location once every hour or so. The WG

54

just doesn't have the computing capacity to register every gun more often than that. I'm hoping that we have a little more time left before they register these."

"Can we get rid of the chips?" Ginger asked as she examined her gun. "Does mine still work?"

"Probably," Gray said. "This one probably does, too." He handed the gun slung over his shoulder to Maeve. "As far as the WG knows, these guns are still in a pile at the hospital."

"We n-n-need to remove the chips," Silas said.

"Can you do that?" Maeve asked.

Ginger looked at Silas. "We probably can. Give us the guns."

Gray looked anxiously out the window as Silas and Ginger each pored over a gun. Maeve watched in silence as they spoke about the computer wizardry in the gun in a language only those with computer knowledge could understand. She walked over to where Gray stood at the window, and laid a hand on his arm.

"Think they can do it?" she whispered.

"They sound like they know what they're talking about," Gray said as his eyes tracked from left to right as he scanned the forest.

"What are we going to do?" Maeve asked.

"I'm not sure." Gray nodded toward Silas and Ginger. "But we need those guns to work to have any chance at all."

Maeve worried the skin on the side of her thumbnail with her teeth and said in a low voice, "What's going on, Gray?"

"I'm not sure." Gray squeezed her shoulder. "But we'll figure it out."

Maeve looked at him with a sheen of tears in her eyes. "How did the world go crazy overnight?"

Gray wrapped his arm around her shoulder and pulled her into his side. "Maybe it was already crazy."

They stood in silence after that, scanning the area outside the window for any threat.

"Got it!" Ginger cried.

Maeve and Gray turned to see Silas holding up a small chip in triumph.

"What about the other guns?" Gray asked.

"We got them all," Ginger said. "It should work now, but we'll have to wait until we need it to test it out." She handed the gun back to Gray.

"Guess we'll just have to trust that it will work," Gray said. "I have faith in you two."

Maeve sank to the floor on the other side of Silas, suddenly exhausted.

"Tell us what happened to you, Silas," Gray said.

"I don't know much, mostly what I've already told you," Silas said with a shrug. "I was walking home when the bombs started going off."

"Were you walking home from school?" Ginger asked. "What did the bombs hit?"

"Yes, and I'm n-n-not sure. I'm pretty sure that one bomb hit the armory and another one blew up in front of WG headquarters. There were more, but I wasn't paying attention. I was just trying to get away."

"Did one hit the school?" Ginger asked

anxiously. Maeve shot Ginger a sympathetic glance as Ginger quickly blinked away tears.

"I'm sorry." Silas looked at the ground. "I really don't know. I was almost home when the blasts started."

"Was it just bombs or was there shooting, too?" Gray asked as he took another look out the window.

"There might have been shooting. I don't know. I was just so scared. People were running everywhere trying to get away. It was all so confusing. I just don't know," Silas said with a helpless shrug.

Ginger looked at Maeve and stood up. "I have to go. My sister is out there somewhere. I have to get her."

"Surely the WG has things under control by now," Maeve said.

Both Ginger and Gray looked at Maeve. "Do you really trust the WG?" Gray asked.

"Maybe," Maeve said as she chewed on her fingernail. "I don't know what to think. In the past, if we did what we were supposed to, then the WG left us alone. Why did that change today?" Maeve shook her head. "I really don't know what to think."

"Maeve, do you really think the way we live is right, with one group of people having all the power?" Ginger asked.

"I've never really thought much about it until recently," Maeve said. "But it seems to work, right?"

"Does what you've seen today look like it's working?" Ginger said. "I don't have time to debate the WG right now. I have to go find Emery."

"Ginger, we don't know who or what is out there.

How do you even know where Emery is?" Gray said.

"I don't care," Ginger said as she got to her feet and grabbed a gun. "Emery is 12. She's smart, but I have to get to her before someone else does. So either help me figure out how to get to her or get out of my way."

"It's your funeral," Gray said.

"Wait," Maeve said as she looked around the dilapidated shack. "You need a better plan than just walking into the school. We don't even know if she's still at the school."

"If I had my computer, finding her would be easy," Ginger said. "I could just follow her tracker."

"Emery has a tracker?" Maeve asked.

"It's in her bracelet," Ginger explained. "I made the bracelet for her out of rolled up bits of paper, and I designed the tracker from leftover bits of electronics I found at the WG. I could find her if I just had a computer."

"I m-m-might have something that will help," Silas said quietly.

"Do you have a computer in your pocket?" Ginger asked dismissively.

"Well, n-n-not exactly in my pocket," Silas said as he fumbled with the black band on his wrist.

"What are you talking about?" Ginger said.

"Um. Well, I kind of like experimenting with odds and ends we have around our house. My dad is an electrician so we always have bits and bobs of stuff that are left over from projects that he's worked on. Usually it's things that don't work, but I like to tinker so, I kinda made a wrist computer," Silas said, holding out his wrist.

58

Ginger grabbed his wrist and looked at the 2-inch-wide armband that Silas wore. The charcoal-colored armband blended in with his skin color so well that no one would notice it unless they were looking for it.

"Does this thing work?" Ginger asked. "And who else knows you have it?"

"Well, m-m-my dad knows since he gave me the stuff to build it, but no one else really knows. Some people might have wondered about the armband if they got close enough to see it, but no one has ever asked me about it. It's pretty basic." Silas shrugged. "It can't do a lot. And, um, it's kinda not allowed by the WG. I mostly just use it to tell me the time and to help do my homework."

"Let me look at it," Ginger said as she held out her hand indicating Silas should hand her the wrist computer.

"You're n-n-not going to turn me in are you?"

"Look," Gray said, stepping forward to get a look at Silas's wrist. "We're not going to turn you in. We're in the same boat you are. We don't know what's going on either, but Ginger needs to find her sister. We just want to figure out what's going on. There's no way to track that thing is there?" Gray swept his eyes over the clearing outside before looking at Ginger for an answer.

"I don't think so. This unit isn't on the WG network so it doesn't carry the tracking software. We should be OK," Ginger said.

"Do whatever it is you need to do with that thing," Gray said. "Then we'll make a plan. Silas, can you shoot?"

Silas's eyes widened. "Do you really think we n-n-need to be able to shoot?"

"People were shooting at us. I'd like to be able to shoot back," Gray said. "Maeve, what about you?"

"No," Maeve said as she backed away from the gun Gray was holding out to her. "I've never held a gun. There was no need for one."

Gray placed the gun in her hands. "Keep it pointed away from yourself and all the rest of us."

Maeve slowly took the gun from Gray and, keeping the gun pointed at the floor, followed Gray back to the window.

"This gun is pretty simple," Gray said. "Point. Shoot. Don't worry too much about aiming. You're not likely to hit anything even if you try since you've never shot one before. Just point it in the direction you want to shoot and pull the trigger."

"OK," Maeve said with uncertainty. "Do you think those people who were chasing us have given up?"

"I don't know," Gray said. "But I want to be prepared if they find us. Go keep watch at the other window while those two work their magic on that armband thing."

CHAPTER SEVEN

"**A**re you two almost done?" Gray asked, never taking his eyes from the forest outside the window.

"It takes time," Ginger said. "Believe me. No one wants to get this thing working more than me, but this isn't exactly cutting edge technology we're working with here."

"Hey, I worked hard on that," Silas said.

"And you did a great job," Ginger said. "But it's still a bunch of junk pieces turned into a wrist computer, and you're the only one who knows how it's built. Give me five more minutes, and I think we'll have it."

"Um, Gray?" Maeve said from her side of the fishing hut.

"Hmm?" he said.

"I think there's something out there."

Gray rushed across the room to Maeve's window. "What did you see?"

"Just a couple of shadows, but I've seen them more than once." Maeve pointed in the direction of the sunset. "At first, I just thought it was because the sun is going down, but I've seen it three times now."

"It could just be an animal. They tend to come out at dusk. Let me know if you see it again," Gray said as he returned to his window.

As the moments ticked by, Maeve strained to see any movement in the forest. She was sure the shadows she had seen were more human than animal, but she didn't want to overreact. Just as she was about to let down her guard, she saw it again, the slight movement of a bush when there was no wind, followed by a vague movement of shadow deeper in the forest.

"Gray, there's definitely someone out there," Maeve said urgently. "I think it's more than one person."

"We need to get out of here. Now. Are you two done?" he said to Ginger and Silas.

"I need one more minute," Ginger replied. Silas looked at Gray with fearful eyes. His whole body seemed to shake.

"W-w-who's out there?" Silas asked.

"I don't know," Gray replied. "But I doubt they're friendly. We need to get out of here without being seen."

"Are we sure whoever is out there is looking for us?" Maeve asked.

"Maeve, do you remember being shot at? Do you really want to walk out that door and ask them if they're friendly?" Gray said.

Maeve shrugged her shoulders. "I just don't understand what is going on. Who would be brave enough to attack the WG?"

"Maybe it's not anyone fighting against the

WG," Ginger said quietly.

"What? You think the WG is part of this?" Maeve said.

"Could be," Gray said. "But we don't have time to talk about this now. We need to get moving. Ginger, keep working as we go."

Maeve froze, contemplating what Ginger had just said. Life in Palumbra wasn't perfect, but it wasn't horrible. They had food, clothing and shelter. Everyone worked. She knew you had to be careful not to criticize the WG and you had to follow all the rules, but if you did that, things were fine. Wouldn't society collapse if the WG didn't impose order?

Maeve's thoughts were interrupted by Silas asking "Where are we going?"

"Into the forest until Ginger tells us where we can find her sister," Gray said.

"How are we going to get out of this hut?" Maeve asked. "There's no way out without the people out there seeing us."

Gray walked over to the corner opposite where they had found Silas huddled in fear. He crouched down and ran his fingers over the rough board of the floor. When he stood up, he had two floorboards in his hands and an opening was next to his feet. "Through here," he said.

"Everybody in," Gray said.

Maeve stared at the tunnel. "Why is there a tunnel under this shack, and how do you know about it?"

Gray motioned toward the tunnel impatiently.

"We don't have time for me to tell you why it's there, but I know about it because my uncle owns this shack. Just be grateful it exists. Now, come on. Everybody in."

"But it's dark," Silas said. "How will we know where to go?"

"I have a light, but there's only one route, so even if it's dark, just keep moving forward."

"Maeve, you go first," Gray said briskly. "Then Ginger. Silas and I will follow you."

"Why do I have to go first?" Maeve mumbled as she moved toward the tunnel.

"Because you have the gun," Gray whispered as she passed him. To Ginger, he said, "Grab the other gun."

"Silas, watch at the window, but don't let whoever is out there see you."

Maeve stopped at the entrance to the tunnel. The opening was narrow, just wide enough for a person's shoulders to fit through. A rough ladder made of what appeared to be sturdy logs was dug into the side of the wall. She lifted the rifle strap over her head and shoulder and gingerly moved the gun to her back before turning her body so she could grab the ladder and start her descent into darkness.

"Wait," Gray said. "Here." He handed her a tiny light that he had removed from his pocket. "Wait for us at the bottom."

Maeve slowly climbed down the ladder until she found herself in a narrow tunnel about 6 feet below the fishing hut. She hunched over to avoid hitting her head, switching on the flashlight to reveal dirt walls and a ceiling supported by rough logs that matched the ones used to make the ladder. The tunnel stretched as far as the light could reach.

Above her, she could hear the muffled voices of the others as Ginger made her way to the ladder. She shone the light on the ladder as Ginger's foot hit the top rung. As she climbed down, Maeve could hear Silas shout.

"Gray! There are people m-m-moving into the clearing."

Maeve heard Gray's footsteps move quickly across the cabin floor. "Who are they?" Silas asked.

"No one who wants to be friends with us," Gray said. "Get moving. We have to get into the tunnel before they get here."

Ginger was only halfway down the ladder when Silas's feet appeared on the top rung. "Move," Gray said.

No sooner had Silas's hands left the top rung than Gray's feet appeared. As Ginger reached the bottom, Gray was pulling the floorboards back across the tunnel opening.

"Turn that light off, and everyone be quiet," Gray said as he quickly climbed down the ladder to join them at the bottom.

They crouched in the inky blackness at the entrance to the tunnel, listening intently.

"Shouldn't we be getting away?" Silas asked quietly.

"If they enter the cabin, I want to hear what they say. Maybe then we can figure out who they are," Gray whispered back.

As he spoke, they heard the door to the fishing hut open and footsteps pound over their heads.

"There's no one here," said a commanding female voice.

"They had to be in here," a male voice replied. "There was no place else for them to hide."

"Well, they're not here now. You must have missed them leaving or they left a false trail. We need to find those kids."

"Why?" the male voice said. "Why are these three kids so important? They don't even know what's going on."

"You know why," the female voice replied. "Arabella doesn't want any witnesses to the hospital attack."

"No. But what do we do now?"

"We keep looking and hope we find them. Get moving."

The footsteps retreated and they heard the door closing.

"What was that about?" Maeve asked. "This makes no sense."

"W-W-Why did they say they were only looking for three kids?" Silas asked. He was the farthest into the tunnel and still shaking with fear.

"I guess they didn't see you enter the fishing hut," Gray said. "I don't think they actually saw us go in. They just followed our path through the woods and assumed we were in the hut. That works in our favor because they'll spend their time looking for us in the

66

forest and won't examine the hut too closely."

"But what about what they said about Arabella?" Maeve asked again.

"I'm not sure, but I can tell you there's been some weird stuff going on at WG headquarters," Ginger said. "We can figure this all out later. Right now, I need to find my sister."

"Is your wrist tracker thing working?" Gray asked.

"Just about. One more command, and I should have it. Shine the light over here," Ginger said as she pressed a sequence of tiny buttons on the wrist strap. "Got it." She examined the strap. "What is she doing there?"

"Where is she?" Maeve asked.

"She's at WG headquarters. I don't understand why she would be there. We have to go get her because those people who were chasing us are clearly part of the WG."

"We have to be careful," Gray said. "They could be using her to lure us to them. They clearly want to get rid of us."

"It doesn't matter," Ginger said as she started walking down the tunnel. "I need to get my sister. Where does this tunnel go, anyway?"

"It comes out in what looks like an old well at the edge of town," Gray said as he stepped into the tunnel. The others followed.

"If you know about this tunnel, how do we know other people don't?" Maeve asked.

"My uncle let me know about it for days like this. I'm sure some other people know about it, but not the WG. Why don't we find Emery and get someplace safe, then I'll tell you what I know."

"Is anyplace safe?" Silas asked. Maeve looked at Silas in the dim glow of Gray's flashlight. His eyes were wide in his face, and she could see that he was holding back tears.

"I don't know what's going on, Silas, but we'll figure it out." Maeve gave Silas's shoulder a comforting pat. "Let's find Emery, then we'll go home and see our parents. Surely they'll know what's going on."

"Maybe," Silas said. "But you didn't see what I saw, Maeve. We may not have homes left to go to."

Gray climbed the ladder of rough-hewn logs first when they reached the end of the tunnel. Maeve watched from her spot at the bottom as he carefully pushed aside the cover on what appeared to be the top of a well. He pushed himself up so just his eyes and the top of his head cleared the edge of the well. It seemed like an eternity to Maeve before he hoisted himself over the edge and disappeared. His head reappeared, and he said "OK, send Ginger up, then Silas. Maeve, you go last."

Maeve wasn't excited to be the last to leave the dank, close tunnel, but she nodded and gave Gray a thumbs up as she moved out of the way for Ginger to start climbing the ladder. Silas followed, and at last, it was Maeve's turn. She slung the rifle over her back and started to climb. Just as she reached the top, Gray's panicked face appeared over the opening. He handed her his and Ginger's rifles, whispered "Stay quiet" and slapped the cover back on the well. Maeve clung to the ladder with sweaty hands, trying to balance her own weight and the weight of all three rifles. She shifted her feet and winced as one of the guns clanged against the wall.

She could hear Gray and Ginger arguing.

"I should go," Ginger said. "I work for the WG. No one is going to suspect anything, and I might find out what's actually going on."

"You and Silas should run while I distract them," Gray replied. "I'm a soldier. We train for this. Maeve can go back through the tunnel and get out through the fishing hut. The people who followed us there will be long gone."

"We shouldn't split up," Ginger argued. "We have no idea what's going on. We just need those people to go away. We don't even know that they're looking for us. We don't even know that the people looking for us know specifically who we are. We just know they're chasing three 'kids'."

"I'm better equipped to get away than you are if they are specifically looking for us," Gray argued back.

"I should go," Maeve heard Silas say. "N-n-no one even knows I'm with you. I can say I just ran out here because I was scared."

"Silas, you've been scared of your own shadow since we met up with you, and now you want to do this?" Gray asked.

"I can do it. I may be scared, but I can do this. N-n-no one will think it's weird that I'm shaking and freaked out. This is freaky."

"This might be our best plan," Ginger said. "Are you sure you can do it?"

"I'm sure," Silas replied. "Stay hidden. And stay quiet."

"We've got your back if things go wrong," Gray said.

Maeve had no idea how much time had passed before Gray removed the well cover and reached down a hand for her to pass him the rifles. He slung the rifle over his back and held the other one in his hand. His other hand returned to help her over the edge of the well. Immediately, he placed the cover back on the well and ran with her to the edge of the tree line.

"What happened?" Maeve asked when they reached the spot where Ginger crouched behind a bush. Gray handed Ginger her gun and Maeve asked, "Where did Silas go?"

"Silas saved our tails," Gray said. "He convinced the WG soldiers that he was scared and ran into the woods. No one knows he was with us, so they didn't suspect we were here. He led them off toward his house. He's supposed to meet us at the entrance to the path behind my house later."

"Do you really think those soldiers were looking for us?" Maeve asked.

"Maeve, do you really think they weren't?" Ginger asked.

Maeve was silent for a moment.

"I don't know what to think anymore," Maeve said.

"Well, you can think about it while we find Emery," Ginger said. "The tracker shows she's not actually inside WG headquarters, but she's close to it. I
70

think she may have gone there to look for me."

"Let's go," Gray said. "We'll try to stay in the shadows and alleys until we have to be out in the open."

Gray strode off, expecting Ginger and Maeve to follow. Ginger fell in line, but Maeve stood for a moment, looking out at Palumbra. Smoke rose from different parts of the city. Maeve shook her head wondered whom she could trust.

Ginger looked over her shoulder. "Are you coming?"

Maeve pulled herself out of her daze. "I'm right behind you," she said as she jogged to catch up. "I just wish I had a better idea of who I'm following and where we're going," she said to herself.

CHAPTER EIGHT

Maeve, Gray, and Ginger kept to the trees, moving slowly, listening for any sign of someone following them. When they neared the edge of the tree line, Gray motioned for them to stop. The three stood side by side and looked out over Palumbra as columns of thick, black smoke rose from the site of the hospital. Farther south, another column of thick, black smoke rose into the sky. Maeve wondered if that smoke hovered over the factory. Scared residents stood in the streets, looking around, bewildered.

In the city center, it looked like a bomb had exploded. The city commons where they gathered to hear announcements from the WG had a crater the size of a bus in it. Storefronts were damaged or destroyed, and buildings that were once several stories tall now lay in pieces. Chaos reigned as people ran everywhere and WG soldiers tried to restore order.

"What happened?" Maeve asked as she turned shocked eyes to her companions.

"The same thing that happened at the hospital. Death and destruction," Ginger said.

"Who did this?" Maeve asked.

"That's the question, isn't it?" Gray said. "Come on. We need to get Emery out of that mess. Where is she, Ginger?"

Ginger looked at her wristband. "She should be just to the east of the WG headquarters. If this is at all accurate, it looks like she's right next to the building."

"Let's go," Gray said. "We should be OK. The chaos will work for us. Just try to stay out of the open areas and away from the WG soldiers. Ginger, you lead the way. Walk quickly and try not to draw attention to yourself."

Ginger started off at a brisk walk, checking her wrist as her legs quickly ate up the ground between their perch on the hill and the chaos of Palumbra. Gray grabbed Maeve's hand and started off after Ginger.

"How did this happen?" Maeve asked.

"I think it might be a long story," Gray said. "My uncle has been acting odd the past couple of weeks. He gave me contingency plans for what to do if something went wrong and showed me the tunnel and a few other things. I can't imagine he was involved in this, but I think he knew something was coming."

"Why do you think the WG would harm their own people?"

"I don't know, but I have ideas," Gray said. "Let's find Emery and figure out what to do next."

"What about my parents?"

"We'll find them, Maeve. I promise."

Ginger suddenly halted at the end of an alley. "Quiet!" she said as she stepped backward farther into the shadows of the alley. She motioned for them to crouch down behind a pile of rubble. They peeked their heads up over the rubble in time to see a unit of WG troops march by.

"The closer we get to WG headquarters, the more troops we're going to see," Gray said. "Keep your eyes open and your heads down. We're sure to be picked up on camera, but hopefully in all the chaos, it will take them a while to notice us. Ginger, how close are we to Emery?"

"We've got another few blocks to go," she said.

"Give me your guns," Gray said.

"Why," asked Maeve.

"It doesn't look odd for me to carry a gun because I'm a soldier. You two will be stopped because civilians aren't allowed to own guns."

Maeve and Ginger handed Gray their guns. He slung them both across his back and motioned to Ginger. "Lead the way."

Ginger walked quickly to the end of the alley, carefully checking all directions before stepping out into the street with her head bowed. Maeve and Gray followed, being careful to keep their eyes moving and their heads down. They walked quickly past several more burning shells of buildings until the white walls of WG headquarters loomed in front of them. As the tallest building in Palumbra at 12 stories, its white stone and glass construction towered over everything below it.

Today was no exception. Despite the chaos around it, WG headquarters stood unharmed, shining brightly in the sun, seemingly unconcerned with the

74

destruction around it. Maeve peeked at the front of the building, noting with concern the large contingent of soldiers that surrounded it.

"How are we going to get to Emery?" Maeve asked. She motioned toward WG headquarters. "This place is crawling with soldiers."

"She's right around the corner," Ginger said.

Keeping to the shadows of the buildings across the street from WG headquarters, Maeve, Ginger and Gray turned the corner. In the midst of a unit of soldiers, Maeve could see several children talking to the WG soldiers and taking snacks from them. She could see Emery's blond curls from where she stood.

"Ginger, Emery's in that group with the soldiers," Maeve said. "How are we going to get her?"

"Ginger is going to go over there and pick her up," Gray said.

"What?" Maeve exclaimed. "Those soldiers aren't going to just let her walk in there and take Emery. They're hunting us, remember?"

"Some soldiers are hunting us," Gray said. "I'm betting that most soldiers have no idea who we are. It's been chaos around here for hours. Even if the WG sent out a notice to be looking for us, not every soldier will have had time to see it and memorize our faces. If Ginger puts her hair up under her hat and doesn't draw a lot of attention to herself, she should be able to get Emery without any trouble. She can even flash her WG badge. Just don't let anyone get too close of a look at it."

"That's crazy," Maeve said. "What if she finds

the one soldier who does recognize her?"

"It's OK, Maeve," Ginger said as she began piling her long, black hair up under her cap. "I'll be careful. Just be ready to grab Emery and run if things go south."

Maeve and Gray watched nervously from the shadows as Ginger made her way across the street. She walked confidently, arms swinging, as if she was simply a concerned sister looking for her sibling. Ginger approached the first soldier and began speaking, angling her head so the soldier couldn't get a good look at her features under her hat. She pointed at Emery who was frantically waving at Ginger from where she stood behind a row of armed soldiers. The children had been corralled into an area where the building created a V. Soldiers stood in front of them, attempting to keep them all in one place. Some WG workers trying to organize the children to play a game or eat a snack.

Ginger continued to talk with the soldier, eventually reaching into her pocket and pulling out her WG badge. Maeve and Gray held their breath. If the soldier knew anything about the events of their morning, now is when it would all break down. The soldier looked at Ginger's badge, glanced at her face and motioned to another soldier. Maeve saw Gray grip his rifle more tightly.

"What will we do if they try to arrest her?" Maeve asked.

"Let's hope it doesn't come to that. We can't fight an entire unit of WG troops. You can't even shoot."

76

The second soldier looked at Ginger's badge, looked a little more closely at her face and nodded at the first soldier. Just as Gray was about to take a step forward, the first soldier motioned to one of the men in front of the children and called out Emery's name. The line of soldiers parted and Emery raced over to hug her sister. Maeve saw Ginger whisper in Emery's ear and grab her hand. The two started to walk away. Just as Maeve was about to breathe a sigh of relief, another soldier yelled for Ginger to wait. Ginger kept a tight hold on Emery's hand and kept walking as if she hadn't heard him.

"Hey, you! Wait!" the soldier yelled again.

Ginger and Emery started jogging toward Gray and Maeve. The soldier who had yelled at Ginger stopped to talk with the soldier who had checked her identification. A female soldier pulled out a handheld computer and typed something into it. When she finished, she nodded to the others, and two soldiers set out in pursuit of Ginger and Emery.

Ginger had already launched into a full-on sprint, dragging Emery and her shorter legs behind her. When she reached Gray and Maeve, they were both already jogging away.

"I think they recognized you," Gray said with a grim smile.

"Yeah. That first guy wasn't too bright, but I could tell the second one had his suspicions. Thank goodness they let Emery go before they realized who I really was. Let's get out of here."

"Hi, Emery," Gray said with a wave as he and

Maeve joined Emery and Ginger in their sprint away from the WG soldiers. "I'm Gray."

"Hi, Gray," Emery panted. "Why are we running?" She looked at Ginger as they darted around a corner.

"The WG don't like us very much right now," Ginger explained as she followed Gray down the street and dodged into an alleyway.

"Did you do something?" Emery stumbled. Maeve grabbed her arm and pulled her along.

Despite their best efforts, the WG soldiers were quickly gaining on them. The soldiers had gotten organized, and now 10 of them dogged the group's steps. Maeve was sure other soldiers were looking for them as well.

"My legs are burning," Emery said as she stumbled again. Maeve pulled the backpack from Emery's back and handed it to Ginger.

"Just a little farther," Maeve said, praying that she was telling the truth. They followed Gray through the alleyways of the city, twisting and turning in all directions. Maeve had no idea where they were or what direction they were going.

Gray led them down a side street that was packed with people. They dodged through the crowd, knocking into people as they ran. Maeve glanced over her shoulder to see the WG soldiers dropping back as the crowd slowed them down.

Fatigue was beginning to set in for all of them, not just Emery, and Maeve didn't know how much longer they could keep up the frantic pace. Gray abruptly stopped next to a building that had been spared in the bombing and began searching the wall in front of him. It looked to Maeve as if he was counting bricks. While she could no longer see the soldiers pursuing them, she knew they were right around the corner.

"Gray, what are you doing?" Maeve cried.

"I'm getting us out of here," he said as he pushed hard on a brick over his head. The wall near his feet swung inward, creating a small opening. Even Emery would have to crouch down to enter it.

"Move!" Gray said. "Emery first, then you two follow. I'll come in last."

As Maeve approached the opening, Gray grabbed her hand and placed a rifle in it. He leaned close enough that she could feel his breath on her cheek. "If I don't make it through the opening, get Silas and go back to the fishing hut. I'll meet you there if I can. Go back into the tunnel. Five hundred feet in, there's a hidden door. Open it and hide there."

"But, Gray," Maeve began. Gray touched his lips to her cheek and gave her a push into the opening. Just as Maeve cleared the opening, the door slammed shut behind her.

Ginger and Maeve stared at the now-closed opening. After a moment, Maeve looked at Ginger, her eyes wide with shock. "Where's Gray?" Ginger asked. "Why did he close the door?"

Maeve began examining the wall, looking for a way to open it for Gray as she explained what had happened on the other side. Maeve put her ear to the wall. "Can you hear anything?"

Ginger laid her ear on the brick wall and shook her head. "The walls are too thick."

Maeve looked around again. They were in a small room that looked like it could have been either a large closet or a small office. The outer walls were brick, and the room was empty, and Maeve had no idea what lay on the other side of the closed, wooden door. As she contemplated their situation, she became aware of a soft crying sound. Turning her head, she found Ginger sitting on the floor with her arms wrapped around Emery.

"It's OK, Emery," Ginger said. "We'll get somewhere safe soon." Ginger rubbed her sister's back as she laid her cheek on her soft, blonde curls. Emery was small for a 12-year-old; she could have easily passed for 9. But what she lacked in stature, she usually made up for in brain power. The WG had put her on a personalized track in school because she was so advanced, but right now, Emery was just a scared 12-year-old, which meant she had a lot in common with the two teenagers who shared the room with her.

"What now?" Ginger asked.

"What choice do we have?" Maeve said. "The WG is clearly looking for us, and we need to get out of here. The problem is I wasn't paying attention to all the turns we made, and I don't know where here is."

"We're in the business district," Emery said as she sniffed and wiped her eyes. "I recognized some of the buildings as we ran."

"OK," Maeve said. "I guess we need to get back to Gray's house to meet up with Silas. Then on to the fishing hut?"

"I wish we could check on our mom," Ginger said. "She must be frantic. And it sure looked like the factory had been hit with a bomb."

"Yeah," Maeve said. "I'd like to find my parents, too. Maybe they have some explanation for all of this. But do we try to find them or do we do what Gray said? He's expecting to meet us at the fishing hut."

"If he's been caught by the WG, we're not going to see him for a while ... if at all," Ginger said.

Maeve touched her cheek where Gray had brushed a kiss before he shoved her through the opening. She shook off the melancholy moment. She would have time to think later; right now, they needed a plan.

"OK. So, we're on the run from the WG. We have a rifle that neither of us really know how to use all that well, a 12-year-old that we're responsible for and no idea where our parents are. Does that sum it up?" Maeve said.

"Yeah, I think that about covers it," Ginger said glumly.

"What do you want to do?" Maeve asked.

"Well, the smart thing would be to get Silas and go to the fishing hut, but my heart says we need to at least make sure our parents are OK," Ginger answered.

"I want to see Mom," Emery said.

"I know, honey," Ginger said as she gave

Emery's arm a quick pat. "Look, our houses are near where we're supposed to meet Silas. I say we head that way and check our houses. If our parents aren't there, then we'll go to the fishing hut and figure something else out."

"If the WG is looking for us, the first place they'll look will be our homes," Maeve said. "Are you sure you want to do that?"

"My mom has done everything for us," Ginger said. "I know it's risky, but we have to try to reach her and make sure she's safe." Emery nodded in agreement. "We'll be careful, but we have to at least try."

Maeve looked at the resolve on Emery and Ginger's faces and slowly nodded. "OK, let's see what's out there."

CHAPTER NINE

Maeve crept over to the door of the room and listened carefully. Hearing nothing on the other side, she cracked the gray, metal door just enough that she could see an open warehouse with large rolling doors on the other side. She thought she had seen a picture once of a place where vehicles were kept, and this looked a lot like that. No one in Palumbra had a vehicle except the WG, and even the WG vehicles were limited. She could only see a small sliver straight ahead of her, but seeing no one, she edged the door an inch wider.

She looked more closely at what she could see of her surroundings. The shiny concrete floor was gray, clean and smooth, and there was nothing between her and those rolling doors. She still didn't hear any people. Slowly, she opened the door wider until there was space for her to slip out of the room. Gripping her gun with both hands, she stepped into the open space and looked up where she saw nothing but lights hanging from the ceiling. The large room was dim but not dark as several high windows let in the fading sunlight. She looked back into the room and whispered to Ginger and Emery,

"Come on. It doesn't seem like anyone is around. Let's get out of here."

Ginger and Emery quickly followed Maeve as she led the way across the empty building. Their footsteps echoed loudly in the cavernous space, and Maeve dearly hoped she hadn't missed anyone in the building. There was no place to hide as they made their way across the room to the door set to the left of the large rolling doors. None of them dared utter a word as they sprinted across the open space.

When they reached the door, Maeve stopped. "Do either of you have any idea where we are?" Maeve whispered. As much as she wanted to open the door and make her way home, she was afraid of what or who might be there when she opened it.

"I do," Emery said. "We're about a half mile east of WG headquarters."

"That puts us just outside the business district. We might be able to lose ourselves in the crowd," Ginger said.

"We'll have to hurry," Maeve said as she eyed the fading rays of sunlight shining through the windows. "Everything will be closing soon, and curfew will kick in. We don't want to be the only ones walking the streets. We'll definitely be found then."

"Do you think Gray is OK?" Emery asked.

"I'm sure he's fine," Maeve said as she touched her cheek again. "He's a soldier. He can take care of himself."

"I hope," she said under her breath. Pushing

thoughts of Gray from her mind, she focused on their task. She needed to get them back to their neighborhood where they could find their parents and hopefully figure out what was going on.

"How do I hide the gun?" Maeve asked Ginger.

"Emery, do you have your long coat in your backpack?" Ginger asked.

"Yes, but I don't know if it's big enough."

"It will have to be. It's all we've got."

Emery dug a long, gray coat out of her bag and handed it to Maeve. "Hold the gun across your arm and throw the coat over it," Ginger said. "Just don't call attention to yourself."

Maeve arranged the coat over the gun and did her best to look natural. "Am I good?"

"You look awkward. Hopefully everyone is too shocked by what happened today to notice three kids walking through the business district," Ginger said.

"OK," Maeve said as she opened the door. "Here we go. Keep your heads down."

Once outside, Ginger, holding tightly to Emery's hand, led the way. They made their way down nearly deserted streets until they reached the business district. Maeve scanned every corner for signs of the WG soldiers. Ginger stopped when they reached the business district, and she and Emery let out audible gasps.

"What?" Maeve asked. She had been following them with her head down and had not seen the main street of the business district when they had.

"It's gone," Emery said.

"What? It can't be gone," Maeve said.

"There's nothing left," Ginger said. "It's been bombed."

Maeve hurried to stand next to Ginger. Together, they silently looked at the burned out ruins of what had once been the heart of Palumbra. All had been reduced to rubble. People mingled together in the middle of the street, some in shock, some in tears. Some dug through the still burning rubble. Maeve saw a little boy in a blue coat who could not have been more than five, tugging on the hand of a woman lying on the ground. Maeve started toward the boy when Ginger caught the back of her shirt.

"You can't," Ginger said.

"Why not? I'm almost a nurse. Maybe I can help," Maeve said.

"You can't," Ginger said again, this time pointing her finger toward a troop of WG soldiers that had started herding all the people to a grassy area that had been untouched by the bombings. "The soldiers will find him. And if you go over there, they'll find you, too."

With reluctance, Maeve turned away. "We need to get out of here," she said. "Emery, what's the best way to get to our street?"

Emery looked around, her brown eyes peering out from under poorly cut bangs. "I think if we go back the way we came, we can circle around to the shortcut you usually take home from the hospital."

"Sounds good," Maeve said. "Let's go. I'll lead. You tell me when I need to make a turn."

86

"Keep an eye out for soldiers," Ginger said. "We don't need to get caught."

The three slowly made their way across town, occasionally dodging WG soldiers. Emery's directions led them to the path to the shortcut. Maeve was pretty sure there were no cameras in these woods, but they would need to be careful.

"OK, let's keep to the path for now," Maeve said. "But listen and keep watch for any sign of other people."

Maeve started down the path toward home with Emery and Ginger close behind. No one spoke. The sound of their feet on the dirt path seemed to echo in the silence, and the faint smell of smoke from the bombings lingered in the air. Not knowing what they would find at the other end made the journey feel like it took forever.

As they passed the place where the box was buried, Maeve gave it a quick glance. She hesitated. With the WG engaged elsewhere, now would be the perfect time to dig up the box. She noticed that the corner of the paper she had found was once again waving in the wind. She looked at Emery and Ginger to see if they had noticed it, but they were both peering into the underbrush on the opposite side of the path. Maeve shook her head. They needed to check on their parents, and digging up the box would take time and might draw attention to them should anyone else pass by. They walked by the box without comment.

As they reached the end of the path, their steps slowed. Gray had said they should meet Silas here, but there seemed to be no sign of him.

"Do you see Silas anywhere?" Maeve whispered to Ginger.

"Who's Silas?" Emery asked.

"A friend of mine who helped us out of a tough spot with the WG," Maeve said. She looked at Ginger.

"I don't see him," Ginger said.

"Should we wait for him?"

"How long can we wait without being noticed?" Ginger asked. "We know the WG is looking for us."

"Maybe we should give it a few minutes," Maeve said.

"We can't stay here long." Ginger looked around anxiously. "We'll get caught. We need to keep moving."

"It sounds like this Silas guy helped you out," Emery said. "I think we should wait for him."

"Ginger's right," Maeve said. "We can't stay here long, but he saved us. We need to give him a little time."

Maeve settled behind a group of bushes and patted the ground next to her. "We'll give him 20 minutes unless the WG soldiers show up."

Ginger looked skeptical but settled in beside Maeve. "You seem sure he'll show up. Maybe he just went back to his parents and has forgotten all about us."

Maeve shifted and swept a rock out from under her leg as Emery sat in the dirt next to Ginger. "I've known Silas for a while. Oh, not well. But he's been a steady presence in my classes for years. He's quiet and he gets picked on because of his stutter, but he's really smart. When he gets interested in something, he sticks

88

with it, and I think he's interested in us."

Ginger swatted a bug away from her face. "I hope you're right because we're wasting time sitting here." She turned to Emery. "How did you end up at WG headquarters?"

Emery dug in her backpack and came out with a granola bar. "When the bombs started going off, our teachers took us to the basement of the school. It's pretty dingy down there, and super crowded with all the kids and teachers in one place. Parents started coming to get their kids." Emery took a bite of her granola bar and continued talking with her mouth full. "It was controlled chaos. Parents coming, teachers calling out kids' names. No one could see much of anything. Hey, did you want some of this?" She waved the granola bar in Ginger's direction.

"No, I'm good," Ginger said. Maeve shook her head, too. "Go on with your story."

Emery took another bite and continued. "When there were only about 50 kids left, a couple of teachers took us back upstairs. Then the WG came. Our teachers argued that we should stay at the school, but the WG soldier said it wasn't safe and they had orders to take us to WG headquarters. He said something about taking care of the kids whose parents didn't show up, but he didn't make it sound like that was a good thing."

"What do you mean?" Maeve asked.

Emery shrugged. "I don't really know. It just sounded kind of menacing. They were about to take the 20 of us that were left into the building when you showed up." She nodded at Ginger. "I was really glad you came when you did."

Ginger hugged Emery and looked at Maeve. Maeve checked her watch and nodded at Ginger. It was time to move on.

Maeve led the way as they left their hiding spot on the side of the path.

"Where to now? Your house or mine?" Maeve asked.

"We could split up," Ginger said.

"I don't think that's a good idea. We split off from both Silas and Gray, and now we can't find either of them," Maeve said.

"I'm with Maeve. We need to stay together. I don't want to be left alone again," Emery said as her voice trailed off to a whisper.

Ginger took Emery by the shoulders, tilted her chin up and looked her in the eyes. "Emery," she said fiercely, "I would never leave you alone."

"But what if something happened to you?" Emery said in almost a whisper.

Ginger hugged Emery close and looked at Maeve with tears in her eyes. "We'll stay together," Ginger said. "Let's go to your house first, Maeve. It's closer."

The three girls carefully made their way down the street, keeping to the shadows as much as they could without looking suspicious. Luckily, no one was out on the street except them. Maeve suspected that the WG had issued a communication that told everyone to stay inside.

Maeve stopped at the end of the sidewalk that led to her front door, knowing she was exposed for everyone to see. She looked at the small house made up of just a bedroom for her parents, a loft for her and a kitchen/living room area. It wasn't much, but it had been her home. Maeve had a funny feeling, it might never be home again. She glanced up and down the street, hoping everyone was too busy dealing with their own problems to notice her, took a deep breath and started up the walk. She knew this was a bad idea, but she had to know if her parents were all right. Some small part of her held out hope that her parents could help her fix this.

"You guys should wait for me in the back yard," she said. "We don't know if the WG has already been here looking for me. If I don't come out in 30 minutes, try to find your mom, then go to the fishing hut. There's a secret hiding room in the tunnel. Look for the door."

Ginger nodded, grabbed Emery's hand, and the two of them dashed around the side of the house.

Maeve took another deep breath and opened the front door, not at all prepared for the sight that awaited her.

CHAPTER TEN

Maeve's parents were sitting at the table, waiting for her. Her dad's eyebrows were drawn together in a look Maeve knew conveyed both worry and anger. Her mom's shoulders were bent forward as if she simply couldn't hold herself upright any longer. She looked at Maeve with sad eyes.

They were alone, but the sadness, worry and anger permeating the air acted as another presence. Maeve swiveled her head to take in the rest of the room – and stopped when her eyes reached the small screen the WG used to send what they called welfare notices. Her picture along with pictures of Gray, Ginger and Emery were on the screen under the words WANTED. Fear stole Maeve's breath. She looked at her parents.

"Hi," she said weakly.

"Maeve, what is going on? And why do you have a gun?" her dad asked as he stood. Though thin, her dad towered over her and with the hints of anger emanating from him, Maeve fought the urge to cower.

"I don't know," Maeve said. "I was at the hospital for the disaster drill when a bomb went off and people started shooting. Gray, Ginger and I ran into the woods and hid because people were chasing us with guns. We escaped and came here. I was worried about you. I know you were at the factory today, and it looked like the factory had been bombed as well."

"It was," her dad said wearily. Maeve thought he looked as if he had aged 10 years since she had seen him this morning. "We were in the other end, away from the bomb. They sent all of us home, and I don't know how many people were hurt or killed." Her dad looked at her closely. "But why does the WG want you?"

Maeve hesitated. She wanted to explain the events of the day to her parents, but something stopped her.

"I don't know." Maeve shook her head for emphasis. "It makes no sense. I was just doing my job."

Her mom rose and hugged her. Maeve breathed in the scent that was uniquely her mom's, flowery and spicy all at once. Her mom looked her in the eyes and said, "Well, you haven't done anything wrong, so you can just turn yourself in and explain. The WG will sort this out."

Maeve reluctantly stepped out of her mom's embrace. The sadness in her mom's face made Maeve's breath catch. She looked at the floor to avoid seeing the disappointment she knew would be in her mom's eyes when she said, "Do you really think so, Mom? Because it seems to me that the WG is part of whatever is going on."

"That can't be true," her dad said emphatically. "The WG is there to protect us, all of us. No harm will come to you if you turn yourself in."

Maeve stared at her father in disbelief. This

93

morning, she might have agreed with him, but so much had happened to her today. She had gone from nurse-in-training to wanted criminal in seconds. A small part of Maeve wanted to turn this whole mess over to her parents, but she couldn't. She had seen too much.

"I want to believe that," Maeve said. "I want life to go back to the way it was, but I can't unsee what I saw today. The WG is involved in whatever is going on here."

"Maeve, how can you know that?" her mom asked. She ran her hand through her hair in exasperation. "If you don't turn yourself in, the WG will assume that you're guilty."

"Guilty of what? I haven't done anything."

"I'm sure you can sort it all out if you just talk with the WG," her dad said. "We'll all be in trouble if you don't."

Maeve gasped. Her eyes moved from her mom's slumped shoulders and tear-filled eyes to her dad's drawn eyebrows and firm mouth. She started to speak, then shook her head. There was nothing she could say that would change her parents' minds about the WG. They had spent too many years doing what they were supposed to do and thinking the way the WG wanted them to think. She watched understanding dawn in her mother's eyes as the tears finally overflowed.

"Maeve." Her mom took a step toward her with an outstretched hand, but Maeve's father waylaid her with a hand on her mom's shoulder. Her mom looked from Maeve's dad to Maeve, dropped her hand and stood silently.

Maeve straightened her shoulders and raised her

chin to look into her father's eyes. "I have to go. If the WG asks you, tell them I wouldn't listen to you."

Maeve walked out the back door with her head held high. As soon as she stepped into the yard, her shoulders drooped as she looked back at her home, taking in the modest blue house for what felt like the last time. She knew she couldn't go back — at least not until she was no longer wanted by the WG.

She spotted Ginger and Emery in the corner of the yard.

"How did it go?" Ginger asked.

"They didn't believe me." Maeve held herself stiffly as if she might break if she moved. "They wanted me to turn myself in. The WG sent out a bulletin with our names and faces saying we're wanted. It didn't include Silas — just you, me, Gray and Emery. Come on, let's go."

Maeve started walking. Ginger waited for a moment as if considering what to say, then shook her head, motioned to Emery and followed Maeve.

"We need to be careful," Maeve said. "I'm not sure my parents won't tell the WG that I was there."

Emery stared at her. "Why would they do that?"

"Because they think the best thing to do is to turn myself in and sort everything out."

Ginger stared at Maeve, as well. "Did you tell them what happened? That's definitely not a good idea."

"That's why I left."

A lone tear dripped down Maeve's cheek, but she said nothing else. The three girls covered the rest of the distance to Ginger and Emery's house in silence.

The Snell house was identical to Maeve's, except it was painted green with colorful wildflowers blooming along the sidewalk that led to the front door. Maeve smiled as she remembered Mrs. Snell digging the flowers up from the woods and planting them there last spring. "I want a moment of happiness when I walk out my front door," she had told Maeve.

"I'll go around back and wait for you," Maeve said.

"We won't be long. I'm going to try to convince my mom to come with us," Ginger said.

Maeve headed toward the back of the house, stopping when she reached the side to watch Ginger and Emery knock on the door. The door opened, and their mom appeared. Ginger leaned down to hug the petite woman. Maeve saw the woman whisper something in Ginger's ear, and Ginger quickly stepped back. She looked over at Maeve with wide eyes and shook her head. Maeve gripped her gun and looked around the yard for an escape route.

Ginger grabbed Emery's hand and her mom's hand and started backing the three of them away from the door. Three WG soldiers appeared in the doorway, guns aimed at Ginger, Emery and their mom. As Maeve watched in horror, Mrs. Snell jerked her hand out of Ginger's grip and rushed at the soldiers.

"Run!" she screamed.

Surprised, the soldiers took a step back. Maeve took off running toward Ginger and Emery. She grabbed their hands and kept running as the soldiers
96

opened fire. She looked over her shoulder in time to see red bloom on Mrs. Snell's chest as she tumbled into the wildflowers.

Time stopped. Maeve couldn't breathe. She couldn't move. The sight of Mrs. Snell falling played on repeat in her mind. She was pulled from her trance by Emery shouting "No!" and twisting her hand in Maeve's. Maeve tighted her grip and pulled Emery away. Maeve's feet felt like lead; every step away from Mrs. Snell hurt. Emery continued twisting and screaming, trying to get free. Maeve held on and pulled both Emery and Ginger with her toward the path to the fishing hut.

Maeve finally found her voice. "You can't help her," Maeve said to Emery. "She died to save you. Don't let that be for nothing."

Ginger was silent. She gripped her gun and ran, wiping away tears with the back of her hand.

Maeve chanced a glance over her shoulder. She tightened her grip on the now-silent Emery and said, "There are three soldiers following us. We need to get out of the open," she said.

No one said anything. Finally, Emery choked back a sob and said, "I know a place."

CHAPTER ELEVEN

With Emery leading the way, the girls fled down the street with feet pounding and WG soldiers not far behind. soldiers in pursuit.

Maeve waited hunched her shoulders, waiting to hear the sound of bullets whizzing by her, but no shots came. She glanced over her shoulder and saw the WG soldiers were gaining ground, but their rifles remained slung over their backs.

"They must have orders to bring us in alive," Ginger said. The tears had dried on her face. "Too bad they didn't have the same orders about my mom. She's dead because of us." More tears slid down her face.

Emery hadn't said a word since she started leading them down the street, but a quick glance told Maeve that Emery's tears had not stopped since she had seen her mother shot. Maeve didn't know what to say. They kept running.

When they reached the corner near Maeve's house, Emery took a quick right. Maeve looked at her house as they ran by and thought she saw her mother's face in the window. For a moment, Maeve gave in to the hope that her parents would help them, but then she saw the blinds snap closed. She was on her own.

Emery led them through a series of back alleys that finally ended at a brick wall. Maeve belatedly wondered at the wisdom of allowing a traumatized 12-year-old to be the leader of their escape plan.

"Are we lost?" Maeve asked.

"No. We're in the right place," Emery said gasping through her tears. "Follow me."

Emery ran to where a trash can sat in the corner where the brick wall met the building. She moved the trash can out of the way, revealing a hole in the ground. With a teary glance at Ginger, she sat on the edge and quickly dropped into the hole. Ginger followed. Maeve hesitated for just a minute. She heard the pounding footsteps of the WG soldiers and dropped in after Ginger and Emery.

The drop was only about 3 feet. Maeve crouched low to keep her head from peeking out of the hole.

"Grab the edge of the trash can and move it back over the hole," Emery said. "Hurry!"

Maeve reached up and grabbed the bottom edge of the garbage can and scooted it carefully over the hole, being careful not to tip it over.

The girls were plunged into immediate darkness.

"What is this place?" Maeve asked.

"It's a secret tunnel," Emery said.

"What's with all the secret tunnels?" Maeve said.

"I don't know," Emery said. "I just found this

one day when I was looking for a place to read. I come here sometimes when I want to be alone."

"How do you avoid the WG?" Maeve asked.

Emery waved her hand. "They don't track the younger kids as much as they do everyone else. It's not that hard to slip away as long as you show up where you're supposed to be when you're supposed to be there."

Ginger nodded. "She's right. The WG doesn't think the kids can cause much trouble, so they don't track them like they track the rest of us." She turned to Emery. "How come you never told me about this place? If anyone caught you here..." Ginger trailed off, leaving Maeve and Emery to fill in the blank.

"Why would it be a problem if they caught her?" Maeve asked. "She's just a kid reading in an abandoned tunnel."

"These tunnels aren't as abandoned as you'd think," Ginger said. She looked at Maeve, and Maeve saw the sadness, anger and weariness on her face. "There's a lot I haven't told you. I couldn't, Maeve. Your parents believe the best way to get along in Palumbra is to blindly follow the WG. You thought so, too, until today."

Maeve looked at her best friend in shock. "I thought we shared everything." Maeve folded her legs and slid down the wall of the tunnel until she was sitting on the floor. "Why wouldn't you have told me?"

"I couldn't risk it, Maeve," Ginger said as she sat next to Maeve. "People's lives were at stake." Ginger looked away. "But keeping it a secret didn't save

100

my mom," she said in a whisper.

Maeve shook off her building anger toward Ginger, and wrapped her arm around her friend's shoulders. Ginger leaned her head on Maeve's shoulder and wept silently. Emery shrugged out of her backpack and sat next to her sister, wrapping her arms tight around Ginger's waist and hiding her face against her back. Maeve used her other arm to pat Emery's shaking shoulder. Wrapped in a group hug, the sisters and Maeve cried out their sorrow. When Ginger's sobbing had turned to silent hiccups, she sat up, hugged Emery and turned to look at Maeve.

"I'm sorry. I should have told you."

Maeve wiped her own tears and shrugged. "You did what you thought was best. I'm not sure I would have believed you before today, anyway." Maeve stared at the wall in front of her and swallowed. "I'm sorry about your mom. She was an amazing lady. I'm going to miss her."

Ginger stroked Emery's hair and sat silent for a moment. "Yeah. We all are."

The silence echoed in the still, dark tunnel until Maeve said, "I'm still not sure what I don't know, but I do know we need to get out of here."

Ginger nodded. "Let's get somewhere safe, and we can talk."

"OK, Emery," Maeve said. "Where does this tunnel go?"

Emery wiped her eyes, shouldered her backpack and stood up. "Under the brick wall, I think. I usually just hang out right here. I bring a candle and read, so I haven't really explored it much. It's a little creepy when you're here by yourself."

"All right, let's follow it to see where it goes," Maeve said. "Any ideas, Ginger, since you seem to know so much about the tunnels?"

"I'm not sure, but I bet Emery is right. This probably goes under the wall and comes up in a safe place. I just hope it's safe for us. Since you have the gun, why don't you lead the way?"

Maeve slowly edged forward in the low tunnel. She held the gun in front of her, more out of necessity than any thought that she could use it in the confines of the tunnel. Strapping it on her back wasn't an option since she already had to stoop over to fit under the low ceiling. Her eyes had mostly adjusted to the darkness, and she could just barely make out the way forward, and she hoped they didn't run into anything unexpected. She could hear Ginger and Emery as they felt their way behind her.

After about 100 yards, the tunnel split. In the darkness, Maeve couldn't discern any difference between the two paths, and she didn't know the city well enough to figure out where she was based on the direction they had traveled.

"Any idea which way we should go?" Maeve asked Ginger and Emery as they came up behind her.

"I think we should go left," Emery said. "That takes us away from the center of the city."

"Are you sure?" Ginger asked. "How do you know?"

102

"We did a project in school last year where we had to map a route around the city," Emery said. "I remember most of the map."

"Of course you do," Ginger said, rolling her eyes. "You and your photographic memory."

"Well, it's kinda useful right now," Emery pointed out calmly.

"Way more useful than when you used it to recite an entire chapter of your math book. But are you sure? We're underground so things can seem different," Ginger said.

"I'm sure," Emery said.

"OK, then, let's go left," Maeve said as she stepped forward.

The girls said little as they walked through the darkness. Maeve wearily put one foot in front of the other, estimating that she had been awake for almost 20 hours by now. Suddenly, the tunnel ended. "This is it," she told the others. "There's no tunnel left. How do we get out?"

"What do you mean there's no tunnel left?" Ginger asked.

"It just ends. There's a wall and nothing else. Maybe they didn't finish it," Maeve said.

"Feel around on the walls. Maybe there's a door or something that we just can't see," Ginger suggested.

All three girls began running their hands over the walls, feeling for some way out of the tunnel. After five minutes, Emery said, "I don't think there's anything here."

"Wait," Maeve said. "Do you hear something?"

Everyone fell silent. They could hear their own

breathing. And then a slight murmuring – like someone speaking a long distance away.

"What is that?" Emery whispered.

Maeve turned in circles trying to decide where the sound was coming from.

"I wonder if we missed another tunnel or a door somewhere back that way," Maeve said. "Let's walk back the way we came. Keep a hand on the wall and feel for a way out."

Slowly, they retraced their steps, feeling along the dirt wall as they walked. "I think I found something," Ginger said after they had walked about a third of the distance back.

"Where?" Maeve asked.

"Right here," Ginger said as she guided Maeve's hand to place it next to her own. Maeve felt what had caused Ginger to stop. Underneath the dirt of the tunnel wall was a board, carefully camouflaged so as to only be apparent if you were feeling for it.

"Everyone be quiet," Maeve said. "Let's see if we can hear that noise again."

Once again, the girls fell silent. The murmuring sound had grown louder and was clearly the sound of voices.

"What do we do?" Emery asked.

"Well, if we can hear them, they can probably hear us, so for starters, we whisper," Ginger said. "What do you think?"

"Ginger, who knows about these tunnels?" Maeve asked.

"Well... It's kind of a long story. The WG knows about some of them, but most of them are unmapped by the WG."

"So, who uses them? And why do you know about them?" Maeve repeated.

"Mostly The Resistance," Ginger said slowly.

"The resistance to what?" Maeve said.

"To the WG."

Maeve turned to stare at Ginger through the darkness. "What?" she said in stunned disbelief.

"Yeah," Ginger said quietly. "That's one of the things I needed to tell you about."

"There are people actively fighting the WG?"

"Right now, it's more of a silent resistance, but that's the eventual plan, yeah."

"Why? Who would risk doing something like that?"

"Maeve, do you really think people like living in a world where the WG controls everything? Do you think it was always like this? Don't you ever just want to do whatever you want to do and not just what you're told to do?"

"Until today, I'd never really thought that much about it. My parents always told me to just do what the WG wanted and everything would be fine."

"That might be why you don't know about The Resistance," Ginger muttered.

Maeve started to speak, but Ginger cut her off. "Sorry. It's not your fault, but this probably isn't the time for this conversation. It's going to take a while to explain it all."

Maeve peered at Ginger through the murky darkness. Maeve started to speak, then stopped. She pushed aside her annoyance and frustration at being left in the dark about so many things and focused on the current problem.

"What are the chances that the people on the other side of that door are part of The Resistance?" Maeve asked.

"I'd say they're pretty good, but I can't be positive," Ginger said.

"What do you think we should do?"

"I think our only choice is to figure out how to open the door," Ginger replied. "If we try to go back and take the other path, we risk running into the WG soldiers if they found the tunnel."

"Emery, we're all in this together. What do you think?" Maeve asked.

"Well... I guess we should try to open the door. We know the WG are back where we came from," Emery said.

"OK. Then let's get this door open."

They began scraping away the dirt camouflaging the door until they could feel the wood. "Dig around the edges to find the hinges," Maeve said as she split her fingernails on the rough wood. She felt a splinter slide into her finger but finally found purchase under the edge of the door.

"Ready," Maeve asked the others.

"Ready," Ginger and Emery replied.

"On the count of three, then." Maeve took a deep breath. "1, 2, 3"

The girls pulled on the door, and it slowly began to open.

CHAPTER TWELVE

"Wait!" Maeve whispered. "When we get the door open, you and Emery stay out here. I'll go first to make sure it's safe. If it is, I'll come back out and get you. If I don't come back, you and Emery run."

"I don't want to leave you behind," Ginger said.

"Your first job is to keep Emery safe. If I don't come back out, make your way back to the tunnel by the fishing hut. There's a door in that tunnel. Gray said it was safe."

"OK," Ginger said slowly. "But be careful!"

The two girls went back to pulling on the door. The door was heavy, but the hinges were well-oiled, making it easier to open. It took all three of them to hold the weight of the door. As the door opened, light began spilling out into the dark tunnel. Finally, the weight of the door caused it to swing open and slam against the tunnel wall, will a dull, soft thump. Maeve, Ginger and Emery let go of the door and jumped out of the way. Maeve shoved Ginger and Emery deeper into the darkness as she got her first glimpse of the room behind the door.

She took a step toward the light. She could hear the voices much more clearly now, and she was grateful the door hitting the wall hadn't made more noise. The lack of alarm from anyone inside gave Maeve the confidence she needed to step into the room where she saw ... nothing. It looked just like the tunnel outside. Worn wooden beams held up the ceiling, and the walls were made of packed dirt. A lone light bulb swung lightly from a ceiling beam. Maeve could still hear voices down the tunnel that branched off from the opposite side of the room. Maeve gripped her gun and slowly and quietly made her way toward the tunnel.

With each step, Maeve fought the urge to run, but where would she run to? Her home wasn't safe with her parents wanting to turn her in, and Ginger's mom was dead. She shook her head to banish the thoughts of her parents and Mrs. Snell. Even though she tried to be quiet, Maeve's steps sounded heavy and loud to her own ears. She looked at the gun she didn't know how to use in her hands. Could she shoot someone if she needed to?

Maeve saw another door at the end of the tunnel, and she could clearly hear two male voices inside, one deeper than the other.

"I have to go find them," the first voice said.

"You can't go there. It's dangerous. I told you it's been compromised," the deeper voice replied.

"We can't just leave them out there."

"Right now, that's what we have to do."

"I'm going. Don't try to stop me."

109

"Think of the bigger cause. Are you willing to throw that all away for a few people you just met."

"I'm going."

"Stay here. I'll be right back."

Maeve backed away just as the door was thrown open. She raised her gun, pointing it into the startled face of Night Cantwell.

Night took a step backward and slowly raised his hands.

"Maeve. How did you get here?" he said, shooting Gray a confused look.

Maeve's hands shook. Night was Gray's uncle, but she also knew he held a high position in the WG. If the WG used this tunnel, then she had to get back to Ginger and Emery and get out. Her eyes scanned the room, looking for an escape route. Another room opened up behind Gray, but Maeve would have to go through Night and whoever else was in the room with him. Her only way out was the door that was now behind her. Her eyes darted nervously from Night to the open door behind him as her hands shook.

"Who's with you?" Maeve asked in what she hoped was an authoritative voice.

"Maeve, why don't you put down the gun, and we can talk this out," Night said.

"No. I've been chased all day by the WG. Gray was captured." She motioned at her gun with one hand but kept the other on the trigger. "I'm not putting the gun down until I know what's going on."

Maeve could just make out the outline of

another person behind Gray. With the light behind the person, she couldn't see his face, just the outline of a body. With her entire body shaking, she moved the gun from Night to the new threat, then back to Night.

"Gray, why don't you come talk to your friend and let her know we're on the same side," Night said.

Maeve's mouth fell open as Gray stepped into the dim tunnel. "Gray?" she said in a small voice.

"Maeve," Gray said, the relief evident in his voice. "We were just talking about how to find you." He gave his uncle a pointed look. "I'm so glad you're OK." He took a step toward her. "Can you put the gun down now?"

Maeve wavered. This was Gray who had sacrificed himself for her to get away. But how had he managed to get away from the WG soldiers? She started to lower the gun. Then stopped.

"Wait. How did you end up here? And what's he doing?" She pointed with the end of the gun toward Night who took another step back as the gun wavered in her shaking hands.

"I guess you're a little more comfortable with that gun than you were when I handed it to you," Gray said. "Look, he's on our side. And he's my uncle. Can we put the gun down and talk about it?" Gray took another step toward and reached out as if to take the gun.

Maeve shook her head. "I don't even know whose side I'm supposed to be on anymore. Until today, I didn't even know there were sides, so why don't you both start by telling me what's going on. How do I even know I can trust you? My whole life I was told to trust the WG. Today, they tried to shoot me. They killed Ginger and Emery's mother. So, excuse me for not just taking you at your word."

"Ok," Gray held his hands up. "We don't have a lot of time, but we can give you the short version. Not everyone believes that the WG has society's best interests at heart. There's a good-sized group of people who believe the WG is simply interested in holding onto power and has been lying to us about the Lost Years and whether anyone else survived the war. Night and I are part of The Resistance – and so is Ginger."

"So why didn't you know Ginger when I introduced you this morning?" Maeve asked as she tightened her grip on the gun.

Gray shook his head. "Maeve, The Resistance is large. I know Ginger's name, but I've never met her before today."

Maeve thought about that for a moment, then nodded, accepting it as plausible. "So why is the WG shooting at me? And why did all the soldiers except you disappear from the hospital this morning?"

"We don't know," Night said. "We're trying to figure it out."

"How can you not know?" Maeve said, as her hands trembled, making the gun waver. "You're Arabella Laughlin's right-hand man."

"She doesn't tell me everything, especially right now." He shrugged. "I don't know if she suspects that I'm helping The Resistance, but she's been much more distant lately. I didn't know about the attacks today, and I had to use all my diplomatic skills to get Gray turned over to me after he was caught by some of Arabella's personal guard."

"Do you think she suspects you're helping us?" Gray asked with a worried look at his uncle. "You could be in danger."

Night's eyes met Gray's. "This whole thing is dangerous, Gray. Look what happened to you today."

"This makes no sense," Maeve said.

"Maeve, I know this is a lot to take in," Gray said, holding out a hand toward her. "Your whole world has been rocked. Everything you knew to be true this morning is not true now, but please believe me, I'm your friend. I care what happens to you. I was just coming to find you."

"Against your uncle's advice," Maeve said.

"I had to consider the good of The Resistance," Night said. "We have to be careful not to risk exposure, especially if Ariella is on to us."

Maeve looked from Night to Gray, considering her options. "I have to trust someone, so it might as well be you," she said, pointing to Gray. "The jury is still out on you," she continued, gesturing with the gun at Night.

"That's good enough for now," Night said. "Can you put the gun down, please?"

Maeve slowly lowered the gun until it no longer pointed at Night, but her hand remained poised near the trigger.

Just as she lowered the gun, she heard the

scraping of feet in the tunnel behind her.

Maeve whirled and lifted her gun as Gray reached for the handgun in the holster at his waist. Night stepped back into the other room.

Another foot shuffled on the dirt path. Maeve and Gray waited.

A small figure stepped out of the shadows.

"Emery!" Maeve shouted, dropping her gun and running toward her. Gray, however, kept his gun trained on the shadow emerging behind Emery. Maeve looked up, expecting Ginger, as the second shadow stepped into the light.

"Silas?" Maeve said. "Where's Ginger? How did you get here?"

"I'm right here," Ginger answered as she too stepped into the pool of light. "Silas stumbled upon us in the tunnel outside. When you didn't come back, we decided we needed to look for you. He came along."

Maeve took a closer look at Silas. He was covered in dust from the tunnel and had a cut on his cheek that was slowly seeping blood.

"What happened to you?" Maeve asked.

"I took a tree branch to the face," Silas said. "I'm glad I finally found all of you. There's no way to get to the 'safe room' through the fishing hut. The WG has soldiers surrounding the hut, so I went back down into the tunnel through the well and found a different door that connected to this tunnel. I was looking for a way back when I ran into Ginger and Emery."

"He literally ran into us," Emery said. "He

114

tripped and fell into Ginger."

"What's he doing here?" Ginger asked, pointing to Gray who had re-holstered his gun.

"It was his voice we heard through the door," Maeve said. For reasons she wasn't sure she understood, she didn't mention Gray's uncle. They hadn't seen or heard him since he disappeared into the other room. Maeve assumed there was another exit there. Maeve glanced at Gray who gave a slight shake of his head to indicate she should leave Night out of their discussion.

"I escaped from the soldiers who caught me. I knew about these tunnels, so I came down here to hide and hopefully make my way back to the fishing hut. But it sounds like that safe zone has been compromised," Gray lied.

"You escaped from the WG soldiers?" Ginger said with skepticism.

Gray shrugged. "What can I say? It wasn't easy, but I managed."

"But who were you talking to," Ginger asked. "It sounded like two voices through the door."

"Nope. Just me thinking out loud," Gray said with a small grin. "Speaking of doors, did you close the one you came through? The WG knows about some of these tunnels, so we need to be as inconspicuous as possible."

"You might want to stop thinking out loud then," Ginger said. "And, yes, we closed the door. I'm surprised you didn't hear it."

"Sound carries oddly in the tunnels," Gray said.

Emery chose that moment to drop cross-legged onto the floor. "I'm hungry," she said. "And tired." She leaned her head against the nearest support timber.

"Walk a few more minutes, and I can find you some food and a place to rest for a few minutes," Gray said. "I think we could all use a rest, and we need to figure out our next steps since it looks like we're fugitives now."

Gray turned and walked into the room Night had disappeared into. Maeve stepped into the room and scanned it for any sign of Night, but he was gone. The room, like most of the tunnels, was lit with a single bare bulb. The only difference between this room and the tunnel was a table and two chairs. A map of Palumbra was spread across the table.

Gray walked to the table, folded up the map and stuck it in his backpack as he continued across the room. "Last one in, close the door," Gray said. Maeve turned to see Silas give the door a shove, and it closed with a thump.

Gray looked over his shoulder as if he were counting heads, gave Maeve a quick smile, then opened a door on the other side of the room and walked through, expecting them to follow.

Ginger grabbed Maeve's sleeve. "Are we sure following Gray is the right thing to do?" she asked. "We have no idea how he got away from the WG soldiers, and no way of knowing where he's taking us."

"Ginger, I have to believe that Gray is on our side," Maeve replied. "He let himself get caught so we
116

could escape. We have to trust someone. We don't know enough about what's going on to make good decisions about what to do. Gray seems to know these tunnels and can at least get us some food and a place to rest. Right now, that seems like our best bet."

"I guess you're right," Ginger said. "Emery needs to eat and rest. We all do. But we need to keep a close eye on him. We don't know what he's been up to."

"We have no idea what Silas has been doing either," Maeve said. "We just have to be careful. But right now, we need food. So, let's go." Maeve strode toward the open door and gestured for Ginger to go first. She stepped through and pulled the door shut with a thunk.

CHAPTER THIRTEEN

Gray led them through a twisting maze of tunnels and rooms. Maeve tried to keep track of each turn, but after 15 minutes of walking through the labyrinth of tunnels, she admitted to herself she was hopelessly lost. She could only hope she wouldn't need to get them out of the tunnels on her own.

No one spoke, but Maeve took stock of her surroundings. The tunnels were all built the same, with worn wooden supports and tightly packed dirt walls. Every so often there was a weathered wood door like the one they had uncovered to enter this section of tunnels. Maeve assumed those doors led to more tunnels. As she put one tired foot in front of the other, she asked, "Why are these tunnels here?"

"We're not sure," Gray said with a shrug. "The WG thinks maybe they were used for mining a long time ago. They pre-date The Lost Years, but they were obviously shored up during the wars." Gray tapped one of the wooden support beams. "These beams aren't nearly old enough to have been here before The Lost Years. Both The Resistance and the WG have added some more supports."

Maeve started to ask another question, but stopped when Emery stumbled. Ginger was watching Emery with concern. Emery was moving slower with each step as the adrenaline from being chased wore off. She looked near collapse.

Maeve touched Gray on the shoulder. "Are we almost there?" she asked quietly. "Emery isn't going to make it much longer."

Silas looked at Emery and, without saying a word, removed her backpack before shouldering it himself. Emery gave him a grateful smile.

"Not long," Gray replied. "It's just around the corner. There's food and a quiet place to rest."

Maeve gave him a thumbs up. It seemed like too much effort to say anything else. Emery wasn't the only one who was quickly reaching the end of her energy.

At last they turned a corner and were met with a door. Gray pulled the door open with little trouble and motioned for Maeve, Ginger, Emery and Silas to go in. Maeve entered cautiously, gripping her gun tightly. After today, she would never rush into a room again.

The room was larger than any of the others they had walked through. Groups of rough wooden tables and chairs were scattered throughout, and a set of bunk beds made out of small logs sat in one corner. Cabinets and a stove-like burner stood in the other corner. Maeve hoped the cabinets contained food.

Maeve, Ginger, Emery and Silas made their way over to a table and dropped their bags. Maeve held onto her gun. They all looked at Gray.

Gray shut the door and walked over to the cabinets. He pulled out five foil pouches and picked up what looked like five canteens then walked back to the table. "It's not real tasty, but it will restore your energy," he said as he passed out the pouches and the canteens.

"What is it?" Emery asked as she peeled back the packaging on her pouch to reveal a solid orange brick of something.

"It's protein paste packed into a bar form," Gray said. "It's what they feed soldiers in the field when we can't get back to base. It lasts forever and will give you enough energy to get through a day. It's not gourmet, but it will keep us going."

Emery wrinkled her nose but bit into the orange bar. "Yuck!"

"I know," Gray said, taking a bite of his own bar. "But it's what we've got."

No one said anything else as they ate and drank. Maeve thought the protein paste bar tasted a lot like mud, but she didn't complain. At this point, anything was better than nothing, so she concentrated on chewing and swallowing and tried to decide which question to ask first.

After they were finished, Gray gathered up their trash and disposed of it in a bag in the cabinet. When he sat back down, he said, "Where do we begin?"

"How about you tell us what happened to you after you sent us into the warehouse," Ginger said. "But first, Emery, you need to go lay down and get some rest. You're dead on your feet."

"I want to hear what happened," Emery said.

"You can listen from over there and if you fall asleep, I'll catch you up. But if we need to move quickly, we can't have you so tired that we have to carry you."

"OK," Emery said as she trudged toward the bed. Ginger followed and helped her climb into the bunk. Maeve saw Ginger lean down as Emery whispered something in her ear. Soft sobs followed, and Maeve saw Ginger wipe her eyes. She started to get up to help, but Gray gently grabbed her hand.

"What happened?" He pointed a thumb in the direction of the crying sisters.

"Their mom was killed protecting them from WG soldiers." Gray's eyes widened and he shot a sad glance toward Ginger and Emery. "I need to go check on them."

"Let them have a moment," Gray said quietly. "They need each other right now."

"Don't you think they need their friends, too?"

Gray's thumb made gentle circles on the back of her hand. "They do. But at just this moment they need to grieve with each other. Losing a parent is hard, but watching your parent die trying to protect you has to be harder."

Maeve knew Gray was speaking from experience about losing his parents, so she sat back down and played with the strap of her canteen.

Without looking up from the canteen, she said, "Sometimes having parents can be hard, too."

"What happened at your house, Maeve?"

"My parents made it clear they thought the only way to deal with things was for me to turn myself in to the WG – even after I told them what had happened today." She looked up. Her eyes glistened with unshed tears. "Why wouldn't they support me?"

Gray took both of Maeve's hands and crouched down in front of her chair. His looked steadily into her brown ones. "Fear makes people do things they would never do otherwise. They love you, Maeve. They were just afraid."

Maeve shook her head. "Ginger's mom died for her and Emery. My parents weren't even willing to risk helping me." She shook her head. "I always thought my parents would be there for me. Instead they betrayed me."

"I'm sorry, Maeve." Gray pulled her from her chair into a tight hug. Maeve laid her head on his shoulder and wept. When her tears subsided, she pushed back from Gray and looked up.

"Your shoulder's all wet." She focused on trying to mop up the wet spot on his shirt with her hand. "Emery and Ginger's mom died. I should be grateful my parents are still alive."

Gray placed his hand over hers, holding it over his heart, then tipped her chin up so she was looking into his eyes. "You get to grieve, too. It's been a hard day."

Maeve nodded and stepped out of Gray's embrace as Ginger walked up to the table, wiping her eyes. Maeve hugged her tightly but didn't speak. They turned to find Gray nudging Silas, who had put his head on the table and

122

fallen asleep while Gray and Maeve were talking.

"W-w-what?" Silas jumped to his feet, looking around wildly. "Oh. I forgot where I was." He ran a hand through his hair and sat back down. The rest of them joined him, and Maeve said, "Why don't you start by telling us what happened to you?" She nodded at Gray. "Then each of us can share our journey here." The others nodded.

"There's not much to tell, really," Gray said. "I was captured by the soldiers. They didn't buy my story that I was looking for you guys. They took me to WG headquarters and stuck me in a cell for a couple of hours. No one came to see me, and I assumed they had forgotten about me. After a couple hours, they took me out of my cell and led me out the back door. I came here."

"That makes no sense," Ginger said. "Why would they just let you go?"

"I assume my uncle had something to do with it," Gray said.

"H-h-how did you know about these tunnels?" Silas asked.

"Believe it or not, I've done some work with the Resistance. I knew this was a safe place for them."

"I feel like there are some holes in your story," Ginger said. "How can we trust you if you won't tell us the whole truth?"

"Look," Gray said. "There are some things I can't tell you because it will endanger people in The Resistance. Just know that I'm here to help. I care about what happens to you." Gray looked at Maeve as he said the last words.

"I guess we'll have to take your word for it, for now," Silas said. "But at s-s-some point, we're going to have to trust each other with everything. I guess, I'll go next."

Silas got up and began to pace. Maeve noticed his hands were shaking.

"When I left you guys at the well, I distracted the WG soldiers by acting scared, which wasn't much of a stretch, and asking them what was going on and what I should do. N-n-no one knew I had been with you so it was easy to just be a scared teenager. I convinced them I was too scared to go anywhere on my own, so they escorted me back to my n-n-neighborhood."

"Did you see your parents?" Ginger asked.

"Yes. They had both been at the factory when the bombs went off. The factory closed and everyone was sent home. They were worried about m-m-me. I didn't tell them where I'd been. I acted like I was going to my room, then snuck out the window to go to the fishing hut like Gray had said."

"You said the fishing hut was surrounded by the WG," Gray said.

"Yes. They had at least a dozen soldiers staking it out. I'm n-n-not very good at being sneaky, so I almost ran into a WG soldier before I realized they were there. Luckily, I heard their voices before I stumbled into them."

"But how did you find these tunnels?" Maeve asked.

"M-m-mostly just luck," Silas replied. "I was backing away through the woods, when I saw a well like the one we climbed out of. I took a chance and looked inside, saw the ladder, wandered through the tunnels and stumbled into you."

"I guess it's my turn," Maeve said. "Or do you want to tell it?" she asked Ginger.

"No, it's awful enough without having to say it."

Maeve told Silas and Gray about outrunning the WG, going back to their homes, then repeated her story of her parents' rejection of the truth and Ginger and Emery's mom's death for Silas. When she finished, her eyes met Ginger's as Ginger raised a hand to her mouth and tears leaked out of her eyes again. Silas laid his hand on top of Ginger's in silent comfort.

A few minutes passed with each of them absorbed in their own thoughts. Finally, Maeve broke the silence.

"So, what do we do now?" Maeve asked. "We still don't know why the WG is after us specifically or why they decided to set off bombs in Palumbra."

Gray stood up and refilled his canteen. "I have some ideas about that," Gray said. "And I bet Ginger has a few things to add."

Ginger nodded. "I actually do. Maeve, do you remember my mom whispering in my ear earlier today?"

Maeve gave Ginger a perplexed look. "I just figured she was telling you to run."

Ginger swallowed hard and breathed deeply as she looked at the floor. When her emotions were under control, she shook her head. "That wasn't all she said."

Maeve, Gray and Silas looked intently at

Ginger. "Go on," Gray said.

"She said The Resistance had evidence that the WG was behind the bombings."

"Did she tell you anything else?" Silas asked as he stood up and began pacing near the back wall of the room.

"No," Ginger said as her voice caught. "There wasn't time."

Gray nodded his head. "That fits with what I was thinking. The question is why would they do that."

"I still can't believe you were both working for The Resistance," Maeve said. "I didn't even know a resistance existed. Why didn't I know? Silas had you heard of them?"

"Yes," Silas said. "My parents would talk about The Resistance after they thought I was asleep. I don't know much, but I think they were a part of it, and they were worried about some of their friends."

"Why am I the only person who has never even heard of The Resistance? What else don't I know?" Maeve said.

"Maeve, until that day you were late coming home from the hospital, when have you ever thought about the WG and how they rule? When have your parents?"

"Never," Maeve admitted.

"Have you ever wondered how the WG came to be?" Gray asked. "Didn't you ever want to do something on your own? Do you really want to be a nurse?"

"I never really thought about it. It's just the way it's always been. I guess I just assumed you wanted to be a soldier and Ginger wanted to work for the WG." Maeve looked over at Ginger who was shaking her head.

"Maeve, what did I always want to do when we were kids?" Ginger asked.

Maeve thought back to days when she and Ginger would walk home from school together dreaming about the future. She remembered Ginger talking about the stars and her crazy imaginings about ships that could reach the stars. Maeve shook her head. Those days seemed so long ago, and Ginger's plans to fly among the stars were farther away than ever.

"You wanted to 'touch the stars,'" Maeve said. "But those were just the crazy dreams of kids who thought anything could happen."

"Sometime crazy dreams are all we have to hold onto," Ginger said.

"We don't even have cars," Maeve said, "and you think you can get to the stars?"

"Never give up on your dreams, Maeve. They might be more possible than you think," Ginger replied.

"I don't even know what my dreams are anymore," Maeve said in a whisper.

Ginger gave Maeve a hug then turned to Gray. "Did you want to be a soldier, Gray?"

"No," Gray replied.

"What did you want to do?" Maeve asked.

"Let me show you," Gray said as he reached in his bag and pulled out a knife with a well-worn handle. He leaned over and started drawing in the dirt floor with the tip of his knife. Maeve and Ginger leaned over in the chairs to watch. Silas walked over to where they

127

sat and stood over Gray as he drew.

When Gray finished, he looked at Maeve, the corners of his lips tipping up into a small smile. Maeve's eyes grew wide, and her mouth dropped. "That's me!"

Gray just smiled.

"That's amazing," Ginger said. "They made you a soldier?"

"N-n-not a lot of use for art in Palumbra," Silas said.

Maeve shook her head. There was so much she didn't know about her friends. She looked at Silas who kept looking from Gray to the drawing and back again as if he couldn't believe that the artwork had come from Gray's hand.

"What about you, Silas," Gray asked. "What do you want to do?"

"I'm pretty easy," he said. "Exactly what the WG is setting me up to do. Work with computers."

"Aren't we quite the group," Gray said. "Only one of us is doing what we were wired to do."

"And now we're back to the question of what we do now," Maeve said with a yawn.

"I think we sleep on it," Ginger said with a yawn of her own. "I know we have a lot to talk about, but we're all so tired, I don't think we're going to come up with any good solutions right now. We should sleep while we can."

"I agree with Ginger," Gray said. "Everybody grab a bunk. We're safe here for now."

CHAPTER FOURTEEN

Maeve opened her eyes slowly, then sat up quickly, eyes darting around the unfamiliar room. Just as quickly, the events of yesterday came flooding back to her, and she relaxed a little. Someone had turned the lights to dim, and she could make out her friends' forms in their bunks. Her eyes slid from one bunk to the next, resting on the familiar outlines of Emery, Ginger, Silas and ... where was Gray? She moved her gaze around the dimly lit room and saw him sitting at the table they had eaten at the night before. Quietly, she pushed the rough blanket aside, shoved her feet into her shoes and joined him at the table.

"Hey," he said quietly.

"Hey, yourself." She glanced over at her sleeping friends to make sure their conversation wasn't disturbing them.

"I thought you would sleep longer," Gray said, looking at her face. "You still look tired."

"I'm good." Maeve brushed her hair out of her eyes. "I've never needed a lot of sleep."

"Me either."

They sat in awkward silence as the minutes

ticked by.

"Gray, what do you know? And why are we keeping your uncle's help a secret?"

Gray gave a sigh. His shoulders slumped, and his eyes looked weary.

"Maeve, there's so much you don't know. I'm not sure where to start. What do you know about The Lost Years?"

"Almost nothing." Maeve gave him a bewildered look. "I thought no one knew anything. In school, they just skim over those years."

"Oh, the WG knows all about them. They just don't want us to know."

"What?" Maeve's brow furrowed in confusion. "Why?"

"If you want to keep people thinking that this is the best life they can have, it's a secret worth keeping. Maeve, The Lost Years are the reason the WG exists. If the WG seized power illegally, do you think they would want you to know that?"

Maeve shook her head. "It's just a lot to take in. What do you know about The Lost Years?"

"Let's wait until everyone else is up, and I'll show you. In the meantime, let's find some food."

Maeve and Gray gathered up enough protein paste bars for everyone and refilled the canteens. By the time they were done, the rest of the group had joined them at the table.

"Everyone, eat up. We're moving on after we finish eating," Gray said.

130

"Where are we going?" Silas asked. "It's safe here. Why do we n-n-need to move on?"

"It may not be safe for long," Gray said. "We know the WG are looking for us, and they know about some of the tunnels. It's only a matter of time before they find us. We'll load up some of the food and take it with us. But we need to start finding answers, and I know just the place to begin."

Gray handed out food and gave everyone a blanket. He grabbed a backpack and tossed it to Maeve as she was the only one who didn't have a bag. They tucked food and blankets in their packs along with some rope. Gray reached into another cabinet and pulled out five large knives with wooden handles and 3-inch-long blades. He put them in sheaths and gave one to each of them, including Emery.

"Are you sure she won't hurt herself with that?" Ginger said.

"Hey," Emery said. "I can use a knife."

"She needs to be able to defend herself," Gray said. "I don't want to give her a gun, but we can't leave her without some kind of weapon. What if she gets separated from us? Plus, she can use the knife to cut food or to cut through things."

"Speaking of weapons," Gray said, "who has a gun?"

"I do," Maeve said.

"Have you figured out how to use it?" Gray asked.

"I haven't had to shoot it yet. You said to point

and pull the trigger."

"Yeah, that's not exactly comforting. We'll work on your gun skills when we have time. What do you have for ammunition?"

"Just what's in the gun," Maeve said. "Is that a problem?"

"We'll get you some more," Gray said as he opened yet another cabinet. This one was sealed with a combination lock. When he opened the door, Maeve saw that it was filled with weapons – guns, grenades, stunners.

"Who does know how to shoot?" Gray asked.

Ginger and Silas raised their hands. Maeve's eyebrows rose. Few people in Palumbra had access to guns.

"How did you learn to shoot?" she asked.

"Everyone in The Resistance learns to shoot. They have a secret range in one of the tunnels," Ginger said.

"What about you?" Maeve said, looking at Silas.

"M-m-my parents taught me. My dad keeps a gun hidden from the WG. He's always been worried that things aren't exactly what they seem. We would sneak out through the woods past the edge of the city late at night, and he would teach me to shoot. He thought I might need to know some day."

"So, I'm the only person who had never heard of The Resistance and doesn't know how to shoot," Maeve said, gesturing toward the guns in frustration. "I feel like I missed out on essential life skills."

"Well, you do know how to help people who are hurt," Gray pointed out. "That's more than most of us."

"Maybe," Maeve said. "But I was just getting

132

started in my training, and I'm not sure I'm all that good at it."

"Well, hopefully, we won't have a reason to test your skills," Gray said as he handed a rifle and a handgun to both Ginger and Silas and held out more ammunition for Maeve. Maeve tucked the ammunition into her pack as Silas and Ginger checked their weapons, slung the rifles over their backs and attached the holstered handguns to their waistbands. "Let's move out," Gray said.

"Where are we going?" Emery asked.

"To find some answers," Gray said.

They shouldered their packs and followed Gray through the winding tunnels for what seemed like an hour. Maeve was hopelessly lost, and she hoped Emery's stellar sense of direction was still working if they needed to escape in a hurry. Every tunnel looked the same − dirt and wooden pillars holding up the ceiling. The complex tunnel system reminded Maeve of the minotaur's maze they had read about in school. She wished she had a ball of string to leave herself a trail back to the entrance. They passed a number of camouflaged doors, but Gray stopped at none of them.

Gray led the way, followed by Emery, Silas, Ginger and Maeve. Talking was difficult as the dirt walls sucked up the sound of voices. They saw no one else, although Maeve thought she heard voices behind some of the closed doors. The narrow tunnels didn't allow for anything other than single-file movement.

"If these tunnels are used by The Resistance, where

is everyone?" Maeve gestured to indicate the empty tunnel.

"Most of The Resistance members just go about living their lives on the surface," Gray said. "They can't be constantly disappearing for no reason. The tunnels are used for meetings of small groups and as an emergency shelter."

"I would think this constitutes an emergency in need of shelter, don't you?" Maeve said.

Gray glanced at her over his shoulder. "If the WG starts going after Resistance members, the tunnels will fill up, but my guess is that hasn't happened yet."

"Gray is right," Ginger chimed in. "The tunnels are a last resort."

"So why do you know so much about the tunnels?" Silas asked Gray.

"I've spent a little time here," he said.

Maeve started to ask another question, but Gray shot her a silencing look and said, "Here we are." They had stopped in front of another door, and they could hear voices on the other side.

"Wait here," Gray said and disappeared through the door.

Maeve looked at Silas, Ginger and Emery who seemed as confused by Gray's actions as she was. Before she could say anything, Gray returned with an older man with a long, gray beard. He reminded Maeve of a picture she had seen in a book once of a wizard.

"Hello," he greeted each of them with a handshake. Maeve shot Gray a confused look. "Who are you?" she said almost rudely.

134

Gray stepped in. "Maeve, Ginger, Silas, Emery, this is John Shield. He's been a member of The Resistance for a long time."

"Almost since the beginning," John said with a smile. "I was a wee lad when my parents became members." His voice held a bit of a burr, which was unusual since no one in Palumbra came from anywhere else.

"What's wrong with your voice?" Emery asked.

"Emery!" Ginger pulled Emery back toward her.

"What? His voice sounds different. I want to know why."

"No worries, lass," John said. "A long time ago, my granddad came here from a place called Scotland. Both he and my da spoke this way. I guess a bit of it has stuck around through the years."

As he spoke, he led them to an area of the tunnels that had wooden walls covering the dirt. A barely visible door was hidden in the wood on the left, kept closed with a lock built into the door that required two keys. John dug into his pocket and pulled out a key. He inserted it into the left keyhole. Then he reached up and tugged a thick string from around his neck. He pulled it over his head where Maeve could see a key dangling from the string. He inserted the second key in the lock. Using both hands, he turned the keys opposite directions at the same time. Maeve heard the lock snick open.

"Gray, here, tells me you lads and lasses are interested in The Lost Years. I was a babe in arms when they took place. I don't remember anything about them myself. My parents and granddad never talked about

135

them around me. They said it was too dangerous for me to know anything."

"But, surely, someone is around who remembers them," Maeve said.

"No one that will talk," John said. "All of us old-timers were just youngsters when The Lost Years happened. Most of those who opposed the WG either died in the fighting during the war or the WG made sure that anyone who knew anything after the war was either killed or just disappeared. No one knows what happened to them. My granddad died when I was 7 in a 'fishing accident,' and my parents disappeared when I was 8. Another Resistance family took me in, but they were too young to know anything about The Lost Years."

While John was talking, Gray and Ginger had pried the door open. John waved toward the opening. "In here, is everything we know about The Lost Years. Gray says you five are trying to figure something out and it might be useful. It's not much, but it's what we've got. Let me know when you're done. Good luck!" With a lift of his hand, John moved back down the tunnel the way they had come.

"Why does he trust you so much?" Ginger asked Gray.

"I've known John a long time. He was a friend of my parents, and he's always kept an eye out for me."

"But you said the tunnels are a last resort," Maeve said. "Why is he down here?"

"He lives down here," Gray replied. "The WG found out he was part of The Resistance, so he came down here. The Resistance made sure it looked like he had struck off on his own beyond The River."

"So what are we doing here?" Maeve asked.

Gray stepped through the open door, and beckoned for the others to follow. Maeve entered the dark chamber last, her eyes struggling to adjust to the darkness. The only light was from the tunnel outside.

"What is this place?" Maeve asked.

"Let me get us a light, and I'll show you," Gray said.

"Is this what I think it is?" Ginger asked.

"I thought this place only existed in legend," Silas said.

Once again, Maeve felt like she was missing crucial pieces of information that everyone else seemed to know. Even Emery chimed in, "Our parents told us about this place."

"Why does everyone know about this place except me?" Maeve asked as she kicked the dirt floor with her shoe.

"Close your eyes," Gray said. "I'm turning on a light."

Maeve squeezed her eyes shut to block out the bright light. When she opened them, she couldn't believe what she saw. One wall was covered with more books than she had ever seen in her life. Another wall was covered in screens. Next to the screens were small cases that looked like skinny books. A bank of electronics sat in front of the screens.

"What is all this stuff?" Maeve asked.

"This is knowledge the WG doesn't want us to

137

have," Ginger answered. "These are books and moving pictures from the Lost Years and before. The Resistance has been collecting them. The idea is that until we understand what happened to create the WG, we can't understand their goals."

"With all these books, surely The Resistance has figured it out by now," Maeve said.

"Not really," Gray said. "Most of these books and moving pictures actually come from before the Lost Years. We have very little information from the Lost Years. We can tell you minute details about what life was like before the Lost Years, but information about those important years is, well, lost."

"How does coming here help us, then," Silas asked.

"It's a place to start. If we're going to figure out what the WG wants with us, we have to figure out what they want in general, and that starts here," Gray said.

"This is overwhelming," Maeve said. "Where do we start?"

"There has to be some kind of cataloging system," Emery said. "Do you know what it is, Gray?"

"I've only been in here a couple of times, but I think things are cataloged by the year they were made. The oldest stuff is over there," Gray said, pointing to his right. "Anything related to the Lost Years would be in this section here." He pointed at a scant section of books to their left. "The moving pictures from the time around the Lost Years are on the bottom shelf."

Maeve looked at the bottom shelf and saw just

three slim cases. "Well, that's not going to be much help," she said.

"I know other people in the Resistance have studied this stuff," Ginger said. "What makes you think we'll be able to see something they didn't?"

"I don't know," Gray said. "But we have to start somewhere, right? Maybe knowing what life was like before the Lost Years can help us understand what happened."

"OK," Silas said. "Let's get started. I'll take the moving pictures. You guys split up the books."

"What are we looking for?" Ginger asked.

"Anything that gives us a clue about how the WG came to power," Gray replied.

"It looks like these three shelves have the most books from the right time period," Emery said. "Let's each take a shelf."

Everyone set to reading and watching. Silence reigned in the library, the only sound the occasional flipping of pages or the scratching of a pencil taking notes. It reminded Maeve of test-taking time in school.

After several hours, Maeve closed the last book on her shelf, set down her pencil and stretched her arms over her head. "That's my last book. How is everyone else doing?"

"I finished all the moving pictures," Silas said. "There was some interesting stuff. Did you know everyone had a car, and there were places called supermarkets where you could go buy whatever food you wanted any time of the day? I'm just not sure how much of it is relevant."

"I'm done, too," Ginger said, standing up and rubbing her back. "My stuff was mostly stories. They seemed too fantastical to be true. People traveled to all sorts of different places. One place was called Paris, and it had a really tall tower that people could climb and look out over the city. And there was a city called New York where millions of people lived. Can you imagine? Surely those books aren't true."

"I'm on the last book," Gray said. "Give me another couple of minutes."

"I finished a while ago," Emery said as she lounged on the ground, using her pack as a backrest, her feet propped on a shelf.

"She speed reads," Ginger said. "Useful at times like this but annoying when she finishes her homework first."

To anyone else, Emery looked like a typical 12-year-old, but Maeve could see her fear and sadness in the way her eyes tracked Ginger every time she moved. Maeve crouched down next to Emery and said quietly, "Are you OK?"

Emery sat up and shook her head. "No," she said as she looked at Maeve, "but having something to do helps." Maeve gave Emery a hug, then stood and dusted off her hands.

"Let's eat while Gray finishes," Maeve said. They sat on the floor in a circle and pulled out protein paste bars. The bars were gone quickly, and they washed them down with water from their canteens. Maeve leaned against the dirt wall and closed her eyes as she waited for Gray to finish. The tension and fear

140

from the last two days washed over her.

"Do you think our lives will ever be normal again?" she said without opening her eyes.

"No," Ginger said. "My life will never be the same. Our mom is dead, and we'll never even get to say goodbye. Whatever happens now, our lives are changed forever. None of us will ever be the same."

"That's assuming we m-m-make it through this alive," Silas said. "My parents don't even know where I am. They support The Resistance, but who knows what will happen to them now that I'm a wanted teen."

"I just want to go home," Emery said in a small voice, reminding Maeve of how young Emery still was.

Ginger leaned over and hugged her. "I know."

Gray closed his book with a soft thump. "You're right, Ginger, nothing is ever going to be the same," he said. "The question is what are we going to do now."

"My life was so much easier when I just did what I was told," Maeve said.

"But is that living, Maeve?" Gray asked in a gentle voice. "Do you really want to just do what other people tell you to do, never making decisions for yourself – just so you can be safe?"

"Is this really better?" Maeve asked. "Running for our lives? Watching people we love die? Never being safe? Not knowing who your friends are?"

"Maybe not," Ginger said. "But at least we're in charge of our lives. And, just maybe, we'll find a way to hang onto that."

"Maybe," Maeve said. "Maybe."

CHAPTER FIFTEEN

G ray stood up and rummaged in his pack. He pulled out a protein paste bar and took a bite. After swallowing, he said, "All right, what have we learned? Silas?"

"There were only three moving pictures. One was clearly just a story. The other two seemed like maybe they were true. I learned that before The Lost Years, people had a lot of stuff. Everyone had cars. They had stores where they shopped for food and clothes. They were allowed to come and go as they pleased. The most interesting thing I found was a section of one of the moving pictures that seemed true talked about a place called the United States creating the ultimate weapon. Just looking at the terrain they showed, it looked a lot like Palumbra."

"That's true," Ginger said. "Lots of people in The Resistance think Palumbra is a piece of what used to be the United States. It was a big place, but Palumbra is just a tiny part of it, somewhere in the center – away from the water."

"That's right," Emery chimed in.

"You sound pretty confident," Ginger said with

a sideways glance. "How can you know for sure?"

"Well, um..."

"Emery, what have you done?" Ginger let out a huff and rolled her eyes.

"I may have hacked into the WG system," Emery said. She quickly averted her eyes as Ginger's mouth dropped.

"You did what?" Ginger shouted. "Are you crazy? What if they had found out you did that?"

Maeve placed a hand on Ginger's arm. "Shh. I know you're mad, but keep it down."

Emery dismissed Ginger's concern with a wave of her hand. "Please, I'm better than that."

"Did you ever think about what would have happened to me or to mom if you got caught? The WG would have blamed one of us for letting you do it!"

Emery went completely still and closed her eyes. She shook her head without saying anything. "I didn't think there was any risk," she whispered. She raised her head and looked at Ginger. "Do you think mom was killed because I did that?"

Ginger rushed over to Emery and wrapped her in a fierce hug. "Oh, Emery, no. Mom knew what she was getting into when she joined The Resistance. Mom dying is not your fault."

Emery sniffed. "I really didn't think too much about it when I did it." She ran a hand through her hair, making the curls frizz. "I didn't get into anything important, just the historical archives. There wasn't much there, mostly maps."

She pulled out of Ginger's embrace. "I probably shouldn't have done it. I don't always think before I do stuff. It just seemed like a challenge."

Ginger gave her another hug and used a corner of her T-shirt to wipe the tears from Emery's face. "It's OK. Why don't you tell us what you found."

Emery nodded and pulled her computer out of her pack. "Let me show you. I kept a screenshot of it."

"That's dangerous," Ginger said. "What if someone at school had searched your computer."

"They wouldn't have found it," Emery said with a small smirk. "I'm better than all the teachers at computer stuff. Here."

Emery turned her computer around so the others could see the map. An unfamiliar outline filled the screen. "I've never seen that before," Gray said.

"It looks huge," Silas said, leaning closer to the screen.

"It is huge," Maeve agreed. "Far bigger than what we've been told exists."

"So what makes you think this is the United States?" Gray asked. He pointed to the screen. "Nothing is labeled."

Emery turned the computer back around and everyone gathered behind her. "Look, here." She pointed to the bottom, right corner of the screen. "See the initials?"

"U.S.A.?" Silas asked. "What does that mean?"

"The first two letters could stand for United States," Ginger said. "But what does the A stand for?"
144

"Who knows?" Maeve said. She sat back down in her chair and placed her chin in her hands. "But how do we even know that has any relation to Palumbra. Nothing on the map says Palumbra."

"N-n-no," Silas stuttered. "But there is an X here in the middle." He pointed to a spot on the map where a small white X stood out.

"Why would this be in the WG archives if it didn't have something to do with Palumbra?" Ginger asked.

"It wouldn't," Gray said. So, let's assume that Palumbra was once part of this United States and that everyone there was rich."

"Well, maybe not everyone," Emery said. "I found plenty of talk in my books about how there were rich people and poor people. There was a lot of debate about whether it was fair that some people were rich and some people were poor. It seems like there were lots of ways to earn money, and if you earned it, you got to keep it."

"That's true," Ginger said. "I had a lot of information on politics in my books. They had something called a democracy where people voted for their leaders, and the leaders talked a lot about either letting people keep their money or doing this thing called taxing, where the government took some of your money to take care of things like build roads, take care of poor people and protect the people."

Maeve stood up and began to pace. "So what happened? My books all talked about entertainment. People had plenty of time to go to moving pictures.

They called them movies. They watched other people play games. They went to places called restaurants where they had other people make them food. And they took time off from work and traveled to other places – London, Paris, Africa. Where are those places?"

Gray followed Maeve's pacing with his eyes as he spoke. "Good question. And do they still exist? The WG has always told us we're the only ones who survived the Lost Years, but what if there are other people out there? Look at that map." He waved his hand in the direction of Emery's computer. "That's a lot of land. How is it possible no one but Palumbra survived? My books talked about work. Apparently, people chose their own jobs. They did things that they liked to do and were good at. No one slotted them into the system."

"All of this is great," Ginger said. "But how does it help us? We still don't know what happened during The Lost Years. If information exists about those years, the WG has covered it up or destroyed it."

Maeve stopped pacing and looked at the four people who had become her only hope of survival.

"I know where we can find information about The Lost Years."

Ginger looked at Maeve and raised her eyebrows. "How could you know anything about The Lost Years? Until today, you weren't even sure the WG was a problem. Why would you be hiding something from them?"

"Well, I found something when I was walking home from work a while ago."

146

"Does this have something to do with the day you were late?" Gray asked.

Maeve looked around the room. Her eyes moved from person to person, as if weighing their trustworthiness. She twirled her hair as she studied her friends, remembering all they had been through in two short days. If she couldn't trust them, then who could she trust? Maeve stopped pacing, looked at Gray, and said, "Yes."

"When were you late?" Silas asked.

"Late to what?" Ginger said.

"Did you get caught by the WG?" Emery asked.

Maeve sat down next to Gray. Gray covered her hand with his, as if to give her courage, and Maeve stared at their joined hands before beginning to speak.

"A couple of months ago, I was walking home through the shortcut, and I found a box. I think it's a time capsule of some kind, buried by kids like us during the Lost Years. I didn't have time to dig it up without getting caught, but I did find a note that said they hoped the contents of the box would lead whoever found it to the truth. I don't know what that means exactly, but it seems like if truth is what we're looking for, then we need to dig up that box."

"You found this a couple of months ago?" Ginger said, shaking her head in disbelief. "And you never said anything?"

"I couldn't," Maeve said. "You work for the WG. How was I supposed to know you were with The Resistance? I didn't even know there was a Resistance."

"Why didn't you go back and dig it up?" Silas asked.

"There was never a good time. There are no cameras on that path, but the WG knows where we are all the time. If I left with a shovel, it wouldn't have taken them long to find me."

"How does Gray know about it?" Emery asked.

Gray squeezed Maeve's hand. "I didn't. I just helped Maeve the day she was late. We made up an excuse about her hurting her ankle. She didn't tell me anything."

"Why were you so concerned about her being late?" Ginger asked.

"Yeah, Gray, why were you so concerned about me being late?" Maeve echoed.

Gray flushed. "Let's just say that I'd had my eye on Maeve for a while, but there was never a good time to get to know her since she and I didn't cross paths," he said with a wink for Maeve. Maeve felt his thumb stroke the back of her hand.

"So, what do we do now?" Maeve asked.

"Obviously, we dig up the box," Emery said, jumping up as if ready to go.

"Wait a minute," Ginger placed a hand on Emery's arm and drew her back into her seat.

"We're wanted fugitives," Maeve said. "We can't just go waltzing down the path and dig up the box."

"Sure we can," Gray said.

Maeve shot him a look that clearly said she thought he was crazy. Gray gave her hand a squeeze and got to his feet.

"Let's go dig up a box."

CHAPTER SIXTEEN

G ray led them through more tunnels to another room. When Maeve stepped through the door, she had to squint her eyes against the sudden onslaught of light from the room. While the room was made of the same timbers and dirt as all the other parts of the tunnels, the dirt walls had been covered with maps of all shapes, sizes and colors. Maeve saw what looked like a blueprint of the WG headquarters next to a map showing the terrain of Palumbra. Other maps included street maps and maps of the forests.

Maeve walked over to a hand-drawn map that covered an entire wall. "This is a map of the tunnels."

"Yep," Gray said as he walked over to join her. "You can see it's unfinished." He pointed to a large blank spot on the paper. "We add to it as we explore more of the tunnel system."

"How do you know which ones the WG knows about?" Silas asked.

"Those are marked in red," Gray said. "We have some friends in the WG who let us know at least some of what they know."

Maeve studied the tunnel maps for a few

minutes, tracing her finger over a few lines. She walked to the map of the city on the opposite wall. After a minute, she pointed. "Here," she said. "This is where I found the box."

The others came over and peered over her shoulder at the spot her finger marked. "It's just off the path, not quite in the woods," she said.

"That would be easy to get to," Emery said. "Look." She walked back over to the map of the tunnels. "This tunnel goes almost directly under that spot, and there's an access to the surface not far away. Except it's red." She pointed at a vertical line on the map.

Everyone's shoulders fell. Eyes that had been bright with hope when Emery began talking turned dull with disappointment. "How do we get there then?" Maeve asked.

"We'll have to risk it," Gray said. "Those tunnels have always been lightly patrolled in the past. It's still safer than dealing with the entire WG army on the surface. We'll need to find some shovels and wait until it's dark."

"We should get some rest, then," Maeve said, setting down her pack and pulling out her blanket. "Wake me when it's time."

Maeve heard light snoring and quiet rustling as she lay with her eyes shut. Despite telling the others they needed rest, Maeve had been unable to shut off her thoughts. She thought she might have slept for an hour. She opened her eyes and looked around. The lights were off, but Gray had left a small battery-powered lantern that shed just enough light to dispel the pitch blackness of the tunnels. She saw human-shaped lumps in different corners of the room. Ginger and Emery were huddled together in their sleep. Silas was a silent, still log across from her. To her left, lay Gray's blanket, but no Gray. She scanned the room, but he wasn't there. Quietly she got up and crossed to the door.

She stepped into the more brightly lit tunnel and looked for signs of Gray. Wishing she had some string to trail behind her in case she got lost, Maeve hesitated. Finally, she shrugged her shoulders and turned left, back toward the way they had come. She wouldn't go far, just down this tunnel a ways.

She wandered for a few minutes, periodically poking her head into empty rooms. Just as she was about to turn back, she heard voices. Once again, she hesitated, trying to pull up the map of the tunnels in her mind. Praying that this was still a Resistance-controlled area, she followed the voices, wishing she hadn't left her gun back with her blanket.

Maeve turned the corner and found Gray talking to his uncle. Gray looked up and reached for the gun at his waist. His startled expression turned to relief as soon as he recognized her and his hand dropped away from his gun. He took a step forward as his uncle eyed Maeve silently.

"Maeve," Gray said. "I thought you would sleep longer."

"Too much to think about," she said. "What are you doing?"

"Filling my uncle in on our plans," he said. "He can make sure the night watches are routed around us while we're digging."

Maeve cocked her head and raised her eyebrows as she looked at Night, noting that he wore clothes that cost more than most Palumbrians made in a year. Working for the Arabella Laughlin clearly had its perks. Maeve wrinkled her nose and said without conviction, "I guess that makes sense."

"Maeve," Night said. "I know you don't trust me, but I can help. We're all working toward the same goal."

"What goal is that?" Maeve asked.

"Getting rid of the WG," Night said.

"I'm not sure that's my goal," Maeve said. "Right now, I just want to figure out how we got to this moment. Then we'll decide how to go forward."

"How can you say that, Maeve?" Gray asked. "The WG wants you dead. How can you not want to get rid of it?"

"Because I hardly know anything about The Resistance." Maeve flung her arms out in frustration. "I'm not from a family of revolutionaries. Until yesterday, I had no beef with the WG. Why are they afraid of me?"

"They're not really afraid of you, Maeve," Night said gently. "You've gotten caught up in something that's bigger than you. The WG is afraid of anyone who wants to think for themselves. Just by being in the

152

wrong place, you're now part of the revolution."

"Is this how revolutions are born? We simply get swept up in events beyond our own making?" Maeve said. "Don't I get a choice?"

"Some revolutionaries are born," Night said. "Some get to choose. And some just get caught by a wave, and it's sink or swim. It's up to you which one you want to be. You've been swept along by the wave today, but I think it's time you made the decision for yourself. I can't give you your life back, but I can give you a safe place to live. It would be lonely and probably kind of boring, but you would be safe and away from all these events. It's your choice."

Gray's ice blue eyes watched her intently. Maeve had the feeling that her decision was as important to him as it was to her.

"But I don't have enough information to even make that decision," Maeve said. "I don't really understand what's going on. Yesterday morning I was training to be a nurse in a well-ordered world. Today, I'm a fugitive for a cause I don't really understand."

Gray looked at his uncle, then stepped forward and took Maeve's hand. Maeve glanced at their intertwined hands and flushed. Her skin where it touched his tingled, and the air seemed to snap around her. She looked into Gray's face, with his slightly crooked nose, those piercing eyes and a mouth that looked as if it always wanted to smile. The thought flitted through her head that she would choose revolution if it meant staying with Gray. But he wasn't smiling now.

Gray stared intently into Maeve's brown eyes. She caught her breath as he said, "Maeve, this choice you have to make is a hard one because you haven't been aware of all that the WG has done. Think, Maeve. Have you ever known someone who just disappeared? Have you ever wondered why the WG watches people so closely? Don't you think it's odd that the WG worries about when a teenager arrives home from a day on the job? The WG isn't keeping watch over us to keep us safe. It's keeping watch over us to keep us from noticing what they're doing."

"And what is that?" Maeve asked.

"Holding on to all the power. Disposing of people who disagree with them or ask questions. And yesterday, they attacked their own people," Gray said.

"How do we know that?" Maeve asked as she let their hands drop.

"Arabella pulled me into her plans today." Night stepped forward. "She got wind of a Resistance plan to attack the WG and decided she wanted to put an end to The Resistance."

Maeve whirled on him. "And you didn't stop her?"

Night held up his hands in front of him as if to ward off Maeve's attack. "I didn't know until it was already done. I've been trying to help those that were hurt and get some Resistance members into hiding."

Maeve looked from Night to Gray. She shook her head. "But why would she bomb her own people? People died. People who had nothing to do with The Resistance."

154

"She wanted it to look like The Resistance had done it to turn the people against The Resistance," Gray replied. "She doesn't just want to capture the leaders of The Resistance. She wants to turn people against it and wipe it out."

"But why?" Maeve asked as she began to pace. "Surely The Resistance isn't that big of a threat. The WG holds all the weapons and controls the food. Why not just round up the leaders?"

"The Resistance is really good at protecting their own people and hiding the identities of whose involved," Night said. He shrugged. "And I do my best to plant misinformation."

"Ideas can be a bigger threat than guns," Gray said. "If all the people of Palumbra turned against the WG, Arabella wouldn't stand a chance."

Maeve stopped and studied Night. She knew Gray trusted him, and she found herself wanting to do the same. "What is the WG planning now?"

Night shook his head. "I don't know, but there's something brewing. I do know Arabella is terrified that someone will find information on The Lost Years. She has something up her sleeve. Something big."

"What do you think it is?" Gray asked, moving to stand next to Maeve. His sleeve brushed hers, and Maeve's breathing hitched as the air between them seemed to crackle.

Night shrugged. "I wish I knew. Arabella is having lots of conversations with General Raisch, who is in charge of the army. I'm not invited to those meetings."

"Why would she be so interested in The Lost Years?" Maeve asked. "I would think the WG would have access to all the information about The Lost Years."

Night nodded. "They do. They keep it locked up tight. Only Arabella is allowed to access it. They found a breach last month, and Arabella went on a tear. She threatened to shoot everyone involved with keeping the information secure."

Maeve's terrified eyes met Gray's and her voice shook as she asked, "Did they figure out who broke into the files?"

Night shook his head as he watched Gray and Maeve intently. "No. Whoever it was covered their tracks, but they're still looking." Maeve let out the breath she had been holding. Night pinned her with a hard stare. "Whoever did it might want to get rid of that computer, though."

Gray nodded. "I'm sure they did. Anyone smart enough to break into the WG system would know to get rid of the computer they used." As he spoke, he intertwined his fingers with Maeve's and squeezed.

"The Lost Years are clearly important to whatever Arabella is planning," Gray said. "We need to know more. Is there any way you can access those files?"

"Not if I want to continue living," Night replied. "After the breach last month, those files are locked up even tighter. We'll have to get information about The Lost Years another way." Night motioned to Maeve. "I hear you think you can help with that."

Maeve nodded. "Did Gray tell you about the box?"

"Just a little bit," Night replied. "I don't want to know all the details. It makes it easier to deny knowing anything if I really don't know it. But information on The Lost Years is important to figuring out whatever the WG is planning. You're the only one who knows where that information is, Maeve. It could be the piece of information we've been missing."

Maeve gave him a skeptical look. "From what I could tell, it was a box with some stuff a bunch of teenagers put in it from The Lost Years. How could that be the key to everything we need to know?"

"We won't know until we find it," Gray said.

"I think you have enough information now, Maeve," Night said. "What are you going to do?"

CHAPTER SEVENTEEN

Maeve was silent for a long time. She tried to order her thoughts so she could make the right choice. She remembered the look in her mom's eyes as she walked out the door yesterday, and she relived her dad's anger at her decision not to turn herself in to the WG. She wondered if she would ever climb the ladder to her loft bedroom again. Even if she chose not to be a part of The Resistance, she knew she couldn't go home. Her parents might never forgive her − and she wasn't sure she could forgive them.

Maeve looked at Gray. Their eyes held − hers filled with confusion, his with hope − and her skin tingled. Whatever was growing between them would be lost if she took Night's offer and walked away. The intensity on Gray's face left no doubt this decision was as important to him as it was to her.

She shifted her gaze to Night and began to chew on the side of her thumb. Maeve didn't know what to think about Night. Gray trusted him implicitly, but Maeve still wasn't sure. It seemed odd that he held a high position in the WG yet knew so little about what had happened. Was he telling Maeve the truth?

It all came down to the box. Did it really hold the key to whatever the WG was planning? Could she walk away and never know?

Maeve's brain felt like it was on overload. She swiped her hand across her forehead, and it came away covered in sweat. She had to choose. The image of Emery and Ginger's mom falling to the ground, blood blooming on her chest flitted through Maeve's mind. She closed her eyes and took a deep breath.

"I'm in," she said quietly as she opened her eyes and looked directly into the ice blue gaze she was coming to know well. Gray's cheeks puffed as he blew out the breath he had been holding and his shoulders relaxed. He grabbed her hand and pulled her in for a hug. "Welcome to The Resistance," he whispered in her ear. Her body tingled as his breath brushed her cheek.

Maeve gave him a small smile and stepped back, but Gray kept hold of her hand.

"What do we do now?" Maeve asked.

"I have to get back to WG headquarters," Night said. "You guys need to figure out how to get that box. I'll do my best to keep the forest clear of patrols tonight. The fewest patrols across the city are between 2 and 5 a.m. The WG feels the mandatory curfew does its job. Only the most foolish would break it."

"I guess he's talking about us," Gray said with a wry grin.

Night walked over to Gray, his blue eyes penetrating Gray's identical ones. "Be careful. There's only so much I can do to keep you safe. No matter what happens, remember I love you." He hugged Gray and gave Maeve's shoulder a pat as he walked to the door. "I'll send word if there's anything you need to know." He lifted his hand in a wave and left.

Gray turned to Maeve, still holding her hand. "Are you ready for this?"

Maeve shook her head. "I'm sure I'm not, but I feel better knowing you're here with me."

Gray tucked a stray strand of hair behind Maeve's ear. "Me too. Let's do this together."

Gray squeezed her hand and smiled. Maeve smiled back. Hand-in-hand they walked out the door to spark a revolution.

When they returned to their sleeping quarters, the rest of the group was beginning to stir. Emery was rummaging through the food to find some breakfast. Ginger sat where she had slept, looking at a map while she ate a protein paste bar. Silas looked up as he packed up his sleeping gear.

"Where h-h-have you two been?" he said as he glanced at their clasped hands and smiled. Maeve smiled back as she left Gray's side to help Emery find something to eat.

"We were talking with my uncle, trying to figure out what our next step is," Gray replied.

"Your uncle?" Ginger's eyes widened. "Doesn't he work for Arabella Laughlin?"

"Yes, but he helps The Resistance," Gray replied calmly. "He's on our side."

Ginger raised her eyebrows at Maeve who shrugged in response.

Gray caught the exchange and blew out a frustrated breath. "He's one of the good guys, I promise."

"We want to believe you, Gray," Maeve said as she returned to his side. "It's just hard."

"Has he done anything but help us since this all happened?" Gray asked as he took a protein paste bar from Maeve.

"No, you're right." Maeve took a bite of her own protein paste bar. It just seems odd. That's all."

"I think right n-n-now we have to believe he wants to help us," Silas chimed in. "I trust Gray, so I'll trust his uncle, too."

Maeve looked at her friends and decided this was not a fight worth having right now. She had no evidence that Night was working against them. She shrugged at Ginger and said, "I guess there's no reason not to trust him right now."

Gray nodded, accepting the olive branch. Ginger just shrugged and went to fill her canteen.

"So, what do we do next, besides sit in this room and eat nasty food?" Emery asked as she held up the protein paste bar Maeve had found for her.

"They're not so bad once you get used to them," Ginger said from her corner. "But what's the plan?"

"We need to dig up the box I found, then we

need to come back here and figure out what to do with whatever is in it," Maeve said.

"Without getting caught by the WG," Gray added.

"No problem," Ginger said with a wave of her hand. She took an intense interest in her protein paste bar as she said in a voice thick with tears, "We'll just stroll into the woods with shovels and dig it up, then saunter back here. It's not like we're wanted fugitives or anything."

Maeve shot Ginger a concerned look. Her friend was quickly reaching the limit of what she could handle, and who could blame her. One night of tears didn't take away the pain of losing her mom. How much longer could she hold it together?

Silas had also taken note of Ginger's tone and moved to sit next to her. He put his arm around her shoulders, offering comfort with his presence. Emery came and sat on Ginger's other side and laced their fingers together.

Maeve started to join them but Ginger sniffed and shook her head. Maeve recognized that Ginger was close to breaking down completely and didn't want to do it in front of everyone, so she turned to Gray and said, "So, how do we get the box? Your uncle said he would take care of the patrols in the forest, but that doesn't help us get there."

"We can get close through the tunnels," Gray said. "Ginger, what were you looking at on that map?"

Ginger straightened and pushed her hair back from her face. She shook out her arms as she stood, as if she could shake the grief out of her body. Maeve shot Gray a look of thanks for giving Ginger something to do. Ginger picked up the map and said, "This is a map of the tunnels, and I assume these red markings mean these tunnels are known by the WG. These tunnels with the green markings should be safe. We'll have to take a roundabout route to get to the forest using these tunnels. It would be much faster on the surface."

"What if we run into a patrol," Silas asked. "Don't we risk leading them to the tunnels they don't know about if we use the tunnels? Then where would we be safe?"

"Are we really safe anywhere?" Maeve asked. "Will we ever be safe again?"

"We're as safe as we can be right now," Gray said, picking up Maeve's hand and giving it a squeeze. "But Silas has a good point about leading the WG to these tunnels. Let me see that map. I think we can get to the forest through the tunnels, but if a patrol catches us on the surface, we need a backup plan to get us back here without leading the WG here, too. Maeve, can you grab that map of the surface that's on the table over there?"

CHAPTER EIGHTEEN

"Who's got the shovel?" Gray whispered as he hunched in the underbrush at the side of the path.

"I-I-I do," Silas replied.

The night was dark with no moon peeking out behind the clouds. The threat of rain lingered in the air. Thunder rumbled in the far distance. As Maeve peered through the darkness toward the path, she hoped the storm would stay in the distance. They didn't need lightning illuminating their activities.

Their trip to the shortcut in the forest had been easier than expected. They followed the tunnels to a surface entry deep in the forest about a mile from the path, not seeing any sign of a patrol. Now, the five of them were hidden in the bushes and weeds at the side of the path just to the south of where Maeve had found the box.

"What do we do now?" Maeve asked.

"I think we should wait a few minutes," Ginger said. "I'm not convinced there won't be a patrol through here soon. I used to see the patrol schedules, and I know there was always one scheduled to patrol this area."

"My uncle said he would keep the patrols away

from here tonight," Gray said.

"I know you trust your uncle," Silas said, "but are you sure he can do that? He didn't even know about the attack on the hospital."

"I'm sure he'll do what he said he would," Gray said.

Maeve looked over at Silas and raised her eyebrows even though he couldn't see her skepticism in the dark. Their whole plan tonight depended on Night's ability to keep the patrols away. Maeve mentally crossed her fingers that he would prove to be trustworthy.

Swallowing her skepticism, Maeve said, "Well, let's go get the box. The sooner we're out of here, the better."

Gray reached over and squeezed her hand, then stepped out on the path with his gun at the ready.

"Maeve, lead the way," Gray said.

The group traveled single file along the dirt path with Maeve in front, followed by Ginger, Emery and Silas. Gray took his spot at the end of the line to guard their backs. Maeve kept a tight grip on the gun she still didn't know how to shoot and cautiously made her way forward.

It seemed to take forever to travel the short distance to the place where they needed to dig. Every crack of a twig and hoot of an owl caused a shiver of anxiety to travel down Maeve's spine.

When they reached the spot where Maeve had first found the box, Maeve dropped to her knees. Ginger knelt next to her.

"Is this it?" Ginger asked.

"I think so. It's tough to be sure in the dark, but I saw the flapping piece of paper when I had just passed that big oak tree over there. I covered it all back up, so we'll have to just feel our way around. I wish we could risk a light."

Ginger looked at Maeve. "Do you really think Night will keep his promise to keep the patrols away?" Ginger asked in a low whisper so Gray couldn't hear.

"I hope so," Maeve said. "We've got big problems if he doesn't."

"Do you trust him?" Ginger said with a glance at Gray.

"Who? Gray? Absolutely. Night? I don't know. There's just something about him that makes me wonder if he's telling us the truth."

"I've never met him," Ginger said as she continued to feel around on the ground for any sign of the box, "but I've heard lots of rumors at WG headquarters."

"What kind of rumors?"

"Just that he's..."

"Any luck?" Gray asked as he came up behind them.

"Not yet," Maeve said. "But it's in this area. Why don't you have Silas and Emery look just over there?" Maeve pointed to the area to her left.

"Ok," Gray said. "I'll keep watch. Find it as fast as you can."

The group was silent as they settled in to their task. The four searchers used their hands to push away leaves and dirt to try to find the box while Gray stood

166

guard.

After 10 minutes of searching, Emery whispered to Silas, "I think I found something."

"Where?"

"Right here." Emery guided his hands to the spot where she had felt something hard in the ground.

"M-M-Maeve," Silas whispered. "We found something."

Maeve stood and brushed the dirt off her hands as she walked over to where Silas and Emery had been searching. "Show me," she whispered.

Emery took Maeve's hand and placed it in the area where she thought she had felt the box. Maeve dug her fingers into the soft earth, her fingers striking a hard surface. "I think this is it. Silas, let me have the shovel."

Silas handed her a small garden shovel. It was the best digging tool they could find in the tunnels. Gray had stopped his patrolling to see what they had found.

"Is it the box?" he asked.

"I think so," Maeve said. "We'll have to dig it up to be sure."

As she spoke, she sank the garden shovel into the ground and began to pull the dirt away. "The ground is soft, so everyone else can use their hands. I don't know how big the box is, so we'll just have to feel our way around it. Gray, you still need to keep watch."

"I don't think there's going to be a patrol," he said. "I could help."

"We can't let our guard down," Ginger chimed in. "We'd all feel better if someone stood watch."

Gray nodded in the dark and stepped back to keep watch while the others dug.

No one spoke as they removed the dirt. The box wasn't that big, but it had been in the ground a long time, making it difficult to remove. Finally, Maeve got the garden shovel under one edge of the bottom of the box and was able to exert some leverage to get it to move.

"I think we've almost got it," Silas said. "Give it one m-m-more lift, Maeve."

Maeve shoved the garden shovel as far under the box as it would go and pressed down as hard as she could on the handle, levering the box up. Silas, Emery and Ginger pushed their hands under the box and lifted, breaking it free from the remaining dirt. They carefully removed it from the hole and set it on the ground. All four of them sat on the ground, sweaty and dirty but relieved to have the box in their possession. In the darkness, it was hard to see, but Maeve could make out the outline of a metal box that was about a foot long in all directions.

"Gray," Maeve said. "We've got it. Let's fill this hole in and get out of here."

"Quiet," Gray whispered. "I think we've got company."

"We've got to get off this path," Gray whispered.

"What about the hole?" Maeve asked.

"We'll have to leave it. Grab the tools," Gray said.

Maeve grabbed the box and the shovel.

"Quiet!" Ginger said in a harsh whisper as the metal blade of the shovel clinked against the box.

They all froze as the echo of metal against metal could be heard through the still night air. In the not too far distance, they heard a shout and the sound of footsteps moving quickly in their direction.

Gray yanked the shovel out of Maeve's hand to avoid any more noise and motioned that everyone should get moving back in the direction of the tunnels. Ginger grabbed Emery's hand and started running. As Maeve glanced over at Silas, she saw he was standing still, frozen with fear. As she started to follow Ginger, she gave Silas's arm a tug, but he remained frozen.

"Gray," Maeve whispered. "Help!"

"Come on, Silas," Gray said, giving Silas a shove on the shoulder. "Get moving."

The shove broke Silas out of his terrified trance. He shook his head and started running, looking back over his shoulder every few steps.

"Go, Maeve!" Gray whispered sharply as he turned to cover their rear. Maeve noticed he was awkwardly trying to hang onto the shovel and his gun at the same time. If they were caught by the patrol, it would be difficult for him to shoot without putting the shovel down.

"Drop the shovel, Gray," Maeve said in a low voice. "What if they find it?"

"So what. It can't lead them to us. It's just a shovel. It doesn't have our names or location on it."

Gray looked at her as he ran. After a moment of deliberation, he dropped the shovel and put both hands on his gun. They could hear the sound of boots crashing through the underbrush behind them.

"Are we going to make it?" Maeve asked.

"Maybe. Can you see the others?"

"No, but I can hear them in front of us. Are we going the right way?"

"Yes. The entrance to the tunnel should be up here on the right. But we need to make sure we're not seen."

As he spoke, Maeve could just make out the shape of the well off to their right. She saw Ginger helping Emery over the top, with Silas on their heels.

"Gray, we're here."

"Hurry!"

As Maeve approached the well, Ginger's head was just visible over the top of the well and Silas was swinging his leg over the top, careful not to kick Ginger.

"Gray, we're not going to make it before they catch us."

"Give Silas the box."

Maeve hesitated. If Night was right, the box was the key to this whole situation. Maeve felt like she could trace the change in her world back to the day she found the box. If she hadn't met up with Gray that day, she would never have escaped the WG when the hospital was bombed. Parting with it made her wary. What if she never found out what was in it?

"Maeve, give it to Silas! We aren't going to make it into the well without being found out. Let him take it to the tunnels. We'll use another entrance. We don't have much time."

Reluctantly, Maeve handed the box over to Silas

as he disappeared into the well. She turned and looked at Gray. "What now?" She could hear the footsteps of their pursuers clearly now.

"Come on," Gray said as he took off into the woods. Maeve followed close on his heels. They ran for what seemed to Maeve like an hour. Gray twisted and turned through the trees until Maeve was hopelessly lost. She knew he was trying to lose their pursuers, but she hoped nothing happened to him because she would never find her way back to the tunnels on her own.

Finally, Gray stopped in front of an oak tree with a trunk so large you couldn't see around it. "I think we're clear," Gray said. "I haven't heard anything for a while. It's probably worth risking getting into the tunnels."

"How do we do that?" Maeve asked, looking around for an entrance.

Gray swiveled his head to look for their pursuers one more time, then reached out and tapped on the tree trunk of the large oak. Three taps and a small hole, barely big enough for a scrunched over person to fit through appeared.

"How did you do that?" Maeve asked.

"It's a door made out of the tree's bark. When it's closed, you can't see the seam. If you know the code and where to tap, it opens. It's some kind of pressure and pulley system. Now, hurry up and get inside."

Maeve unstrapped her gun as there was no way to squeeze through the door with it on her back. She pushed it into the hole in front of her, then doubled herself over and made an ungraceful roll through the

171

small opening. As soon as she was out of the way, Gray followed, slithering in on his stomach. As soon as he was inside, he tapped the wall and the door slid closed.

Gray looked her over to make sure she was unhurt, then reached for her hand. Electricity snapped between them. Even though Maeve knew the danger was still out there, for the moment they were safe. She smiled at Gray. Gray's arm circled her shoulders in the cramped space and pulled her head to his chest. He rested his cheek on her hair. They sat like that for a few moments, recovering from the harrowing chase.

"For a minute there, I didn't think we were going to make it," Gray said.

Maeve looked up at him. "I don't know what I would have done if something had happened to you. I have no idea where we are." She looked down and shrugged. "I feel so unprepared for this."

Gray rubbed her shoulder. "You're doing great. I've trained for situations like this, even before I became a soldier. My uncle was big on survival training. He always said we had to be prepared."

"I just can't believe that I was so oblivious to everything going on around me. My best friend and her mom were part of The Resistance, and I never knew it. I feel kind of stupid."

"You're definitely not stupid." Gray tilted her chin up so she could see his face. His eyes held determination, as if whatever he had to say was important. "Your parents taught you to take the path of least resistance in this society. It kept you and them
172

safe. But when you found out there was another option, you chose to stand up and fight. Never forget that you made a choice."

Maeve was silent for a moment. "Did I choose to fight or did I simply choose the path of least resistance again, the one that let me stay with you?" she asked quietly.

Gray gave her a small smile. "As flattering as that is and as glad as I am that I may have factored into your decision, think about when you really chose to fight, Maeve. It wasn't in that room with me and my uncle. It happened long before that."

Maeve's eyebrows drew together as Gray's words sank in. "I don't know what you're talking about."

"Sure you do." Gray continued to run his palm up and down her back in comforting strokes. "The minute you chose to walk away from your parents and everything you had ever known, you chose to fight. There was never any chance you were going to take my uncle's offer to live a life in hiding. That's not who you are."

Maeve turned Gray's words over in her head. She nodded. "You know, I think you're right. But I needed Night to offer me that choice. I didn't really feel like it was my choice until I said it out loud."

She fell silent again. When she spoke her voice caught. "But I've lost my parents, my home. What if I never see them again? My last moments with them will be ones of anger and betrayal."

"We just have to hope that when this is over, you can settle things with them." Gray fell silent, letting

Maeve have a moment to process all that had happened to her. She sniffed and wiped her eyes, suddenly realizing Gray was still holding her. What had been easy and comfortable just a moment before became slightly awkward and charged with anticipation.

Finally, Maeve lifted her head. When she did Gray's eyes bored into hers as if asking permission. She nodded slowly. He lowered his head and kissed her.

Maeve had never been kissed before. She put her arms around Gray's neck and kissed him back, enjoying the feel of his lips on hers. Gray drew back, dropped a kiss on her forehead and stood up, pulling Maeve up with him. "OK?" he asked.

Maeve touched her lips. "That was more than OK," she thought. Out loud, she simply said, "OK."

Gray grabbed her hand. "Come on. The others will be wondering where we are."

"Oh no!" Maeve grabbed Gray's sleeve, pulling him to a stop. "I can't believe we just stood here talking when they could be in danger."

"I'm sure they're fine," Gray reassured her. "They made it into the tunnels before the soldiers saw them. I wouldn't have stopped here if I thought there was any danger to them." He started walking down the tunnel again.

Maeve blew out a breath and followed, her mind returning to the kiss they had shared. Despite their circumstances, she grinned, feeling slightly giddy inside at knowing she had experienced her first kiss. It didn't take long, however, for her mind to turn to the question

174

that had been burning her brain before her interlude with Gray. Finally, she asked Gray, "Why was there a patrol? I thought your uncle was going to keep them away from that area?"

"I don't know. Clearly something went wrong. I hope my uncle is OK."

"Gray, are you sure your uncle is on our side?"

"How can you ask that?" He dropped Maeve's hand. "Of course he's on our side. He raised me. Do you really think he would set a patrol on me?"

"Gray, I don't know your uncle that well, but it seems like he might have his own agenda that doesn't necessarily line up with ours. How much do you know about what he does for the WG?"

"I can't believe we're having this conversation." Gray lengthened his stride and walked stiffly down the tunnel. Maeve had to jog to keep up. "He's the only parent I had after my parents died. There's no way he would betray me or turn me over to the WG patrols. Something had to have gone wrong."

He shrugged.

"Maybe he didn't know about this patrol. Maybe the patrol wasn't supposed to be there. I don't know, but my uncle loves me. He wouldn't do anything to harm me."

Maeve started to speak, stopped, then opened her mouth to speak again. "I hope you're right."

Gray gave her a cold look and quickened his pace even more. Maeve followed, the joy of their kiss lost in the silence.

CHAPTER NINETEEN

"What's going on with you and Gray?" Ginger asked quietly.

"Nothing," Maeve answered.

"Doesn't seem like nothing. You aren't even speaking."

Maeve looked at Gray, sitting in a chair across the room. They had arrived back at the room in stony silence. Gray appeared to have forgotten all about their kiss in the wake of their argument about his uncle. He had returned to the room, passed out protein paste bars and water and taken a seat – all in silence. Maeve had had enough. They had work to do. She hadn't given up everything she knew to let opening the mysterious box take a back seat to an angry boy. She and Gray would have to work through their issues another time.

Maeve stood up, rubbing her hands together to get rid of the last of the protein paste crumbs. "Let's open the box," she said, with a glance at Gray.

Gray raised his eyes to meet hers and nodded – a silent agreement to set aside their argument for the moment. Everyone made their way to the table in the center of the room where Silas had placed the box.

Emery picked up the plastic bag that Maeve had opened once before. She pulled out the paper inside and read:

To the people of the future:
We have left this time capsule for you to open. We hope that what is in this box leads you to the truth.
The students of Preston High School

"What is Preston High School?" Emery asked. "There's no school with that name here."

"I know there used to be a town called Preston near Palumbra," Silas said. He walked over to the map on the wall. "It was right here." He pointed to a spot on the map that was well outside the limits of Palumbra, beyond The River.

"How do you know that?" Ginger asked.

"I like to look at old m-m-maps," Silas said. "There aren't very many of them, but my dad found a couple one day in the trash outside our neighbor's house. I don't know why he had them or why he would throw them away. M-m-my dad brought them home, and I've m-m-memorized most of them. But we'd be in big trouble if anyone caught us with them. Some of them are from the Lost Years."

"I want to see them," Emery said. "Someday."

"You got it," Silas said. Ginger looked at him with soft eyes and a slight curve of her lips. Maeve assumed she was thankful that Silas was acting like there would be a future day when he could show Emery the maps. Right now, Maeve couldn't think beyond the next few hours.

"Well," Gray said. "Let's get this thing open. I think you should do the honors." He held the box out to Maeve. As she took the box from him, their fingers brushed, and Maeve felt that same jolt she felt every time they touched. Gray must have felt it, too because his eyes met hers. He gave her a small smile.

Maeve looked at the square, gray metal box. She had never seen one like it before, but very few things in Palumbra were made out of metal. It was too expensive to use for something as mundane as a storage box. She looked at the clasp. She pushed the small, metal button next to the clasp. Nothing happened.

She tried it again. The button moved infinitesimally, but the box didn't open.

"Is it stuck?" Emery asked.

"Maybe you're not doing it right," Ginger said.

"I don't know," Maeve said.

"Try moving the button up or down or left or right," Gray said. "My uncle had one of these when I was younger. I think the button actually moves."

Maeve flinched at the reminder of the person at the center of her argument with Gray, but she reached out her hand again. She tried to move the button up and down, but it didn't budge. Next, she tried moving it to the left. Still nothing. Finally, she edged the button to the right. It moved slightly. She applied more force, and the button slid to the right at the same time they heard a click.

A crack appeared between the lid and the box.

178

Maeve held her breath and slowly lifted the lid.

Maeve blew out the breath she was holding.

"What's in it?" Emery asked impatiently.

"It looks like a photo, a map and a disc," Maeve said.

Carefully, she lifted each item out and set them on the table. The photo was curled on the edges and cracked in the middle, but the image of a building was clear. The map was folded into fourths, and the paper was yellowed with age. The disc was in a plastic case and looked much like the discs in the room where all the information about the Lost Years was kept.

"What is that building?" Ginger asked. "I don't recognize it." She picked up the photo and looked at it from all angles, even turning it upside down. Maeve could almost see Ginger's brain picking apart every detail of the building, trying to match it up to something she had seen in Palumbra.

"I don't recognize it," Silas said. "I wonder if it's one of the ruined buildings beyond the edge of town. If it's in Palumbra, it clearly doesn't look like this anymore."

The building in the photo was taller than anything in Palumbra. The roof was shaped like a pyramid with a spire on top. Scalloped artwork adorned the four sides of the roof, giving the building a storybook appearance. Maeve was reminded of an old drawing she had seen once of a house made out of candy, but this was no candy cottage in the woods. This building was at least 30 stories tall. Most buildings in the city had just one or two floors except for WG headquarters, which had 10.

"Are we sure this building is here?" Maeve asked.

"Well, if it's anywhere else, we'll never find it," Gray finally chimed in. "Nothing exists outside of Palumbra. We're the only people left."

"It only makes sense that this building is here," Ginger said. "Or it was. The people that left this note clearly lived near here. Why would they leave us a photo of a building that was somewhere else?"

"Maybe the map will show us where the building is," Emery suggested.

Maeve unfolded the map, being careful not to tear the brittle paper. Gray came up behind her and peered over her shoulder. His closeness unnerved her, but she laid the map on the table. As Gray leaned over her shoulder for a closer look, their eyes met, and he gave her an apologetic smile. Maeve's lips quirked into a smile in return, and they both turned back to the map. Ginger, Silas and Emery leaned in for a closer look.

"This isn't Palumbra," Emery said. "It's far too big. And, look, this looks like water." She pointed to a big blue expanse on the map.

"I think you're right. But what could it be a map of?" Ginger said. "And what's this smudge spot here?"

"Wait. I think Palumbra is on this map. It's just that Palumbra was part of something much bigger then," Silas said. "Look, this looks like the middle of the city." Silas pointed to a spot in the corner of the map. "Everything spreads out to the..." Silas stopped, tilted his
180

head, looked at the corner of the map and finished, "east. When you look at just this small part of the map, it kind of matches up with the map on the wall."

Gray looked at the map on the wall and back to the map on the table. "I kind of see it. But we know that there's no land east of here." Gray pointed to a place on the map several miles from Palumbra.

"Do we know that or do we just know that because that's what they told us in school?" Silas challenged.

"Silas is right," Maeve said. "We've never been there. We don't know what's beyond the city's edge."

"But, surely, my uncle would have told me if there was more out there," Gray said.

Maeve walked over to Gray and put her hand on his shoulder. She crouched down so her eyes were level with Gray's while he was sitting in the chair. "Gray, I know you want to believe in your uncle, but I think we can all agree that your uncle hasn't told you everything." She shrugged. "Maybe he had a good reason not to tell you."

Gray's ice blue eyes bore into her own green ones as if trying to read her soul. Defeat and uncertainty flitted through his eyes before he nodded and turned back to the map.

"Look," Gray said, pointing at the smudge mark Maeve had noticed before. "There's a marking here."

"Are you sure that's not just a smudge?" Maeve asked.

"No." Silas rubbed his finger over the smudge.

181

"Gray's right. That's an intentional mark. Maybe that's what these people wanted us to find."

"Why didn't they just mark it with an X?" Emery asked. "That's what they do in all the pirate books. X marks the spot."

"Maybe because this isn't a pirate book," Ginger said. "I bet they wanted it to look like a smudge to protect themselves if the box was found early."

"So, we have a photo of a building we don't recognize, a map to somewhere we haven't been and a disc? And these are the keys to The Lost Years and fighting the WG?" Gray said. "I was kind of hoping for more."

Maeve saw the disappointment in his eyes and despite their earlier argument took his hand in hers. He gave her a surprised look, but intertwined their fingers. Maeve gave his hand a quick squeeze then picked up the disc and put the map and the photo back in the box.

"Let's go see what's on this disc," she said as she handed the box to Silas. "Maybe it will have more answers for us."

Maeve stopped when she reached the end of the tunnel. She looked at Gray and squeezed the hand she was still holding. "Which way?"

Gray turned left and took the lead with Maeve trailing behind him. Silas, Emery and Ginger followed silently.

When they reached the room that held The Resistance's meager Lost Years archive, Gray opened the door, released Maeve's hand and motioned for them all to enter. When they were seated inside, Gray shut
182

and locked the door. Maeve raised her eyebrows when the lock clicked into place.

"We don't know what's on that disc, and we don't know who we can trust," Gray said by way of explanation. Maeve nodded and slipped the disc into the disc-playing machine. Immediately, a group of teenagers appeared on the blank wall that served as a screen.

"If you're watching this, it means you found the box we buried," said a young, blond woman who looked to be about 16. She might have been pretty once, but she was clearly ill-fed and in need of a bath. The teens surrounding her looked no better. Their eyes were haunted – as if they had seen too much and were weary of it all. "We don't have much time, but we want you to understand our world. We won't know how this all turns out, and we'll probably all be dead by the time you find this. But if things go as badly as they seem to be going, your world is going to be a difficult place."

"Start at the beginning, Emma," said a dark-skinned girl with braids all over her head who stood behind the blond girl who was talking.

"Ok, Grace. The beginning. It seems like so long ago. We lived in a great place. Our land had cities and farms and everything you could need. We were connected by technology. We had phones we could carry in our hands that connected us with anyone, anywhere. There was talk of landing people on Mars. We had already been to the moon. There was enough food to feed everyone. We lived in a world of plenty." She paused. "We had no idea how lucky we were."

"But then it all went bad. That technology that connected us to everyone also allowed us to share ideas. But it turned out that no one really wanted to hear ideas that conflicted with their own beliefs. People became more and more entrenched in their 'side' of things. Because we had so many options for getting information, people only listened or read information that supported what they already thought. It got to the point that the intelligent exchange of ideas became impossible. Arguments in public became common. Then the brawling started. It became dangerous to go anywhere. To say anything. People stayed home. They had everything delivered. They worked from home. They accessed information from home. They no longer had real-life relationships with other people. They could say anything they wanted and only listen to the people they wanted to listen to because they never met anyone in real life."

The blond girl named Emma looked at the dark-haired guy standing next to her. He took over. "Then the real fighting started. Those with guns formed groups. Militias, they called themselves. They were created on all sides of the issues. Supposedly they were designed to 'protect' people from people on the 'other side.' They were a disaster. All it took was one day. One group started shooting at another group and all hell broke loose. The military was called in, but it didn't matter. By then, people were just shooting at each other for no reason. There was no order and no chance of restoring it. It happened all over the world. People killing each other because they didn't agree with each other."

184

He shook his head.

"Governments fell. And that's when the real trouble began. Different militias got their hands on powerful weapons, and it became a worldwide war. Countries were obliterated. We were on the verge of being wiped out."

Emma stepped back to the center of the screen. "Until our government had a 'bright' idea. They started rounding up the children and teenagers."

There was a loud boom from the screen. "We have to go," the girl named Emma said. "Find the place on the map. Go to the building in the photo. You'll find the truth there."

The screen went black.

Emery was the first to speak. "How did they know things would be bad now?"

"They knew what their government was planning," Gray said. "They figured it had to be bad."

"But how?" Ginger asked. She pointed at the now silent screen. "They were just teenagers like us. How would they know?"

"They were part of it somehow," Silas said. "They had to be. They probably took a great risk to warn us."

"Maybe," said Maeve. She paused. "Can you imagine the world they lived in before? With technology that connected them around the world? Food for everyone?"

"Sounds like that technology was what destroyed their world," Ginger said. "And created the one we live in now. No wonder the WG suppresses opposing ideas so quickly. They know about this. They know how locked into one idea people can get – and the trouble it can cause."

"But it wasn't the different ideas that caused the problem," Maeve argued. "It was an unwillingness to listen to other ideas. I don't think having lots of different ideas is bad. But not listening, not treating other people as humans is where they got into trouble."

"And the isolation," Gray said. "When they stopped interacting with each other in person. It's easy to see the other side as animals if you never actually 'see' the people who hold those different ideas."

"Well, it's landed us in a m-m-mess now. What are we going to do?" Silas asked.

CHAPTER TWENTY

Everyone looked around. No one seemed to know what to do. Maeve removed the disc from the player and placed it back in the box.

"We could do nothing," Silas said. "We could pretend we don't know any of this and just walk away from Palumbra. It wouldn't be easy, but it's an option."

"Silas is right. We can just end this now and go live our lives as outcasts. It would be hard, but it would be safe," Ginger said with a glance at Emery.

"Would we really be safe, though?" Maeve asked. She picked at the skin on the side of her thumbnail with her teeth. "Is there anywhere that's truly safe in this world? I used to think I was safe in my parents' house, but look where I'm standing now."

"Maeve is right," Emery said. "I don't think anywhere is safe, especially if the WG find out we know this stuff. They're already after us, and they don't even know about the box." Emery took Ginger's hand. "I know you want me to be safe, but we can't run from this. There's nowhere to hide."

Ginger looked at Emery with glistening eyes. She swallowed. "We've lost so much already. I can't lose you, too."

Ginger hugged Emery to her as the tears spilled down her cheeks. Maeve, Silas and Gray were silent as the two sisters mourned together. After a few minutes, Ginger wiped her eyes, squeezed Emery's hand and said, "We need a plan."

Gray nodded and said, "We have two places we need to find – this building and whatever that place is on the map. We have two choices. We can all go together to each place or we can split up. It will be faster and less noticeable if we split up, but there's safety in numbers if we stay together."

"I think we should stay together," Maeve said. "You're my family now. I don't know what I would do if something happened to one of you."

"I'm with Maeve," Ginger said. "We have to stick together."

Gray looked at Silas. "I think we should split up. We're being hunted by the WG. We have to figure this out quickly and splitting up is the best way to do it. Plus, we'll be less n-n-noticeable in groups of two and three than as a pack of five."

"I'm with Silas," Gray said. "Splitting up is more efficient and less noticeable. We're more likely to be found if we stay together."

"Well, that's a tie vote," Ginger said. "What do we do now?"

"There's one m-m-more person," Silas said as he pointed to Emery.

"She's 12," Ginger said. "I don't think she gets to

make life and death decisions. I know what's best for her."

Emery rolled her eyes at this pronouncement.

"Ginger," Gray said, pointing at Emery, "she's in as much danger as the rest of us. And from what I've learned about Emery, she's not your typical 12-year-old. I think she deserves to get a vote."

Ginger looked at Maeve. Maeve nodded slightly. With a sigh, Ginger looked at Emery and said, "What do you think we should do?"

Emery looked at her sister and chewed on her lower lip. In a low voice, she said "I'm sorry, Ginger. I think we should split up."

Ginger nodded and pulled up a chair at the table. The other four did the same. "So, what's our plan?" Ginger asked.

Gray pulled the map and the photo out of the box and placed them in the center of the table. "Clearly, one group of us will go find the building and the other group will look for the place on the map. We need to decide how to get to those places and how we're going to split up."

"I think you and Maeve should go look for the spot on the m-m-map," Silas said. "We at least have some idea where we might find the building, but the m-m-map is kind of a mystery. Ginger and I at least know where the building ruins are."

"Ginger, what do you think?" Gray asked.

"I'm fine with that plan." Ginger leaned in to get a better look at the map. "It's definitely going to be harder to find the spot on the map. Plus it's a longer journey. Emery and I aren't splitting up, so it makes the most sense for the group with two people to take the harder task."

"Maeve, are you on board with that?" Gray asked.

"Yes, that sounds good to me."

Gray looked warily at Maeve before he spoke again. "I think we should talk to my uncle."

Maeve looked up and locked her eyes on Gray's gaze. "Are you sure that's a good idea after running into the patrol last night?"

"Maeve, I know you don't trust him, but he's my uncle. He practically raised me. I can't believe he'd want to harm me. He's part of The Resistance."

Maeve shrugged her shoulders. "I always believed my parents wanted what was best for me, but look how that turned out."

"Maeve..." Gray trailed off as his shoulders slumped.

"I think Gray is right," Ginger said. Maeve's stunned gaze met hers. "But I think we should be careful. We can talk to Gray's uncle and give him some information but not all of it."

"How can we do that?" Silas asked.

"We can tell him we found a map, and we want to find out where it leads," Ginger said. "We don't have to tell him where. Heck, we don't even know where it goes. We don't have to tell him about the photo or the disc. We need his help. He knows what the WG is doing. Trapped down here in the tunnels, we have no idea what's going on."

"Ginger is right," Silas said. "We need supplies,

190

and we need to avoid the WG. The only person who can help us with that is Gray's uncle. We'll have to trust him − at least a little."

"Plus this will be a good test," Emery chimed in. "If we give him just a few bits of information, we'll know if he uses it to try to catch us."

"I don't really think we need to test my uncle," Gray said through gritted teeth. He shook his head. "But I can see why you guys wouldn't want to tell him everything. What do you think, Maeve?"

"I can live with it. Why don't you contact your uncle."

Maeve stood against the wall in the room the group had come to call home, idly gnawing on the skin at the side of her thumbnail. It was a habit she had worked to break in school, but one she returned to in times of stress. She watched Gray as he paced on the other side of the room. Emery, Silas and Ginger were still in what they had taken to calling The Lost Years Library, watching the disc again to see if they could gather any more clues. There was a thick silence standing between her and Gray, broken only by the rhythm of Gray's boots hitting the floor as he paced.

"Gray, are we going to talk about it?" Maeve said as she dropped her hand to her side.

"Talk about what?" Gray shrugged. "You don't trust my uncle. I do. What else is there to talk about?"

"How about that kiss?" Maeve spoke quickly, as if trying to push the words out.

"What's the point?" Gray waved his hand as if brushing aside the memory of their kiss. "You don't trust my family. How do we get past that?"

"Gray, you have to admit it's a little suspicious that those soldiers almost caught us," Maeve said in an intentionally calm voice.

"But we're here now, and my uncle knows it." Gray kicked at the loose dirt on the floor. "No one has found us down here."

"Don't you think that would be a bit obvious?"

"Maybe he didn't know about the patrol," Gray said. "He doesn't know everything."

"Maybe," Maeve conceded. "I just think we should be cautious about what we tell him. How can that hurt? If he doesn't know exactly what we're doing, then he can't get in trouble for knowing about it if he is on our side. He even said he preferred it that way."

"I just can't believe he'd betray us." Gray took a deep breath. "He's raised me by himself since my parents died. He loves me."

"I thought my parents loved me, too."

Gray looked at her then, those ice blue eyes seeming to pierce into her soul. Tears formed in the corners of her eyes, but she forced them back. Gray sighed.

"I know, Maeve. I know." He walked over to where she was leaning against the wall and held out his hand. "Let's agree to be cautious in telling my uncle
192

everything. It doesn't matter what our reasons are right now. Truce?"

Maeve looked at his outstretched hand and slowly placed her hand in his. His hand closed over hers and he tugged her into in his arms. Maeve buried her head in his chest, willing to borrow someone else's strength − just for a moment.

"I know I should be grateful," Maeve said. "At least my parents are alive. Just misguided. Ginger and Emery watched their mom die in front of them."

"Don't," Gray said as smoothed his hand over her hair. "Your loss is as real as theirs − just in a different way. You deserve to be able to grieve, too."

Maeve began to cry. Slow, silent tears that dripped down her face onto the front of Gray's shirt. She grieved for everything she'd lost in the past few days − a home, a relationship with her parents, Ginger and Emery's mom and the loss of the simplicity of her life. She had no idea how long she stood there, tears streaming down her face and Gray stroking her hair and whispering all those nonsense things you say to someone when you don't know what to say.

Finally, she stepped back and wiped her eyes with one hand while Gray still held onto the other one. Although she was sure her eyes were puffy and her face was red, her body felt lighter and the gnawing feeling around her heart had eased. "Thanks," she said.

"Any time, Maeve."

Gray used his other hand to wipe the last tears from her face, kissed her on the forehead and led her over to the table.

"Let's eat something and figure out what we're going to tell my uncle," he said as he tossed her a water and a protein paste bar.

Night Caldwell strode through the door with an air of authority about him. His eyes flickered over Maeve and landed on Gray. He wrapped Gray in a fierce hug. "I'm so glad you're safe," he said. "I heard this morning there was a patrol out last night in the area you were in. Did you have much trouble?"

"We almost got caught," Maeve said. "I thought you were going to keep the patrols away."

Gray shot her a dark look, and Maeve closed her mouth. She'd let Gray handle it.

"What happened with the patrol?" Gray asked his uncle.

The lines around Night's mouth tightened. "They decided to send out a patrol to that part of the path. It wasn't on the schedule. I didn't know about it until this morning."

"Why are they leaving you out of the loop so often?" Gray asked. "It seems like Arabella used to tell you everything, but now she hardly tells you anything." Gray paused. "Do you think they suspect you're with The Resistance?"

Night shook his head and sat heavily in a chair. "You're right. There's a lot I don't know, and that's starting to worry me. Something weird is going on, and they're shutting me out. I'm trying to figure it out, but I have to keep a low profile."

Gray shot Maeve a triumphant look. Night's explanation clearly made sense to him. Maeve raised one eyebrow at him but remained silent. Night watched the interplay between them with interest.

"But you called me here for a reason." Night stood. "What can I help you with?"

Maeve nodded at Gray, letting him give his uncle the agreed-upon information. "We've found a few interesting things, but we need some information, and we need you to help us figure out the safest way to get to the ruins at the edge of Palumbra."

For a split second, Night's eyes showed a flash of anger or frustration. "Why would you need to go there?" Night asked. "There's nothing out there except death and decay. The WG doesn't even patrol out there anymore."

"We just need to look at something," Gray said. "We think it will help us to figure out some papers we found."

"What papers?" Night asked. "Did you find something important in the box?"

"It was just a note written by some teenagers – a kind of time capsule thing," Maeve said. She shrugged. "You know teenagers. They do things just for fun. They probably thought it would be funny to write a note to the future."

"Can I see it?" Night asked eagerly.

"Silas has it right now," Gray said. "He wanted to see if he could figure out what some of the words we didn't know meant. They're probably some kind of slang from years ago."

"What time period is it from?" Night asked.

"We're not sure," Maeve lied. "It didn't have a date on it. We'll show it to you some other time. It just mentioned the buildings out where the ruins are, and we wanted to go see if we could figure out what they were talking about. It's probably a waste of time, but it's better than sitting around and waiting to get caught."

"But you could get caught wandering around out by the ruins," Night challenged.

"Not if you help us." Maeve moved to stand next to Gray, a united front to get what they needed from his uncle.

"Maybe," Night conceded. "But remember, Arabella is clearly not telling me everything. What do you need from me?"

"You're the only one who can get us a schedule of patrols," Gray said. "We also need to know whatever you can tell us about that area. What it used to be. Danger to avoid. That kind of thing."

Maeve and Gray had decided to leave out all mention of the map, the photo and the disc. And they didn't tell Night they were searching for two things. The groups would stay together until they were out of the heavily patrolled territory then split up.

"I don't know much about that area," Night said, pulling out a chair and straddling the back of it. "It's not
196

even mentioned on any of the WG maps. I'm not sure how much help I can be. If I suddenly take an interest in those buildings, it will look suspicious and might actually draw attention to you." Night tapped his fingers lightly on the back of the chair. "We don't patrol out there that I know of. It's just a bunch of ruined buildings that date back to before The Lost Years."

He looked from Maeve to Gray. "Are you sure you want to do this?"

Maeve and Gray nodded.

"I can get you the patrol schedule. I'll leave it in the nook as you leave the tunnels. You know what I'm talking about?" He looked at Gray who nodded in response.

"I'm pretty sure you're not telling me everything," Night said as he stood and pushed the chair back into the table. "I don't know if you're trying to protect me or if you're worried I'll tell someone what you're doing. Either way, it's probably the smart thing to do."

Night placed a hand on Gray's shoulder. "I love you. No matter what, remember that. I can't come back here. I've slipped away too many times lately, and someone might decide to follow me. I'll leave that patrol list for you, but there's not much else I can do right now."

"That's fine," Gray said. "We'll figure this out. Then we'll get everything back to the way it should be."

"I hope so, Gray. I hope so."

CHAPTER TWENTY-ONE

"This is the list of patrols for the next two days," Gray said, setting a single sheet of paper on the table. They were gathered around the table in their living space, eating another meal of protein paste bars and water.

"That seems like a short list," Maeve said.

"My uncle left a note saying the WG has pulled in most of the patrols, especially the ones outside the city center." Gray tapped the list. "I guess there's a bit of chaos up there after the attacks the other day. Most of the soldiers are needed to control the city center."

"That makes sense, I guess," Maeve conceded.

"He also said that the five of us are at the top of the list as far as fugitives go. Everyone is looking for us."

"That's just great," Silas said. "Nothing like m-m-making this easy."

"Apparently, they're very interested in you two," Gray said, pointing at Ginger and Emery. "Why do you think that is?"

"I have no idea," Ginger said.

Emery shifted her eyes to look at the floor. "No

idea," she mumbled.

Ginger looked at her. "What have you done?"

Emery's eyes widened. "Why do you think I did anything?"

"Emery." Ginger put on her big-sister voice. "We need to know. All our lives are on the line here. We can't fight blind."

"Well, you know how I was working to write some new code before all of this started?"

"Yes." Ginger cocked her head in thought. "But you said it was just a project for school."

"Welllll," Emery stalled, "it might have been a program that can hack into the WG computers and take control."

"Emery!" Maeve bumped the table as she jumped to her feet. "Why would you do something so dangerous?"

Emery shrugged. "I wanted to see if I could do it." She looked at the floor and mumbled, "I wasn't actually planning to use it."

"Wait," Gray said. "How does the WG even know you created it?"

"I may have mentioned it to one of my teachers − not exactly what it was, but enough that a smart person could put two and two together." She glanced from Gray to Maeve to Ginger. "I was stuck and needed help. I had no idea he would rat me out."

"He may not have done it willingly," Gray said. "The WG isn't known for asking questions kindly."

"Oh no!" Emery's eyes traveled around the room

as if looking for her teacher. "Mr. Maynes was so nice. I hope they didn't hurt him."

Maeve and Gray exchanged a look. Maeve reached over and rubbed Emery's back. "It's OK, Emery. I'm sure Mr. Maynes is fine. He probably told them what they needed to know and they let him be."

"Do you really think so?" Emery asked, her eyes glassy with unshed tears.

Maeve closed her eyes, took a deep breath and said, "I really do."

"Do you still have that program, Emery?" Gray asked.

"Yes, it's on the computer in my backpack."

"You have your computer in your backpack?" Maeve asked, her eyes wide with alarm. "Gray, remember what your uncle said? We have to get rid of it."

Emery ran over to her pack and hugged it to her chest. "No way! I have way too much stuff on here."

Gray approached Emery. "Emery, my uncle said they had figured out that someone had hacked into the WG's archive regarding The Lost Years. He seemed to think they could trace it back to you."

"Please," Emery rolled her eyes. "I'm so much better than that. I disabled the tracker in the computer the day they gave it to me. And they might think they can trace me, but there's no way. I covered my tracks."

Maeve blew out a breath. "You're sure?"

"She's sure," Ginger said. "I double-checked it yesterday. I even had Silas look at it. It would take them years to track through all the false trails she laid."

Maeve looked at Silas for confirmation. Silas nodded. "I don't know anyone who could trace the hack back to her. I certainly couldn't do it."

"OK. We need to keep that computer safe," Gray said. "Who knows when we might need that program."

"I think you should keep it, Gray," Silas said. "You're the strongest and the most knowledgeable about how to outwit the WG."

"But I don't know how to use the program. Emery does, so it has to stay with your group. I think you should carry it," Gray said to Silas.

"M-m-me?" Silas pointed to himself. "You'd trust me with that? What if we meet a patrol and I freeze like last time?"

"Silas," Ginger said. "You can do this. Emery and I trust you. You're braver than you think. You could have just stayed at your house. No one knew you were with us. But you chose to be part of this, so give yourself some credit."

Silas sat up straighter as Ginger spoke. He nodded his head. "I still think it would be safer with Gray and M-m-maeve, but I'll do my best."

Gray laid his hand on Silas's shoulder. "That's all we can ask."

"I thought I'd be better at this," Maeve said in disgust.

"Why, exactly, did you think that?" Ginger

asked. "You've never even fired a gun before."

True to his word, Gray had brought them all to a room in the tunnels where they could practice shooting without causing damage to anyone or anything. Ginger and Silas were fairly steady shots, but Maeve consistently shot 10 feet to the left of the target.

Gray gently took the gun from Maeve. "You've been doing this for two days, and you haven't shot yourself or anyone else. I'd say you're doing just fine."

Maeve shook her head. "But I need to be good at it. I need to be able to defend myself."

Gray handed Maeve his canteen. As she took a large gulp, he said, "You'll figure it out. But remember, shooting at a target is a lot different than shooting at a person."

"Could you do it?" Maeve asked.

"Shoot a person? Yes," he answered briskly. "But not everyone can. And those that can have to live with it." Gray busied himself with cleaning and storing the guns. Maeve wondered what had happened to make him so certain. She shared a glance with Silas, but Silas just shrugged his shoulders and began taking down the targets.

"What about you, Ginger?" Maeve asked as she brushed her hair out of her eyes.

Ginger was quiet for a moment, her thoughts clearly lingering on the day her mom died. She shook her head and tucked a stray hair behind her ears. "Probably." She shook her head again. "No, definitely. If someone I loved was in danger, I could definitely do it." Ginger dropped her eyes and turned to pick up her own canteen.

"What about you, Maeve?" Gray asked quietly. "Do you think you could shoot someone?"

Maeve took another long swallow from the canteen and handed it back to Gray. "I don't know. I think maybe I could. Like Ginger, I'm pretty sure I'd do it if someone I cared about was in danger."

Maeve picked up her gun and shouldered her backpack. As she turned to exit the room, she heard Gray whisper, "I hope you never have to find out."

"Does everyone have everything?" Gray asked as they stood outside the door of their living space in the tunnel they had come to know so well. Maeve looked at her friends. Each one had a backpack and a rifle slung onto their backs − except Emery who had been given a knife. Despite several trips to the room The Resistance used as a shooting range, Emery had not gotten the hang of shooting. Maeve's skills with a gun still hadn't improved much, but she thought she could probably hit something in the general direction of her target.

"Yes, Gray," Emery said. "You checked our packs like 12 times."

Everyone laughed as Emery sounded like a regular 12-year-old annoyed with an older brother. Gray ruffled Emery's hair. Maeve smiled.

"OK, let's go," Gray said. "We'll stay in the tunnels as long as possible. When we go topside, we'll travel together until just before we reach the ruins. Then

Maeve and I will break off to try to follow this map. You guys find that building, discover what you can and make your way back here. If Maeve and I aren't back within a week, go find my uncle."

Ginger, Silas and Emery nodded. "We've got it," Silas said. "Lead the way."

The group made their way through the now-familiar maze of tunnels. Gray led them to the end of a long tunnel near what Maeve knew to be the outskirts of the city center. A rickety-looking wooden ladder was built into the side of the tunnel. "This ladder goes up to the edge of the forest on the south side of the city. From there, Silas, Emery and Ginger will keep heading south toward the ruins. Maeve and I will head north toward where we think that spot is on the map. Since none of us know exactly where we're going, keep your eyes open. Try to stay out of areas where there are people. Keep to the shadows. And avoid the patrols at all costs. Silas, do you have the patrol list?"

"Yes," Silas said. "And Emery has it memorized."

"Ok. Everyone be careful. We'll meet back at our home base."

"What if we can't get back?" Emery asked quietly.

"We'll make it back, Emery," Ginger said.

"I hope so." Emery's lip trembled. She took a shallow breath and blew it out. Peering at Ginger from lowered eyelids, she said, "But I bet mom thought everything would be fine, too."

Ginger shrugged out of her pack and dropped to

her knees next to Emery. She took hold of both her arms and looked directly into her eyes. "Emery, I promise I won't let anything happen to you. Keeping you safe takes priority over everything else." She thought for a moment. "Would you rather stay here? I'm sure you could stay with another Resistance member, maybe that John guy that we met." Gray nodded his head when she looked to him for confirmation.

Emery shook her head and sniffed. "I would just worry about you and be scared of being with a stranger. You promise we'll all be OK?"

Before Ginger could make a promise she wasn't sure she could keep, Silas stepped in. "We're going to be just fine." He ruffled her hair. "We'll all watch out for each other and everyone will meet back here before you know it."

Ginger gave Emery a long look. "Are we good?"

Emery sniffed once more and nodded. Ginger picked up her pack and gave Gray a nod.

"All right." Gray motioned toward the ladder. "Let's get up the ladder and get going. I'll go first to make sure it's clear. Maeve, you're last up. Guard our backs."

###

Standing on a hill at the edge of the forest, the group took a last look at the city center. They could hear short bursts of gunfire and saw plumes of smoke rising from the city center. On the edge of town closest to where they stood, they saw several patrols going door to door in a neighborhood. As they watched, one patrol pulled a person out of a house, forced him to kneel.

Ginger grabbed Emery and hugged her tight. "Don't look," she whispered. A gun shot reverberated through the afternoon silence.

Maeve's horrified gaze met Ginger's shocked one. "What is going on," Maeve said as she took a step back from the bloodshed. "Why would the WG do that?" Her hands shook, and she turned to run.

Gray stopped her with a hand on her shoulder. "We can't run," he said quietly. "The WG will notice us."

Tears formed in the corner of her eyes. With hands still shaking, she reached up to wipe them away. "What is happening?"

Ginger still held Emery close, and Silas was sitting on the ground with his head on his knees.

"They're rounding up members of The Resistance," Gray said as he ran his hand soothingly up and down Maeve's arm. "I only hope there's still a few left when we get back."

"How can your uncle be a part of this?" Maeve asked. She sucked in a shaky breath. "They're shooting people in cold blood."

Gray paused and breathed in deeply. "I have to believe he's doing his best to hide as many members as he can, but he can't raise too much suspicion. They're already treating him oddly. We don't want them to just shoot him, too."

Gray left Maeve's side and offered his hand to Silas and pulled him to his feet.

"Come on," Gray said. "We have to get out of here before they notice us. The only good thing about what's going on in the city is that means there's not a lot of extra manpower to put into patrols outside the city center."

"But what about my parents?" Silas said.

Gray placed a hand on Silas's shoulder. "We can't do anything to help them right now. Our job is to figure out what this building and this map have to tell us about what's going on."

Gray motioned toward the forest to urge everyone to start walking.

"But what if they don't tell us anything? What if this is all a wild goose chase?" Silas's voice rose with every question. "What if this is just how life is going to be from now on?"

"Silas." Ginger moved to stand in front of Silas. "We have to believe that we're going to find something that will help us. Those kids on that disc looked desperate – just like us. Whatever they wanted us to find has to help somehow."

"But how are we going to stop this?" He motioned toward the city below them.

"I don't know," answered Maeve. "What I do know is this. We've all sacrificed something to choose to follow this path. I lost a relationship with my parents. You chose danger over safety. Gray chose to protect us when I'm sure his uncle could stash him somewhere safe. Emery and Ginger lost their mom. If we don't follow through on this, we'll have lost all of that for nothing. We have to keep going. We have to figure this out."

"Maeve is right, Silas," Ginger said. "We have to keep going so that we can make our losses count for something. I know it's hard because you don't know what your parents are going through, but we can't fix that right now. What we can do is figure out this puzzle. OK?" Ginger held out her hand.

Silas took a look back at the city center then slowly reached out and took Ginger's hand.

CHAPTER TWENTY-TWO

"This is where we split up," Gray said as they reached the top of yet another hill. They had been walking for hours. By Maeve's estimate, they had covered about 10 miles. They could just see faint plumes of smoke in the distance where the city center stood. Only one patrol had come anywhere near them, and it was one that Night had put on the list, so they easily avoided it.

Gray pointed to the south. Just in the distance, they could see the outline of what may have once been some tall buildings. "That's your destination," he said to Ginger, Emery and Silas. "Hopefully, you'll find the building we're looking for over there. It should take you another day to reach it on foot. Be careful and watch for patrols. If the WG is hiding something, they won't leave it unguarded."

"What about you two?" Ginger asked.

"We're headed that way," Gray said, pointing off to the east.

"What's out there?" Emery asked.

"I have no idea," Gray said. "As far as I know, the map of Palumbra ends another 10 miles north of here. Beyond that, this map is the only guide we have. Our only option is to take our best guess, and based on what little we can decipher of this map, I'm guessing what we're looking for is in that direction."

"But if you're not sure of the m-m-map, how will you find what we're looking for?" Silas said.

"A lot of guessing and praying," Maeve said.

"Not sure I believe anyone's listening to those prayers," Ginger said.

"Maybe not, but I think faith might be the only thing we have to hang onto right now," Maeve said.

"Maybe," Ginger said with a shrug.

"It's time to get going," Gray said. "We'll meet back up in less than a week."

Maeve hugged Ginger. "Be careful. Remember how we used to dream about big adventures when we were kids? This might not be your trip to the stars, but it definitely qualifies as an adventure," Maeve said.

"Yeah," Ginger replied. "This might be a bigger adventure than I was planning on. Take care of yourself."

Maeve moved on to Emery. She hugged her tight. "Take care of your big sister. I'll see you in a week."

"See you in a week," Emery said with a sniff.

"Do I get a goodbye?" Silas asked.

"Absolutely." Maeve wrapped him in a hug. "Please take care of them. They've been through so much already. And take care of yourself, too. I've gotten kind of used to having you around."

"I'll do m-m-my best. You guys be careful, too."

Maeve and Gray watched as Silas, Emery and

Ginger made their way down the south side of the hill.

"Do you think they'll be OK?" Maeve asked.

"I hope so," Gray said. "We did the best we could to get them ready. Ginger and Silas are decent shots, and Emery is smart and quick. Hopefully, they won't run into any trouble in the ruins."

"I hope you're right," Maeve said. "I really do."

Gray took Maeve's hand. "We should get moving. We're really exposed on this hill. Just because we haven't seen a patrol doesn't mean they aren't out here."

"We need to look at the map," Maeve said. "And we need to eat."

"Let's walk to that stand of trees." Gray pointed to a group of trees about a half mile to the east of the hill they were standing on. "That will give us some cover and some shade. We'll eat and figure out our next move."

When they reached the trees, Gray began pulling food from his pack, and Maeve removed the map from hers. Gray handed Maeve a protein paste bar and a canteen.

"I'm going to look around to make sure we're in the clear," he said.

Maeve took the food and water and nodded. She unfolded the map as Gray walked away. As she ate, she turned the map in all directions, trying to make sense of the odd markings. When Gray returned, she had the map in her lap and was tracing something on it.

"We're clear," Gray said as he dropped down next to her. "What are you doing?"

"Trying to figure out this map. We can't follow it

211

if we don't know what we're looking for. I haven't been able to identify much, but I think this is The River." She pointed to the spot on the map she had been tracing.

"That seems much too long for The River," Gray said. "We've always been told The River empties into the lake on the edge of Palumbra."

"But what if it doesn't? The WG has lied to us about just about everything else. What if they lied about this as well."

"But why?" Gray asked as he took the map from Maeve. "Why does it matter if The River stops at the edge of Palumbra or not?"

"What if they didn't want anyone to check? What if there's something else outside of Palumbra?" Maeve took the map and scooted next to Gray so their thighs were touching. Gray looked up. Maeve spread the map out across both their laps, trying to ignore the warmth of Gray's thigh pressed against hers.

"Look," she pointed at The River. "What if The River keeps going? That means you could live outside of Palumbra, right? Maybe that's why they want everyone to believe The River stops at the edge of Palumbra. If there's no water, then you can't live out there. To be safe, you have to stay in Palumbra."

"I guess," Gray said slowly.

"Think about it, Gray. We've been told our whole lives that The River is the reason that Palumbra was able to exist after The Lost Years. It was what saved us. Clean water was key to the city's revival. And if that clean water was only available to Palumbra, then

Palumbra was the only place that could have survived, right? But what if that's not true? What if this map takes us to someplace outside of Palumbra?"

"But that would mean that we aren't the only ones that survived The Lost Years. There could be other people out there somewhere."

"Exactly."

"But why haven't we ever heard from them? Surely if there are people out there, we would have seen some sign of them."

"I don't know," Maeve said. "But I think we should follow The River." Maeve's hand brushed Gray's as she took the map from him and folded it. Gray grabbed her hand.

"Maeve," Gray started.

Maeve looked into the depths of his blue eyes. "Yes?" she said quietly.

"I'm not sorry I kissed you."

"I'm not sorry you did either," she said with a shy smile. "I am sorry we don't see things the same way when it comes to your uncle."

"Me too. I just can't believe he's capable of betraying me." Gray looked out over the uninterrupted field of green grass and trees that stood between them and their goal.

"Gray, I don't want to think that he could betray you, either, but you have to admit it's suspicious that that patrol nearly found us. What if he thinks he's keeping you safe by having you get caught?"

Gray plucked a piece of grass from the ground

and began to shred it between his fingers. "How would that keep me safe?"

Maeve twirled her hair, then tucked it behind her ear. "At least he would know where you are, and he probably thinks he could get you out of trouble if you got caught."

Gray shook his head and stood up. "I just don't know, Maeve."

"I think we should just be careful around him, that's all." Maeve stood and brushed some lingering dirt off her pants.

Gray gave a hesitant nod. "I guess that's the smart thing to do ... for now."

CHAPTER TWENTY-THREE

"I think this might be it," Silas said as he looked at the shell of what was once a building of more than 20 stories.

"I don't think so," Ginger said. "It's the wrong shape. And where's the spire that was on top?"

"No, look," Emery said, "I think Silas is right. When the top stories fell, they sheared off this piece here." Emery pointed to a spot on the photograph where the building exterior protruded.

Ginger looked again. She tilted her head. Then shook it. "I still don't see it, but if you two both think this could be the place, we should probably check it out."

They stood in the middle of a ruined city. All around them loomed the remains of buildings that once teemed with life but were now nothing but crumbling shells. Ginger thought it odd that no weeds or vegetation had sprung up in the cracked and shattered buildings. She marveled that this clearly once-bustling area could have ended up like this.

"Are you coming?" Emery asked, breaking into Ginger's thoughts.

Bringing her mind back to the task, Ginger

nodded and followed Emery and Silas. Their trip to the ruins had been uneventful. It took a day longer than Gray had estimated because of their need to avoid the WG patrols. She and Silas had shared the watch on the two nights they had spent sleeping in the open. Ginger's neck prickled, and she had a feeling their luck might not hold much longer.

"Come on," Emery said impatiently as she followed Silas through a gap in the ruins. Ginger fingered the strap of the gun thrown over her shoulder and followed her sister.

Once inside, all three of them stopped. Even though the building had fallen, they could tell it had once been a grand piece of architecture. The towering atrium's walls were covered with pictures made out of small tiles. A large statue of a man on a horse had fallen on its side in the center of the atrium.

"I wonder who he was," Emery said.

"I don't know," Silas said. "But let's hope we don't end up like him. Come on."

Ginger followed Silas through the piles of rubble to the other side of the atrium. Emery trailed behind, trying to take it all in.

"Where are we going?" Ginger asked.

"It looks like there are stairs over here, behind that big pile of concrete," Silas answered as he pointed to his left.

Emery looked to where Silas was pointing. "I'm not sure those are stairs," she said.

"Well, let's go find out," Ginger said, striding

quickly toward the pile of rubble.

They approached the broken pile of concrete but still couldn't see behind it. "How do we get around?" Ginger asked.

"There's a spot right there that looks like one of us could fit through," Emery said, pointing at a small opening near the bottom of the pile.

"I'll never fit through there," Silas said.

"Me either," Ginger said.

"I can fit," Emery said, dropping her backpack. Before Ginger could stop her, Emery slipped into the darkness of the opening.

"Emery," Ginger yelled, "come back here. We don't know what's in there."

"I'm fine," Emery yelled back. "But toss me a flashlight. I know Gray made sure we had them."

"How do we get her out?" Ginger asked Silas.

"I don't think we do," Silas answered. "We'd better just give her the light, so she'll come back faster." Silas began to rummage through his backpack.

"Emery," Ginger said, "please come back out here."

"Ginger," Emery said. "I'm fine. There's no other way to get through. I looked on our way in. If we want to find out why this building is so important, we have to go this way. Now, toss me a light."

Silas stepped up to the opening and reached the light as far into the opening as his arm would go. "Emery, here's the light. Take a look around and come back here − quickly."

"OK," Emery said. "Don't worry. I'll be fine.

Ginger, I can do this."

Ginger looked at Silas as she tucked a stray strand of hair behind her ear. "What if something happens to her?" she whispered. "She's all I've got left."

Silas wrapped Ginger in a hug. "It's going to be OK. She's a smart kid. And she's right. Look around. There's n-n-no other way through, and she's the only one who can fit. Let's see what she finds, and we'll figure out a plan from there."

Ginger rested her forehead against Silas's shoulder for another moment then took a deep breath and stepped back. "Thanks," she said quietly. "I know she's smart and capable. She's just my baby sister, and she's already been through so much."

"Letting her do this will make her feel like she's an important part of what we're doing."

"What are we doing, Silas? How did we get here?"

"I'm not so sure. I was obviously in the wrong place at the wrong time. Or maybe the right place. I don't know. What I do know is that I'm still terrified, but it appears that we're the only people who can figure this out."

"Are we really, though?" Ginger ran her fingers through her long ponytail. "We're just a bunch of kids. I'm hauling my 12-year-old sister through the ruined shell of a building after we watched our mom die. Why are we the ones doing this? Surely, The Resistance would be better suited for this."

"But would they? The WG is already looking to destroy The Resistance. My parents have to be super careful not to do anything out of the ordinary. The WG looks for any excuse to arrest those they think are part of The Resistance. And now it's even worse." Silas walked over and looked in the opening for any sign of Emery as he finished talking.

Ginger sat down next to a pile of rubble. "What's your story, Silas? Why are you here? Really? You had the chance to stay with your parents, and you chose to come back with us. Why?"

Silas sighed and sat down next to Ginger. He picked up a rock and began to toss it in the air and catch it. He watched the path of the rock as he spoke, being careful not to look at Ginger.

"I wanted to be part of something important, I guess. I've always taken the safe route. Kept m-m-my head down. Stayed off of anyone's radar. I stutter, as I'm sure you've noticed. I always chose not to talk m-m-much. Other kids would m-m-make fun of m-m-me, so I learned to become invisible. And mostly I lived in fear."

Ginger watched him throw the rock and catch it. She nodded so he would know she was listening, but Silas's eyes stayed on the rock.

"M-m-my parents have always tried to protect me from their work with The Resistance. The only reason I know they're part of it is because I heard them whispering about it one night. They never saw m-m-me as someone who could be useful."

"I'm sure that's not true, Silas," Ginger said. "Your parents were probably just trying to protect you. Belonging to The Resistance is dangerous. If you didn't know about it,

219

then you wouldn't be of interest to the WG."

"M-m-maybe," Silas said, "But I'm pretty sure the WG would have arrested all three of us if they got caught. Anyway, after I helped you guys out that day, I went home. And I realized I could make a choice. I could keep living my safe life or I could help you guys − not because I wanted to be part of any great cause, but because you guys noticed m-m-me. And it didn't matter if I stuttered. For the first time, I felt what it was like to be a necessary part of something. So I came back."

Silas caught the rock and turned to look at Ginger.

Ginger took the rock from Silas, leaned over and kissed him on the cheek. "Good choice, Silas. Good choice."

"Ginger, Silas!" Emery's voice came from a distance.

Ginger and Silas leapt to their feet and raced to the opening where Emery had disappeared. "Emery, are you OK?"

"I'm fine." Ginger could almost hear her rolling her eyes. "I'm coming out."

Ginger and Silas watched as a faint beam of light grew stronger and Emery shimmied out of the opening. Ginger grabbed Emery in a fierce hug. "Don't you ever do something like that again. Next time, we make a plan together, OK?"

Emery looked away. "I'm sorry, Ginger. I didn't think you would let me go, and it was the only way. Next time we'll talk about it."

220

"Let's hope there's not a next time to worry about," Silas said, pulling Emery into a hug of his own. "We're glad you're safe. What did you find?"

Ginger stepped back and took a good look at Emery. "You're covered in dust." She started brushing concrete dust off of Emery's shoulders and hair.

Emery shrugged and said, "The only narrow space is right at the beginning. If we could clear away some of that debris, you guys could make it through the rest. Silas was right. There are stairs, but not right behind the rubble. You have to walk a ways."

"Did you find anything that might indicate this is the right building?" Ginger asked.

"It's hard to tell, but I did look in several rooms. This was clearly an office building of some kind, and it looks like people just left everything where it was. I don't know what happened, but everyone left in a hurry. The computers and stuff obviously don't work anymore, but we might find something in one of the offices that would help us figure this out."

"I guess we should get to work m-m-making this opening bigger then," Silas said.

They walked over to the pile and started to work.

"I think it will be tight, but we should all be able to fit," Ginger said. "Silas, you may have to carry your pack in front of you through the first area."

"OK, let's go, then," Emery said.

"Lead the way," Silas said, handing Emery the flashlight.

Emery disappeared once again into the opening,

followed by Ginger and then by Silas who, in fact, did have to carry his pack and his gun in front of him and turn sideways to make it through the opening. About 20 feet in, Ginger watched as Silas slung his pack and his gun to his back and stood up straight. "You're right, Emery. This isn't so bad."

"Come on," Emery said. "The offices are this way."

She led them through the dim tunnel of rubble to a door that hung half off its hinges. "Stairs are through here," she said. "Be careful. There are a few railings missing."

Ginger walked through the door and stopped so abruptly Silas bumped her from behind. "Emery! You climbed these stairs?"

The stairs were missing nearly all their railings and stood open to a sheer drop. Ginger couldn't tell how far down the drop went, but she was sure it was at least a full story to the basement. The stairs themselves were crumbling with gaps of one, two and in some places three stairs. "What if you had fallen? We wouldn't even have known what happened to you."

"I'm fine, Ginger. It's fine. Just be careful," Emery said as she started up the first flight of stairs, careful to hug the wall and avoid the gaps.

Silas nudged Ginger. "Go on. We have to know what's in here. Otherwise this whole journey has been for nothing."

Ginger nodded, swallowed hard and slowly began to climb the stairs. Silas followed a few steps behind.

222

"You can do it, Ginger," Silas said quietly. "Afraid of heights?"

Fear stole Ginger's voice, so she nodded.

"I'm right here," Silas said. "I won't let you fall."

They reached the first floor without incident and began to explore the offices. "I think we should split up," Emery said even as Ginger shook her head. "No, listen, we'll be much faster if we split up. There's no one here but us. We'll be perfectly safe."

"Emery is right," Silas said. "We can cover m-m-more ground if we split up. If everyone stays on this floor, we can look through all the offices and move on. This place gives m-m-me the creeps, so the sooner we're out of here, the better."

Ginger reluctantly nodded her head in agreement. "OK, but stay on this floor," she said with a hard glance at Emery.

"OK, OK, I get it. Stick together. I won't leave this floor."

They each entered a different office. Ginger looked around hers. Offices were the same in every generation, Ginger thought to herself. The technology might change, but the basic accoutrements of an office were the same – the desk, the chair, the drawers for filing things. She picked up a dust-covered stapler off the desk and wondered about the person who had once worked here. What had happened to him or her? Did they survive The Lost Years? Did they fight in the wars that must have occurred? Did they have a family?

Ginger's musings were interrupted by a shout

from Silas. She hurried out of her office and into the one Silas had chosen.

"What did you find?" she asked as Emery also entered the room.

"Look," Silas said. "These are plans for massive weapons."

"How do you know that?" Ginger asked, taking the papers from him. "What do you know about weapons?"

"N-n-not much," Silas said. "But, look." He spread out the large roll of paper on the desk and pointed to a long line on the page. "I think this is the gun part." He tilted his head. "But it's not like any weapon I've ever seen. There's no place for bullets or ammunition of any kind. What does it shoot?"

Ginger looked at the page and idly fiddled with her ponytail. "I kind of see it. But does this mean anything? This building is old. These plans have to be as old as when this building was destroyed, and surely that was during The Lost Years. So, do these plans even mean anything now?"

Emery took the plans from Ginger and studied them thoughtfully. "This is all technology that still exists today. If someone got their hands on these plans, they could easily build this today." She looked at Ginger. "And I'm not sure this building was destroyed during The Lost Years. I think it was more recent."

"What are you talking about?" Ginger asked. "Why would there be a whole area of Palumbra that no one knows about?"

"Why do you think that, Emery?" Silas asked.

224

"Come look," she said as she walked out the door.

Silas stuffed the papers into his pack and followed Emery into the next office. Ginger tucked in behind Silas.

"See," Emery said as she held up a coffee cup and what looked like a woman's bag. "There's sludge in the bottom that looks like the remnants of coffee. And this bag contains spoiled food. If this building dated back to The Lost Years, this stuff would be long gone. I think this was a WG building, and it's only recently been destroyed."

"That's crazy," Ginger said. "Surely we would have noticed the WG blowing up an entire city."

Silas walked over to the window and looked out in the direction of the center of Palumbra. "But would we?" Silas asked. "Or could we have been distracted?"

"The bombings!" Ginger said. "We couldn't figure out why the WG was bombing their own people. It was a distraction to keep us from noticing activity and smoke in the distance. We were too busy worrying about what was going on right in front of us."

"No one knew this place existed. Why would they need to get rid of it?" Emery asked.

"M-m-maybe they don't need it anymore," Silas said. "The best way to hide what was going on here would be to destroy it."

"But why did we think these buildings were already in ruins?" Ginger asked. "My whole life, I've been told the buildings on the edge of Palumbra were destroyed during The Lost Years."

225

"But did anyone ever check? Maybe some of the buildings were destroyed and the WG was using the remaining ones to develop weapons."

"But weapons for what?" Ginger walked to stand next to Silas. "There's no one else out there."

Silas stared out the window. "That we know of," he said quietly.

Behind them Emery placed the coffee cup back on the desk and said, "Come on. Let's see what else we can find."

Emery, Silas and Ginger continued to look through the offices. They found similar papers about weapons in each office, but nothing to tell them what the WG was going to use the weapons for. When they reached the fourth floor, Silas stopped.

"Look." He pointed at the footprints in the dust on the floor. "Someone else has been here."

"How did they get up here?" Ginger asked. "There were no footprints on the steps or on the other floors."

"Maybe there's another way up," Emery said.

The footprints led all over the fourth floor from office to office.

Silas pulled his gun over his shoulder and motioned Emery and Ginger forward. "Be careful, and be ready to run."

The group quietly followed in the path of the footsteps, with Silas carefully peering around each corner before motioning Ginger and Emery to follow. They reached the last door in the corridor. Unlike all the other doors, this one was closed. Silas motioned for

Ginger to stand on the other side of the door. "The footprints only go in," Ginger whispered. "They don't come out."

Silas nodded as he slowly turned the knob and the door swung open. Both Silas and Ginger pointed their guns through the door.

"Don't shoot!" said a weak voice from the corner of the room. Slumped against the wall was a middle-aged man with a sheaf of papers in one hand, bleeding from a wound in his side.

Without lowering his gun, Silas said "Who are you? Why are you here?"

The man shifted and grimaced in pain. "I worked here," the man said slowly. "I was trying to gather papers that proved what was going on here. We had been told to evacuate, but I hid, and I stayed. Someone needs to know what's going on, what the WG is planning. Someone needs to save the children."

"What?" Ginger said, lowering her gun. She walked slowly over to the man. "Let me see," she said, motioning to his wound. "Maybe I can help."

"It's too late for me," the man said. "You have to take these." He shoved the papers at her. "Save the children."

Ginger ignored the papers and knelt next to the man. "Let me help," she said as she pushed back his shirt to better see the wound. He batted her hand away and waved the papers in Ginger's face.

"Take these, please," he whispered.

Ginger took the papers and handed them to Silas.

"Please let me help," she said to the man as she placed a folded T-shirt from her pack against his wound.

The man nodded weakly. "There's not much you can do. It's too late for me."

Silas knelt next to Ginger and Emery came around to the other side of the dying man. She picked up his hand and held it.

Ginger's eyes filled as she said, "At least tell me your name."

"It's Elton Price," the man whispered.

"Nice to meet you, Mr. Price," Emery said.

Ginger held pressure on the make-shift bandage. "Tell us a little about you."

Elton's eyes fluttered open. "I worked here – because the WG said I had to. We were sequestered here for months. No one was allowed to come or go. My wife and kids don't even know where I am. I just told them I would be gone for a few months for work." He winced and closed his eyes again.

"I wish Maeve was here," Ginger whispered to Silas. She motioned at the prone man. "I don't know what to do."

Silas put his hand on Ginger's. "There's nothing we can do. He's right, it's too late. All we can do now is stay with him and make him comfortable." Silas peeled Ginger's hands away from Elton. Ginger tried to pull away, but Silas held firm. "Ginger, we can't fix this. There's no help nearby. At least he won't die alone."

Emery still held Elton's hand as she leaned over close to his ear and said, "Tell us about your family."

228

Elton's eyes opened once more but this time they focused on a point on the ceiling as if he were looking at something none of the rest of the could see. "My wife, Greta, and I fell in love during school. We've known each other since we were kids. When we met the minimum age for marriage, we got permission and started our life together."

Elton began to shiver. Ginger didn't know what else to do, so she asked, "What about your children, Mr. Price?"

Elton's breathing evened out and the shivering subsided a little. "Twins," he said in a voice so soft Ginger had to lean over to hear him. "They're 3. Girls. Curly blonde hair. They're a handful, but so sweet." His voice tapered off and his breathing slowed.

Emery continued to hold his hand while Ginger and Silas sat quietly. Ginger was wishing she had gotten the opportunity to tell her mom goodbye when Emery began to sing softly, an old lullaby that their mom had sung to them. Ginger joined in and Silas hummed along.

Elton opened his eyes one more time and give Emery's hand a slight squeeze. "Thank you." His eyes closed again and the hand Emery was holding went limp. Emery locked eyes with Ginger as Ginger felt for a pulse, shook her head and stepped away. "He's gone."

Emery let go of his hand, placing it next to his still body. Tears leaked out of the corners of her eyes. Ginger wiped her bloody hands on her pants and opened her arms. Emery ran into them. Sobs wracked Emery's body as she said, "Why does everyone have to die?"

"Shh, Em." Ginger stroked her hands up and down on Emery's back in a soothing motion. "We're going to be OK. We'll make sure Mr. Price's family knows what happened to him."

Emery sniffed and wiped her eyes. Silas stepped over to her, crouched down and looked into her eyes. "Emery, it stinks that Mr. Price died, but we're going to get out of this situation and you're going to grow up and do great things. Mr. Price died trying to save something important. We can't let his death go to waste." He looked at Ginger's pale face. "And as much as I hate to say it, we can't spend much more time here."

Ginger walked back over to Elton, knelt down and searched his pockets. When she saw the horrified look on Emery's face, she said, "I'm just getting any personal stuff he had in his pockets for his family."

Emery nodded as Ginger returned to the desk carrying a wallet and a well-thumbed photo of two little girls. She held it up for Emery and Silas to see then stuck both items in her pack. As she stood, she caught sight of the bloody smears on her pants where she had wiped her hands. She froze and her hands began to shake violently.

"Ginger?" Silas said sharply. He took her hand and led her over to the desk. "Stay with us." He squeezed her hand. "We can't do anything else here. Let's look at these papers and get out of here."

They spread the papers out on the desk. "Silas?" Ginger's voice trembled as she pointed at the papers.

Silas picked up one of the papers. "What does

this mean?" he asked. "Why do these papers contain the names of all the teenagers in Palumbra?"

"What?" Emery said as she joined them at the desk. "What else does it say?"

"Nothing," Ginger said. "It's just the names of teenagers split into different groups. But there's no information about what the groups mean."

"What should we do?" Emery asked. She sniffed and wiped her nose with the back of her hand.

"I think we should check the rest of the offices on this floor and then head back to the meeting point," Silas said. "See what the others have found."

"I agree," Ginger said, looking over her shoulder where Elton's body lay. "I just wish we could have done something more for him."

Silas patted her shoulder. "We can," he said. "We can save the children."

CHAPTER TWENTY-FOUR

"Get down, Maeve," Gray whispered frantically. "They'll see you."

Maeve ducked down next to Gray. They were hiding behind a wall of low bushes. A WG patrol had stopped for lunch not 500 yards from them. After days of not seeing a patrol, they had almost stumbled onto one.

"What are they doing this far out from Palumbra?" Maeve asked, keeping her voice low. "We're almost to where The River is supposed to end."

"Maybe that's why they're here," Gray answered. "To make sure no one gets to The River's end."

"What are we going to do? They don't look like they're moving on any time soon."

"We wait. What else can we do? We might as well eat, too." Gray handed Maeve another of the seemingly never-ending supply of protein paste bars. Maeve was most looking forward to having a meal of real food when this was all over. While they didn't get much from the WG, they did always get a ration of meat and vegetables. Her mom was a master at stretching that ration to give them some meat and produce for most of the month. Maeve's shoulders slumped slightly as she remembered the look of pain in her mom's eyes the last time she saw her.

Maeve and Gray ate and watched the WG soldiers. After an hour, the soldiers started to pack up. One soldier split off from the group and headed toward their hiding spot.

"Gray," Maeve whispered intensely, shoving him with her elbow. "What do we do?"

"Just wait," Gray answered, "maybe he'll go in another direction."

Maeve looked around. Their bushes were the only cover except for a stand of trees about 300 yards to their right. Maeve nudged Gray. "If we have to make a run for it, head for those trees. Maybe we can lose them in the forest."

Gray nodded but never took his eyes off the approaching soldier. He was so close now that Maeve could see the color of his eyes – a muddy brown. "I bet he needs to pee," Gray said. "This is the only vegetation around. Be ready to run when I say go."

Maeve maneuvered into a crouch with her gun at the ready. As Gray did the same, a twig cracked under his boot. The soldier looked straight at her and raised his gun.

"Go!" Gray yelled as he grabbed her hand and took off for the trees. Maeve heard the crack of gunfire as she sprinted for the safety of the forest. Shouting and more gunfire rang out behind her, but she didn't waste time turning to look. She dropped Gray's hand and ran as fast as she could. She could hear Gray's feet pounding next to her and thought he was returning fire. Everything sounded as if it was happening a long distance away. She could see the trees in front of her. Another 100 feet and she would reach them. Gray gave a grunt next to her. She slowed and looked at him, but he motioned her on.

They ran through the trees, dodging back and forth to confuse their pursuers. Gray had taken the lead, and Maeve followed behind. Her side was aching, and just when she thought she couldn't run any farther, Gray made a hard right and disappeared into an opening between two rocks. Maeve followed and found herself in a low cave. Gray pulled her to the ground next to him and put a finger on his lips. They could still hear their pursuers. Maeve listened to Gray's heavy, somewhat labored breathing. She looked at him closely, but he seemed fine.

She held her breath as two WG soldiers walked so close to their hiding spot that she could count the eyelets on their boots. The soldiers passed by without investigating their enclosure. Maeve knew she, too, would have missed the opening if Gray hadn't found it. They waited. Every minute seemed to take an hour to pass. Even when they could no longer hear the soldiers, they waited. The only sound was Gray's heavier than normal breathing. Finally, Maeve could take it no longer, and she rolled to her side to look at Gray. While her breathing had evened out, his was still ragged. Sweat dripped off his forehead, which was a ghastly shade of white along with the rest of his face.

"Gray!" Maeve exclaimed. "What's wrong?"

"I...got...shot," Gray said before his eyes rolled back in his head, and he passed out.

Maeve quickly scanned Gray's body, looking for the wound. Seeing nothing, she touched his shoulder, intending to roll him over, but her hand came away wet and red with blood. His black jacket had hidden his bleeding from her.

Maeve knew if he was going to survive, she had to get the bleeding stopped.

"Don't you dare die on me," Maeve whispered fiercely. "We're in this together."

Quickly, she stripped his jacket and shirt off, thankful he was unconscious to spare him the pain. Blood gushed from the wound. Maeve dug in her pack and grabbed a canteen and a T-shirt. She lifted his shoulder and was relieved to see blood pouring from the back of his shoulder as well. At least the bullet had gone all the way through.

She ripped the T-shirt in half making two pads then poured water over both the front and back of the wound. She knew keeping the wound clean was key to avoiding infection, but she also knew a dirty cave wasn't the ideal place to bind up a wound. She pressed the pads she had made firmly to both the front and back of his shoulder and prayed that the pressure would be enough to stop the bleeding. Almost immediately, the T-shirt pads were soaked through. Maeve used her knee and one hand to keep pressure on the wounds while she rummaged in Gray's pack and found his extra T-shirt. She used her teeth and one hand to tear the T-shirt in two and quickly replaced the pads she had been using with new ones. These pads soaked up the blood but didn't become saturated.

Maeve kept continuous pressure on the wounds until she couldn't feel her hands. She didn't dare remove the pads because she knew the bleeding could pick up again.

"I need something to tie these on with," Maeve said to herself. She took a chance and removed her hands from the wounds and rummaged through her pack for her spare pair of pants. Unable to tear the tough fabric, she folded them into a workable length and wound them around Gray's shoulder, holding the pads in place. When that was done, she slumped against the wall of the cave and prayed.

After a few minutes, Maeve lifted her head and looked at Gray's still form. She checked the make-shift bandage and surveyed her handiwork. She looked at her bloody hands and shook her head in amazement. Despite being designated as a nurse by the WG, she had spent most of her time at the hospital running errands for doctors and shuffling papers. She had learned about treating wounds like Gray's, but she had never done it herself.

Maeve wondered what Arabella Laughlin would think about the WG having trained her so she could save Gray. She smiled slightly at the thought. She cleaned her hands as best she could with the T-shirt she had discarded. She didn't dare use any more of their precious drinking water. She could only hope they could find a stream soon
236

where she could wash them well.

As she wiped away the blood, Maeve pondered the life of a nurse. She couldn't deny the thrill she got from having stopped the wound from bleeding, and it was an adrenaline rush. But was that because she was working on Gray or because she would really enjoy the work?

Maeve shrugged. She didn't know the answer. The WG had told her to be a nurse, so that's what she did. But she had never really considered whether it was something she wanted to do.

Maeve yawned as the adrenaline rush from their close escape began to wear off. She wasn't sure she wanted to be a nurse forever, but today, she was grateful she was.

Maeve let out a relieved sigh when Gray's eyes fluttered open, their ice-blue depths filled with pain and confusion. He tried to sit up but let out a groan and quickly laid back down.

"What happened?" he said in a raspy voice. Maeve grabbed a canteen and helped him drink it.

"You got shot," Maeve said. "I packed the wound, and it's finally stopped bleeding. But those are our spare T-shirts, so you're stuck with what you're wearing."

Gray glanced at his bare chest. "Well, that's not much."

Maeve grinned. "I still have the T-shirt you were wearing when you got shot. It's not in great shape, but it will work. Not sure you can get your arm through it, though."

"Is the bullet still in there?" Gray asked.

"No. It went all the way through," Maeve answered. "I'm worried about infection, though. This isn't exactly a sterile place to bind up a wound. I did the best I could."

Gray picked up Maeve's hand. "You did great. I would have died if you hadn't got the bleeding stopped. Any more patrols?"

"Not that I've seen, but that doesn't mean they're not looking for us. We need to move on as soon as you feel up to it."

"How long was I out?"

"About three hours, I think."

"Then we really need to move. Help me get dressed."

"You need to eat first." Maeve handed him a protein paste bar and some water. "You're of no use to me if you pass out from hunger and blood loss."

"How are we on supplies?" Gray asked with his mouth full of protein paste.

"OK," Maeve said. "We've got enough bars left, but we're running low on water. We'll have to find a well or a stream to refill the canteens."

Gray looked at her as he munched on his protein paste bar. "What?" Maeve asked.

"Just thinking about how much you've changed in the time I've known you," Gray said.

"How have I changed?" Maeve asked.

"When I met you, you couldn't even lie to the

WG without help. Now, you're counting supplies, treating bullet wounds and planning subversion. While I like this new Maeve, I can't help but feel sad you had to change at all."

"We don't always get to pick the path we want," Maeve said quietly. "Sometimes, the only choice is to change."

"I know," Gray said and reached over and gave her hand a squeeze. He finished the protein paste bar, balled up the wrapper in his hand and used his good arm to push himself to a sitting position. "We need to get moving. I don't think I can get that T-shirt over my arm. I'll just wear my jacket."

Maeve grabbed his blood-soaked jacket and helped him into it, wincing every time he grimaced in pain. "I'm sorry, Gray. You should be resting in a hospital, not finishing this search. I could leave you here, go search and come back for you."

"No. We stick together. There's no way I'm sending you out there by yourself. I may be injured, but no one else knows that. We're better together." Gray sent a grin her way.

Maeve grinned back as she transferred supplies from Gray's pack to hers.

"What are you doing?" Gray asked.

"I'm putting everything we need in one pack," she said. "I need you to carry a gun, and your shoulder won't bear the weight of both the pack and the gun."

"I can carry it," Gray said.

"No, you can't," Maeve said sharply. "You're

injured, and I need you to be able to get to the place on the map and back to safety, so we're not putting any more strain on that shoulder than we have to. I need you alive and healing, Gray." She softened her tone. "I don't know what I would do out here without you."

Gray looked away and blew out a breath. "OK."

"I just hate this."

Maeve placed her hand on his arm. "I know, but right now you need a little help. Let's go." She grabbed her gun in one hand and Gray's hand with the other. She took a step forward, but Gray pulled her back toward him and embraced her with his good arm.

"What?" Maeve said as she looked up into his face.

"Thank you," Gray said quietly.

"For what?"

"Taking care of me, keeping us safe, making sure I don't overdo it." He lowered his head toward hers until their foreheads were touching. "For being brave and doing what has to be done."

Maeve leaned in until her head was on his shoulder. "I don't think I'm any of those things," she said. "I'm just scared and doing what has to be done to stay alive. I'm not brave or strong. I'm just Maeve."

"Well, I'm a fan of 'just Maeve'," Gray said as he kissed her. Maeve pushed up to her tiptoes and leaned into the kiss. It was a gentle kiss, one that made Maeve feel treasured and important. Gray broke the kiss and held her for another minute. Finally, Maeve stepped back, took Gray's hand, leaned up to kiss his cheek and said, "Let's get going. We have work to do."

240

CHAPTER TWENTY-FIVE

The going was slower than Maeve would have liked. While Gray was upright, he wasn't steady. As the day went on, his breathing became more labored and Maeve worried that his wound was causing more trouble than he was letting on.

At last, they reached where The River ended in a lake and Maeve tried to force him to let her look at his shoulder. Gray shoved past her and insisted that they keep going, saying there was nothing she could do for it anyway. Maeve gave him a hard look but didn't argue, falling in behind him as he carefully placed one foot in front of the other. She knew he was right, but that didn't make it any easier to watch him struggle, his movements becoming less sure with each step forward.

Maeve turned her focus toward the lake. This was the moment of truth. On the other side of the lake, they would see if The River continued on like on the map or if the WG was telling them the truth about The River ending and Palumbra being the only civilization left.

The lake was not large, but they couldn't see to the other side. Even with Gray's labored pace, they traversed the ground around the lake quickly, being careful to stay in the cover of the trees. They had not encountered a patrol since they left the cave, but they had seen the places where patrols had recently camped.

When they reached the other side, Maeve let out a shocked gasp. A large dam held back the water to form the lake at the top of a hill. The River stretched out from the dam into the distance well beyond the horizon. "Gray?" Maeve asked in a whisper.

"I know, Maeve," he said as he settled his arm around her waist, drawing her into his side. "I know."

"Why, Gray? Why are they lying to everyone? Why didn't your uncle tell us about this?"

"I don't know, Maeve. It's possible that what's out there is so dangerous that they don't want anyone venturing farther than this point. But it's also possible that the WG wants to hide whatever is out there from us."

"I don't understand," Maeve said. "What can be so terrible that they need to hide it? And if it's so important that we don't go farther than this point, why is this area unguarded?"

"It's a good question, Maeve. I don't know. The only thing I can come up with is that my uncle moved the patrols around to protect us."

"How would he know we were coming here? We never said what direction we were heading."

Gray stared out over the lake as he said, "I may have left him a note."

"What?" Maeve stepped back and stared at him with her mouth open. "Why would you do that? You could have endangered all of us."

"Maeve," Gray said heavily, "he's my only family. I wanted him to know which direction we went in case we didn't come back."

"What if he's using that information to set us up?" Maeve began to pace. "I can't believe you would be so reckless."

Gray leaned against a rock on the bank of the lake. "Maeve," he said quietly. "When my parents died, I didn't know what to do. I was 8 years old and all alone. My uncle was just someone who visited every now and then and that my parents told wild stories about." Gray looked up with a small smile. "Apparently, my uncle was something of a rebel even when he was young."

Maeve continued to pace. "I know you have fond memories of him, Gray, but we don't know whose side he's on."

"I know it looks bad, Maeve." He tapped his hand on the rock behind him. "But he wouldn't hurt me. When he took me in, he gave up so much. He was 8 years younger than my dad. He went from being a single young guy with few responsibilities to raising a traumatized 8-year-old who spent most of his time acting out because his parents were dead."

Maeve stopped pacing and joined Gray at the rock. "I bet you were a handful," she said with a wry grin.

"I was, but Night always had time for me even though his job got more and more important as Arabella rose through the ranks of the WG. He made me feel like I was the most important thing in his life."

"What happened with Arabella?" Maeve asked. "Why would Night work for her if he'd always been a rebel?"

Gray shrugged. "He really believed in her at first. He told me more than once that he thought she could really change things."

Maeve shifted to look at Gray. "So what happened?"

Gray shook his head. "I don't know where things went wrong. Maybe my uncle just misjudged her." Gray looked at Maeve, his intense blue eyes piercing all the way to her soul. "All I know is that my uncle has never done anything except protect me. He would never intentionally put me in harm's way. I don't know where I would be if he hadn't taken me in."

Maeve was silent as she studied the ground in front of her. She chewed on the side of her thumbnail as she took in all that Gray had told her. Finally she spoke.

"I know you love him, Gray. And I believe that he loves you, too. I just don't know if we can trust him." She paused. "I wish you hadn't left him that note, no matter how much you trust him. It was a betrayal of my trust."

It was Gray's turn to study the ground. "You're right. I just couldn't imagine having something happen to us out there and not having my uncle know where I was." Gray gestured toward the horizon. "I needed to leave a note that said thanks for all he did for me and letting him know what happened." Gray put his hand on his injured shoulder and pinned Maeve with his gaze. "In case we don't make it back."

Gray picked up Maeve's hand. "But I should have talked to you about it. I broke your trust and possibly endangered you. That wasn't fair. Can you forgive me?"

Maeve looked at their clasped hands and nodded. "I guess I can understand. But I do wish you had talked to me about it. No more making decisions that affect us both without discussing it, OK?" She looked up at him.

Gray squeezed her hand. "You got it. From here on out, we make decisions together."

Maeve looked at the map again, unsure which way to go. They had followed The River for several miles, but now they had to leave it to find the spot marked on the map. Maeve had kept a wary eye out for patrols that might be following them, but she had to admit that maybe Gray had been right about his uncle keeping the patrols away. Once they had passed the lake, they had seen no signs of any other people.

She glanced at Gray as he sat in the shade of a tree, eating another protein paste bar. He had little appetite, but Maeve kept encouraging him to eat. She knew that if they didn't find their destination soon, Gray would be in real trouble and unable to make it back to the tunnels. She had checked his wound earlier. It was red, swollen and hot to the touch, all signs of infection along with the fever. They needed to get that wound clean and find a way to lower Gray's fever before much longer.

"I think we should go this way." Maeve pointed to the east. "We should be able to find this place before dark. I just wish we knew what we were looking for."

Gray slowly got to his feet, cradling his arm. "I hope it's a building and not buried treasure," Gray said. "I don't think I've got enough strength to dig for loot."

Maeve gave him a worried look then started off in the direction she had pointed. Gray followed in her wake, concentrating on putting one foot in front of the other.

"I think this is it," Maeve said wearily. They had slowly covered the remaining ground to the building in front of them. Gray had leaned heavily on Maeve for the last mile. Maeve knew she was going to have to do something about that wound and the fever before they tried to head back. While his fever didn't seem super high, it was persistent.

"What do you think it is − or was?" Gray asked slowly as if each word cost him energy. He he eyed the crumbling brick structure that had once been a two-story building that stretched for most of the block. The glass in the windows was long gone, and weeds had begun to climb up the exterior. The roof existed only in patches, but most of the exterior was still standing, although the bricks were beginning to crumble.

"Do you think we should go in now or wait until morning?" Maeve asked.

"We need to do it now," Gray said with a tired sigh. "The sooner we find what we came for, the sooner we can head back. Something about this place is making

246

my spine tingle. It's almost as if we're being watched."

Maeve looked around and gripped her gun. "I thought I was just being paranoid," Maeve said. With another glance around, she started walking toward the entrance to the building. "Let's get this done," she said.

Once inside the double doors, Maeve noted the office that stood to one side just as you entered the building. The walls had once been glass but were now just frames. A hallway stretched out before her.

"Should we stay together or split up?" Maeve asked Gray.

"It will be faster if we split up but safer if we stay together," Gray said as he swayed on his feet.

Maeve took his hand and announced, "We'll stay together."

They slowly made their way down the hallway, stopping to peek into the rooms on either side.

"Gray, I think this was a school of some sort," Maeve said.

"Why do you think that?"

"Look. There's the office when you come in. Then there are classrooms on either side of the hallway, all the way down. What else could it be? I think we should investigate the office." She led the way back to the office they had seen on the way in.

They stepped through the broken window panes into what had clearly been the front office of a school. Now that they were in the office, Maeve could see the faded logo – a tiger surrounded by the words Preston High School – painted on the wall.

"Gray, this is the high school those kids were from," Maeve said.

"What kids?"

Maeve spun to face Gray. She quickly took in his unfocused eyes and sheen of sweet on his brow. He pulled his eyebrows together in concentration and struggled to focus on her face. Maeve reached into her pack and handed him a canteen. Gray took a long swallow. His hand shook as he gave the canteen back to her.

"Come on, Gray. Stay with me." She gave his good arm a little shake. "We're talking about the kids in the video. The ones that left the note and the map. This is their high school. There has to be something here they want us to find."

Maeve walked to the other side of the desk and began opening drawers and cabinets. "There's nothing here," she said in frustration. "Everything is empty. Are we going to have to search the whole school to find what we're looking for? That could take days!"

"I think I'm what you're looking for," said a voice from the doorway.

CHAPTER TWENTY-SIX

Maeve and Gray pivoted quickly, guns at the ready. A woman stood in the doorway. Her face was worn and grizzled; her back was stooped. She leaned heavily on a tree branch, cut down to work as a cane. She carried no weapon other than the cane. It was hard to tell how old she was, but Maeve guessed she was near 80.

"Who are you?" Gray demanded with his gun still pointed at the intruder.

"I'm Emma," she replied.

"Emma? Who's Emma?" Gray asked.

Maeve peered at the woman for a moment, the set of her eyes and the smile lines around her mouth had remained the same through the years.

"Gray, I think she's the girl from the video," Maeve whispered. She turned to the woman. "Did you make the video we found in the box on the path in Palumbra?"

"That was me," the old woman answered. She sighed. "That was so long ago."

"Why are you living out here?" Gray asked as he lowered his gun but kept it at the ready.

"Where else would I go?" Emma asked. "All my friends were either caught or killed in the war. I fought, but when it became apparent we were all going to lose, I hid. There was a bunch of us who hid in the caves up in the hills around here. I'm the only one left."

Maeve eyed the old woman, then looked at Gray. She noted the sweat on Gray's forehead and the way Emma kept shifting her feet. One of them was going to collapse soon if she didn't get them to sit down. She motioned to the few remaining chairs in the room. "Let's sit down. I think we have a lot to talk about."

Emma sank gratefully into the chair. Maeve could see the relief in her eyes. Gray acted as if he would continue standing. "Sit down before you fall down," Maeve whispered as she walked by him. His eyes widened at the order, but he followed her direction.

Maeve handed out canteens and protein paste bars, noting their dwindling supplies. "How are you surviving on your own?" Maeve asked.

"When you've lived out here as long as I have, it's not hard," Emma replied. "At this point, I don't really know any other way to live. It's been 70 years."

"70 years! Why didn't you go live in Palumbra?"

"Oh, my dear, there was no place for me in Palumbra. I know the truth. Think about it. Do you know anyone who is as old as me in Palumbra?"

Maeve thought for a moment. "No. Now that you mention it, I don't. Why is that?"

"They killed them all," Gray said quietly.

Maeve jerked her head toward him. "What?

Why would they do that? And how do you know that?"

"Because The Lost Years can't be lost if anyone knows about them, right?" Gray said as he looked at Emma for confirmation. "I just figured it out right now."

"Unfortunately that's true. They didn't want anyone around who knew the truth about The Lost Years. They either killed us or sent us to live outside the boundaries of Palumbra, which was a death sentence in itself. Only a very small band of us survived ... because we hid. No one knew we were here. Until you. I guess you found our time capsule, huh?"

"Yes," Maeve said. "We followed the map. Our friends are trying to find the building in the photo."

"Are there any adults in your group?" Emma asked.

"No. Gray's the oldest. There's only five of us."

"Where are the other three?" Emma asked as she looked around the room.

"We split up," Gray said. Maeve noticed him wince as he raised the canteen to his mouth. "They went to look for the building you gave us a photo of."

"Ah, yes," Emma said, tapping her finger on the top of her walking stick. "I hope they have as much luck as you are."

"I don't know how lucky we are," Maeve said. "He got shot, and we're about out of food." She opened her pack to show their meager rations.

Emma placed both hands on top her walking stick and used it to push herself to her feet. She wobbled slightly, then caught her balance.

"I think that you two should come with me," she

said as she turned toward what was left of the door. "There's nothing to be gained by staying here, and your young man needs some medical attention."

"Can you help with his wound?" Maeve asked. "I did the best I could, but it's infected."

Emma patted Maeve on the arm. "I'm sure you did, dear. But I have some things in my home that can help with the infection. Let's get him fixed up and then I'll tell you all I know about The Lost Years."

"Drink that − all of it," Emma said sternly to Gray. Gray eyed the cup of steaming liquid suspiciously.

"What is it?"

"It's willow bark tea. It's an old remedy for fever. Drink up, and you'll feel better."

"Will it put me to sleep?" Gray asked warily.

"No. But it will help with your fever and should help with the pain in your shoulder."

Gray still looked skeptical.

"For goodness sake, Gray, drink the tea." Maeve stood up and took the cup from Emma. "If I have to, I'll hold your nose and pour it down your throat. You're no good to anyone if you fall over from fever. I can't carry you back to Palumbra. We have to get you steady on your feet." She walked over to him, leaned down to where he was sitting and whispered into his ear, "I need you. We're in this together, remember?"

Gray nodded and reached for the cup.

Maeve sat down next to Gray and looked around Emma's "home." They were in a deep cave cut into the side of the hill. The entrance was cleverly hidden by what looked like an avalanche of rock. Only if you knew where to look would you see the gap that was the opening to the cave. Maeve was stunned at how much the interior of the cave resembled a small apartment. Firelight and candlelight danced on the stone walls, and a table and chairs sat on one side of the room next to a cabinet that held dishes and cooking utensils. A rug covered the dirt floor. On the other side of the room, Maeve and Gray sat on a single bed with a wrought iron frame. The bed had been covered with a patchwork quilt, which was now wrapped around Gray's shoulders as he shivered from the fever. Several other chairs and even a small couch were gathered around the fire in the center of the cave. Emma had clearly mastered the art of cave living.

"How long have you been living here?" Maeve asked as she surveyed the room.

"About 50 years now," Emma answered. "It didn't look like this when we started. For the first year, we pretty much had a fire and a blanket. Over the years, we scavenged stuff from the ruins around us. There are six caves in this area, and we had four or five people living in each one. There were other bands of survivors in different areas. But I'm the last one left in our group."

"But you said you've been living out here for 70 years," Gray said skeptically. "What did you do for the other 20?"

"I was on the run," Emma said. "Living the life of the most wanted, moving from place to place every night to avoid detection. After 20 years, they stopped sending patrols all the way out here, and we could settle in one spot. But we still needed to stay hidden, so we made the caves our home. I was 16 when we made that video and went on the run."

"Wow," Maeve said. "Can you tell us what happened to cause such destruction?"

Emma got up and took Gray's now-empty cup to the counter. "I lived a normal teenager life until the war," Emma said as she placed a pot over the fire. A tempting aroma quickly rose from the pot, and Maeve's stomach grumbled.

"Then the war came. I was just a kid. The world was the way it was. We didn't interact much face to face. We lived life through our devices. We kept company with people who thought the same way we did. We went to schools that taught a particular political ideology. We didn't associate with anyone who thought differently."

Emma stirred the pot and shook her head. "We were actually taught that people who thought differently were the enemy. Well, you can imagine that if you're raised thinking someone else is the enemy, then eventually you don't feel bad about attacking that enemy. That's how the war started. Someone took offense at an idea someone else had, and they decided to start shooting. Who that actually was is lost to the mists of history, but once it started, it spread. There was no stopping it. The world descended into chaos and bloodshed."

"That's terrible," Maeve said as she joined Emma at the table. "Why didn't anyone stop it?"

"Oh, my dear," Emma said as she patted Maeve's shoulder. "There was no one left to be the voice of reason. People who spoke out against the war were the first to be killed. Dissenters were rounded up and executed. There was no such thing as a pacifist. If you weren't for the war, you were either dead or in hiding. But that wasn't the worst of it."

Gray stood and walked to the chair next to Maeve. He winced as he lowered himself into the chair. Maeve took his hand. "How much worse could it be?" Gray asked.

"They started using the teenagers," Emma said as she stirred the pot over the fire.

"Using the teenagers?" Maeve asked, shaking her head in confusion. "What do teenagers have to do with it?"

"That school where you found me? The one we attended? They used us to create weapons. They harnessed our collective brain energy and used it to make an energy weapon more powerful than anything anyone had ever seen."

"What?" Maeve exclaimed. "That makes no sense. How can you harness energy from someone's brain?"

"I never understood it all, but there were thousands of us. They hooked us all into the same contraption and the power from our brains created a force that couldn't be replicated. It's how Palumbra survived the war."

Gray raised his eyebrows and looked at Maeve as she chewed the edge of her thumbnail. The WG had a lot of power, but Maeve couldn't imagine that even now her friends in Palumbra would agree to hook themselves up to a machine that became a weapon.

"Eat your stew," Emma said. "Then I'll show you what's left of their terrible experiment."

Maeve and Gray entered the ruins of the high school once again, following in Emma's wake. She led them to what was once a massive room with thousands of seats in it. It reminded Maeve of her high school auditorium, only on a much larger scale. In the center sat the ruins of a large black machine that reminded Maeve of an octopus − if an octopus had hundreds of arms. The arms were broken and twisted but Maeve could see that they reached into the air over each section of the auditorium.

"What is that?" Maeve asked as she walked to the base of the machine.

"That's what they used to capture energy from our brain waves," Emma answered.

"But how did that work?" Maeve asked. "We studied the brain a little in my nursing training. Brain waves emit really low amounts of energy. Even if there were thousands of you, it still wouldn't produce the kind of power you're talking about."

"Well, the way I understand it," Emma

explained, "is that they would have us all work on what seemed to be an unsolvable problem. It was either a math problem or a brain teaser or a riddle. Since the machine connected us all together, and we were focused on the same problem, the machine was able to take our brain waves and boost the energy to astronomical proportions. They harnessed that energy for their weapon."

"But why would you agree to that?" Maeve asked. She waved her hand at the machine. "This thing is creepy."

Emma leaned heavily on her walking stick. "They told us we were part of an experiment that could change the future. We were told the research they were conducting would end the war and create a new world where everyone lived in peace." Emma shrugged. "We were so tired of the war. We believed them."

"Didn't anyone protest?" Gray asked as he examined one of the machine's arms.

"Some kids said they didn't want to be part of The Experiment, but those kids eventually stopped coming to school." She shook her head. "I don't know if they quit coming on their own or if the government did something to them. It was easy to just disappear in the chaos of the war. No one would really come looking for you."

Emma waved her hand at the auditorium. "The worst part is we were just one cog in the machine. There were hundreds of these schools all focused on the same thing."

"Why didn't you just pretend you were working on

the problem and think about something else?" Gray asked.

Emma sank into one of the few remaining chairs. "At first, we were excited to be a part of this fantastic new research. We felt special, and we thought we were making a difference. Later, when the excitement wore off, they would offer incentives – food, blankets, clean water – luxuries during the war. You did what you had to do to survive."

Maeve took a seat next to Emma and leaned forward. "So, why did you and your friends decide to make the video? Did you know you were being used to create massive energy weapons?"

"At first, we didn't know. They just told us it was research and that it was important to end the war. Plus we liked the extra food and things. But then my friend Trent overheard one of the teachers talking about it. When we found out what we were really being used for, we knew we had to figure out how to tell someone the truth. And we knew we had to stop it."

"What did you do?" Gray asked.

"We started a rebellion. Slowly at first, but then it grew. We stopped coming to school. As more kids heard about what they were being used for, more kids stopped going. We went into hiding. One night we snuck back into school to use the video equipment because we knew we needed to leave a tangible item for people to find, so we decided on the disc instead of a digital file. There was less risk of getting caught with a disc. Digital files have a way of ending up where you don't want them – even after they've been deleted."

"But you almost got caught," Gray pointed out as he slowly made his way over to where Emma and Maeve sat.

"Yes. That was a terrible night." Emma's eyes took on a far-off look. "Trent did get caught – and he was executed on the spot. He wasn't the last of my friends to die at the hands of the government."

"Why did you risk going into Palumbra to bury the box?" Maeve asked. "Why not just bury it here?"

"It was obvious that Palumbra was going to be the one place left standing. We knew by then that we couldn't keep the government from using the weapon, but we wanted to leave a message in the place where it was most likely to be found in the future."

Emma struggled to her feet and moved toward the door. "Everyone of importance was being moved to Palumbra, and all of the supplies were being routed there. We figured if anyone was going to be around in the future, it would be in Palumbra."

"So what happened? You started a revolution, but the WG still won," Gray said.

"By the time we figured out what was happening and started to get organized, what became the WG had already won. They had used the energy weapon to win the war." Emma turned and looked from Maeve to Gray. "People just gave up. After so many years of war, they were happy to live in Palumbra and be taken care of. The WG hunted down the rest or we went into hiding."

"But weren't people worried about a weapon this

259

powerful?" Maeve stood and held her arms out to encompass the room.

Emma patted her arm. "My dear, people were tired and hungry and they had lost so much. The WG promised not to use the weapon again and they promised to give everyone what they needed. That sounded really good to a lot of people."

"But why was it so important to pass this information to the future?" Maeve asked. "The war is over. No one is using teenagers as weapons. This technology has been destroyed."

"Are you sure?" Emma asked as she made a sweeping gesture with her hand. "You don't think once they knew how to do this they would just stop, do you? The future − that's you − needed to know so you can keep it from happening again."

CHAPTER TWENTY-SEVEN

"Are you sure you don't want to come with us?" Maeve asked Emma two days later as she shoved the last of her meager belongings into her backpack.

"No, dear," Emma replied. "I've lived out here so long that I think I'll finish my days here. I would just slow you down and be in the way."

Maeve started to speak, but Emma held up in her hand.

"But you would worry about protecting me, and that wouldn't serve your purpose. Plus, I don't think your young man completely trusts me."

"Gray's suspicious of everyone – except his uncle," Maeve said wearily. "I'm suspicious of that man."

"Trust your instincts, dear," Emma said as she hugged Maeve. "But leave room for second chances."

"Are you ready?" Gray asked as he walked into the cave. "We need to get going."

"I guess," Maeve answered. "Are you sure you're ready? I don't like the look of that wound." Maeve placed a gentle hand on his forehead. "And you're still running a fever. Maybe we should wait another day."

"Maeve, we can't wait any longer." Gray pushed her hand away. "I feel better. We have the willow bark to make tea. We have to go now. Silas, Ginger and Emery will be worried about us. We have to get this information back to the others. I'll be fine."

Gray slung his pack over his good shoulder and held his other arm close to his body. Maeve resigned herself to nursing Gray as they traveled back to Palumbra.

Emma held out her hand to Gray. "Be careful, young man," she said. "You remind me of my friend Trent. Think before you act, and give your trust only when it has been earned."

They shook hands, and Emma turned to Maeve. She gave her another hug and whispered in her ear. "Trust yourself. Trust your friends. Be wary of anyone else. Good luck."

As they walked away, Maeve turned to look at Emma standing in the hidden opening of her cave. She waved at the same moment she heard a high-pitched whine. Maeve scanned the sky, looking for the source of the sound as Gray grabbed her hand and began sprinting for the cover of some nearby trees.

"What is it?" Maeve asked as she ran.

"That's the sound of a WG drone," Gray said.

"A drone? What's that?"

"Nothing good. It's an unmanned flying bomb."

"Oh no! What about Emma?" Maeve asked.

"She should be OK in her cave," Gray said. "The bigger question is what is a WG drone doing all the way out here? Did they follow us? Or are they
262

looking for the remnant of people from The Lost Years? And why would they do that now when they've left them alone for all these years?"

As they talked, the high-pitched whine got closer and louder. Maeve could see a dozen drones in the sky, converging over what had been the high school.

"Gray, look! What are they doing?"

Maeve's words were drowned out by a huge explosion as the 12 drones dropped their bombs onto the school. Maeve pushed Gray farther into the trees to shelter from the flying debris. When the dust finally cleared, a massive crater filled the space where the school had once stood. Maeve glanced over to Emma's cave, relieved to see the opening was still there. As she watched, an arm appeared, giving her a wave. Maeve breathed a sigh of relief knowing that Emma was safe from the attack.

"What do we do now?" Maeve asked. "With WG drones in the area, do we risk heading back? Can those drones see us?"

"I don't know a lot about the drones," Gray said. "They're kind of a top secret thing. My uncle told me about them before we left. It was the first time he's ever mentioned them." Maeve lifted her eyebrows when Gray paused and looked at her. "He said they're mostly used for surveillance and bombing. But they've been kept secret from the people of Palumbra. Only a handful of people know about them. If they're still in the area, they might be able to detect us, but their surveillance capabilities are limited to taking photos of the area. They can't find us by picking up our body heat or our movement."

"Gray, why did your uncle tell you about them before we left?" Maeve stared at the destruction and scanned the air for any sign of the drones, but they had disappeared as quickly as they had appeared.

Gray stared at the ground. "I don't know, Maeve. Maybe he was trying to warn me. He was very specific about what they could and couldn't do." He lifted his eyes. "You don't think he sent them, do you?"

Maeve shrugged. "Who else knew we were out here?" She shouldered her pack and began to walk through the woods. Gray stopped her with a hand on her sleeve.

"I don't know why Night tried to warn me about the drones, but he wouldn't have sent them after us, Maeve."

Maeve spun around, leaves flying out from under her feet. "Listen, Gray. I don't know what your uncle is doing. He doesn't seem to want to confide in us any more than he wants us to know. That makes me not willing to take him at his word. I know you love him and trust him, but something here doesn't add up."

Gray straightened and gripped the strap of his pack more tightly. "I won't give up on him. I know he wouldn't intentionally harm us."

"But what about unintentionally?"

Gray didn't say anything. He just stood there, gripping his pack until his knuckles were white. He slowly shook his head and his chin dipped toward his chest. "I really don't know."

Maeve took in the sheen of sweat on Gray's forehead and the damp spots under his arms and deliberately relaxed her shoulders. She took a step toward Gray, trying to bridge the distance that had opened between them that was much greater than the 3 feet that physically separated them. She held out her hand, bit her lip and waited.

Gray stared at her hand, then lifted his eyes to hers. "What do we do now?"

Still extending her hand, Maeve shrugged her shoulders and said, "I guess we head back to Palumbra and see if we can get some answers." Even though Maeve's arm was getting tired she refused to drop her hand. Gray would have to deliberately snub her offer of reconciliation before she gave up. "For what it's worth, I hope you're right about your uncle. I wouldn't want him to betray you. I know what that feels like. I wouldn't wish that on you."

Gray looked from her face to her outstretched hand, and Maeve knew he could see the pain in her eyes. Gray nodded and slowly took her hand in his, intertwining their fingers and pulling her toward him with his good arm. He leaned down until their foreheads were touching. "I'm sorry," Gray said quietly. "I would never have wished that for you, either."

Maeve swallowed and nodded. They stood in silence, hands intertwined and foreheads touching, until Maeve stepped back. She had no idea how much time had passed, but the storm between them seemed to be over.

"Come on," she said. "We need to get back.

How do we avoid these drones if they come back?"

"We do our best to keep to the cover of the trees to avoid being seen. And we hurry," Gray said.

"What are we going to do?" Ginger asked Silas as she stared at the drones above her head. Crouched in the forest behind some bushes, she hugged Emery close. "Do you think they're looking for us?"

"M-M-Maybe?" Silas said. "I've never seen anything like them. What do they do?"

"They're drones," Emery said. "I saw a picture of them in an old book once. They can do surveillance, drop bombs and shoot missiles, but there's no one on board. They're run by remote control. I didn't know they still existed. The book I saw them in was from before The Lost Years."

"The bigger question is why are they here, and how do we avoid them?" Ginger said. "Any ideas?"

They had made it to the top of the hill outside the ruins of the city before they had seen the drones. Not knowing what they were, they had immediately taken cover in the forest then watched as the drones headed into the ruins and hovered over the buildings they had just left. The drones dropped their bombs, and the ruins went up in smoke and flame.

"Do you think those drones belong to the WG?" Ginger asked.

"I don't think anyone else would have that kind

of fire power," Silas replied.

"Definitely the WG," Emery said with a nod. "And we're in trouble because those drones haven't left."

"Why do you think they're sticking around?" Ginger asked.

"I think they m-m-might be looking for us," Silas answered.

"How would they know we're out here?" Emery asked.

"I don't know," Ginger said, scanning the sky with anxious eyes. "But it seems like too much of a coincidence for the WG to suddenly decide to bomb buildings at the same time we're looking for a building. What should we do now?"

"We should keep to the cover of the trees and try to m-m-make our way back to the tunnels. We can probably get there in a day. But we can't be seen. Those drones aren't a joke."

"OK," Emery said as she grabbed Ginger's hand. "Let's go."

At the edge of the forest, they stopped. One hundred yards of open land with nowhere to hide stood between them and the entrance to the tunnels. After traveling for most of the day, the sun was setting to the west. Silas shook his head.

"There's no way across without exposing ourselves to the drones," he said.

"Are we sure the drones are still out there?" Ginger asked. "We haven't seen them since this morning."

"N-n-no," Silas said as he frowned. "But there's no way to be sure."

"We need to get this information back to Palumbra and meet up with Gray and Maeve," Ginger said. "We can't sit here and wait forever. The longer we're out here, the more likely it is we'll run into a WG patrol."

"One of us could try to cross the open space to see if it's safe," Ginger suggested. Her gaze traveled all around the clearing.

"I can do it," Emery said.

"You are definitely not doing it," Ginger said. "It will either be Silas or me."

"But, I'm the smallest and the fastest," Emery pointed out. "It makes more sense for me to do it than either of you. I'm carrying less weight and I don't have to worry about a gun."

Ginger looked at Silas. "Tell her why this is a bad plan."

Silas's gaze traveled from one sister to the other. He shook his head. "Emery, it's just too dangerous. I believe you could do it, but we can't let you go out there by yourself." He locked eyes with Ginger. "We should all cross together. It's the only way."

Ginger nodded and took one last look at the sky. "OK, the sky looks clear. Let's go."

Silas led the way out of the edge of the woods. The sky remained silent and clear. They jogged toward the center of the clearing together, with Silas and Ginger scanning the sky. Emery's gaze was locked on a tree on the other side as she jogged slightly in front of

Silas and Ginger.

A high-pitched whine caused both Silas and Ginger to slow and scan the sky, allowing Emery to get even farther ahead. Three drones zoomed out over the tops of the trees they were heading toward. Ginger reached for Emery only to find she wasn't there. She raised her eyes in horror as the drones bore down on her sister.

"Emery!" Ginger cried. She froze as Silas quickened his stride and closed the space between them and Emery. "Come on!" he yelled over his shoulder. Ginger began running and could only watch in horror as the drone dropped its cargo. Silas leaped for Emery, snagging her around the waist, throwing her to the ground and covering her with his body. The bomb exploded.

Ginger pulled her gun forward and began firing at the drones. "Come on, Ginger. You can do it," she commanded herself. She stopped running and took careful aim. As much as she wanted to get to her sister and Silas, she had to get rid of those drones first.

Her first shot missed completely. "You can do it," she whispered. Her second shot clipped the edge of the drone that had dropped the bomb. It wobbled in the air before plummeting to the ground. "One down, two to go," she told herself.

As the two remaining drones turned back toward her, she steadied her gun and pulled the trigger. She scored a direct hit. As the drone spiraled into the ground, she was already lining up her next shot. But the third drone moved back over the trees in retreat. Ginger sprinted for Emery and Silas, keeping a wary eye on the sky.

"Emery! Silas!" Ginger called as she ran.

"I'm here!" Emery called back. "Hurry! Silas is hurt!"

Through the smoke from the bomb, Ginger could just make out Emery leaning over someone on the ground. "What's wrong with him?" Ginger panted as she reached Emery.

Before Emery could reply, three more drones appeared in the sky. "Emery, grab his other arm. We have to get into the cover of the trees. We're sitting ducks out here."

"Ginger, he's too heavy," Emery said. "We can't move him."

"Emery, we have to − even if it hurts him. We'll all die out here."

They tugged and pulled Silas the last 25 yards to the trees as the drones settled above them. "Why aren't they dropping any more bombs?" Emery asked.

"I think they're watching us, hoping we'll lead them to our hiding place," Ginger said as she leaned over with her hands on her knees trying to catch her breath. "Or maybe they're just keeping track of us so the WG can find us. Once we get under the trees, we should be OK for a bit. The trees are too close for those things to fly low. As long as they don't drop another bomb, we'll make it."

"What if they can find us through the trees?" Emery asked.

"That's a chance we're going to have to take," Ginger said as she leaned over to examine Silas. He was covered in blood and burns, but the worst was a wound to his abdomen where a piece of shrapnel from the bomb was lodged. Ginger looked out over the clearing and saw the trail of blood where they had dragged him. Her heart sank. They were being hunted, and she was no doctor. She quickly felt for a pulse and was relieved to feel a faint thump-thump.

"We have to get the bleeding slowed down," Ginger said. "Give me something to bandage this wound with. I don't want to pull the shrapnel out until we have him in a safe place."

Emery handed Ginger a t-shirt from her pack. As Ginger pressed down on Silas's wound in an effort to staunch the blood, Silas moaned and his eyes flickered open. "What happened?" he whispered.

"You saved Emery," Ginger said as she continued to press down on the make-shift bandage. "But you took the brunt of the bomb. I'm trying to stop the blood so we can get back to the tunnels."

Silas tried to sit up but fell back to the ground with another groan as pain glazed his eyes.

"Silas, I know it hurts, but we have to move you. We have to get back to the tunnels before the WG find us. Emery and I will help you, but we have to get you to your feet."

Ginger used her belt to hold the makeshift bandage in place around Silas's abdomen, then shifted to provide support as he once again made the effort to sit. Together with Emery, Ginger somehow got Silas to his feet. She and Emery half-carried, half-dragged Silas toward the secret entrance to the tunnels. Ginger silently prayed they would encounter no WG patrols because she couldn't reach her gun.

"The entrance isn't far, Silas," Emery said. "You can make it."

Silas grunted and hung his head, trying to mask the pain.

"Ginger," Emery whispered. "We're a day away from the tunnels."

"No, we're not. If I remember the map correctly, there's an entrance up ahead."

Emery thought about it for a minute as if looking at the map in her head. "But that tunnel isn't marked safe."

"It can't be any more dangerous than out here. We'll just have to take our chances."

Step by painstaking step, they made their way to the tree that marked an entrance to the tunnels. When they reached the tree, Ginger nodded at Emery to go first. Emery slipped into an almost unnoticeable gap in the trunk. Ginger pushed Silas through the gap next and, with a last look around, she slipped in as well.

Emery had already begun descending the ladder in the hollow trunk while Silas was propped up against tree trunk near the opening. "Silas, we have to get down this ladder. I'm going to go first. When I get two steps down, you follow. I'll support you on the way down. Can you do it?"

Silas remained silent, but he slowly nodded his head.

272

With extreme caution and a lot of grunting and sweating, they made their way down the ladder. Ginger breathed a sigh of relief when they reached the safety of the tunnels.

"Where are we?" Ginger asked Emery as she supported Silas. His breathing was shallow and his bandage was soaked through with blood.

"I think we're north of our regular quarters," Emery said. "It doesn't look like this is a WG-controlled area of the tunnels."

"Lead the way," Ginger said. "I'll help Silas."

Emery set off at a slow pace in deference to Silas's condition. Ginger put both arms around Silas, careful to avoid his wound and hauled him along down the seemingly deserted tunnel. It wasn't until they turned the corner that they came face to face with five people pointing guns at them.

"Who are you?" said the dark-skinned teen at the front of the group.

Emery slowly raised her hands and looked at Ginger.

CHAPTER TWENTY-EIGHT

"Who are <u>you</u>?" Ginger asked as she pushed Emery behind her with the arm she wasn't using to support Silas.

"You're in our tunnel," the boy said. Ginger took in his muscled arms and the large gun he was pointing at her. With her arms full supporting Silas, she hoped they were friendly as she had no chance of getting to her gun. And they had even less chance at running away.

"Look," Ginger said. "I don't know who you are. I'm hoping you're not with the WG, but if you are, there's nothing I can do about it. My friend needs help, and I don't have time to stand around talking about it. I'll take it from whoever I can get it from."

The dark-skinned giant's eyes widened in surprise when she mentioned the WG. "We're definitely not with the WG. The WG is after us."

"Well, welcome to the party. Pretty sure we're enemies numbers 3, 4 and 5. My friends who are still out there somewhere probably rank 1 and 2. Now, will you help me?" she said as Silas slumped against her.

"How do we know he's really hurt and this isn't all just a ruse to infiltrate The Resistance?" he asked.

"You don't, but do we look like we're faking it? The longer we stand here, the more blood he loses. I'm pretty sure he's unconscious now. Either help us or get out of the way. If my friend dies because you delayed us, you'll live to regret it."

"OK," he finally relented and lowered his gun. "We'll help you, but know that we're watching your every move."

"Great," Ginger said. "Watch away. Now get us to some medical supplies."

The muscled teen nodded to two of his cohorts, and they hurried over to help Ginger with Silas. They quickly made their way through the tunnel to a brightly lit room on the right. As they stepped through the door, all conversation in the room came to a halt as the occupants of the room stared at the newcomers.

"We need a medic!" the boy yelled as he entered the room in her wake. Immediately, a girl with braided hair and a white tunic stood along with a boy of about the same age with matching hair color and facial features. They made their way to the table where the two helpers had laid Silas's limp form.

"These are your medics?" Emery asked. "They're not that much older than me."

"They know enough," the boy said. "They've had plenty of practice."

Ginger stood next to Silas, holding his hand and praying they had gotten help in time.

"Come on, Silas. Hang on," she whispered.

The two medics gestured to a few other people

in the room and they quickly joined them at the table. "We're going to have to take that shrapnel out," said the boy medic. "And he's going to lose more blood. He may not survive it."

"What's the other choice?" Ginger asked.

"There is no other choice," the girl with the braids said. "If we leave it in, he'll die. If we take it out, he has a chance. But even if he survives the blood loss, he still has burns to worry about it. And then there's infection. We'll do our best, but he's in a bad way."

"Silas," Ginger said as a tear crept down her cheek. She leaned down and whispered in his ear. "You can't die. You saved Emery. You have to live."

When she stepped back from the table to let the medics do their work, she saw Emery at another table with her head buried in her arms on the table. Ginger sat down next to her and stroked her back. "This is all my fault," Emery said through her tears.

"Oh, Em," Ginger said. "You didn't do anything wrong. Don't blame yourself. Just pray Silas makes it." Emery laid her head on Ginger's shoulder and began to cry quietly. Suddenly, food appeared in front of them. Ginger looked into the coffee-colored eyes of the boy from the tunnels. With Ginger sitting down, he seemed even larger than when she had been staring into the end of his gun.

"I thought you might be hungry," he said, taking the seat next to her. "You three look like you've been through a lot."

"I'm not really hungry," Ginger said. "Too

worried about him." She tilted her head toward the area where Silas was being worked on by at least six people. "Thanks for your help."

"Sorry I was so harsh," he said. "I'm Tristan, by the way. We can never be too careful down here. But he's clearly not faking it."

"I'm Ginger. This is Emery. That's Silas."

"Nice to meet all of you," Tristan said with a little wave. "Want to tell me your story?"

"I can't tell you everything, but we got caught in a WG drone attack," Ginger said as she rubbed Emery's back and tried to work up some enthusiasm for the food in front of her.

"Drones?" Tristan pushed his chair back in surprise. "The WG has drones? We had no idea. Can you describe them?"

Ginger spent the next five minutes slowly eating and giving Tristan a detailed description of the drones. To her surprise, most of her meal was gone when she finished talking.

"I have to share this information with The Resistance leaders," Tristan said. "Don't go anywhere."

As soon as he left, Ginger looked up to see the girl with the braids standing next to her. "You need to come," she said quietly.

Ginger grabbed Emery's hand and they followed the girl to where Silas lay. "We've done everything we can," she said sadly. "He lost so much blood, and we have no way to replace it. We have no facilities for a transfusion, and even if we did, we can't weaken the healthy to save the dying."

Emery stumbled at the word dying. Ginger steadied her and said "Silas can't be dying."

"I'm so sorry," the medic said. "He's awake and is asking for you. Stay with him as long as you want."

"Silas?" Ginger whispered as she and Emery approached the table that was serving as a make-shift hospital bed. The room was cleaner than any of the other tunnel rooms they had seen. Rows of cots lined the room, but Silas's cot was the only one occupied. A couple of medics stood in the corner talking quietly and watching them. Where there had been a flurry of activity earlier, now there was just Silas, Ginger and Emery. Ginger took his hand.

"Hey," Silas said in a thready, weak voice. "Why the long face? It's going to be OK."

"Oh, Silas," Ginger said. "I'm so sorry we dragged you into this."

On the other side of the bed, tears streamed down Emery's cheeks. "I'm sorry, Silas. I never meant for you to get hurt. I didn't know you and Ginger had stopped."

"N-N-No worries, sport," Silas said. "You thought the drones were gone. I'd do it again if I needed to. I guess no one will call me a coward any more." The corners of his mouth lifted in a weak grin.

"Silas, you were never a coward," Ginger said with force. "You're one of the bravest people I know. Thank you for saving my sister."

Silas's eyes fluttered and his breathing became

more labored. "Emery, can you go find m-m-me a glass of water?" Silas asked. Emery looked at Ginger. She gave a slight nod.

"OK. Don't go anywhere until I get back." She leaned over and kissed Silas on the cheek. "Thank you." She hugged his shoulders and backed slowly away. One of the medics who had been talking on the other side of the room took her hand and led her away, leaving Ginger and Silas alone.

"Ginger?"

"I'm here."

"It's getting kind of dark in here, don't you think?" Ginger looked at the lights on the ceiling blazing brightly.

"They turn the lights down when it's time for bed," she lied.

"You're a terrible liar. I'm dying, aren't I?"

Ginger nodded as a single tear slid down her cheek. "I'm sorry, Silas. They did everything they could."

"I know." He grasped her hand tighter. "Just don't leave me, OK."

"Never!"

"It was quite an adventure wasn't it." Silas coughed. "Wish I could see it through to the end." He coughed again, and Ginger offered him a sip of water. She started to speak but found her throat had closed, so she squeezed his hand instead.

"My dad always told me to never leave a job unfinished. I hate to disappoint him."

Ginger found her voice. "You're definitely not

disappointing your dad. He's going to be really proud of what you've done."

Silas closed his eyes. "I'm afraid of the dark." He struggled to catch his breath. "I always have been. When I was little, my mom would tell me stories at bedtime when it was time to turn out the lights. They were stories about brave boys who stood up for what's right."

"Sounds like you have a great mom." Ginger helped him take another drink of water.

"It's getting dark, Ginger." Silas grasped her hand tightly. "Tell me a story about someone brave."

Ginger swallowed and took a deep breath. "Once upon a time, there was a boy named Silas..." Ginger spoke until her voice was hoarse. She told of a boy named Silas who slayed dragons and saved princesses. The whole time, Ginger watched the slow rise and fall of Silas's chest.

Silas's eyes fluttered open. "Ginger," he said. "Finish the job. For me."

His eyes fell closed again. His breathing slowed. Ginger held tight to his hand until it went slack in her grip, and still she held on. She had no idea how long she had been sitting there when the girl medic with the braids came over and gently pried her hand away. "He's gone," she said.

Ginger laid her head on the table next to Silas and wept.

CHAPTER TWENTY-NINE

"Ginger, Ginger! Wake up," Maeve said.

Ginger sat up abruptly, briefly disoriented. "What? Who?" She looked around and found Maeve and Gray kneeling next to her pallet on the floor.

"Maeve!" Ginger threw herself into Maeve's arms and began sobbing.

Maeve hugged Ginger close as Gray looked on helplessly. "Tristan told us about Silas," Maeve said, reaching up to wipe her own eyes. Ginger continued to sob, and Maeve wondered if she would ever stop.

"Shh," she whispered as she rubbed circles on Ginger's back. While Ginger comforted Maeve, Emery crept over to Gray's side and tugged on his hand. Gray winced as the movement caused pain to tear through his shoulder.

"It was my fault," Emery whispered.

"What?" Gray knelt knelt beside Emery. "I doubt that."

Emery nodded and wiped her nose with the back of her hand. "I got too far ahead. He had to run after me and then he threw himself on top of me when the bomb went off."

Ginger's sobs had subsided and she and Maeve were watching the exchange between Emery and Gray. Gray turned questioning eyes toward Maeve. Ginger shook her head, stood and pulled Emery into a hug. "It wasn't her fault. No one did anything wrong. We just got caught by WG drones."

"He was the bravest of all of us," Maeve said as she wiped away her own tears. "And he always thought he wasn't."

"He knew in the end though," Ginger said. "I made sure of it."

"He was lucky to have had you two by his side," Gray said while looking at Emery. "He wouldn't have wanted you to think his death was your fault."

Emery nodded but didn't look convinced. Maeve squeezed Emery's hand in reassurance, but she knew it would be a long while before Emery believed them.

"Ginger, you said the WG drones dropped bombs on you?" Gray said. "Were you in those buildings when they dropped the bombs?"

"No. We were on our way back to the tunnels. They definitely targeted us."

Gray held up a hand before Maeve could say anything. "I know what you're going to say. I still say my uncle wouldn't harm us, but I agree we have some questions for him."

Ginger gaped. "You think his uncle sent those drones after us?"

"I don't know if he did it intentionally, but he's

the only one who knew where we were going," Maeve said with a shrug.

Ginger drew her eyebrows together and cocked her head. "How did he know?"

Gray looked at the ground. "I might have left him a note."

Ginger's gaze skittered from Maeve's resigned face to Gray's sheepish one and back again. "I think we have a lot to talk about. How did you guys even find us, anyway?"

Gray blew out a breath and said, "It's a long story. Let's find some food, and we'll tell you all about it."

"We need to have a service for Silas," Emery said without looking up from her breakfast. "The Resistance leaders insist we can't bury him. They burn all bodies, but we need to do something to remember him."

"She's right," Ginger said. "We can't just let his death go unmarked. I know we have important things to do, but Silas was important, too."

"Let's do something tonight," Maeve suggested as she took a seat next to Ginger. "I don't think it's safe to go above ground, but we could go back to our original quarters and have a private moment."

Everyone nodded in agreement. The solemn quartet had found a table off to the edge of the room to eat their breakfast. The Resistance members left them mostly alone, not wanting to intrude on their reunion or their grief.

They ate in silence, the only sound the clinking of their forks against their plates, until Gray said, "I know we're all missing Silas, but we have to talk about what we've learned. The WG is definitely looking for us, and I don't know how much longer it's going to be before they find these tunnels."

"Did you guys find the building? Did you find anything to help us?" Maeve asked.

"We found it," Ginger said. "But it's not an old ruin. It's a recent one."

"What?" Maeve turned to face Ginger. "Are you sure?"

Ginger nodded. "The WG was using that building for some kind of research. Then they bombed it themselves to make it look like a ruin. We met a guy. His name was Elton. He died, too." Ginger paused. "He told us to 'Save the children,' and we found a list of names."

Emery pulled the list from her pack. "It's all the teenagers in Palumbra," she said. "We have no idea why the WG wants all the teenagers, but they made a list."

"And I think Elton wanted us to save them. But from what?" Ginger asked.

Maeve and Gray exchanged a look. "I think we know."

"We met Emma," Maeve said.

"Emma? Who's Emma," Ginger asked.

"Emma from the video?" Emery chimed in.

"Yes, Emma from the video," Gray said.

"But she must be almost 90 by now," Ginger said.

"She is," Maeve replied. "She's been living in hiding for the past 70 years."

"We found the school that was in the video," Gray said. "Emma told us that when she was in high school, the government used all the teenagers to create powerful energy weapons."

"What?" Ginger said. "That doesn't make any sense. How could teenagers make energy weapons?"

"They didn't make them, Ginger," Gray said. "They were the energy weapon."

"What? How?"

"They harnessed the energy from their brain waves and boosted them to create an energy weapon," Maeve explained.

"Wait," Emery said. "Brain waves don't produce a lot of energy. Sure, theoretically, you could harness the power of brain waves to make some energy, but certainly not enough to create a powerful weapon."

"I know," Maeve said. "But they hooked thousands of teenagers to this big machine and somehow it took the energy from their brain waves and magnified it to make an energy weapon. That's how Palumbra survived The Lost Years."

Emery looked thoughtful. "I guess it's possible. Did the machine still work?"

"No," Maeve said. "And it doesn't exist any more."

"Why not?" asked Ginger.

"Because the WG drones dropped bombs on it when we were leaving," Gray said.

"So you think the WG is trying to recreate this

weapon somehow?" Ginger asked, bringing the focus back to their discussion.

"Based on the information you found and what we saw, I think that's the most likely scenario," Gray said. "What we don't know is why the WG is doing this. If Palumbra is the only place left, who are they going to fight?"

"Maybe we're not the only ones left," Maeve suggested.

"What do you mean?" Ginger asked.

"Ginger, The River doesn't end at the edge of Palumbra," Maeve replied.

"What?" Emery exclaimed. "How is that possible? On every map, it ends in the lake."

"It keeps going on the other side," Gray said. "Our map shows it continuing on. We followed it and found the school and Emma."

"Why does the WG not want anyone to know what's out there?" Emery asked.

"It's a good question, Emery," Gray said. "One we need to find the answer to."

"Who wants to start?" Maeve asked.

They were gathered in their original quarters in the tunnels, each holding a paper flower that Ginger had fashioned out of scrap paper. The Resistance medics had patched up Gray's shoulder the best they could. He was continuing to drink the willow bark tea Emma had given them, and the medics had given him a shot to ward off infection, but Maeve was still worried he would end up like Silas. She shook her head. She couldn't think about that now.

"I will," Emery said.

"Silas was the best. He watched out for me. And he did brave things even when he was afraid. He was the reason we found Elton. He was the reason I'm alive today. I'm going to miss him." She placed her flower on the table. She shook her head, unable to go on. Ginger hugged her close and rubbed her back.

"Silas was my friend for a long time," Maeve said. She swallowed hard and sniffed. "I wish I had made more of an effort to know him better before this all started. He struggled to express himself with words, but he proved to be the bravest and most loyal of friends. This wasn't his fight, but he made it his − because of us. Rest well, Silas." Maeve dropped her flower on the table next to Emery's.

"I didn't know Silas long," Gray said as he put his good arm around Maeve. "But he made an impression. He stood up for what was right − even when he didn't have to." He paused and took a deep breath. "He wasn't a soldier, and he didn't think he was brave. But when it came time to make the right decision, he didn't hesitate. You will be missed." Gray gently set his flower on the table with the other two.

"I didn't really know Silas until he joined our group." Ginger walked up to the table. Her flower shook in her hand. "In the time I knew him, he was the bravest person I've ever met. This whole thing terrified him, but he led the way. And he saved my sister at the cost of his own life." She swiped a hand over her face. "I'll never forget you, my friend." Tears overflowed down Ginger's cheeks as she set the flower on the table with the others.

The four friends formed a circle. "May God protect and keep your soul – until we meet again," Maeve said as they hugged in silence.

"What now?" Maeve asked the next morning at breakfast. They had slept in their original quarters but had returned to The Resistance end of the tunnels for breakfast. Gray sat next to her, slowly rotating his injured shoulder.

"How does it feel?" Maeve asked.

"Not good," Gray answered.

"Maybe you should have it looked at by the medics again."

"Not much more they can do. It just has to heal."

Maeve noted Gray's pale face and a few sweat drops on his forehead. She touched his forehead. "Gray, you have a fever again. You have to get help."

"I'll be fine. It's not as bad as it was on the way back."

"How was your trip back?" Ginger said. "You never told us."

288

"It was pretty bad," Maeve said at the same time Gray said, "It was fine."

Maeve stared at him in disbelief. "It was not fine! You could barely walk for half the trip. If we'd been discovered by those drones, we both would have died. You couldn't carry a gun or a pack, and I could barely get you to put one foot in front of the other."

"OK, so maybe fine isn't the best description," Gray conceded.

"Finally, on our third day back, the tea Emma had given us seemed to work and his fever broke. So, I'm a little concerned that it's back. I thought you were on the mend."

Gray waved off her concern. "I'll be fine. Let's talk about what we should do next."

Maeve and Ginger exchanged looks, but they silently agreed to change the topic.

"I think we need to check in with my uncle," Gray said.

"Yeah, you can ask him why those drones came after us," Maeve said bitterly.

"That's definitely a question on my list. We also need to find out what's going on in the city since the bombings."

"I can help with that," Tristan said as he placed his plate on the table.

"This is Tristan," Ginger said.

"We've met," Gray said. "He helped us find you when we got back."

"How did you find us?" Ginger asked.

"We got back to our original area in the tunnels and found John," Gray explained. "He had heard about the two girls and the wounded boy that had stumbled into this end of the tunnels. He contacted Tristan and Tristan led us here."

"Well, Tristan and I met when he pointed a gun in my face as I tried to help Silas into the tunnels," Ginger said.

"Not my best moment." Tristan hung his head. "In my defense, I had no idea who you were. I am sorry about your friend, though. He seemed like a good guy, and I know he got hurt protecting you." He nodded in Emery's direction. Emery nodded and turned her head away. Maeve reached over and patted Emery's hand.

"How do you all know each other," Tristan asked.

"Maeve and I have been friends since we were kids," Ginger said. "Gray's a new addition."

"I keep thinking you look familiar," Tristan said to Gray. Gray nodded. "You might know my uncle. Night Cantwell."

"Your uncle is Night Cantwell? He's a huge asset to The Resistance."

"Glad you think so," Gray said with a touch of sarcasm that Maeve knew was directed at her.

Ginger stepped in before Maeve could say anything. "Can you tell us what's been going on in Palumbra for about the past week? We've been out of the loop, you could say."

"Well, you know about the bombings, right?"

Four heads nodded in unison.

290

"Since then everything has been on lockdown. Curfews in place. Soldiers patrolling the streets. You have to have a reason to be out, and even then you need papers to prove it. Everything except essential businesses are shut down. The WG put out the word that the bombings were done by The Resistance. Except they weren't. We had nothing to do with them. We would never bomb innocent people."

"We know," Ginger said. "The WG bombed the buildings themselves."

"What?" Tristan exclaimed. "Why would they do that?"

"We're not exactly sure," Gray stepped in before Ginger could say any more. Ginger looked at him with questioning eyes but said no more.

"What is The Resistance doing?" Gray asked, turning the conversation away from territory that could lead to their more recent adventures.

"We're lying low. It's too dangerous up there for us. More and more of our members are congregating down here." Tristan waved a hand around the room. "The WG has been rounding up known Resistance sympathizers."

"So, what's your role?" Maeve asked.

"I'm part of The Resistance leadership. That's how I know about his uncle."

Maeve looked at him skeptically. "Aren't you a little young?"

"Look around, Maeve," Tristan said with a sweep of his hand. "We're all young. Most of the older leadership of The Resistance was captured before we could get the warning out. What's left are the people the WG didn't know about. Mostly young people."

"Do you know if Silas's parents made it?" Emery asked softly.

"I don't, Emery. But I can find out."

"Please do," Ginger said. "They need to know about Silas."

"You guys are welcome to join The Resistance," Tristan said as he stood. "We need more people like you. Find me if you need anything."

Silence reigned for several minutes after Tristan left as they each ate their breakfast and worked their way through their own thoughts.

"Can we trust him?" Maeve asked Ginger.

"I think so. He's been nothing but kind to us after I convinced him we weren't WG plants."

"OK," Gray said. "We need to talk to my uncle, then put a plan into place to keep the WG from completing their plans to recreate the energy weapon of The Lost Years."

"Are you sure, Gray?" Maeve asked gently. "It wasn't coincidence that those drones found all of us."

"Maeve." Gray took her hand and rubbed his thumb over her knuckles. "Trust me. I have to believe my uncle isn't out to harm us. And we need to know what the WG knows. It's our only hope of destroying their plans."

"I agree with Gray," Ginger said. "I'm not 100 percent sure about his uncle, but he's our only link to
292

the inner workings of the WG."

"Me too," Emery chimed in. "I think it's our only workable plan."

"OK," Maeve gave in. "I just hope we don't regret it."

CHAPTER THIRTY

Maeve and Gray entered the room, followed by Ginger and Emery. The lights were low in this room in a part of the tunnels Maeve didn't recognize. "Where are we?" she whispered to Gray.

"I'm not exactly sure," Gray replied. "I've never been to this part of the tunnels, but this is where my uncle said to meet."

"I don't like this, Gray. There are too many things we can't control."

"It will be OK, Maeve. My uncle will help us."

Maeve gave Ginger and Emery a wary glance. Ginger nodded at Maeve and squeezed Emery's hand.

Before Maeve could speak, Night stepped out of the shadows. He was dressed in the uniform of the WG government. Gray trousers, white shirt and black jacket with the WG insignia on the pocket. Maeve looked at her own rough trousers and compared them to the fine fabric of Night's ensemble and felt a twinge of jealousy and anger that Night was reaping rewards from working for the WG.

"Gray!" Night exclaimed as he pulled Gray into

a fierce hug. "I'm so glad you made it back."

"Not all of us," Ginger said bitterly.

"What?" Night said. "Where's your other friend? Silas, I think it was?"

"Dead," Ginger said bluntly. "The WG killed him."

"But how is that possible?" Night swept his gaze around the room as if hoping to see Silas. "I kept the patrols away from the areas where you would be."

"Yeah. Well, that didn't work out so well for us," Maeve said. "But it was those drones that really set us back."

"Drones?" Night wrinkled his forehead in confusion. "We didn't send out any drones."

Night looked Gray over from head to toe. "What happened to you?" he asked when he noted the stiff way Gray held his arm away from his body.

"I took a bullet in the arm from one of those patrols we weren't supposed to run into."

"That's not possible." Night shook his head as he examined Gray's arm. "I specifically moved the patrols out of your way."

"Well, one of them didn't get the message," Maeve said as she stepped toward Gray. "Gray got shot by your non-existent patrol, and Silas was killed by a drone you didn't send."

"I don't understand," Night said as he took a step back, his eyes wide with bewilderment. He held his hands out palms up. "I didn't know anything about any of this."

He turned to Gray. "Are you OK? Do you need

295

medical attention?"

"We've done the best we can," Gray said. "There aren't a lot of medical supplies available down here. But I think the infection is gone. It just needs to heal."

Night paled. "Infection? You could have died."

"That's what happens when you get shot," Maeve said.

Night sat. "Oh no," he said. "I never meant for this to happen when you got involved. I was sure I could protect you."

Maeve felt a tingle up her spine. She looked around uneasily. The only door was behind them. She motioned with her hand for Emery and Ginger to start backing toward the door. Carefully, she took a step back, grabbing Gray's hand as she did.

Gray looked at her, then at Emery and Ginger. He shook his head, disbelievingly. Maeve knew the instincts honed in his training as a soldier had to be tingling. Slowly, he took a step backward.

"I'm so sorry, Gray," Night said as he stood up. Tears shimmered in his eyes as he stepped forward. "You were never supposed to get hurt."

Suddenly, soldiers appeared out of the shadows of the dimly lit room, blocking the exit. Guns pointed at them from all sides. Maeve slowly raised her hands.

"This wasn't the plan," Night said as the tears spilled over down his cheek. "You were supposed to stay out of the way down here in the tunnels. I could have kept you safe. But you," he pointed at Maeve, "discovered something we didn't know existed. Now
296

you know too much. I'm so sorry."

Gray looked at his uncle in disbelief. "But I thought you were helping us. Why would you do this to me? After all we've been through together? Was it all a lie?"

Night put his hands on Gray's shoulders and looked intently into his face. "I love you, Gray. More than you even know. I've been trying to keep you safe. I really have."

Gray motioned to the soldiers. "This is keeping me safe? Us safe?"

Night pulled Gray in for a hug and whispered in his ear, "Trust me. It will all work out."

Night stepped back and squeezed Gray's shoulders. "I'll come see you as soon as I can. Just do what you're told, and you'll all be fine."

Soldiers had surrounded Maeve, Ginger and Emery while Gray and his uncle were talking. Maeve stared at Night and Gray with wide, scared eyes. "Gray?" she said. The soldier behind her poked her with the end of his rifle and told her to be quiet.

Gray looked at his uncle. "I can get you out of this," Night said. "But I can't free them." Night motioned to Maeve and the others. "You have to choose."

Gray stared at his uncle. Maeve chewed her lip as Gray cocked his head as if he didn't understand what his uncle was asking, then he locked eyes with her. Gray shook his head. "I'm not leaving my friends."

Night's shoulders fell. "All right," he said to the soldiers. "I have no choice. Take them away."

The soldiers stripped Gray of his gun. Maeve

had left her pack with all the information they had gathered with The Resistance. The soldiers pushed Gray toward the group near the door. Emery huddled into Ginger's side. Maeve glanced at Ginger and tipped her head toward the door.

A soldier pushed his gun into Maeve's back. "You first, missy."

Maeve moved through the door with the soldier at her back.

As she stepped through the doorway in front of the soldier, a hand grabbed Maeve, pulling her to the side. The soldier that followed her through met with a swift and silent end. The same thing happened three more times until Maeve, Emery, Ginger and Gray were having their ties cut and being handed guns. Maeve smiled when she saw Tristan's familiar form.

"Hi, Maeve." Tristan gave her a mock salute.

The hallway had descended into chaos as the soldiers realized their prisoners had been stolen. Gray assessed the situation and motioned Maeve to keep moving. Looking at Tristan, he said, "How did you know we were in trouble?"

"Let's just say a night owl told us that we need to abandon the tunnels and get you guys out, too."

Maeve stopped suddenly and said, "Night told you to come get us?"

Gray fired his gun back toward the approaching soldiers as they ran.

Tristan motioned for Maeve to keep running as he, too, fired back toward the soldiers. Maeve resumed running, but asked again, "Night really told you we needed help?"

Tristan nodded. "We got a message not long after you left. It said the tunnels have been compromised and gave a location where you were headed. It matched what Gray had told me, so I decided you could use some backup."

Maeve stumbled as a bullet whizzed by her.

Gray grabbed her arm to keep her from falling. "We're a little busy right now. Can we get all the details later?" He gave her a gentle push to get her moving faster as he turned to fire behind him again..

About 30 Resistance members were fighting with the remaining soldiers. An alarm sounded in the distance. "Fall back," Maeve heard Tristan shout as a group of WG soldiers rounded the corner. The Resistance fighters were quickly becoming outnumbered. "Move!"

Maeve alternately ran and shot at the WG soldiers. She heard a thump and The Resistance member next to her fell to the ground. Maeve grabbed the girl's arm and hauled her to her feet. "Come on. Keep moving."

Gray appeared on the other side of the girl and they helped her down the tunnel. Two more Resistance soldiers took their places to help the girl when Maeve shouted over the din, "Where are we going?"

"We have to get out of the tunnels."

"Got any ideas?" Tristan shouted from behind them.

"Just one," Gray said.

"In here," Gray said as he darted into a room. Maeve entered the room with Ginger, Emery and Tristan right behind. Tristan slammed the door shut and wedged a piece of wood in the handle. It wouldn't hold the WG soldiers off long, but it might buy them some time.

"What about the others?" Ginger asked.

"They'll be fine," Tristan said. "They're trained fighters. They'll head to the surface, lose their pursuers and head to the backup safety zone on the surface."

"Why didn't we do that?" Emery asked.

"Because you guys are too valuable," Tristan answered. "The WG will follow you wherever you go. Apparently, you know too much. And you've made them look bad. Your faces are all over the official WG communications." Tristan glanced around the room, looking for another exit. "All of Palumbra is looking for you. It's safer for The Resistance if they think you're hiding out somewhere different."

Something hammered at the door. Maeve looked around frantically for an exist. "Gray! We're trapped. What were you thinking?"

Gray crouched on the floor and started moving dirt away with his hands. Tristan knelt next to him and began doing the same.

"Ginger," Gray said. "Keep a gun trained on that door. Shoot anyone who comes through. Maeve, Emery, help us."

When Maeve crouched next to Gray she saw the outline of a trap door. She began moving dirt with her hands. "What is this?"

300

"Our way out," Gray said as he quickly shoved the dirt aside. "I was just hoping this was the right room. My uncle showed it to me once."

"Where does it go?"

"Into the lower tunnels. No one has been down there in years."

"But won't the soldiers notice it once we've uncovered it?" Emery asked

"Maybe," Gray said, "but we can lose them down there. No one has mapped it."

"What if we get lost?" Maeve muttered under her breath.

Gray heard her. "You have a better idea?"

Maeve hung her head and pushed dirt aside faster. "No."

"Guys?" Ginger said frantically. Maeve looked at the door. It was starting to bend under whatever force was being applied from the other side. "You might want to get that door open. Now!"

"We've got it," Gray said as he and Tristan lifted the trap door. "Emery, go!"

Quickly, Emery climbed into the hole and descended into the darkness. A short scream echoed from the hole.

"Emery!" Ginger cried as she knelt next to the hole.

"I'm fine," Emery's shaky voice answered. "Be careful. The ladder is missing a rung after the fourth one."

"Ginger you're next," Tristan said from the position he had taken guarding the door.

As Ginger's head disappeared, Gray motioned

for Maeve to go. As she lowered herself down the ladder, she heard the sound of wood splintering. Gray's feet appeared on the rung above her hands. "Move it, everyone," he said. "They broke the wood holding the lock. We have to get out of here."

Maeve scrambled down the ladder as quickly as she could. The rungs were broken in some places, missing in others, making the mad dash downward treacherous. She heard the trap door slam shut and heard Gray say, "Can you wedge something into it?" but she was unable to make out Tristan's reply.

Finally, Maeve's feet hit solid ground. She stumbled away from the ladder to make room for Gray. Tristan followed quickly. "Is everyone here?" Gray asked in a voice that was more out of breath than Maeve thought it should be after the climb down the ladder.

"Yes," Emery said. "And I found the light I carry in my pack." She turned the light on. Maeve looked into the scared faces of her friends. Gray was sweating and pale and holding his injured arm stiffly. Maeve thought she saw blood seeping through his shirt on his injured shoulder.

"Let's move," Gray said. "It won't be long before they find that trap door." As if on cue, they heard a thump from above and dirt fell from around the ladder.

"I shoved a piece of wood I grabbed from the room in the handle, but it won't hold them long," Tristan said. He motioned to Gray. "Lead the way."

Gray snagged the light from Emery and moved off down the tunnel to the left. The tunnels were covered in cobwebs, and many of the timbers were rotting, causing the ceiling to sag in places. Dirt sifted down into their hair as they moved through the tunnel. The limited illumination from the light Gray held revealed places where parts of the tunnel ceiling had fallen to the ground, leaving a pile of earth they had to step around. Maeve could hear the skittering of tiny paws as she walked, and she shuddered as she wondered what creatures lived down here. Jogging to catch up with Gray, she said, "Do you know where we're going?"

"Away from the WG soldiers," Gray said with a grin. "But, yes, vaguely. I know there's another trap door in the room next to the one we used originally. I just need to figure out how to get there from here."

Behind them, they heard voices. "Kill the light," Tristan whispered.

Gray shut off the light, plunging them into darkness. Maeve reached for Gray's hand, needing the reassurance of another person in the Stygian blackness. Gray squeezed her hand in reassurance.

"We need to keep moving," Gray whispered.

"Go," Tristan replied. "I'll stay in the back."

"How can you see?" Maeve whispered.

"I can't," Gray replied. "Everyone put your hand on the person in front of you. Stay together. We can't afford for any of us to get separated."

Maeve tucked her fingers into Gray's belt loop, and she felt Emery's hand on her arm. She gave it a reassuring pat. She only hoped Ginger and Tristan were behind Emery. "We've got this, Emery. Stay close."

Slowly, Gray started to move. Maeve could tell he was keeping one hand on the wall to their left and one hand stretched in front of him.

Progress was slow. They made turn after turn until Maeve was hopelessly lost. The voices behind them grew fainter and fainter until Maeve could no longer hear them. "I think we've lost them," Maeve whispered to Gray.

"Maybe," he whispered back. "But we'll stay quiet and keep the light off for a bit longer."

Maeve bumped into Gray when he stopped and abruptly stepped back, causing a chain reaction with those behind her. "Ouch," she heard Ginger exclaim.

"What's going on?" Tristan asked.

"Um," Gray said. "I think we have a problem."

"We're wandering around in the dark in abandoned tunnels being chased by people who want to kill us," Ginger said. "How many more problems can we have?"

"We could fall into a big pit," Gray replied.

"What?" Tristan exclaimed. "Scooch over. Let me through."

Maeve stood on her tiptoes and peered over Gray's shoulder. She couldn't see anything, just darkness. "How do you know there's a pit?" she whispered.

"I stepped out and there was nothing," Gray said. "I almost fell in. We need to see how big it is, but I don't want to risk turning on the light."

"What if we covered the light with something?"

Emery asked.

"Like what?" Tristan asked.

Ginger dug in her pack and pulled out a dark T-shirt. "If we cover the light with this, the fabric should let enough light through that we can see without immediately giving away our location if those WG soldiers are still following us."

Gray took the shirt, knelt down and covered the light with it. He turned the light on, then pulled the shirt tight at the bottom to avoid letting large beams of light out. A dim glow filled the tunnel. As her eyes adjusted to the added light, Maeve saw Gray's pit ahead of them. The hole was deep and covered the entire floor of the tunnel except for a 6-inch-wide ledge on the right-hand side.

"What are we going to do?" Maeve asked. "Is there another way?"

"There might be," Gray said. "But I know we're headed in the right direction now. I'm not sure how long it will take us to find another tunnel that goes this way without getting lost down here ourselves."

"Plus, the WG is back there somewhere," Emery said.

"Do you think that ledge will take our weight?" Tristan asked.

"Only one way to find out," Gray said, stepping toward the ledge.

"Wait!" Maeve cried.

Gray turned back toward her, questions in his ice blue eyes.

"Shouldn't we tie a rope to you or something?

That way if the ledge crumbles, we might still save you?"

Tristan pulled a lightweight rope from his pack and one end of it to Gray. "Tie this around your waist. I'll hold the end until you get across."

Gray tied the rope around his waist. "Make sure you keep the rope out of my way," he said. Tristan nodded.

"Be careful," Maeve said and stood on tiptoe to kiss his cheek. "We can't do this without you."

Gray nodded and turned to the ledge.

Slowly, he placed one foot on the ledge, turning his body sideways to keep his back to the wall. Dirt crumbled beneath his foot. He moved his other foot to the ledge and began scooting his way across with excruciating slowness. Dirt crumbled every time he moved, and each step seemed to take an eternity. Finally, he was across. He untied the rope and looked around.

"I'm going to tie this end of the rope to that rock." He pointed to a large boulder that partially blocked the tunnel. "That way, I can keep my hands free to help when you guys get close."

Tristan wanted Emery to go across next. Emery backed away from the pit. "I can't," Emery said. "I'll fall."

Tristan knelt and looked Emery in the eye. "Emery, you are not going to fall. You can hold my hand as far as it will reach, and Gray is waiting to help you on the other side. The rope will catch you if you stumble." He tucked her hair behind her ear. "This is the only way across. You can do it."

Emery looked at Ginger, who nodded. "You can do it Em."

Emery nodded as Tristan tied the rope around her waist then took her by the hand and led her to the ledge. Emery bit her lip and Maeve could see her hands shaking as Ginger hugged her and whispered something in her ear. Emery slowly put a foot on the ledge. Dirt crumbled as she put her weight on the ledge. Emery whimpered.

"You're doing great, Emery," Tristan said. "Just keep going."

Emery clutched Tristan's hand so tightly that Maeve saw him wince, but inch by painstaking inch, she shuffled her way across.

"You have to let go now, Emery," Tristan said. "My arm won't reach any farther. Two more steps and you'll be able to reach Gray."

Emery whimpered again but released Tristan's hand – and froze. "I can't," she said in a trembling voice.

"Emery, you can," Ginger said. "It's just two steps."

"I can't. I can't move."

"Emery, listen to me," Ginger said calmly. "You have to move. It's just two steps. You can do it."

"I'm sorry, Ginger." Emery's voice caught. "I really can't."

"Remember when we were little and we would get scared of something? What did mom always say?"

"Don't let fear win."

"Right. Don't let fear win, Emery. It's two steps. Don't let mom down. She'd be so proud of you and how you've been so brave. Don't let fear win when we've come so far."

In the dim light, Emery looked at Ginger. And

started to move her feet.

Maeve breathed a sigh of relief when Gray's hand clasped Emery's and she made it the rest of the way across.

Ginger crossed next with no problems, but Maeve could see the weight of the others had caused some of the ledge to crumble away. As she tied the rope around her waist, she whispered to Tristan, "Is that ledge going to hold?"

"I hope so since I'm last. Just focus on getting across. Gray won't let you fall."

Maeve edged her way onto the ledge, keeping her back flat against the tunnel wall. She could hear dirt showering down into the pit every time she moved her feet. She was nearly across when she felt a large chunk of dirt loosen beneath her foot. Frantically, she grabbed for a handhold. Just as she found a divot in the wall, the earth fell away beneath her. She let out a shriek as she dangled by one hand over the abyss.

"Gray!" Maeve's terrified eyes met his horrified ones. She felt her fingers slipping as she tried to hold her bodyweight with one hand. Her feet swung in open space as she kicked out looking for a foothold.

"Hold still, Maeve," Gray said. He was quickly pulling the slack out of the rope tied around her waist.

"I'm going to fall," Maeve said. Her free hand skittered along the wall in a vain attempt to find another handhold. Her arm began to ache.

"No you're not. I've got you. Just hold on. You're almost here. It's not far. You can do it."

308

Maeve looked to her right and saw the edge of the pit 2 feet away. "I can barely hold on," she said. "How am I going to get over there?"

"You're going to swing your body just a little and let go."

"What?"

"Maeve, I've got you. I'm not going to let you fall. You just have to get your foot on the edge. We can work together. When you start swinging, I'll pull you with the rope. You can do this."

Maeve's hand slipped and her whole body jerked.

Gray tightened his grip on the rope and said, "On the count of three. 1, 2, 3."

Maeve swung her body slightly to the left just as she lost her grip on the divot. Her foot struck the ground. She had made it, but the momentum of her body pushed her forward and she stumbled. As she tried to right herself, the ground shifted again. Gray dove at her, pulling her to safety as the edge of the pit where she had been standing fell away under the force of her landing.

Maeve's whole body shook. She looked up into Gray's eyes and smiled. "Well, that was exciting."

"More excitement than we needed." Gray helped her to her feet and held onto her arms until her legs decided to support her weight. "Don't scare me like that again," Gray whispered into her ear. "We're in this together, remember?"

She was finally able to stand on her own, and Gray released her.

"Um, guys?" Tristan said from the other side.

"What do we do now?" He pointed at the 2-foot-long gap between the ledge and the other side.

"We need to bridge the gap somehow," Gray said. "Give me a minute."

Gray took the light behind the boulder. Maeve heard something breaking, and Gray came back with a board. It was old and looked nearly rotted. She gave the board a skeptical look. "Are you sure that's safer than him just jumping the gap?"

"No, but it's all we've got," Gray said. He placed the board over the gap. "OK, Tristan, give it a go."

"Shhh," Tristan held up his hand. "Do you hear that?"

In the far distance, Maeve could hear voices. "Tristan, you have to move!" she whispered.

"Kill the light," Tristan said. "It's giving away our position."

"But you can't cross in the dark," Ginger exclaimed. "You'll fall."

"We have to kill that light," Tristan said. "Otherwise we're all going to be dead."

Gray nodded and doused the light. In the pitch black, Maeve could hear Tristan moving toward the ledge. She prayed silently that he would cross safely. Gray placed the rope in her hands for extra support should Tristan stumble then they held their breath and waited. Maeve could hear the voices growing closer as she listened to Tristan's shuffling steps move slowly across the gap.

A board cracked. The rope went taught.

"Tristan?" Maeve whispered.

"I'm fine," his low voice answered. "The board cracked a little, but it's holding. I'm almost there."

Another crack sounded as Maeve heard Tristan hit the dirt hard.

"Tristan?" Ginger cried.

"I'm good," Tristan replied. Maeve could hear him getting to his feet and dusting off his hands. "The board broke and I had to dive for the ground, but I made it. Now, let's get out of here."

CHAPTER THIRTY-ONE

The group slowly navigated the twisting turns of the tunnels. The voices behind them grew fainter until they could no longer hear them. After what seemed an eternity, Gray turned the light back on. It was a relief to be able to see again, but what they saw was not encouraging. The tunnels here were in much greater disrepair, with fallen support beams and dirt crumbling from the ceiling.

"Gray," Maeve asked. "Do you have any idea where we are?"

"Mostly," Gray replied. "If I'm right, and I could definitely be wrong, we should be just under The Resistance tunnels. Hopefully, there's an entrance into the next level soon."

Maeve hoped he was right. She was tired and cold. After the rush of adrenaline from crossing the gap, weariness had settled on her shoulders like a heavy cape.

Emery's voice spilled out of the darkness. "Hey, what's this?"

Gray shined their meager light in Emery's direction. "What do you see?"

"It looks like a ramp," Emery said. "But it's blocked."

When Gray shined the light where Emery pointed, Maeve saw a skinny tunnel that branched off the main one. The ground sloped up slightly for about three feet before it was blocked by debris.

"This looks like it might be our ticket out of here," Tristan said.

"But look at all that debris," Ginger said. "It will take hours to remove it. What if the WG soldiers find us before we clear it?"

Emery was studying the debris intently. She walked over to where the debris was stacked and gave it a shove. The whole pile moved slightly.

"I don't think this is a pile of debris," Emery said.

"What are you talking about?" Ginger said. "Of course it is. These tunnels are old and that one caved in. It's unfortunate that that's the tunnel we need to use."

Maeve had joined Emery at the wall of debris. She, too, gave it a shove. Once again, the entire pile moved slightly.

"I think she's right," Maeve said. "Bring the light over here, Gray."

Gray moved to the wall and held the lantern higher so Maeve and Emery could examine the edge of the debris pile. They whispered together for a moment, then Maeve said, "You tell them, Emery. You figured it out."

"It's not a pile of debris. It's a door," Emery announced.

"What?" Gray said.

"How do you know?" Tristan asked.

"No way," Ginger said, disbelieving.

"Look," Emery said, pointing at the edge of the pile. "It's cleverly disguised, but there are hinges right here. We just have to figure out how to open it."

"How did you figure that out, Emery?" Ginger asked.

"Look at the debris," Emery said. "It looks too perfectly placed. If it had just fallen down, it would have been smashed and there would be big clumps of dirt from the ceiling. But none of these beams are broken, and there's just not enough dirt for it to have been a collapse. When you push on it, the whole pile moves, not just one or two pieces. Whoever did this, disguised it well enough to fool people who were just walking by. You'd have to be looking really closely to figure out it's not exactly what it looks like."

"So how do we open it?" Gray asked.

"I'm not sure yet," Emery said. "Got any ideas?" she asked Maeve.

"There has to be a latch or a trigger somewhere. The hinges are on the left, so let's try looking on the right."

"Shhh," Gray said, holding up a finger.

Everyone stopped talking. For a moment, the air was thick with silence then Maeve heard the low murmur of voices from a long way off.

"They must have found a way around that gap," Gray whispered. "We have to get that door open fast. This light is a dead giveaway to our location. Be quiet and find that latch!"

314

Everyone began feeling the edges, top and bottom of the debris pile, looking for the mechanism that would open the door. Maeve could hear the low murmur of voices getting closer. "Gray," Maeve whispered. "We need to douse the light. We're going to have to figure this out in the dark."

Gray looked at her with a solemn expression, then nodded. "I'm going to turn out the light," Gray told everyone. "Keep feeling for that latch."

Maeve moved her hands steadily along the top edge of the debris. Splinters dug into the palms of her hands, and her fingers and arms were going to bear the scratches from this endeavor for several days. The voices were steadily getting closer. They were close enough now that Maeve could begin to make out the words.

"Stupid kids. Why are we stuck in this tunnel chasing teenagers?"

Maeve frantically moved her hands, pushing and pulling on anything that protruded from the wall of debris. Her hand moved over something smooth. She paused. The rest of the debris pile had been rough. Tentatively, she pushed on the smooth area. Nothing happened. She moved her fingers over the smooth section, trying to figure out the size and shape. It felt like a small square about 3 inches on each side. She tried pushing it again. Nothing. She felt around the edges and found a gap. The smooth piece stuck out just enough for her to get her fingers under it. She tucked her fingers around the edges and pulled. The smooth square moved −not much, maybe just a centimeter −

but it moved. Maeve prayed she didn't pull the whole tunnel down on top of them, then pulled harder. The door shifted.

"What was that?" Gray whispered.

"I think I found the latch," Maeve replied in a low voice. "But it's stuck."

"Let me help. Where are you?"

"Over here. Just follow my voice."

Gray made his way over to Maeve as she kept talking. Maeve knew he was near when she felt his body heat share space with her own. She held out the hand that wasn't holding the possible latch to keep him from bumping into her. Maeve heard Gray inhale sharply when her hand landed on the muscles of his chest. He took her hand and stepped up next to her. "Where is it?" he breathed into her ear.

"R-r-right here," Maeve said a little shakily as she guided his hand up to where hers was.

"Um, guys?" Tristan said in a harsh whisper.

"What?" Gray whispered impatiently.

"I can see a light. If we're getting this door open, we need to do it now."

Gray placed his hand over Maeve's on the latch. "How does it work?"

"We have to pull. I got it to move a little, but I'm not strong enough to pull it all the way."

"Let's do it together. Ready? 1, 2, 3."

Maeve and Gray pulled with all their strength. Slowly, the latch began to move, and the door began to shift. Inch by agonizing inch, Maeve and Gray pulled the latch toward them as the door moved away from them.

"Just a little bit more," Ginger whispered. "We can almost get through."

"Hurry!" Tristan said urgently. "They're coming this way."

"That's it!" Ginger said. "There's just enough space. Let's get going." She shoved Emery through the small space into the unforgiving darkness.

"Oof," Emery said quietly as Maeve heard Emery's knees hit the dirt on the other side. "See if you can find the latch that closes the door. The one on this side was a smooth square," Maeve whispered as Ginger disappeared through the gap.

"Go!" Gray whispered as he gave her a gentle shove in the direction of the gap. Maeve could see light coming down the tunnel behind her. She crawled through the gap with Tristan on her heels. Gray followed.

"We have to get this door closed," Gray whispered.

"I've got it," Emery said. "It's the same mechanism. I just felt for the smooth square."

Gray and Tristan followed Emery's voice. Maeve could see a faint beam of light through the gap and could clearly hear the voices of the WG soldiers.

"Get it shut!" she whispered. "They're almost here."

Tristan and Gray heaved on the latch and the door slowly swung closed. Maeve prayed the owners of that light hadn't seen the debris pile move.

Maeve sat with her back against the

camouflaged door, trying not to make a sound. Her heart raced, and she could feel sweat pooling in the small of her back. No one moved. She could hear the soldiers on the other side of the door.

"Did you hear something?"

"Like what?"

"Like a scraping sound. Sounded like something being dragged across the ground."

"I didn't hear it. Where was it coming from?"

"Right around here. I heard it as we turned the corner."

"You think those kids were trying to dig through this debris pile?"

"Maybe. But nothing looks like it's been moved."

"They definitely came this way, though. Look at the dirt on the ground. It's all stomped down."

The soldier's voice got louder as he came closer to the debris pile.

"Don't let him touch it. Don't let him touch it," Maeve chanted under her breath.

"Maybe they tried to move something and realized it was too heavy. They're just kids."

"You're probably right. There's no way they moved this debris out of the way and then moved it back. Let's keep looking."

The soldiers' footsteps and voices got fainter and fainter as they moved on. Maeve let out the breath she'd been holding.

Gray pulled her to her feet and motioned for her to follow him. Still unwilling to light the lamp again, the group lined up and put their fingers through the belt loops of the person in front of them. Gray led the way, and Ginger brought up the rear.

They walked for 20 minutes before Gray felt safe enough to re-light the lantern. The group gave a collective sigh as light penetrated the inky blackness. After walking in the darkness for so long, Maeve's eyes took several minutes to adjust to the light.

"Where are we?" Ginger asked.

"I think we're almost to the next level of tunnels," Gray replied.

"But where, exactly?" Tristan asked. "Those tunnels could be dangerous now that they're compromised."

"I'm pretty sure we're just under the room we used as our first base," Gray said.

"But are those tunnels safe?" Maeve asked. "We've been down here for hours."

"Maybe," Gray said. "I don't know, but it's our best bet for getting out of here."

Gray stopped underneath a wooden hatch in the ceiling. "I think this is our way out."

Maeve looked at the hatch. "How are we going to get up there?"

"I'll go first. Then Tristan can lift you girls up to me. He can use the handholds on the wall to pull himself up until we can grab him." Gray pointed to some notches cut into the wall.

"Ok. Be careful." Maeve squeezed Gray's hand as Tristan stepped forward and cupped his hands. Gray placed his foot into Tristan's hands. Tristan gave a mighty boost, and Gray balanced precariously on one foot, relying on Tristan's strength to hold him as he worked the latch on the hatch with his good arm. "OK. Give me another boost."

Tristan pushed his hands upward. His arms trembled with the effort to give Gray the leverage he needed to open the hatch. Maeve chewed on her the side of her thumb and prayed Gray didn't fall. Hampered by only being able to use one arm, his balance was precarious. The hatch opened and light flooded into the passageway. Gray scrambled over the edge as Tristan's arms fell to his sides.

Minutes later, Gray's head appeared in the opening. "We're clear, but I can hear fighting close by. We need to move fast."

Maeve turned to Tristan. "I thought you said The Resistance evacuated the tunnels. Why is there fighting?"

Tristan shrugged. "They probably left a contingent of The Resistance behind to make sure everyone else got out safely. Those should be the last members of The Resistance down here. They'll head to the surface as soon as they can get away from the WG soldiers."

Maeve nodded and turned to Emery. "Let's go Emery." She helped Emery onto Tristan's shoulders. He stood and Emery reached for Gray's hand. Using only his good arm, he helped Emery over the edge.

"Ginger, you're next," Tristan said. He cupped his hands and boosted Ginger up in the same way he had lifted Gray. Ginger grabbed the edge and swung herself over.

320

"Gray, are you all right?" Maeve heard Ginger ask. Worried now, she hurried over to Tristan. "Boost me up," she said.

Tristan cupped his hands and propelled her upward. She grabbed the edge and pulled herself up. Gray stood with his gun at the ready, but Maeve could see blood seeping through his shirt where the wound had opened again.

"What happened?" Maeve asked.

"It tore open when I pulled myself up."

"We have to rebandage it." Maeve moved toward him to look at the wound.

"We don't have time."

"We don't have time for you to bleed to death!"

"Hey guys, can we argue about Gray's death in a minute?" Tristan asked. "I could use a little help."

Maeve rushed to the opening and motioned to Ginger. They both leaned in and grabbed Tristan's arm, but Tristan's weight was too much. Tristan was tall and muscular, and his size threatened to pull both Maeve and Ginger back through the hatch. Gray reached over Maeve and grabbed Tristan's jacket with his good arm. Together they pulled Tristan to the edge where he was able to scramble over the edge.

As they closed the hatch, they could hear gunfire closing in on their position. "Gray, we have to get that bleeding stopped," Maeve said.

"There's no time," Gray said. "We have to get to safety."

"What about my pack?" Maeve asked. "We left

321

it with The Resistance."

"We're going to have to trust that they got it to safety," Tristan said. "They knew how important it was. Come on!"

"Where are we going?" Ginger asked as she grabbed Emery's hand and followed Tristan at a trot.

"Like I said earlier, we have a back-up plan. It's always been just a matter of time before the WG found us, so we have a safety zone on the surface that should be safe."

Tristan wove through the tunnels at a quick pace. The fighting remained behind them, but they could hear it getting closer. Finally, they came to a ladder. Tristan quickly climbed the rungs followed by Ginger and Emery. Gray was breathing heavily and Maeve noted the gray cast to his skin. They needed to get that bleeding stopped now.

"Gray?" she asked.

"I'm fine."

"Can you make it up the ladder?"

"I think so."

"You go first. I'll follow you."

Rung by painful rung, Gray hauled himself up the ladder. Maeve could hear gunfire and the sounds of hand-to-hand fighting creeping ever closer as she followed Gray up the ladder, her gun at the ready.

Maeve's feet had just cleared the edge of the opening to the outside world when she heard fighting at the bottom of the ladder. "Let's get out of here."

Tristan led the way through the dark night. The

ladder had dumped them into the outside world just on the outskirts of the city. Maeve had no idea what time it was, but she knew it had to be after curfew from the lack of people in the streets. For once, luck had turned its face toward them and the moon was covered by clouds. Though it was dark, they could see just well enough to not need a light.

In front of her, Gray stumbled. Maeve moved to his side and peered into his ashen face. Despite the darkness, Maeve could tell Gray was on the brink of collapse. She felt his shoulder, and her hand came away wet and sticky with blood. Gray stumbled again.

"Tristan," Maeve hissed. "We have to stop."

"I'm ... fine," Gray said with a heavy breath. "Maeve, we have to keep going."

"You're not going to be going anywhere soon. If you pass out, you'll slow us all down."

"I'm already slowing you down," Gray said heavily. "You should just hide me and leave."

"We're not leaving you. So stop talking about it."

Maeve looked up as Tristan approached. "What's wrong?"

"Gray is about to pass out. We need a place to bandage his shoulder and stop the bleeding."

"We're too exposed here. Can you make it another quarter mile?"

"Yes," Gray said with a grimace.

"I'll help him," Maeve said, placing his arm around her shoulders.

"Maeve," Gray whined, "I can walk."

"Not from what I've seen. Shut it and start moving."

Tristan returned to the front of the line as they slowly made their way farther from the city. They kept to the shadows as much as possible, the blackness of the night working as camouflage. Each step they took elicited a deep, pained breath from Gray. Maeve could feel his heart beating quickly and prayed they made it somewhere safe soon.

Finally, Tristan stopped and ducked behind a tree. Ginger and Emery followed. When Maeve and Gray reached the tree, Maeve could see a shallow cave carved out of the large rock face behind the tree. Unless you were standing at just the right angle, the tree blocked the cave from view. Maeve and Gray quickly entered the small shelter, and Tristan moved to the opening.

"I'll keep watch," he said. "Get him fixed up, and let's get moving. We're still far too close to the city."

Maeve looked at Ginger who dropped her pack and began handing Maeve their limited medical supplies. Maeve stripped off Gray's jacket and shirt, worried by the blood she saw there. The bandage was soaked through. She quickly removed the bandage, and Gray hissed in pain.

"Sorry," she said apologetically. "I know it hurts."

"Just get it done," Gray said through gritted teeth as he leaned his head against the rock wall and closed his eyes.

When Maeve finally saw the wound, she gasped. The stitches had torn and blood was pouring

324

out of the hole. She leaned over to look at the exit wound and found blood dripping down his back as well.

"I don't have any way to stitch this back together, so we just have to hope we can get the bleeding at least slowed down."

She swiftly packed bandages on the wound and applied pressure in both the front and back. "Emery come hold this," Maeve said, pointing to the bandage she had folded and pressed against Gray's back. Emery took her place next to Gray and held the bandage in place.

Maeve wrapped strips of bandages around Gray's shoulder to hold the pressure packs in place. She handed Gray his shirt and helped him into it and his jacket, wishing she had something clean to offer him. She looked at her own hands, realizing they were covered in Gray's blood. Her hands began to shake and her vision blurred.

"Is he going to be OK?" Ginger asked.

"I don't know." Maeve shook her head and swiped her hair off her forehead with the back of her hand. She looked at Ginger, her heart in her eyes. "He's lost a lot of blood, and he's still bleeding." She paused and looked at Gray again. She hadn't really known him that long, but he was quickly becoming one of the most important people in her life. Ginger poured water from Tristan's canteen over Maeve's bloody hands. Maeve raised her eyes to meet Ginger's concerned gaze. "I've only just found him," Maeve whispered. "How can I lose him?"

"Hey," Gray said in a whisper of a voice. Maeve turned her head, feeling a little awkward since she didn't realize he could hear her whispered words. "I'm going to be fine. How could I not be when I have such a great nurse." He gave Maeve's hand a squeeze and struggled to his feet. "Let's go."

Tristan gave him a skeptical look as he wobbled on his feet. "Ginger, you're going to have to be the rear guard. Maeve is going to need both hands to keep him on his feet. Emery, you stay right next to me."

Ginger gave Tristan a mock salute and took her position at the end of the line. Emery moved next to Tristan. With a wave of his hand, Tristan left their hidden enclave and walked away from the city.

As they walked, Maeve struggled to keep Gray on his feet. After about a mile, she was carrying most of his weight as he shuffled along beside her. "Tristan, how much farther do we have to go?"

"About half a mile. How's he doing?"

"Not good. I think he's floating in and out of consciousness. And he's heavy. If he passes out, there's no way I can carry him."

"I'm good," Gray said, his voice thready. "I'll make it."

"We have to go on," Tristan said, turning concerned eyes to Maeve. "We haven't run into any WG patrols yet, but once they realize we made it out of the tunnels, the patrols will be swarming. We need to get to safety before that happens."

Maeve nodded and continued to put one foot in front of the other. Her shirt was plastered to her back with sweat, but she didn't know if it was from exertion or from being so close to Gray. His fever had returned. Every five minutes, she forced some water down him. "I wish we had some of that willow bark tea," she said.

"We do," Gray said. "In my pack. But we don't have time to stop. We can get it when we reach safety."

Their progress was slow but steady, and they finally stopped when they came to the cliffs that indicated the eastern border of Palumbra. Like The River in the west, they had all been taught that all life ended at the cliffs. Maeve watched as Tristan tapped lightly on a portion of the cliffs. A piece of rock moved backward and Tristan motioned for them to step through.

Maeve and Gray walked through the opening into an airy, open space filled with people. She recognized some from their earlier time spent with The Resistance. She heard Tristan enter behind them and the opening shifted closed. "What is this place?" she asked.

CHAPTER THIRTY-TWO

Suddenly, Gray's weight all landed on Maeve. She staggered under the sudden increase in her burden. She hadn't realized how much of his own weight Gray had been carrying. Tristan grabbed Gray before Maeve could fall. "We need a medic," Tristan called.

The girl with braided hair that Maeve had met in the tunnels hurried toward them. "Bring him over here," she said, leading the way to an area in the back of the cave where several people sat or laid on cots. Some had bandages covering their arms or faces. Others appeared to be sleeping.

"We suffered some injuries in the tunnels," she said to Tristan. "But most of our people had already moved here. It was a good call to evacuate the tunnels before you went to find them."

Tristan looked at Maeve as they gently lowered Gray to an open cot. "Maeve, this is Cicely. She's one of our best medics."

Maeve looked at the girl again. This time, Maeve could tell she was older than she looked, probably a year or two older than Maeve. "I'm Maeve.

Think you can help him?" she asked, gesturing to Gray's still form. "I did the best I could, but I'm just training to be a nurse, and we had limited supplies."

"What happened to him?"

"He split the stitches open on his gunshot wound."

"No new injury?"

"No. But I think that one is infected. He's burning up."

"I can clean it and stitch the wound closed, but we don't have much here to deal with infection." She waved her hand toward the sparse medical facilities. "The best we can do is cut out the diseased tissue and work to get his fever down. Hopefully, the infection is just in the wound and hasn't spread."

As she spoke, Cicely removed Gray's jacket and unwound the bloody bandage. Her facial expression remained unchanged as she took in the redness around the wound.

Maeve touched the angry red area, but quickly pulled her hand back as if burned. "It's so hot."

"Remember, that's his body fighting the infection. We just have to help. Can you get me some clean water?" Cicely motioned in the direction of a sink off to the right.

"You have running water in a cave?"

"This place was designed as a refuge," Tristan said. "Water is one of the things necessary for survival. So we made sure we had it. It draws from an underground spring beneath the cave."

"There's some willow bark tea in Gray's pack,"

Maeve said to Cicely. "It helped with the fever before."

"Get me the water, then make that. We'll see if we can get it in him."

Maeve and Cicely worked together to clean and stitch Gray's wound. An hour later, they both stepped back from the cot. "We've done all we can do," Cicely said. "Your job from here on out is to keep the wound clean and keep giving him that tea. Hopefully, he hasn't lost too much blood. We have a lot of things here, but no equipment to give him a transfusion − and no way of knowing what blood type he is."

Maeve cleaned herself up and went back to Gray's cot. A chair had been placed at the side of it for her. When she sat down, the adrenaline that had been keeping her on her feet suddenly disappeared. She was exhausted − and hungry. Almost as if she had conjured it, a protein paste bar appeared in front of her. She looked up and saw Tristan holding out the food and a glass of water.

"Thought maybe you could use this," he said.

"Thanks," Maeve said wearily. "Pull up a chair and tell me about this place."

Tristan grabbed an unused chair from next to a nearby cot, flipped it around and straddled it, leaning his arms on the top of the chair.

"This is our last refuge," Tristan said. "The Resistance always knew our days in the tunnels were numbered. We couldn't dodge the WG soldiers forever. We knew when things got difficult, we'd need a place to harbor our people." He looked around. "Remember,
330

until a few weeks ago, we were all living normal lives above ground. We were only using the tunnels as a place to meet and make plans. When people needed to live there, it became much riskier."

"But when did The Resistance build this?"

"The Resistance has been around a lot longer than you think," Tristan continued. "After The Lost Years, when the WG first came into existence, there was a group of people who thought a government with complete power was a bad idea. People were so shell-shocked by all that had happened to them during The Lost Years that they allowed the WG to take as much power as they wanted. Most people were just happy to be alive."

"So The Resistance started that long ago?"

"Not really," Tristan said. He got up and began to pace around the bed. "A group of families were wary of the WG, but everyone was really just focused on survival. At first, it made sense to have a central group in charge of distributing the resources. But those families who were skeptical felt like they needed a shelter if something went bad. No one was really sure the war was over. And no one but those in power knew if there was anything else out there. So they built this cave. It was meant to simply be a refuge for their families. A place to escape another war."

"So what happened?"

"The WG became more powerful. Information was restricted. Those same families began to question whether the WG was actually looking out for their best interests. They became the core of The Resistance. Over the years, this cave was expanded and stocked with enough supplies to harbor everyone in The Resistance."

"But how? The WG controls everything."

"Everything they know about. There are Resistance members who work in all areas of Palumbra. They were able to squirrel away everything from food to clothing to plumbing supplies over the years. No one notices one or two missing cases of protein bars or a shirt that got sent to the reject pile because of a 'tear' in the fabric. It took a long time, but this place is fully stocked to support us for a while."

Maeve looked around the cavern. There were probably 250 people in the space that reminded Maeve of large warehouse. The area had been sectioned off into separate spaces for families, so each family unit had its own place. In the center were long wooden tables where people sat and ate, talked or where children played games or did lessons.

"How did you get everyone out?" Maeve asked as she picked up a cool washcloth and began to wipe Gray's forehead and face.

"When we came looking for you, we sent the rest of the group out here. They used the entrance you came in. We sent them out in small groups and managed to get everyone out except those who volunteered to fight. Those small groups worked their way to the cave, hiding until they were sure the WG wasn't watching. We don't think anyone saw us."

Tristan returned to his chair and took the cloth from Maeve. "You need to go get some rest. Go with

Ginger. She'll show you to your quarters."

Maeve looked around and saw Ginger and Emery standing 10 feet away. She got wearily to her feet. "He needs some more tea in half an hour," she said to Tristan. He nodded and waved her toward Ginger.

Maeve concentrated on persuading her tired legs to move. Ginger grabbed her arm as she swayed on her feet. "Come on. You need some sleep."

With one last look at Gray, Maeve let Ginger lead her away.

Maeve woke still feeling like she could sleep for a week, but she thought she might be able to keep her eyes open. She hauled herself out of the cot in the small area she had been assigned and went to check on Gray.

"You're awake!"

"Barely," Gray said in a thready voice. Maeve had to lean close to hear him. "Thanks for getting me here."

Maeve took his hand. "You would have done the same for me."

"What's the plan now?"

"The plan is for you to stay in this bed and heal." She felt his forehead. "You still have a fever."

"Maeve, I want to help."

"Right now, the only person you need to help is yourself. You can't possibly hold a gun or run, so until you can do those two things, you're out of the fight. Let other people handle it."

"But I somehow feel responsible. No matter my uncle's long-term intentions, he brought the WG to The Resistance tunnels."

Maeve squeezed his hand. "What happened back there? What game is your uncle playing?"

Gray was silent, considering his words. "I don't really know, but we have to trust that he knows what he's doing. He put us in a bad position, but he sent Tristan to get us out."

Maeve dropped Gray's hand and began to pace next to his bed. "But he didn't know that things would work out, did he? What if we hadn't found that trap door? We'd be sitting in a WG prison − if we weren't already dead."

Gray studied her thoughtfully. "I really don't know, Maeve," he said wearily. "I truly believe that my uncle is looking out for us − even if his protection isn't perfect. He's walking a fine line. If Arabella believes he's working with The Resistance, she won't hesitate to kill him."

Maeve returned to her seat. "I don't know what to think, Gray." She bit her lip. "It seems like your uncle is playing a game with our lives. He may have a bigger plan in mind, but it would be much easier if he would just share it with us."

"I know, but I have to believe in him. I know you don't know him very well and his actions have certainly not always seemed helpful. We just have to trust."

Maeve shook her head. "You trust. I'm going to go see what The Resistance is planning."

"I want to be included in whatever gets planned.

I still feel responsible that my uncle's plans got us into this mess."

"We'll see." Maeve rose to go find Tristan and see what exactly was being planned. Gray tugged on her hand, pulling her back down.

"Please, Maeve. I need to be part of this."

Maeve nodded, squeezed his hand and walked off to find Tristan, Ginger and Emery.

"There's Sleeping Beauty," Ginger said as Maeve approached the table where she, Emery and Tristan were poring over a map.

"Feeling better?" Tristan asked.

"A little. I still feel like I could sleep for a week."

"Don't we all," Ginger replied.

"What's going on? What are you guys looking at?"

Ginger pointed at the map. Maeve had seen it before. As a matter of fact, she had followed it when she and Gray had found Emma. "My pack made it safely here."

"Yep," Emery said and pointed to the pack at her feet.

"Good. That's one less worry. What are you looking at on the map?"

Tristan pointed to the area where she and Gray had found Emma. "We're wondering why they had the drones bomb the high school."

"I thought they were trying to kill us."

Emery shook her head. "That makes no sense. You weren't even in the high school when the bombs dropped. Those drones probably had infrared imaging in them. They could tell you weren't there."

"I think they wanted to hide what you had already seen. The machine in the high school," Tristan said.

"But why?"

"Well, if you were going to recreate a weapon and you didn't want anyone to know about it, wouldn't you get rid of the first one?"

Maeve stared at Tristan. "You think they're rebuilding the exact same weapon? Why? Who are they going to use it against?"

Ginger swept her arm over the map. "This map shows a lot more world than just Palumbra. What if there are other people out there?"

Tristan pointed at an area of the map farther west than any of them had gone. "What if there's another city out here?"

Maeve looked at the area he pointed to. "Why would you think that? There's nothing there."

"Nothing that we recognize," Emery said. "But look at these lines." She pointed to lines that looked a bit like a wheel with spokes. "What do you think those are?"

"Rivers?"

"I think they're roads," Emery said. "The city is in the center and the roads lead out. It's like a hub."

"So you think there's a civilization there like Palumbra?" Maeve wrinkled her forehead and drew her eyebrows together. "Why have we never heard from them?"
336

"Who says we haven't?" Ginger said. "We have no idea what the WG has been hiding from us."

"But surely we would have had some inkling that they existed. Shouldn't people have traveled from there to here."

"But would they?" Tristan asked, pointing to another spot on the map between Palumbra and the hub city. "According to this map, this area is nothing but desert. Why would you cross it if you don't think there's anything else out there?"

Maeve stood up. "Who have you told about this?"

"No one," Ginger said. "But there's a Resistance leadership meeting in an hour. We've been invited to share what we know. We need a plan for defeating the WG."

"We need to share this with Gray. See if he can remember his uncle talking about anything that might have been related to this."

"Gray?" Maeve gently shook his shoulder. His eyes fluttered open. Maeve noted that his skin was still warmer than it should be, but his eyes looked clearer.

"Maeve? What is it?" He looked over her shoulder and saw Tristan, Emery and Ginger arrayed behind her. "Is something wrong?"

"No, we're all fine," Maeve said.

"We just have some questions we need to ask you before we meet with The Resistance leadership," Tristan said.

"OK," Gray winced as he struggled to sit up. Maeve moved his pillows to form a backrest and handed him a glass of water.

"What do you want to know?"

"Did your uncle ever mention the possibility of there being life outside of Palumbra?" Ginger asked.

Gray shook his head. "No. He always talked like we were the only ones left. Why? Have you found something?"

Emery stepped forward and spread the map on Gray's lap. "This map is of much more than just Palumbra."

"I know that. Maeve and I figured that out when we were looking for the high school. But that doesn't mean there's anyone else out there other than pockets of survivors like Emma."

"But look here," Emery said as she pointed to the hub city. "We think this is a city. See the way the roads all lead away from a central area. It's like a hub."

"Sure," Gray said. "But why do you think anyone is left? This is a map from a long time ago when there were more people in the world."

"But that's just it. We think the WG is recreating that weapon we saw, but why would the WG need a weapon if we're all alone?" Maeve said. "They've already started rounding up the teenagers of Palumbra to create a weapon like the one we saw with Emma. Why would they need that if there's no one else out there?"

"Think, Gray," Tristan said. "Surely your uncle said something that might lead you to think there are other people out there."

338

Gray gave him a pained look. Maeve knew he was still confused by his uncle's actions. "I don't know." Gray looked at the map in his lap. "We didn't talk a lot about what he did for the WG. We mostly talked about stuff I cared about and things around the house."

Maeve took Gray's hand. "It's OK. We just wanted to check to see if he had ever mentioned anything about the hub city or anywhere else."

Gray's hand tightened on Maeve's. "What did you just say?"

Maeve pointed to the area on the map they thought was a city. "We've started calling it the Hub. It looks like a wheel with the hub at the center. Why?"

"My uncle did talk about the hub. I just assumed he was talking about WG headquarters, but what if he was talking about this city?"

"What did he say about," Ginger asked.

Gray frowned then squeezed Maeve's hand. "He talked about The Hub being the center of things. And he said it was dangerous."

Gray shrugged. "He was part of The Resistance. I just assumed he was talking about the WG. It made sense in the context. But what if he was giving me information he knew I would need?"

"When did he say this?" Maeve asked.

"After I met you on the day you came home late. Maybe a week or two later. We were talking about the WG and how they had consolidated power. He just slipped that in the middle of the conversation."

Maeve stood up and shook her head. "But why

would he give you that information and then turn us over to the WG?

"Maeve, you know that wasn't his long-term plan," Gray said. "He sent Tristan after us."

Maeve whirled on Gray. "I just don't like other people taking calculated risks with my life − or your life."

"Calm down, Maeve," Ginger said gently. "No matter what Night did, we all made it out in one piece."

"Except for him." Maeve pointed at Gray's shoulder. "And Silas certainly didn't make it out in one piece. It just seems that Night's plans come with a lot of risk − for us."

Tristan placed a hand on her shoulder. "It wasn't the best plan, but maybe it was the best he could do under the circumstances. The WG hasn't found us here yet, so we know Night hasn't given them this location."

"Is anyone searching these hills for us?" Gray asked.

"No. We have patrols stationed at the entrance. They've seen no one."

Gray sent Maeve a triumphant look. "My uncle isn't out to betray The Resistance. If he was, he would have sent search parties into these hills. It's the most logical place for hideout. We have to trust that he has a plan."

"Gray, I know you want to believe in your uncle. He's the only family you have left. But he's put our lives at risk too many times. How could we ever trust him again?" Maeve said.

"I just can't believe that the man who took me in after my parents died would just abandon me like that. There has to be a bigger plan. We just can't see it."

340

Tristan looked at his watch and placed his hand on Maeve's shoulder. "The meeting starts in 10 minutes. We should get going."

Maeve let out a huff of frustration. She squeezed Gray's hand, then stepped back from his bed.

"Emery, you stay here with Gray," Ginger said. Before Emery could protest, Ginger held up a hand. "I know that you found The Hub on the map, but they won't let you in the meeting. You're too young. I promise we'll tell you everything."

Emery flopped into the chair next to Gray's bed. Gray smiled at her. "I guess it's just you and me, kid." Emery rolled her eyes but grinned at Gray as the others walked away.

Maeve sat with Ginger and Tristan at the back of a crowded "room." About 30 other people, all adults were crammed into the small area that had been sectioned off from the rest of the cave complex with sheets and rocks. Maeve knew their voices would carry to the rest of The Resistance in the cave, but the sheets and rocks gave the impression of privacy.

A tall, thin woman with coffee-colored skin and dark, straight hair stood at the front of the room. She clapped her hands once and conversation in the room died down.

"Who is that?" Maeve whispered to Tristan.

"Cleo," Tristan whispered back. "She's the head

of The Resistance. She's been on the run for a long time. We've kept her hidden in safe houses for the past 20 years."

"Wow." Maeve shook her head. "How old is she?"

"Probably around 45, but I don't know."

"As most of you have realized," Cleo began in a clear, low voice, "the time has come to fight openly. For decades we've been fighting in the shadows, doing what we could to infiltrate the WG and protect the people of Palumbra. But now, the WG led by Arabella Laughlin have given us no choice but to fight openly. We've been driven out of our homes and treated like criminals. We must stand up and fight back."

A young man in his 20s stood up. "We have no chance against the WG army. How are we going to fight? It was one thing when we were fighting in secret. It's another to take them on head on. We don't have the numbers or the equipment."

Others in the room nodded in agreement. Maeve realized that these people, like her, had lost everything. They needed to know that there was a chance of winning before they could move forward. Unfortunately, Maeve agreed with the 20-something young man. There was no way they could defeat the WG army in a head-to-head fight.

Ginger tapped Maeve on the arm, and Maeve looked away from the debate taking place at the front of the room to see what Ginger wanted. To her surprise, Emery was standing next to Ginger. "You need to hear this." Ginger waved for Maeve and Tristan to follow

342

her and Emery out of the room.

Maeve followed Emery and Ginger out into the cave. Emery carried a computer. "I thought you were keeping Gray company," Maeve said.

"I did more than keep him company," Emery said. "We figured out a way to defeat the WG."

"What?" Maeve said, looking at Ginger who just nodded enthusiastically.

"Gray and I were talking about what it would take to stop the WG, especially if they were already rounding up our friends to use them as a weapon. We realized we don't have to beat the WG soldiers. We just have to beat their weapons."

"Where did you get the computer?" Maeve asked.

"It's mine," Emery said. "Remember, it was in my pack. It's totally off the WG network."

Maeve nodded and motioned for her to go on. "So, The Resistance keeps a log of all the WG weapons and what they know about them. Gray and I pulled up the specs on the WG weapons that The Resistance has gathered. We know every WG weapon has a computer chip in it. They can disable any weapon that gets out of their control like Gray said they did with his gun back at the fishing hut until you guys removed the chip. "

"OK," Tristan said. "But we can't disable them. We don't have the code."

"No," Emery replied. "But you have me."

"Gray told me about the chip and how they work. I already know how to hack into the WG computers. All we have to do is upload a code that will shut down their weapons. We can win this war without firing a shot." Emery's eyes shone with triumph.

"What's the catch, Emery?" Ginger asked with a wary look on her face.

"What makes you think there's a catch?"

"I know that look and that tone. I've been your sister for 12 years. I can tell when you're holding something back."

"Well, um. To upload the code, we'd have to be at the main WG server inside WG headquarters."

"What?" Ginger exclaimed. "No. Definitely not. You're to go nowhere near WG headquarters."

Emery began to argue, but Tristan held up his hand. "Stop." He pulled up a chair, spun it around and straddled it. "Emery, are you 100% sure you can do this."

"Yes," Emery answered confidently. "I can." She looked at Ginger and took a deep breath, drawing herself up to her full height. "It's our best option. Lots of people will die otherwise, and we'd probably lose. We can't let our friends be used as weapons, Ginger. If we do that, then mom and Silas died for nothing."

"That's a low blow, Emery." Ginger stood and turned her back to the group. "Just because I want to keep you safe doesn't mean that I've forgotten about mom and Silas."

Emery hung her head. "I didn't mean it like that," she said. "But if we know we can do something that will prevent more people from dying, shouldn't we do it?"

Ginger gripped her hands together and studied Emery thoughtfully. "Mom would be proud of you,"
344

she said quietly. After another moment of silence, Ginger nodded. "Well, I guess we'd better go tell Cleo what we know."

CHAPTER THIRTY-THREE

They re-entered the room with The Resistance leadership where the debate about engaging the WG army continued. Tristan walked to the front of the room and whispered something in the ear of a short, sturdy middle-aged man. He nodded and stood.

"I think we should hear from Tristan and his friends," the man said. He returned to his seat as Cleo turned to look at Tristan.

"You want us to hear from the people responsible for the WG finding out where we were?" Cleo said to Tristan.

"I don't think that's a fair claim, but I do think you should hear from them," Tristan said clearly for everyone to hear. "They have risked their lives to bring new information to us. I think we could learn something if we listened to what they have to say."

Cleo eyed Tristan for a moment, then nodded. "OK, you have the floor."

Tristan stepped forward and motioned for Ginger, Emery and Maeve to join him. Maeve chewed on her thumbnail as the four of them stood surrounded by the curious eyes of The Resistance leadership.

"Friends," Tristan said, "the WG has plans beyond what any of us even began to imagine. At this moment, they are rounding up children and teenagers and planning to use their brain waves to power a weapon beyond our imagination."

A low murmur of disbelief could be heard around the room. "That's impossible," a man shouted.

"How do you know this?" a woman holding a baby shouted.

"Maeve and Ginger, can you tell them what you know?"

Maeve dropped her hand to her side, straightened her shoulders and stepped forward. "I know it's hard to believe," Maeve began, "but it's true." Ginger told the crowd about finding the list of teenagers in the ruined city, and Maeve told her story of meeting Emma and seeing the weapon from The Lost Years. They skimmed over the parts of their stories when Silas died and Gray got shot. When they finished, the crowd stood in silence.

"How do we know this is true?" shouted a man in the back of the room.

"You don't," Maeve said. "I can't prove anything. I have very little physical evidence. We have a video from The Lost Years along with a map. And Gray is out there in a hospital bed with a gunshot wound in his shoulder. You'll have to take our word on the rest."

"But so much was destroyed in the war. How does the WG have this technology?" shouted an older woman from the side of the room.

"Think about it," Tristan said. "If the WG knew this was out there, then they could have spent years working on it. We would never have known. People have disappeared over the years. We thought they were dissenters, but it's possible the WG kidnapped people who would be able to help them build this thing and held their families hostage as leverage." Maeve thought about Mr. Tomkins, their neighbor who had been taken away. He had been a scientist. What if he hadn't been part of The Resistance? What if he was taken to help build the weapon?

"How does knowing this help us?" asked the short, sturdy man Tristan had talked to first.

"It doesn't," said the young man in his 20s. "It just makes our cause more hopeless."

"I think you have more to tell us," Cleo said in a quiet, calm voice.

Tristan nodded. He pulled Emery forward. "This is Emery. She has a solution to our problem of taking on the WG."

"You want us to rely on a 10-year-old?," shouted a voice from the back.

Tristan raised his eyebrows. "She's 12, and she's one of the smartest people I've met so far." He stepped back and motioned for Emery to start speaking.

Emery stared at the ground, then at Ginger. Ginger nodded, and Emery began to speak. "Um. Well, I was talking to Gray, and we think we've figured out a way to disable the WG soldiers' weapons."

348

"No way," said a woman in the front row. "I'm supposed to believe a 12-year-old kid figured this out?"

"Why don't you let her tell you about it, and we can decide if it's realistic," Cleo said in a quiet authoritative voice that left no doubt about who was in charge.

"Well, the WG weapons all have a locater chip in them. That chip can also disable the weapon if you have the right code. We can hack into the WG system and send a new code to the chip disabling the weapons."

"What's to stop the WG from just re-enabling them?" Cleo asked.

"The code we would send would permanently shut the weapons down. There would be no way to remove the command. Kind of like a self-destruct button."

A man in the front row stood. Maeve recognized him as John from the cave. "Aren't most of our weapons stolen from the WG? How come they've never shut them down?"

A murmur of agreement came from the crowd. Cleo raised her hand for silence and stepped forward again.

"Many of our weapons are from the early days after The Lost Years when the technology didn't exist to put a chip in every gun," she said. "We have a few guns in our possession that have the chips, and they don't work because the WG disabled them."

Cleo turned to Emery. "You can create this code?"

"I know I can do this. We just need a way to get me into WG headquarters. This has to be done from the main server."

"OK," Cleo said. "Tristan you can stay, but the

rest of you need to step outside while we discuss what you've told us."

Maeve glanced at Ginger and Emery and saw that they were as startled by this command as she was. If they were going to put Emery in harm's way, then they thought they should be part of the conversation. Tristan motioned toward the exit with his head, silently telling them to go. Slowly, the girls left the room.

"Emery, you did a great job," Maeve said. "Can you go check on Gray?"

"What do you think of all of this?" Maeve asked Ginger when Emery was out of earshot. "Do you trust them?"

"I don't know," Ginger said. "I trust Tristan, but I don't know the rest of them. They seemed pretty skeptical about our story."

"Ginger, I lived it, and I'm skeptical about our story. It seems too fantastic to be true."

"I guess you're right," Ginger said with a shrug. "I'd just feel a lot better if Gray was on his feet and able to help protect Emery."

"Me too," Maeve replied. "Me too."

###

Maeve was helping Gray eat his dinner when Tristan finally returned.

"Where are Ginger and Emery?" he asked as he pulled a chair over to the side of Gray's bed.

"Getting some dinner. They'll be back in a few

minutes," Maeve said.

"How was the meeting?" Gray asked.

"I think they're convinced that what you saw is real, but persuading them that a 12-year-old girl is their best bet for victory has been a little tougher."

"What other options do we have?" Gray asked as he chewed a mouthful of protein paste.

"None, really," Tristan said. "We can't meet the WG army head-on. We'd be annihilated, and there's no one else within The Resistance with the skills Emery has. We have some people who worked in the technology sector of the WG, but no one understands the coding like Emery."

"The WG tightly controls access to computers," Maeve chimed in. "There aren't a lot of opportunities to learn. Emery's talent was so obvious that they had put her in a track at school to become a technologist for the WG."

"And she's pretty much a genius," Gray added, "so she learned a whole bunch of things that weren't in the curriculum once she had access to the computer. Still, it's a lot to ask from a 12-year-old."

"Is someone talking about me?" Emery asked from where she stood behind Maeve holding a plate containing protein paste and what looked like some kind of potato.

"We were just waiting for you two to get back so Tristan can tell us what the plan is," Gray said.

Maeve pointed at two chairs on the other side of Gray's bed. "Grab a seat."

"So, what's the plan for not getting my sister

killed?" Ginger asked Tristan.

Tristan dropped his gaze. "Well, there's a plan. I'm not sure it's a good one."

"Go ahead and tell us about it," Maeve said.

"The Resistance leadership wants to get Emery in the building by offering to talk to the WG."

"How's that going to work?" Ginger asked. "No one is going to believe that we sent a 12-year-old to negotiate peace."

"True," Tristan agreed. "They're proposing that each side bring a group of children as a gesture of good will and peace. The theory is that no one will try to attack if there are children involved."

"So we're not just putting Emery at risk?" Maeve said. "We're going to involve other people's children as well? What are they thinking?"

"Isn't there a way to get in the building without going through the front door?" Gray asked. "We'll have no chance to slip away with Emery if she's part of a group of kids that are being watched. How do they propose she gets to the servers?"

"I think they were hoping she could ask to go to the bathroom or something, then slip away." Tristan shrugged his shoulders helplessly. "I told you it wasn't necessarily a good plan."

"This plan is guaranteed to fail and could get Emery killed," Ginger said. "That's not going to happen."

"So, what do you propose instead?" Tristan asked.

352

"I say we go in the back way," Gray said.

"The back way?" Maeve asked. "Where's that?"

"My uncle used to go to WG headquarters at night. There's a back entrance that only WG officials use. It's not super heavily guarded — or at least it wasn't. You need an access key to get in, but the server rooms aren't far from the entrance — just down a flight of stairs to the basement."

"But what if they've added more guards since the battle with The Resistance in the tunnels?" Ginger asked.

"We could send out a team of people to do some surveillance and find out," Tristan said. "I doubt they've increased the guards at that entrance. The WG thinks they've won. The Resistance is in hiding, and they know we don't have the manpower to take them on. Our patrol teams say the WG isn't even really looking for us — but they are still looking for you."

"But how will we get an access key?" Ginger asked.

"We steal one," Maeve said.

"From who?" Ginger asked skeptically.

"Well, we know a high-ranking WG official, and we have inside information on where he keeps things. I say we snatch one from Gray's uncle," Maeve said.

"Maeve..." Gray began.

"What? Do you have a better idea?"

"Can't we just get a message to him and see if he can let us in the building?" Gray asked. "Seems like that would be easier than stealing his key."

"I don't think it's smart to let him in on our plan," Tristan said. He held up his hand before Gray could protest. "I agree with you that Night is still trying to protect us, but I also agree with Maeve that his methods have a tendency to put us at risk. There's enough risk in this situation without adding your uncle as a wild card."

Maeve nodded. "Gray, every one of us has lost someone in the past few weeks. Ginger and Emery's mom died. Silas died. My parents betrayed me. Is it so hard to believe that your uncle might not have our best interests as his top priority?"

Gray looked from Maeve to Tristan and slowly nodded. "OK. But it won't be easy. He keeps his access card with him almost all the time."

"So when doesn't he have his access card with him?" Ginger asked.

"When he's sleeping," Gray replied. "But it's on his nightstand, so he can find it if he gets called in in the middle of the night."

"What if we steal the card and he has the access code changed?" Emery asked.

"He won't," Gray said confidently. "We just have to make sure he knows that we took it."

"Are we sure that's smart?" Tristan asked. "We don't know what he'll do with that information. What if he messes up our plan?"

"Are you willing to risk him changing the codes?" Gray asked.

Maeve held up a hand to stem the brewing argument. "As much as I hate to admit it, I think Gray is right. We need to let Night know we took it and pray he doesn't do something to get us killed."

Tristan nodded. "So what do we leave behind?"

Gray dug in his pocket with his good hand. "Here." He handed Maeve a photo. "That's the only picture I still have of my parents. Just leave it on his nightstand."

Maeve took the photo of a handsome, brown-haired man and a young woman with a bright smile holding a baby. She smiled at baby Gray and slid the photo into her own pocket.

"Are you sure about this?" Tristan whispered to Maeve as they crouched in the darkness outside the home Gray had shared with his uncle.

"No, but we have to do it. The Resistance is going to get Emery killed. We need that access card."

The two had been waiting outside the house for hours, watching as Night ate dinner and prepared for bed. All the lights in the house had gone out two hours before. "I think it's time," Maeve said. "Whistle like a bird if you see anything."

"Good luck," Tristan said as he gave her a quick embrace. "Be careful."

Maeve slowly slid out of the shadows and crossed to the first-floor window that had been left open a crack. Gray had told her his uncle always left the family room window open a crack to let in the night air. As quietly as she could, Maeve pushed the window open far enough that she could fit through and hoisted herself up and over the sill. Her boot caught the side of the window and she winced at the clunking sound it made. She crouched in the shadows in the corner of the room, making sure she hadn't woken Night.

When all remained silent, she quietly made her way through the kitchen to the hallway where Gray had told her she would find Night's room. The house was slightly bigger than her own home that she shared with her parents. She figured Gray probably slept in the loft like she did. The days of sleeping in her own bed seemed like a far distant past to Maeve, and she wondered if she would ever sleep there again.

Shaking her head to clear her thoughts, Maeve crept down the hallway. There were only two doors — one leading to Night's bedroom, the other leading to the home's only bathroom. Slowly, Maeve eased open the door on the right. In the glow from the moon, she could see Night's form in the bed and could hear him breathing heavily. Leading with her rifle, she tiptoed her way close to the right side of the bed. As she reached the nightstand, Night shifted in his sleep, causing Maeve to freeze. There was nowhere to hide in the small room, so she held her breath as Night settled back into sleep.

She scanned the nightstand, looking for the ID badge that also served as a key to the WG headquarters. She spied it sitting next to Night's comm device. She quickly grabbed it and stuck it in her pocket. She reached her hand into her other pocket and removed

Gray's photo of his parents and placed it in the same place where the ID badge had been. She turned to go, but something made her look back at the man who had raised Gray – and put them in so much danger. She wanted to shake him awake and ask him how he could claim to love Gray and still endanger his life multiple times, but then she remembered her own parents had betrayed her, and she turned to leave. As she did, the floorboard beneath her boot let out a squeak. Night mumbled in the bed. Maeve froze. Night settled again, and Maeve crept out of the room.

She quickly made her way back to Tristan.

"Everything go OK?" Tristan asked.

Maeve nodded and held up the ID badge. Tristan reached to take it from her and froze. A light came on in Night's house and he opened the front door. Tristan and Maeve shrank back into the cover of the trees. A twig snapped under Tristan's foot. Silhouetted in the doorway of his house, Night raised his hand and saluted them.

CHAPTER THIRTY-FOUR

"**D**id you get it?" Gray asked.

Maeve held up the access key. "He definitely knows I was there."

"Does he know it was you?"

"I left the photo." Maeve went on to tell him about his uncle saluting them in the darkness.

"Good job." Gray used his good hand to push himself to a standing position.

"What are you doing?" Maeve asked.

"Getting up. I'm tired of sitting in bed while you put yourself at risk."

"You almost died. You need to rest."

"Maeve, the future of the world is at stake. I'm not going to spend the fight for it in bed. Let's go see Cleo."

"You did what?" Cleo thundered.

"We stole Night Cantwell's access key to WG headquarters," Maeve said quietly. "Gray says there's a back entrance we can use to get in."

"Why would you do such a thing?"

"Because your plan was going to get my sister killed," Ginger said evenly.

"And this one is so much better?" Cleo asked.

"You could have been killed. And what makes you think the WG won't just change the access codes once Night realizes his key is missing?"

"We made sure he knew it was us. He'll leave the codes as they are," Gray said confidently.

"Are you sure?" Cleo asked skeptically. "It seems to me Night is playing a game that none of us know the rules to. I don't want your possibly misguided loyalty getting people killed."

Gray held up his good hand. "Just hear me out. I know my uncle tried to turn us over to the WG, but he didn't have any choice without blowing his cover. He couldn't take on the whole WG army himself. Turning us over was his only option to protect his position."

"Why hasn't he tried to contact us then?" Tristan asked. "We could definitely use some intel on what's going on inside the WG right now."

"How did he contact you before?" Gray asked.

"He got word to us in the tunnels and we would meet him," Tristan answered. "We had a drop in the tunnels where he could leave a note. He'd set a time, and we'd meet."

"Then there's not really any way to contact us now, is there?" Gray said.

"That might be true, Gray," Ginger said. "But are you willing to risk Emery's life over it?"

"No, but I'm willing to risk mine."

###

"This is nuts," Maeve muttered as she crouched next to Emery, who was sandwiched between her and Tristan. Ginger covered Emery's back. At 3 in the morning, all was quiet as they hovered in the shadows of WG headquarters. "This is never going to work. He's going to get himself killed."

The five of them had cautiously made their way into the city and to their current position, dodging WG patrols. With every breath, Maeve expected a WG soldier to pop out of the shadows. From where they crouched, they could see Gray approaching the back entrance. No guards appeared.

"This is too easy," Maeve whispered to Tristan. "No way that entrance is left unguarded."

"Shh, Maeve. We don't know what the situation is here in the city. All of our informants fled to the cave. Maybe the unrest has died down, and the WG have gotten careless."

"Or maybe it's a trap," she said bitterly.

"It could be," Tristan said. "That's why we have backup. The Resistance is ready to come to our aid if things go wrong." He patted the radio on his belt.

"This is nuts," Maeve muttered again as Gray swiped the access key. In the silence, Maeve could hear the bolt click open.

Gray gave them a thumbs up and motioned for them to join him.

When they reached the door, Gray pulled it open and they silently entered the WG headquarters, with Emery firmly ensconced between Tristan and Ginger.

360

Ginger, Maeve and Tristan scanned the hallway with their rifles at the ready, but no one sounded the alarm.

"There have to be cameras watching us," Tristan said. "There's no way our entrance has gone unnoticed. We have to move fast."

"This way," Ginger said. "I've been in this part of the building before. The staircase to the server room is down this hallway." She began moving down the hallway, leading with her gun.

The group moved swiftly down the deserted hallway until Ginger found the staircase door. Gray swiped the access card, and they made their way down the concrete stairs to the bottom floor.

"Where are we?" Gray asked.

"We should come out just to the left of the server room," Ginger replied.

"There's no way that room is empty," Tristan said. "Let me go first." Tristan and Ginger switched places. Maeve took Emery's arm as Gray drew his pistol.

"Can you even shoot with that hand?" Maeve asked.

"I'm not great, but it's better than going in unarmed," Gray replied. "Maeve." Gray placed his hand on Maeve's arm.

Maeve turned her face up to meet his gaze. "Yes?"

"Thanks for saving my life. Not sure what I would have done without you."

Maeve stared into those ice blue eyes. "Thanks for protecting me from the WG soldiers that day on the path. We're definitely better together. I know we might not make it out of here. I just want to say..."

"Hey, you two, save it for later," Tristan said with a roll of his eyes. "We need to move."

Gray winked and squeezed her arm. "Later, OK?"

"Later," Maeve agreed and turned to follow Tristan.

Tristan gently turned the handle on the door. It opened just enough for him to see through. "I think we're clear," he said. He turned to Ginger. "Cover me," he said as he burst through the door.

Maeve kept herself between Emery and the door and braced herself for the sound of gunfire, but all remained quiet as Ginger slid through the door. Maeve followed while Emery and Gray slipped in behind her. They stood in a room lined with computer servers. "Why so many servers? No one has computers."

"Clearly there's more going on in WG headquarters than we know about," Gray said. "But the bigger question is, where is everyone?"

"Who cares?" Ginger said. She motioned to Emery. "Get started so we can get out of here."

Emery carried her computer over to a server, pulled out a cord, plugged it in to the server and began typing. Tristan took up a position at the door. "Ginger and Gray, stay with Emery. Maeve, check around the room for another entrance."

Maeve carefully made her way around the room, looking behind computer equipment for hidden doorways. "This is the only door," she said as she returned to Tristan. "What do you think is really going on? Why is no one around?"

362

"I think we've walked into a trap," Tristan said. He motioned toward the door with his gun. "But what else could we do?"

"What do you think our chances of making it out of here are?"

"Not great. Let's focus on the job. We'll worry about getting out of here after Emery finishes."

Maeve walked over to Gray and Ginger. "How much longer?"

"It's going to take a bit," Emery said. "I have to hack through their defenses – and they're pretty good."

"Can you do it?" Ginger asked. "If you can't, we should get out of here. I don't think we're going to be alone much longer."

Tristan held up a hand and placed a finger over his mouth to indicate the need for silence. The only sounds were the hum of the servers and the tapping of Emery's fingers.

The door to the server room slowly swung open. Night Cantwell stood in the entrance – his face set in a stern expression. Maeve and Tristan pointed their guns. Gray and Ginger closed ranks in front of Emery.

"Keep typing," Ginger whispered.

Night raised his hands and said "Hello, Gray."

"Night," Gray acknowledged with a tip of his head.

"You look much better than the last time I saw you."

"No thanks to you."

"Ah, Gray, I'm so sorry, but I did what needed to be done. I knew your friend would take care of you." Night tipped his head in Tristan's direction.

"But you couldn't know that we would be fine when you turned us over to those soldiers. What were you thinking?" Gray asked, eyeing Night warily.

"I was thinking of the greater good," Night said steadily. Deliberately, Night looked up toward the ceiling.

Night motioned to Ginger and Tristan who were still pointing their guns in his direction. "Can we put the guns down? I just want to chat."

Gray glanced at his friends and said, "No. The last time we 'chatted' I almost died."

"Come, Gray, there are at least a hundred soldiers headed this way. You didn't really think your entrance went unnoticed, did you?"

"Why did you let us get away with your access key if we were just going to walk into a trap?"

Night approached Gray. "I know you don't understand my methods. Just know that I've had to protect more than just you."

Maeve took a step toward Gray, but he motioned her away.

"But shouldn't protecting me have been your top priority?" Gray asked in a pained voice. "We're the only family either of us has left."

Night shook his head. "I wish it were that easy, Gray. I love you and would never have put you in harm's way if I had a choice, but you got involved in things I couldn't protect you from."

"Why are we so important to the WG? What value do we have? The WG has been chasing us since the hospital bombing."

364

"That is the question, isn't it, Gray?" Night stepped toward Gray, and Tristan motioned him back with the end of his rifle. Night stepped back and continued, "What makes the five of you so special? Maybe the fact that you've gotten this far. Maybe it's that we learned something from our ancestors about the power of the teenage brain. The truth is, Gray, you and your band of friends are a bigger threat to the WG than the entire Resistance because you hold the key to The Lost Years. You learned the truth. The WG can't let that get out."

Maeve could hear Emery's fingers tapping away on the keyboard. She hoped Emery was making progress quickly because they were running out of time. She kept her eyes trained on Night, looking for any sign that he had something harmful planned.

"Why did you lead the WG to the tunnels?" Tristan asked. "We trusted you."

"Of course you did," Night said, turning toward Tristan. "Why wouldn't you?" He turned back and looked steadily at Gray. "I am who I have always been."

Gray blinked. Maeve remembered Night looking toward the ceiling, so she turned her eyes upward and scanned the corners of the ceiling, looking for cameras. She found one in each corner. The WG was watching this exchange.

"Emery?" Maeve whispered. "Are we close?"

"Two more minutes."

"We know about the weapon," Maeve said, trying to buy Emery more time. She knew WG troops would be called in the minute Night was done with them.

"So you figured it out. The diabolical plan of the WG – to harness the brainpower of the children to rain down destruction on others."

"But you said there was no one else out there," Gray said.

"No," Night replied. "I let you assume there was no one else out there. It's safer that way."

"But the WG is planning to kill them," Maeve said.

"Before they kill us, yes."

"But we could work together," Maeve said. "How do we know they're not friendly?"

"Oh, Maeve, you have a lot to learn about the world. Why would those in power willingly give it up?"

"You mean the WG is going to destroy an entire city just because they don't want to share power?"

"You learn quickly."

Tristan turned toward the door and raised his gun. Three WG soldiers rushed through the door and surrounded Tristan. Time slowed. Maeve saw the WG soldier's finger move to the trigger on his rifle. Without thinking, she aimed and fired and watched in horror as one of the soldiers fell to the ground, blood blooming on his chest. Time stopped. She dropped her gun and covered her mouth. She heard Gray shouting at her, but his voice sounded as if it were coming from inside a cave. Moments passed, chaos exploded around her, but Maeve wasn't aware of any of it. Her world had narrowed to the young soldier lying dead on the ground.

When she became aware of the people around her again, Night stood between the WG soldiers and her friends, his hands outstretched, one toward each group. Gray was tugging on her hand to get her to move away from the soldiers, and Emery was frozen with her hands still over the keyboard.

Night was talking urgently to the WG soldiers when the door swung open again and a tall, fit woman with graying hair dressed impeccably in a gray skirt and a WG blazer walked in.

"Arabella," Night said.

CHAPTER THIRTY-FIVE

"Night." Arabella said in a clipped, aristocratic tone. "Thank you for leading our friends here. You will be amply rewarded."

Gray turned toward his uncle in horror. "Did you lure us here to turn us over to her?"

Night stood silently, his eyes fixed on Arabella. Maeve saw a sneer flicker across his face, but he quickly masked his expression.

"Nothing to say?" Arabella asked snidely.

"Arabella." Night repeated himself. "I was just going to call you."

"Really?" Arabella replied as she began to circle Night. Maeve heard Emery's fingers begin to click on the keys again. She coughed to cover the sound, hoping Emery was well-hidden behind Tristan and Ginger. Arabella shot her a hate-filled look the sound but continued talking to Night. "You were in this room with them a long time without calling it in. I thought we agreed you would let me know as soon as you found them."

Night shrugged. "I wanted a moment with my nephew. He's like a son to me. I was trying to persuade him to turn himself in."

Maeve decided the cameras must not have the ability to transmit sound.

"And did you succeed?"

Gray stepped forward. Night frowned at him. "Not a chance," Gray said. "We're going to stop you."

Arabella laughed, a shrill, high-pitched sound that sent shivers down Maeve's spine. "You?" She pointed at his arm. "You can't even hold a gun properly. How do you think you're going to manage that."

Arabella stepped closer to Gray and held out her hand. The soldiers pointed their guns at Gray. "Give me the gun since it's of no use to you." Gray started to raise his gun, but Night shook his head in a warning. Gray gritted his teeth and laid the gun in Arabella's outstretched palm.

"Thank you," Arabella said politely.

Maeve was torn between moving closer to Gray and staying where she was to protect Emery. She glanced at Tristan who gave her a shooing motion with his hand, encouraging her to get closer to Gray.

Maeve slowly began to inch her way forward, trying to avoid Arabella's notice.

Arabella wrapped her hand around Gray's injured arm. "Did you think your uncle would save you this time? What a poor, misguided young man you are." She squeezed Gray's arm. Gray's face tightened in pain, but he remained silent. Night watched with an impassive look on his face. "I'm in charge here. Night only does my bidding. Even he doesn't know the full extent of my plans."

"What plans are those, Arabella?" Night asked.

"Did you think my schemes ended with destroying our nearest neighbors?" She laughed that high, shrill laugh again. "Do you know what's out there?" She gestured toward the door. "So many more places to conquer, and with our latest weapon and the help of all our teenage friends in Palumbra, we will rule them all."

Maeve heard Emery drop something at Arabella's last pronouncement. Arabella looked around the room for the source of the sound. Quickly, Maeve stepped forward and asked, "But I thought we were the only ones left."

Arabella turned toward her and stepped away from Gray. Gray frowned and rubbed his arm. "Do you believe everything your government tells you, sweetheart?" she said in a sickeningly sweet voice. "What a sweet girl you once were. It's too bad you had to go digging into things that didn't concern you."

She dismissed Maeve with a flick of her fingers and turned back to Night. "But the question right now is what to do with you?"

"Arabella, I delivered the kids to you. What more do you want?"

Arabella put her face inches from Night's and said with deadly calm, "Loyalty, Night. I want loyalty." She stepped back. "And yours is definitely suspect."

She tapped her chin with her perfectly manicured fingernail. "I think since your loyalties seem to lie with your nephew that you should share the same fate."

370

She turned and walked to the door. "Shoot them," she said without emotion. "Start with him." She pointed at Gray and left the room.

Time seem to stop. Maeve watched a soldier raise his gun and aim it at Gray as if in slow motion. Tristan fired first, but the shot went wide. The soldier fired. Maeve screamed. At the last minute, Night threw himself in front of Gray, knocking both Gray and Ginger to the floor.

Maeve watched blood begin to seep out of Night's abdomen. Gray's wound had opened again and began to leak blood as well. Maeve couldn't see Gray, but Ginger began to sit up and reached for her gun.

Emery let out a short scream as Tristan moved between her and a WG soldier. Tristan aimed and fired, taking down the soldier who had been headed for Emery. Maeve and Tristan trained their guns on the remaining WG soldier who, realizing he was outnumbered, dropped his gun and raised his hands.

"Ginger," Maeve said. "Shut the door and lock it. Emery, please tell me you're almost done."

"I'm done now," Emery said as she hit a key. "All their guns should be disabled."

Tristan grabbed the WG soldier's gun and ordered him to sit with his hands on his head.

A groan came from the direction of Night and Gray. Maeve nodded at Tristan who was using an electric cord to secure the hands of the WG soldier and rushed over to where Night and Gray lay. Maeve was afraid to look down, afraid of what she would see.

"Maeve," said a hoarse voice. "Help me."

Maeve looked toward the voice and saw Gray kneeling over his uncle trying to put pressure on his uncle's wound with his one good arm as blood trickled down his other arm. Maeve rushed over to Gray, pulling off her jacket as she went.

"Emery, transmit a message to Cleo to let the rest of The Resistance know the guns are down. Tristan, keep an eye on that door. Ginger, see if you can't get Gray's bleeding stopped."

Maeve looked into Gray's ice blue eyes. "I've got it from here." She took her jacket and moved Gray's hands out of the way, replacing them with her jacket and applying pressure with both hands. "Let Ginger look at you."

"Is he going to be OK?" Gray asked in a quiet voice.

Maeve looked down at Night who moved his head slightly left to right. Blood poured out over her hands, despite her best efforts to staunch the flow. "I'm doing my best, Gray."

Night licked his lips. "Maeve," he whispered. "I never wanted this to happen. I love Gray. I... was... protecting... him... the... only... way... I... could."

Maeve thought Night's idea of protection could use some work, but in the end he had protected Gray from a bullet. She wasn't going to argue with a dying man.

"Shhh," Maeve said. "You're not helping yourself by talking."

"I'm... dying," Night said as he struggled to take a breath. "Take... this." He pressed a key into her hand.
372

"Bottom... drawer."

"Where?"

"At... the... house."

Night struggled to draw another breath. Blood continued to gush from his wound. Maeve's jacket was soaked. Maeve pressed harder on the wound.

"Gray," Maeve said. "Come here."

Gray made his way over to Maeve. She absently noted that his wound had stopped bleeding, but his face was ashen.

Maeve's eyes met his. "I'm sorry," she said.

Gray took Night's hand. "Uncle," he said as tears formed at the corner of his eyes.

"Sorry... Gray. I... really... was... protecting... you. I... love... you."

The hand Gray was holding went limp.

"No, Night, please, no."

Maeve reached out a bloodied hand and took Gray's hand in her own. "I'm so sorry, Gray. I tried to save him."

Gray looked at her and she could see the heartbreak in his eyes. Gently, she placed her arms around him as he laid his head on her shoulder.

"Guys," Tristan said. "I know this is a bad time, but we need to get out of here."

Maeve nodded and slowly helped Gray to his feet. Gray gave his uncle one last look, shook his head, wiped his eyes and grabbed his gun. Maeve motioned to Emery to follow Tristan and Ginger out the door.

CHAPTER THIRTY-SIX

The operation to round up the WG leadership was swift once the WG's guns were disabled, but Maeve's group let others handle that. They made their way back to the cave, and Maeve surrendered Gray to Cicely's care. She knew they needed to talk about what had happened, but he needed to have his wound taken care of first.

"What now?" Ginger asked. "What about the teenagers and the weapon?"

"Hopefully, we'll find out where they're keeping it and where they've taken the children once The Resistance has cleaned out WG headquarters," Maeve said.

She, Tristan, Emery and Ginger were sitting around one of the tables in the cave, eating protein paste bars. Maeve knew she needed to go see Gray again, but she also needed a moment to gather her thoughts. She still hadn't told the others about the key. She just thought Gray should hear his uncle's final thoughts first. She really had no idea what to make of what he had told her.

Resistance members were beginning to straggle into the cave with reports of easily overtaking WG soldiers throughout the city. Once other citizens of Palumbra realized the WG was weaponless, they joined The Resistance and the battle was swiftly over. The WG leadership was being held at WG headquarters until The Resistance could figure out what to do with them. Unfortunately, Arabella was not among them. The WG leadership was hopeful she would be found, but after meeting her and seeing her in action, Maeve was sure the WG leader had a plan to get away.

One of the latest arrivals, an older man with olive skin and a handlebar mustache announced that a group of Resistance fighters had found where they were holding the children. A cheer went up around the room. The Resistance was helping to reunite the teenagers with their families. Maeve managed a smile despite her weariness and sense of loss. She nodded to Ginger and made her way back to the area being used as an infirmary. Other than Gray, there were relatively few people being treated. It seemed Emery's virus had done its job, keeping the bloodshed to a minimum.

When Maeve approached Gray's cot, he appeared to be sleeping. For a moment, she simply stood and watched him breathe and was flooded with gratitude that he was still alive. She pulled up a chair next to his cot and gently took his hand. His eyes fluttered open.

"Sorry," Maeve said. "Didn't mean to wake you."

"You didn't. I wasn't asleep. Just thinking."

"I'm so sorry about your uncle, Gray."

Gray squeezed her hand. "Thanks. It still seems

unreal. I keep thinking about what he said."

"He really did love you, Gray."

"I know, but that's not what I was thinking about. It was something he said earlier – 'I am who I have always been.' What did he mean by that?"

"I think he was telling the truth."

"The truth about what? So much of what he said was a lie."

"The truth about protecting you."

"Why would you think that? Do I look like he protected me?" Gray asked, gesturing to his wounded arm.

"Because before you came over, he told me he loved you and he was protecting you. And he gave me this." Maeve held up the key he had given her and said it was to the bottom drawer."

"The bottom drawer of what?"

"He just said 'at the house.'"

Understanding dawned in Gray's eyes. "Do you know what it's to?" Maeve asked.

"Yes. He kept his gun in the bottom drawer of his night stand. I was never allowed to open that drawer. It was always locked – even after I became a soldier."

"Why would he give you the key to his gun?"

"I don't know. I guess we'll have to find out."

The next week flew by. Maeve, Ginger, Gray, Emery and Tristan were hailed as heroes by The Resistance and the people of Palumbra. They had to tell

376

their account of what happened in WG headquarters over and over. Maeve turned over the contents of the box that had started it all to The Resistance leadership, but she kept the key in her pocket. She and Gray had decided not to tell anyone about it until they knew what was in the drawer.

Gray's shoulder began to heal. There was a memorial service for all those who had been killed, including Emery and Ginger's mother. Now that the constant threat of danger was over, both Ginger and Emery were taking time to come to terms with their grief. Tristan, Maeve noted, was never far from Ginger's side as she and Emery struggled to cope with being alone in the world.

Gray silently mourned his uncle. To the rest of Palumbra, he was a part of the WG, but Maeve knew that Night was still the only family Gray had left. They took long walks, sometimes talking about what had happened and sometimes just strolling hand in hand in silence. On one such walk, Maeve brought up the soldier she had shot.

"I didn't believe I would ever kill someone," she said as she kicked a pebble on the ground.

Gray stopped and turned her toward him. "If you hadn't killed him, he would have killed Tristan. You had no choice."

Maeve shrugged. "I tell myself that every day. It doesn't make the nightmares go away."

Gray pulled her into his arms and Maeve leaned her head against his chest. "Will they ever go away? Will

I ever not see that soldier's face when I close my eyes?"

Gray laid his cheek on the top of her head. "Maybe," Gray said honestly. "But it will forever change who you are."

Maeve shook her head. "I'm never picking up a gun again."

Gray nodded. "I hope you never have to."

The loss of Emery and Ginger's mom and Gray's uncle also had Maeve thinking about her parents. On another of their walks, Gray asked, "Maeve, what about your parents?"

Maeve dropped his hand and turned her head away to look at flower near the path. Sometimes those piercing eyes saw more than she wanted him to see. "What about them?"

"Are you going to go see them? I know they've been asking The Resistance leadership about you."

"Gray, they were going to turn me over to the WG. What would I say to them? They were willing to betray me just to save their own skins."

Gray placed his hand on her shoulder and turned her to look at him. "I don't think it's that simple. They were scared, and they were scared for you. Their whole lives they had been conditioned to trust the WG. They were just doing what was the most natural thing for them. They probably truly thought you would be safe."

"The WG was trying to kill me. And my parents

were willing to just turn me over," Maeve said bitterly.

"Maeve, they're your parents. And of all of us, you're the only one with parents left. Don't throw that away. Please."

Maeve looked at him and shook her head. "I don't know. Maybe it would be easier if they weren't around. What am I going to say to them?"

"I don't know, Maeve, but I think you should see them. At least hear what they have to say."

Maeve nodded. "Will you go with me?"

"If you want me to."

"I do."

"Then let's go."

"Now?" Maeve's voice rose. "You want me to go now?"

"No time like the present. It will just get worse if you put it off. Go talk to them. Listen. Then decide if you want to have a relationship with them."

Maeve nodded and Gray led the way to their neighborhood. When they got to the front door of her house, Maeve pressed the key into Gray's palm. "I think I want to do this myself. And I think it's time you found out what's in that drawer. I'll come to your house when I'm done."

Gray nodded and squeezed both her hands then leaned down and gently kissed the top of her head. Maeve took a deep breath and opened the door.

"Maeve," her mom exclaimed. She came rushing toward Maeve but stopped abruptly as Maeve kept her hands in her pockets and stood on the threshold.

"We're so glad to see you. Aren't we Harold?"

Maeve's mom said to her dad who was seated at the table.

Her dad looked up in surprise from the papers he was poring over and nodded warily.

"Come in," her mom said.

Maeve took a step toward her mom and said, "I think we have some things to talk about."

Maeve's mom nodded glumly. "I'm so sorry, Maeve. We didn't know all of the things about the WG. We thought we were doing the right thing."

Maeves dad stood and put his arm around her mom. "We didn't want you to get hurt, but you were involved in things that could have hurt our entire family."

Maeve looked at her dad, and she felt sorry for him. His whole world had been built on a lie. "But I did get hurt. Some of my friends died, their parents died. I killed someone. Do you know what that's like?"

The question hung in the air. Maeve's mom's eyes had widened in horror when Maeve announced she had killed another person.

Her mom stepped toward her, with her hand outstretched. "I don't, Maeve. But I," she gestured toward Maeve's dad, "we, love you. I know we don't deserve it, but can you forgive us? Can we try to rebuild our relationship?"

Maeve looked from her mom's outstretched hand to the door, deciding whether to stay or leave. Her mom held her breath. Finally, Maeve took her mom's hand and said, "We can try."

###

Maeve found Gray sitting on the floor of his uncle's bedroom. Papers were spread around him. He looked up as she entered and Maeve noted the tear tracks on his cheeks. Stepping carefully so as not to disturb the papers, she made her way across the room and took a seat next to him.

"How did it go?" Gray asked.

"Better than I thought it would. They truly thought they were doing the right thing by turning me over to the WG. I don't understand, but I forgive them. I don't think our relationship will ever be the same, and I certainly don't want to go back to living with them. I'm just too different now. But we're going to keep seeing each other. They're my parents, and I love them. They love me, too."

Gray hugged her with his good arm. "I know that was hard, but I'm glad you talked to them."

Maeve nodded. "What's all this?" She swept her arm out to encompass the papers Gray had spread across the floor.

"Records. Of everything. My uncle kept a whole file of what was going on at the WG. He noted who was involved in leading the projects and who was just doing their job to keep the WG from going after their families. This will help The Resistance sort out who the people who truly need to be punished are. But this is the second most interesting thing here." Gray handed her a folder.

Maeve opened the folder and started reading the single sheet of paper inside. As she read, she started to smile. "He really did this?"

"Yes. I think this is what he was trying to protect by staying with the WG."

"He uploaded a virus to the weapon? It was never going to work."

"It was never going to work," Gray agreed.

Maeve threw her arms around Gray. "This means he wasn't ever working against The Resistance. He was working to destroy their weapon. That should clear his name."

Gray smiled. "At least he'll be a hero."

"He was already a hero. He saved your life."

Gray nodded as a tear made its way down his cheek. "I know."

Maeve hugged him again. "You said this was the second most interesting thing."

"Yeah. Check this out." He handed her another folder that was much thicker than the first.

"What is this?" Maeve asked as she pulled out a map. "Is this..."

"Yeah," Gray said. "It's a map of the land between here and the other city, the one we were calling The Hub."

"But this means we know how to get there. Why would the WG keep this hidden. And why hasn't The Resistance said anything about there being other cities out there?"

"Because it would start a panic. People have been told their whole lives that we're alone. To introduce the idea that there are other people out there during an already turbulent time would create even

382

more panic. My guess is that they're waiting until things settle down in Palumbra."

"What are you going to do with all this?"

"I'm not sure. Maybe I'll give it to The Resistance. But right now, I think I'll just hold onto it."

Maeve helped Gray pick up the papers and put them back in the folder.

"What do we do now?" Maeve asked.

"I'm not sure," Gray replied, taking her hand in his. "But whatever it is, we get to choose."

EPILOGUE

Maeve and Gray stood on the shore of the lake that was fed by The River. They had taken the day to retrace their steps to the edge of Palumbra. Two months had passed since The Resistance had overthrown the WG. Palumbrans were still sorting out how to deal with a new government that allowed more freedom. The people had even voted in the first elections that anyone could remember. Cleo had been elected as the new president of the Palumbran government, and each quadrant of the city had an elected representative. The government was working to create a more free society without creating chaos, so progress was slow. But it was coming. That thought made Maeve smile.

All of them were healing inside and out. Gray's shoulder was as good as new. Maeve still had nightmares about the WG soldier she had killed, but they came less frequently.

She was talking with her parents more but had moved in with Ginger and Emery. Emery was back in school, and Gray, Maeve, Tristan and Ginger had been tapped by the new government to help introduce the children and teenagers to the idea of freedom. It was a task they embraced while they dreamed of a world where one day Gray could pursue art and Ginger could touch the stars.

But at the moment, Maeve stood in front of Gray with his arms wrapped around her as they both looked out over the lake. While they were surrounded by forest on this side of the lake, she could see for miles on the other side.

"What do you think is out there?" Maeve asked as she turned in Gray's arms.

"I don't know," Gray said.

"Think we should find out?"

"One day we will."

"Together?"

"Together."

What happens when Maeve and her friends meet survivors from The Hub?
*Find out in **The Hub**, available for pre-order now!*

About the Author

L.D. Fairchild lives in one of the only big cities in Kansas with her husband, two daughters and two dogs. When she's not dreaming up new ways for the world to end, she loves reading, creating things and spoiling her dogs.

Since she spends her days in imaginary worlds, she loves meeting people in the real one. Be sure to look her up on Instagram and Facebook or drop her a note at booksbyfairchild@gmail.com.

booksbyfairchild.wixsite.com/ldfairchild

Made in the USA
Monee, IL
03 January 2024

51078999R00229